The

WARSAW
ORPHAN

Also by Kelly Rimmer

TRUTHS I NEVER TOLD YOU
THE THINGS WE CANNOT SAY
BEFORE I LET YOU GO

For additional books by Kelly Rimmer,
visit her website, www.kellyrimmer.com.

The
WARSAW
ORPHAN

1

Roman
28 March, 1942

THE HUMAN SPIRIT IS A MIRACULOUS THING. IT IS THE STRONGEST part of us—crushed under pressure, but rarely broken. Trapped within our weak and fallible bodies, but never contained. I pondered this as my brother and I walked to a street vendor on Zamenhofa Street in the Warsaw Ghetto, late in the afternoon on a blessedly warm spring day.

"There was one right there," he said, pointing to a rare gap in the crowd on the sidewalk. I nodded but did not reply. Dawidek sometimes needed to talk me through his workday, but he did not need me to comment, which was fortunate, because even after months of this ritual, I still had no idea what to say.

"Down that alleyway, there was one on the steps of a building. Not even on the sidewalk, just right there on the steps."

I fumbled in my pocket, making sure I still had the sliver of soap my stepfather had given me. Soap was in desperate demand in the ghetto, a place where overcrowding and lack of running water had created a perfect storm for illness. My stepfather ran a tiny dentistry practice in the front room of our apartment and needed the soap as much as anyone—maybe even more so. But as desperate as Samuel's need for soap was, my mother's need for food eclipsed it, and so there Dawidek and I were. It was generally considered a woman's job to go to the market, but Mother needed to conserve every bit of strength she could, and the street vendor Samuel wanted me to speak to was blocks away from our home.

"...and, Roman, one was behind a big dumpster." He hesitated, then grimaced. "Except I think we missed that one yesterday."

I didn't ask how he'd come to that conclusion. I knew that the answer was liable to make my heart race and my vision darken. Sometimes, it felt as if my anger was simmering just below the surface—at my nine-year-old brother and the rest of my family. Although, none of this was their fault. At Sala, my boss at the factory on Nowolipki Street, even though he was a good man and he'd gone out of his way to help me and my family more than once. At every damned German I laid eyes on. Always them. Especially them. A sharp, uncompromising anger tinged every interaction those days, and although that anger started and ended with the Germans who had changed our world, it cycled through everyone else I knew before it made its way back where it belonged.

"There was one here yesterday. In the middle of the road at the entrance to the market."

Dawidek had already told me all about that one, but I let him talk anyway. I hoped this running commentary would spare him from the noxious interior that I was currently grappling with. I envied the ease with which he could talk about his day, even if hearing the details filled me with guilt. Guilt I could handle; I probably deserved it. It was the anger that scared me. I felt like my grip on control was caught between my sweaty hands, and at any given moment, all it would take was for someone to startle me, and I'd lose control.

The street stall came into view through the crowd. There was always a crush of people on the street until the last second before seven o'clock curfew. This was especially the case in summer, when the oppressive heat inside the ghetto apartments could bring people to faint, besides which, the overcrowding inside was no better than the overcrowding outside. I had no idea how many people were inside those ghetto walls—Samuel guessed a million, Mrs. Kuklínski in the bedroom beside ours said it was much more, Mother was quite confident that it was maybe only a hundred thousand. All I knew was that ours was not the only apartment in the ghetto designed for one family that was currently housing four—in fact, there were many living in even worse conditions. While the population was a hot topic of conversation on a regular basis, it didn't actually matter all that much to me. I could see with my own eyes and smell with my own nose that however many people were trapped within the ghetto walls, it was far, far too many.

When the vendor's table came into view, my heart sank: she was already packing up for the day, and there was no produce left. I was disappointed but not surprised: there had been little chance of us finding food so late in the day, let alone food that someone would barter for a simple slip of soap. Dawidek and I had passed a store that was selling eggs, but they'd want *zloty* for the eggs, not a tiny scrap of soap.

"Wait here a minute," I murmured to my brother, who shrugged as he sank to sit on an apartment stoop. I might have let him follow me, but even after the depths our family had sunk to over the years of occupation, I still hated for him to see me beg. I glanced at him, recording his location to memory, and then pushed through the last few feet of people mingling on the sidewalk until I reached the street vendor. She shook her head before I'd spoken a word.

"I am sorry, young man. I have nothing to offer you."

"I am Samuel Gorka's son," I told her. It was an oversimplification of a complicated truth, but it was the best way I could help her place me. "He fixed your tooth for you, remember? A few months ago? His practice is on Miła Street."

Recognition dawned in her gaze, but she still regarded me warily.

"I remember Samuel, and I'm grateful to him, but that doesn't change anything. I have no food left today."

"My brother and I…we work during the day. And Samuel, too. You know how busy he is, helping people like yourself. But the thing is, we have a sick family member who hasn't—"

"Kid, I respect your father. He's a good man and a good dentist. I wish I could help, but I have nothing to give you." She waved to the table, to the empty wooden box she had packed up behind her, and then opened her palms toward me as if to prove the truth of her words.

"There is nowhere else for me to go. I can't take no for an answer. I'm going to bed hungry tonight, but I can't let…" I trailed off, the hopelessness hitting me right in the chest. I would be going home without food for my mother that night, and the implications made me want to curl up in a ball, right there in the gutter. But hopelessness was dangerous, at least in part because it was always followed by an evil cousin. Hopelessness was a passive emotion, but its natural successor drove action, and that action rarely resulted in anything positive. I clenched my fists, and my fingers curled around the soap. I pulled it from my pocket and extended it toward the vendor. She looked from my palm to my face, then sighed impatiently and leaned close to hiss at me.

"I told you. I have nothing left to trade today. If you want food, you need to come earlier in the day."

"That's impossible for us. Don't you understand?"

To get to the market early in the day one of us would have to miss work. Samuel couldn't miss work; he could barely keep up as it was—he performed extractions from sunup to curfew most days. Rarely was this work paid, now that money was in such short supply among ordinary families like his patients, but the work was important—not just because it afforded some small measure of comfort to a group of people who were, in every other way, suffering immensely. Every now and again, Samuel did a favor for one of the Jewish police officers or even a passing German soldier. He had a theory that, one day soon, those favors were going to come in handy. I was less optimistic, but I understood that he couldn't just close his practice. The moment Samuel stopped working would be the moment he had to perform an honest reckoning with our situation, and if he did that, he would come closer to the despair I felt every waking moment of every day.

"Do you have anything else? Or is it just the soap?" the woman asked me suddenly.

"That's all."

"Tomorrow. Come back this time tomorrow. I'll keep something for you, but for that much soap?" She shook her head, then pursed her lips. "It's not going to be much. See if you can find something else to barter."

"There *is* nothing else," I said, my throat tight. But the woman's gaze was at least sympathetic, and so I nodded at her. "I'll do my best. I'll see you tomorrow."

As I turned away, I wondered if it was worth calling into that store to ask about the eggs, even though I knew that the soap wasn't nearly enough for a whole egg. It wasn't enough for even half an egg here on the market, and the stores were always more expensive than the street vendors. Maybe they would give me a shell? We could grind it up, and Mother could drink it in a little water. We'd done that for her once before. It wasn't as good as real food, but it might help a little overnight. It surely couldn't hurt.

As I spun back toward our apartment, a burst of adrenaline nearly knocked me sideways. Dawidek hadn't moved, but two Jewish police officers were now standing in front of him. Like me, my brother was tall for his age—an inheritance from our maternal grandfather that made us look bizarre when we stood with Samuel and Mother, who were both more diminutive. Even so, he looked far too small to be crowded into the doorway of an apartment by two officers. That situation could turn to bloodshed in a heartbeat. The Kapo operated on a spectrum from well-meaning and kindly to murderously violent, and I had no way of knowing what kind of Kapo were currently accosting Dawidek. My heart thundered against the wall of my chest as I pushed my way back to them, knowing even as I approached that intervening could well get me shot.

For everything I had been through and for everything I had seen, the only thing that kept me going was my family, especially Dawidek. He was my favorite person in the world, a burst of purity in an environment of pure evil. Some days, the only time I felt *still* inside was when he and I were playing or talking in the evenings—and that stillness was the only rest I got. I could not live without him; in fact, I had already decided that if it came to that, I wouldn't even try.

"Dawidek?" I called as I neared. Both Kapo turned toward me. The one on the left, the taller one, sized me up as if an emaciated, unarmed sixteen-year-old was any kind of threat. The smart thing to do would have been to let Dawidek try to talk his own way out of this. He was nine years old but used to defending himself in the bizarrely toxic environment of the ghetto. All day long, he was at his job alone, and I was at mine. He needed his wits about him to survive even an hour of that, and I needed to trust that he could handle himself.

But I couldn't convince myself to be smart, even when I knew that what I was about to do was likely to earn me, at best, a severe beating. I couldn't even stop myself when the Kapo gave me a second chance to walk away. They ignored me, returning their attention on my brother. "Hey!" I shouted, loud enough that my voice echoed up and down the street, and dozens of people turned to stare. "He's just a kid. He hasn't done anything wrong!"

I was mentally planning my next move. I'd make a scene, maybe push one of the Kapo, and when they turned to beat me, Dawidek could run. Pain was never pleasant, but physical pain could also be an effective distraction from mental anguish, which was the worst kind. Maybe I could even land a punch, and that might feel good. But my brother stepped forward, held his hands up to me and said fiercely, "These are my supervisors, Roman. Just supervisors on the crew. We were just talking."

My stomach dropped. My heartbeat pounded in my ears and my hands were hot. I knew my face was flushed raspberry, both with embarrassment and from the adrenaline. After a terse pause that seemed to stretch forever, the Kapo exchanged an amused glance, one patted Dawidek on the back, and they continued down the street, both laughing at me. Dawidek shook his head in frustration.

"Why did you do that? What would you do, even if I was in trouble?"

"I'm sorry," I admitted, scraping my hand through my hair. "I lost my head."

"You're always losing your head," Dawidek muttered, falling into step beside me, as we began to follow the Kapo back toward our own apartment. "You need to listen to Father. Keep your head down, work hard and hope for the best. You are too smart to keep making such dumb decisions."

Hearing my little brother echoing his father's wisdom in the same tone and with the same impatience was always jarring, but in this case, I was dizzy with relief, and so I messed up his hair and let out a weak laugh.

"For a nine-year-old, you are awfully wise."

"Wise enough to know that you didn't get any food for Mother."

"We were too late," I said, and then I swallowed the lump in my throat. "But she said that we should come back tomorrow. She will set something aside for us."

"Let's walk the long way home. The trash cans on Smocza Street are sometimes good."

We were far from the only family in the ghetto who had run out of resources. We were all starving, and any morsel of food was quickly found, even if it was from a trash can. Still, I was not at all keen to return to our crowded apartment, to face the disappointment in my stepfather's gaze or to see the starvation in my mother's. I let Dawidek lead the way, and we walked in silence, broken by his periodic bursts of commentary.

"We picked one up here... Another over there... Mordechai helped me with one there."

As we turned down a quiet street, I realized that Dawidek's Kapo supervisors were right in front of us, walking a few dozen feet ahead.

"We should turn around. I don't want any trouble with those guys," I muttered. Dawidek shook his head.

"They like me. I work hard and don't give them any trouble. Now that you have stopped trying to get yourself killed, they won't bother us, even if they do notice us."

Just then, the shorter policeman glanced toward the sidewalk on his right, and then he paused. He waved his companion ahead, then withdrew something from his pocket as he crouched low to the ground. I was much too far away to hear the words he spoke, but I saw the sadness in his gaze. The Kapo then rose and jogged ahead to catch up with his partner. Dawidek and I continued along the street, but only when we drew near where he had stopped did I realize why.

We had been in the ghetto for almost two years. Conditions were bad to begin with, and every new day seemed to bring new trials. I learned to wear blinders—to block out the public pain and suffering of my fellow prisoners. I had walked every block of the ghetto, both the Little Ghetto with its nicer apartments where the elite and artists appeared to live in relative comfort, and through the Big Ghetto, where poor families like my own were crammed in, trying to survive at a much higher density. The footbridge on Chłodna Street connected the two and elevated the ghetto residents above the so-called Aryan Poles, and even the Germans, who passed beneath it. The irony of this never failed to amuse me when I crossed. Sometimes, I crossed it just to cheer myself up.

I knew the ghetto inside and out, and I noticed every detail, even if I had taught myself to ignore what I saw as much as I could. I learned not to react when an elderly man or woman caught my hand as I passed, clawing in the hopes that I could spare them a morsel of food. I learned not to so much as startle if someone was shot in front of my eyes. And most of all, I learned to never look at any unfortunate soul who was prone on the sidewalk. The only way to survive was to remain alert so I had to see it all, but I also had to learn to look right through it. The only way to manage my own broiling fury was to bury it.

But the policeman had drawn my attention to a scene of utter carnage outside what used to be a clothing store. The store had long ago run out of stock and had been repurposed as accommodation for several families. The wide front window was now taped over with hessian sacks for privacy; outside that window, on the sidewalk, a child was lying on her stomach. Alive, but barely.

The ghetto was teeming with street children. The orphanages were full to bursting, which meant that those who weren't under the care of relatives or kindly strangers were left to their own devices. I saw abandoned children, but I didn't *see* them. I'd have passed right by this child on any other day. I couldn't even manage to keep my own family safe and well, so it was better to keep walking and spare myself the pain of further powerlessness. But I was curious about what the policeman had given the child, and so even as we approached her, I was scanning, looking to see what had caught his attention and to try to figure out what he'd put down on the ground.

Starvation confused the normal growth and development of children, but even so, I guessed she was two or three. She wore the same vacant expression I saw in most children by that stage. Patches of her hair had fallen out, and her naked stomach and legs were swollen. Someone had taken her clothing except for a tattered pair of underwear, and I understood why.

This child would not be alive by morning. Once they became too weak to beg for help, it didn't take long, and this child was long past that point. Her dull brown eyes were liquid pools of defeat and agony.

My eyes drifted to her hands, her palms facing upward, as if opening her hands to God. One was lying open and empty on the sidewalk beside her. The other was also open but this palm was not empty. *Bread.* The policeman had pressed a chunk of bread onto the child's hand. I stared at the food, and even though it was never going to find its way to my lips, my mouth began to water. I was torturing myself, but it was much easier to look at the bread than at the girl's dull eyes.

Dawidek stood silently beside me. I thought of my mother and then crouched beside the little girl.

"Hello," I said, stiff and awkward. The child did not react. I cast my gaze all over her face, taking it in. The sharp cheekbones. The way her eyes seemed too big for her face. The matted hair. Someone had once brushed this little girl's hair and had probably pulled it into pretty braids. Someone had once bathed this child and tucked her into bed at night, bending down to whisper in her ear that she was loved and special and wanted.

Now, her lips were dry and cracked, and blood dried into a dirty black scab in the corner of her mouth. My eyes burned, and it took me a moment to realize that I was struggling to hold back tears.

"You should eat the bread," I urged softly. Her eyes moved, and then she blinked, but then her eyelids fluttered and fell closed. She drew in a breath, but her whole chest rattled, the sound I knew people made just before they died—when they were far too ill to even cough. A tear rolled down my cheek. I closed my eyes, but now, instead of blackness, I saw the little girl's face.

This was why I learned to wear blinders, because if you got too close to the suffering, it would burn itself into your soul. This little girl was now a part of me, and her pain was part of mine.

Even so, I knew that she could not eat the bread. The policeman's gesture had been well-meaning, but it had come far too late. If I didn't take the bread, the next person who passed would. If my time in the ghetto had taught me anything, it was that life might deliver blessings, but each one would have a sting in its tail. God might deliver us fortune, but never without a cost. I would take the bread, and the child would die overnight. But that wouldn't be the end of the tragedy. In some ways, it was only the beginning.

I wiped my cheeks roughly with the back of my hand, and then before I could allow my conscience to stop me, I reached down and plucked the bread from the child's hand to swiftly hide in my pocket. Then I stood and forced myself to not look at her again. Dawidek and I began to walk.

"The little ones should be easier. I don't have to ask the big kids for help lifting them, and they don't weigh anything at all. They should be easier, shouldn't they?" Dawidek said, almost philosophically. He sighed heavily and then added in a voice thick with confusion and pain, "I'll be able to lift her by myself tomorrow morning, but that won't make it easier."

Fortune gave me a job with one of the few factories in the

ghetto that was owned by a kindly Jew, rather than some German businessman only wanting to take advantage of slave labor. But this meant that when the Kapo had come looking for me to help collect the bodies from the streets before sunrise each day, the only other viable person in our household was my brother.

When Dawidek was first recruited to this hideous role, I wanted to quit my job so that I could relieve him of it. But corpse collection was unpaid work, and my factory job paid me in food—every single day, I sat down to a hot lunch, which meant other members of my family could share my portion of rations. This girl would die overnight, and by dawn, my little brother would have lifted her into the back of a wagon. He and a team of children and teenagers, under the supervision of the Kapo, would drag the wagon to the cemetery, where they would tip the corpses into a pit with dozens of others.

Rage, black and red and violent in its intensity, clouded the edges of my vision, and I felt the thunder of the injustice in my blood. But then Dawidek drew a deep breath, and he leaned forward to catch my gaze. He gave me a smile, a brave smile, one that tilted the axis of my world until I felt it chase the rage away.

I had to maintain control. I couldn't allow my fury to destroy me because my family was relying on me. *Dawidek* was relying on me.

"Mother is going to be so excited to have bread," he said, his big brown eyes lighting up at the thought of pleasing her. "And that means Eleonora will get better milk tomorrow, won't she?"

"Yes," I said, my tone as empty as the words themselves. "This bread is a real blessing."

2

———

Roman

"CLEVER BOYS. YOU ARE SO CLEVER," MY MOTHER SAID, CRA-
dling the bread in her spare hand, the other busy supporting my
newborn sister, who was suckling desperately at my mother's
breast. "How did you do this? Was it the street vendor?"

"She was very sympathetic," I said, carefully avoiding both
the truth and a lie. Dawidek and I hadn't discussed the need to
hide the origins of the bread. We didn't need to.

My mother beamed at us, and from his place beside her on the
mattress on the floor of our room, my stepfather smiled proudly,
too. I would have to tell him later that I still had the soap, because I knew that as soon as my mother finished the bread, he
would immediately turn to worrying about how we would
provide for her tomorrow, unless I told him that I had a plan
in place. But for now, I just enjoyed the happiness in his eyes.

"A miracle," my mother declared. "Today, we are blessed."

Before the war, my family had been the sole occupants of
a spacious, three-bedroom apartment on bustling Miła Street,

right in the center of the Jewish Quarter of Warsaw. My stepfather was the principal dentist at his very own clinic a few
blocks away, and his parents owned the apartment above ours.
We weren't wealthy by any means, but we did enjoy a comfortable existence. I had skipped several grades in elementary
school and was traveling to and fro across Warsaw by tram to
attend high school, and Dawidek was in the early years of his
education at a Jewish school just a few blocks away from home.
My mother kept the house and volunteered at a soup kitchen
in her spare time.

Today, that same three-bedroom apartment on Miła Street
was now home to our family, Samuel's parents, their elderly
friends Mr. and Mrs. Kukliński, and the Frankel and Grobelny
families. The Grobelnys once lived in a small apartment on the
same floor as Samuel's parents, right above us. When the first
big influx of people came, they made the mistake of coming
down to visit us and left their door open. By the time they went
back, two other families had invaded their space, and they never
got it back. They were a family of five then, but Mr. Grobelny
was shot on the street just a few weeks later, and then their two
older children died of influenza the following winter. Mrs. Grobelny was so forlorn she barely functioned anymore, and her
toddler, Estera, relied heavily on the other adults for care. Mrs.
Grobelny and Estera shared the dining room in our apartment,
sleeping together on a sofa each night.

The Frankels were a Hungarian Roma family, consisting of
Laszlo and Judit, and their seven-year-old twins, Imri and Anna.
It had been crowded before Grandfather came home with the
Frankels the previous autumn. He apologized profusely even
as he laid down the law as the unofficial head of our crowded
household. He'd seen Laszlo begging in the street while Judit
sat with the children, sheltering behind a trash can to get out
of a bitter wind.

"It is not right that those children should sleep on the street over winter while we could find room for them in our household."

We had done our best to fairly apportion the apartment—the Grobelnys in the dining room, my entire family in what was once Samuel and Mother's room, the Frankels in my bedroom, and the grandparents and the Kuklińskis were in Dawidek's former room. What was once the front room now served as Samuel's clinic. Every apartment in every building in the ghetto was now crowded with multiple families, as the Germans brought people from all over Europe to cram them in behind the walls with us.

When the ghetto wall had gone up, the water was shut off, and now we could only get water from the station faucet. Given Mother was busy with Eleonora, my grandparents and the Kuklińskis were old and frail, and everyone else was working during the day, it had fallen to Judit to fetch the household's water. Morning and night, she would make the trip with a bucket in each hand. It wasn't nearly enough. Like everything else, water had to stretch, and not a single drop could be wasted. Judit was a master of reuse. Sometimes she'd boil scraps of food to soften them, then use the same water to launder clothes, then use it again to flush our toilet.

How had it come to this? Once upon a time, I'd had hot showers every day and enough food that I didn't even realize a person could feel a hunger so intense it became a throbbing pain in their stomach. Even after two and a half years of occupation, including almost two years walled within the ghetto, I sometimes managed to convince myself that the complete collapse of our lives was some kind of dream. The nightmarish existence of life within the ghetto sometimes did take on a surreal, dreamlike quality. How could it possibly be real? How could we have slipped from the life we knew to this one in such a short period of time? How could I have taken a chunk of bread from the hands of a dying child to give it as a gift to my mother? And how could it be that my mother would be so hungry that that small, crusty piece of bread could inspire tears of joy?

I tried not to think about the little girl's vacant eyes and the cracked, bloodied skin at the corner of her lips, but every time I looked at the bread, her face appeared. To help distract myself, I hovered near my mother and then motioned toward the baby that rested in her arms. Mother smiled at me, and Samuel took the bread from my mother's hand so she could pass me my baby sister.

Eleonora. The miracle child who made our already complicated lives all that much more complex. The streets were rife with stories about women who were forced to end their pregnancies, women who were shot on sight simply for being pregnant, even newborns murdered by the SS, right in front of their families.

Grandmother had assumed the role of family rations collector when Mother's belly became too big to hide. The rations were a form of torture, too—generally, what was called a *family serving* of an oatmeal-like sludge, ladled into our kettle by the Kapo under close German guard. We were enduring a slow-motion extermination by starvation. The collective rations of our entire household would barely meet the nutritional needs of a single adult.

Samuel said with Mother's malnutrition, a successful pregnancy was an actual miracle, a verification that God had wanted to bless us with the child. I loved Eleonora, but I felt so conflicted about her presence. Breastfeeding was draining the life from my mother, besides which it was increasingly evident that she was not producing enough milk to sustain Eleonora anyway. My sister had been unsettled constantly since her birth six weeks ago, but I was noticing that the periods where she was quiet and still were becoming eerily prolonged.

I told myself that this was because Eleonora was getting older and that as babies got older, they just learned how to be quiet.

Deep down inside, I knew that I was fooling myself. The so-called miracle bread had probably bought us a little more time, but tragedy was hovering at our doorstep. The thought of Dawidek having to lift Eleonora's tiny body onto that wagon made me want to tear the world apart.

There was nothing I could do to change our situation, nothing beyond the daily struggle to get just a little food, to buy just a little more time.

"I removed a bad tooth from a woman today," Samuel told us, as Mother began to nibble on tiny bites of the bread. "She said she'd heard a rumor that we're all going to be moved to the East, and soon."

"To the East?" Mother replied, frowning. "What's in the East?"

"A work camp. At Treblinka, near the forest. She heard that the Germans have built large factories where we will *all* work to produce goods for the Germans, not just the small number of us with work permits."

I waited, knowing what was coming next. There were always rumors, and Samuel always heard them first because, like Dawidek, he was friendly and often cheerful, and the nature of his work meant that his patients quickly came to trust him. We had a conversation like this every few weeks, and while the rumors changed, the progression of the conversation did not. Samuel never disappointed. He drew in a deep breath, then his face stretched into a broad smile, and he gave my mother a re-assuring hug.

"You see! It's like I told you, Maja. The Germans have realized their mistake, putting so many of us in these conditions. Soon, they will relocate us to the forest where there will be enough space and food and water for us all, and we can earn our keep for them properly. They want us for labor, right? So it makes sense that they would move us somewhere where we can be strong to work for them." Samuel looked across to Dawidek, who was pushing pebbles around on the floor as if they were toy cars. Then he looked to me, and he smiled again. "You'll see, Roman. Things will get better soon. It's only a matter of time."

My mother silently broke off another piece of the bread, catching the crumbs that rained down onto her skirt. When she had finished her mouthful, she licked her finger and collected the crumbs from her skirt. Finally, she looked at me, and her gaze spoke volumes. She was tired of this—tired of our situation and tired of Samuel's stubborn refusal to acknowledge the simple, obvious fact that we were, effectively, doomed. She rarely said as much aloud anymore. I noticed that over the course of her pregnancy, and in the weeks since Eleonora's birth, my mother had become less and less vocal about her thoughts on what the German end goal might be. When we were first walled in, she was full of fight and carefully looking for a way out. But time had worn down her spirit in the same way that it had worn down her physical reserves, and now my mother was a shadow of who she once had been. I knew that Samuel saw it, too, and I often wondered if he wasn't compensating for the hopelessness of our situation when he went off on these ridiculously optimistic tangents.

"And if what awaits us in the forest is not better than this, but worse?" my mother said carefully.

"Worse?" I repeated incredulously. I couldn't imagine anything worse. It was, to me, as close to hell on earth as a person could imagine.

"Dawidek, darling, could you please go out to the bucket to fetch me a cup of water to have with this delicious bread?" Mother asked, her tone all at once sweet and gentle. Dawidek carefully set his pebbles down on the floorboards and left the room. My mother looked right into my eyes, and she whispered, "There are many rumors. You know this—they come and they go. I don't want you to panic, but Judit told me today that there are those at the market who say that a man escaped from a camp at Chełmno. She says that he saw proof that the Germans intend to be rid of us."

"Rid of us? How many of us?" I said, frowning.

Mother looked away before she murmured, "Maybe all of us."

"That's absurd," Samuel said dismissively. He shook his head, then exclaimed, "They need us for labor, Maja! Why would they kill us all when they need us for labor? They are trying to expand the Reich throughout all of Europe, and in this ghetto alone the factories are producing enough clothing for their entire army, not to mention the munitions we are producing. Besides which, why would they have allowed us to live until now, only to kill us all later? And how *could* they kill us all? It is impossible. It is a ridiculous notion."

"Is it really so impossible?" Mother asked him impatiently. "After everything they have done to us, how can you believe they wouldn't be capable of that?"

"Because they are still *human*, Maja!"

It was Samuel's turn to raise his voice, and he did so just as Dawidek returned to the room, wide-eyed, holding a cup of water in front of him like a shield. None of us moved, even as I felt a shiver of fear run down my spine. In all of the years that Samuel had been in my life, I had only ever heard him raise his voice twice. The first time was a shout of joy when my mother announced that she was pregnant with Dawidek. The second time was when they argued just before the Germans walled in the ghetto. Mother wanted to flee the city. Samuel was convinced he would still be allowed to operate his dentistry practice back in his old clinic, and that in doing so he could sustain the family.

"They *aren't* human, Samuel," I said, throat tight. "How can you even think they are, after what we've seen?"

Samuel closed his eyes, but his breathing was ragged. In the dim light, I saw that his hands were clenched into fists. After a moment, he exhaled unevenly, and then he whispered, "I need to believe that there is some hidden depth of grace within these men who torture us, because if there isn't, then all hope is lost. And it's not just lost for us, Roman, but for humanity, because even once all of this is over, this evil could emerge from the souls of men again and again and again."

Dawidek finally moved to offer Mother her water. She gave him a sad, apologetic smile as she took it, then murmured her thanks. My brother walked back to his pebbles and resumed his game. The conversation seemed over, so I startled when Samuel suddenly added, "Have you heard anything?"

I looked up to find the question was, bewilderingly, directed at me.

"How would I have heard anything?"

He shrugged.

"Don't the boys at the workshop talk?"

I suppressed a wince. The boys at the workshop did talk; I just didn't engage unless there was no way to avoid it. It was different in the beginning. Sala had taken a dozen of us into his employ on the same day. I made three friends in that cohort: Leonard, Gustaw and Kazimierz. We all learned to operate the machines together, and soon I found myself looking forward to my work. Leonard had a wicked sense of humor and was forever making me laugh, and Gustaw wanted to be a lawyer just as I did—if we were ever able to return to our education. He and I found plenty of intellectual topics to keep our minds active. Kazimierz was well connected and knew all kinds of ways to access black-market food and other resources.

Leonard was the first to go—he contracted typhus and died within days of falling ill. Gustaw simply disappeared. I went to his house when he stopped coming to work, and his parents had no idea what had happened to him. Losing Kazimierz was the hardest: our merry gang of four had been just two for months, when one day the Gestapo came into the factory and dragged him away, kicking and screaming. Having seen Gustaw's parents' agony at his unexplained absence, I took it upon myself to go to Kazimierz's mother to explain what had happened. After that, I made a determined effort to avoid friendship. I'd learned the hard way that loneliness was difficult to survive, but grief was infinitely worse.

I sat at a table working a sewing machine opposite another boy about my own age. Although we had worked together for over a year and he had made many attempts to talk to me, I still didn't know his real name. The other boys called him Pigeon. I had no idea if this was an insult or a compliment or even where the nickname originated. I avoided a friendship with him purely because I'd heard the rumors—he, like many of the young men in the factory, was flirting with the underground. I had already watched one friend dragged away by the Gestapo, and should that happen again, I would make sure it happened to a stranger.

I did empathize with those who worked with the Resistance. I'd thought of it myself, but these were childish fantasies, and I knew I'd never act upon them. No resistance activity could save my family from what they were going through; in fact, connecting with the Resistance could only bring my family pain. Besides which, every time the subject came up, Samuel made me promise I would never get involved. I knew his determination to avoid the underground came not from a philosophical objection to resistance, but from a philosophical objection to facing our reality.

After all, if Samuel was right and sooner or later the Germans would correct the hellish existence they had forced us into, there was little point in risking our lives to fight them.

"I keep to myself at work," I said abruptly. Baby Eleonora was beginning to wriggle, so I shifted her in my arms, lifting her higher and rocking gently, the way I had seen my mother do.

"Perhaps you could ask around," my mother said. She gave me a slightly pleading look. "Something is coming, Roman. You know Mrs. Grobelny's second cousin is on the Council, and she said that he hinted things are soon to change. I know that there is not much we can do to protect ourselves, but if we just knew what was coming…" She trailed off, and then she added weakly, "If only we knew what was coming, at least I could sleep at night. Even if it is bad, I'd rather know."

Straightaway, Pigeon came to mind. My mother's request was simple and one I really couldn't decline.

3

Emilia

I NEVER SET OUT TO BE REBELLIOUS. I WAS CURIOUS, NATU-
rally, maybe a little stubborn…and I was *definitely* out of my
depth in Warsaw, hundreds of miles away from the village I'd
always called home.

But rebellious? No. That trait was not in my nature. If you'd
asked me why I was rebelling, I might have given you a blank
look, and I'm quite certain I'd have had no clue what you were
referring to. My deception was innocent, as much as such a
thing is possible. Every single aspect of my life had fallen out of
my control, and at not-quite fourteen years old, I was somehow
both wise beyond my years *and* emotionally stunted. Unable
to process or to even understand my own confused feelings, I
had begun to crave autonomy desperately enough that I was
driven to seek even the illusion of it. I made dozens of small
decisions each day, but I made each of them under the watch-
ful eye of my adoptive parents, Truda and Mateusz—except for
the decisions I made in the glorious hour between five thirty

and six thirty each evening. That's when I would leave Truda cooking our dinner, and I'd ostensibly walk down the flight of stairs to the lobby, where I would open a back door to access the little courtyard that only the residents of our building were allowed to use.

Truda didn't like me to visit the courtyard at all, and she was adamant that I not go there during the day. It backed onto an alleyway that was a shortcut for people walking to the nearby market, and our apartment was only a few blocks from the walled Jewish district, so German soldiers sometimes wandered by. But by six o'clock the market was closed, and the foot traffic in the alleyway had slowed to a trickle. Truda and Mateusz were determined to keep me safe and had gone to extraordinary lengths to do so, but even Mateusz could see that I couldn't live locked up inside of a third-floor apartment.

"It's one thing to keep her safe," Mateusz had said, "but surely our goal should be to keep her safe *and* sane. She needs at least a little time outside each day, and she really needs a taste of independence."

And so it was decided that I could visit the courtyard every single evening. I was pleased with this, even after Mateusz pulled me aside to warn me that it was a privilege, not a right.

"You know how much is at stake, so be careful. Just enjoy the peace and quiet in the courtyard, don't speak to anyone, and come straight back. Okay?"

"I promise," I had said, absolutely determined to honor their trust.

Except that…within a week, with only the lonely apple tree and a slightly overgrown boundary garden to amuse me, I was bored silly, so I went looking for something else to entertain me. Ever since, as soon as our apartment door closed behind me, I would turn right to visit with Sara, the woman who shared the third floor of our building with us.

Every now and again I would wonder if Truda wouldn't mind

at all that I was visiting Sara. After all, Sara was a nurse and a
social worker, an accomplished woman by any standards. And
while I knew almost nothing of her story, I did know that she
was alone, and I had a feeling my visits brought her a measure
of comfort. Besides, most of the time, she was giving me lessons from her nursing textbooks or allowing me to assist her
with her endlessly ambitious cross-stitch or knitting projects.
Our time together was entirely innocent, and there was likely
no need for me to keep it a secret, except that I *liked* that hour
being hidden from my parents. Sara spoke to me as an adult,
not a child, and she very rarely refused to answer my questions,
even if they were awkward or uncomfortable. It was Sara who
warned me about the likely arrival of my monthly courses just
before it happened for the first time, and she who had explained
the basic mechanics of sex.

The unlikely bond she and I forged over several months had
become far too important to me to risk.

And so, each afternoon, I waited until Truda was busy preparing supper. I'd dress as if I were leaving the building, call out
a farewell and then, as quickly as I could, reach into the small
drawer in the hall table by the front door. I'd withdraw Sara's
spare key, just in case she was running late from her job, and
then I'd slip out into the hallway that joined our apartments,
and instead of turning left, I'd turn right.

It was one small thing I could control. One small thing I
could be responsible for. One small measure of power. And, it
turned out, that was enough.

There was nothing to suggest that that night was going to
be any different from any of the other nights I had spent with
Sara. We had worked on unpicking a sweater so that she could
reuse the good yarn for another project, and we had discussed
the kinds of books she liked to read. She offered to lend me a
tattered copy of the first part of *Nights and Days*, by her favor-

ite author, Maria Dąbrowska. I panicked at this generous offer, wondering how I would explain the book's presence in my hand when I returned home to Truda and Mateusz.

"Or, if you already have plenty to read, you could borrow it some other time," she had said, when my panicked pause stretched too long.

When the grandfather clock in her sitting room had almost reached six thirty, I carefully set down the yarn, and Sara walked me to the door. I had to leave right on time, because Mateusz ran on a militant schedule and always arrived home between six thirty-five and six forty.

"I'll see you tomorrow," I said as I pulled the door open, but to my surprise, I saw my adoptive father standing there, holding a small package in his hand. He looked every bit as startled as I.

"Elżbieta…" he said, using the false name I adopted when we arrived in Warsaw. Even after all of those months, I still hated that name. My natural mother died during labor, but my father once told me that all throughout her pregnancy, he'd hear her talking to me, calling me Emilia right from the outset. Answering to Elżbieta now felt like a betrayal, even though I recognized I had no choice. But that was the least of my worries, because Mateusz's gaze skipped between me and Sara, then narrowed. "I am surprised to see you here." His frown was as intense as any I'd ever seen.

"I… I was just… It was…"

For once in my chatty young life, I was completely lost for words. I kept glancing between Sara and Mateusz, trying to figure out how to draw the strands of my two falsehoods together. Was there some way I could explain this to Mateusz without betraying to Sara that I was not supposed to be in her apartment?

If there was, I couldn't think of it.

"Ah, is the package from Piotr? Thank you, Mateusz. This will be the extra sugar I asked him to find for me," Sara said, leaning past me to take the parcel from Mateusz's hand. But then she turned her attention to me, and she correctly read the strained silence, then said lightly, "But…young Elżbieta, were you not supposed to be here?"

I felt my face flame hot, and the air in Sara's small entryway felt too stale. I panicked, pushed past Mateusz and ran back to my room.

"What were you thinking, Elżbieta?"

"I don't know."

"But why would you do this?"

"I don't know."

"Do you not understand how risky it is for you to disobey us?" Truda cried, her hazel eyes shining with unshed tears. "After everything we have done for you, why would you betray us like this?"

Truda's dramatics did not move me, although I was well aware that beneath the histrionics lay a kernel of unavoidable truth. When Truda, Mateusz and I first left our village of Trzebinia, we traveled to the city of Lodz. At that stage Mateusz hadn't seen his brother in years, but we were desperate, and we had nowhere else left to turn. Uncle Piotr's foreman at his factory in Lodz explained that Piotr was setting up a new business in Warsaw, and so on we went, until we found him here, living in a hotel. I'd stayed in hotels with my real father several times before the war began, but I'd never known anyone rich enough to live in one. As soon as we found Uncle Piotr in that hotel, he accepted me as his niece and changed his entire life without question—renting an apartment for us all to share, and somehow magically sourcing false identity papers for me to ensure I could be safe here.

We didn't even know if I needed to live under a false identity, but Uncle Piotr was determined. "If there is any risk at all, it is better to adopt a false name," he assured us, and then he made it happen.

Mateusz found work with an accounting firm, but his wages were minimal, and I was aware that Uncle Piotr had been supporting us ever since we arrived. Disapproval from Truda and Mateusz stung, but Uncle Piotr's disapproval felt like a soul-deep ache. He was a jovial sort, always quick with a smile or to whip out the vodka to celebrate or commiserate. I'd never seen him angry before. I didn't realize he was capable of it. But there he was, staring at me over the rim of his wire-framed glasses, his jaw set tight.

I was deeply embarrassed as I crossed my arms over my chest and tucked my chin in as if to make myself smaller. I felt like I had been blushing for the entire hour since Mateusz had caught me out. The scolding lasted for about the same length of time.

"Sara said that you have been visiting her almost every day for weeks. If you want a friend, I'll arrange for you to play with Katarzyna!" Truda exclaimed. Katarzyna was the twelve-year-old daughter of one of Mateusz's colleagues. She was nice enough, but to me, she seemed bewilderingly dull and immature.

"Katarzyna is boring," I exclaimed impatiently. "She is a child!"

"*You* are a child," Mateusz pointed out, mild and calm as always, even as his gaze told me he was just as frustrated as Truda and Uncle Piotr.

"A person doesn't stare into the dead eyes of their brother and remain a child. A person doesn't watch their innocent father die before the eyes of their entire community and *remain a child*."

For just a moment, the adults all stared at me in silence, the scolding stuttering to a stop as they looked upon me with sudden pity.

"We barely know Sara," Truda added, her tone softening. "Just because you like her doesn't mean you should trust her."

"I agree that Katarzyna would be a more sensible choice for

Elżbieta, but I also want you to know that Sara is no threat to us," Uncle Piotr interjected cautiously.

"With all respect, Piotr—" Mateusz began, but Uncle Piotr shook his head and spoke over him.

"Believe me, Sara is too well regarded to be working with the Germans. She's a kind, generous woman—a nurse, who works with the Department of Social Welfare and Public Health."

"She is my friend. She has been teaching me so much, even about…" In my determination to defend Sara, I had been about to say that she had been giving me anatomy lessons, but when I met Truda's eyes, it suddenly occurred to me that my adoptive mother might not be so excited about that. "About knitting. And cross-stitch."

"I am sorry, Elżbieta. I can see you have become very fond of Sara, but you have disobeyed us, and you've betrayed our trust. You simply must respect our wishes," Mateusz said slowly.

I pushed my chair back from the table and stood. I wasn't even sure why I was so heartbroken, but the thought of losing the *one* thing in my life that I could control was utterly devastating. And so, I did what most teenagers do when they are embarrassed and ashamed and disappointed and frustrated: I lashed out at the people who cared about me the most.

"I hate you! Both of you. You've ruined my life! I wish—"

"Emilia," Uncle Piotr said flatly, and the sound of my real name was so rare that it startled me into silence. When I looked at him, his expression softened just a little. "Allow me to give you some advice, child. Never say things in anger that you will regret in calm. Take yourself to your bedroom, and let me speak to Truda and Mateusz."

I left the room, tears prickling my eyes. I threw myself on my bed, all sorts of hotheaded thoughts running through my mind. I contemplated running away but dismissed this thought. I thought about sneaking out to visit Sara anyway, then dismissed this thought, too. I could tell from Truda's and Mateusz's reactions that my brief periods of freedom had come to an end.

And soon enough, my frustration and embarrassment gave way to new emotions: shame and regret. Truda and Mateusz hadn't ruined my life, they had saved it, and if anything, in doing so they had ruined their own. My father was executed right in front of our village at the start of the war. That same day, Truda and Mateusz took me into their family. Trzebinia, like the rest of our great country, had become a difficult place to live, but despite the circumstances my adoptive parents had carved out a relatively comfortable existence for themselves, even through the war. Like Uncle Piotr, Mateusz had inherited a textiles factory from their father, and he earned a tidy income through it. Our home in Trzebinia was large and beautiful, our friends warm and plentiful.

But last year, my brother, Tomasz, had come to our house in the middle of the night, unannounced, and by lunchtime the next day, everything had changed. Tomasz had been aiding Jews in hiding, and the penalty for that was execution—both for him, and his immediate family. My brave, brilliant brother was stuck. He had been exposed, and to save his fiancée, he knew he had to turn himself in, but that would mean certain death, and as the last remaining member of his family, I was at risk, too. We had no idea if the Germans knew I existed, if they knew who my new family was or whether they were looking for me at all. But Mateusz and Truda chose to flee as though my life were in immediate danger. They willingly gave up everything just to ensure my safety. But for Uncle Piotr's kindness, we would be destitute, having left behind everything in Trzebinia.

By the time a soft knock sounded at my door and Mateusz entered, I was sobbing tears of shame. When he sat on the edge of my bed, I sat up and threw myself into his arms. He embraced me and murmured softly, "Emilia, I know this is all so hard on you, but it really is so important that you do not lie to us. You understand the need for secrecy. I know you do."

"But it has been months," I said, weeping softly. "Can we not relax just a little now?"

"The minute we relax is the minute we will regret our complacency." I tensed, and Mateusz contracted his arms around me. "I am telling you this because I want you to be paranoid—that is the best way for us to keep you safe. Truda and I love you more than I can explain. When you came into our family, you completed it. If we are protective of you, we are only being protective of our own hearts. I understand that you and Sara have become friends, and Piotr assures me that she is a safe and trustworthy person…that perhaps you have been bringing her some comfort, too."

"I think she is lonely," I said, blinking tears from my eyes. "And…maybe I am lonely, too."

"Then, you may continue spending time with her, but you must promise that you will respect our rules. I only want what's best for you. I thought… I had hoped that, by now, we would have shown you that."

"You really have. And I am grateful. It's just that sometimes…"

"You miss Alina."

I felt a pang of sadness in my chest at the mention of her name. Alina was Truda's little sister, but I thought of her as *my* sister, too, because she and Tomasz were engaged. Just before he turned himself in to the Germans, Tomasz had helped Alina to flee Poland, smuggled from our village in the back of a supply truck. God willing, she was safe in England now. I was glad for that. But I also wished that she'd stayed because I had no idea how to navigate this upheaval without her.

"Alina always let me talk," I said, my throat tightening. "She listened to me, even when I asked her questions she couldn't answer. She let me get them out, and I felt better when they were out."

"And Sara does this for you?"

"Well, no. Because I can't tell her who I really am or why we are here. And we don't even talk about the Germans, I promise you. We just talk about books and crafts and music, and she has been teaching me a little about…science."

I finished school at the end of grade four, and Truda tried to homeschool me, but we had mixed success: her own schooling was limited because her family had been unable to afford to send her to high school. Mateusz, who had completed high school and had even been to university, was sympathetic to my desire to learn, and I saw understanding dawn in his eyes.

"Okay, Elżbieta," he murmured. "We will allow you to continue to visit with Sara each night, but you must promise that you will never lie to me again. And you must promise you will *never* tell her the truth about our family."

"I promise."

I truly meant that promise. I was lucky to be allowed to continue to spend time with her, and I had no intention of taking any more risks. My friendship with Sara was one bright spark in an otherwise gray existence.

4

Roman

"HELLO," I SAID. ACROSS THE DESK FROM ME, AT A MACHINE identical to mine, Pigeon blinked as he returned from his trip to the restroom. It had taken me several hours to figure out how exactly I could initiate a conversation. I was well out of practice with small talk.

"Me?" he asked, pointing to his chest.

I scowled at him.

"Who else would I be talking to?"

He gave me a wry smile.

"Roman, we have worked opposite one another for over a year, and you've never spoken to me before. Not once. Do you even know my name?"

"Pigeon."

"It may surprise you to learn that Pigeon is not actually my name," he said and chuckled. I cleared my throat and glanced down at my machine again, adjusting the tension of the thread to tighten it, then loosen it, just to appear busy. I was embarrassed to have already made a meal of the conversation. My workmate laughed again, freely and lightly. "I'm Chaim, and it's nice to properly meet you at last."

I nodded curtly, then turned my attention to my machine. All day long, Sala's factory turned out *Stiefelriemen*, simple leather bootstraps German soldiers used to tighten their shoes around their ankles. With high-quality boot leather harder and harder to come by, soldiers were forced to make do with whatever boots were on hand, regardless of sizing. Our boot straps enabled a soldier to wear a pair of shoes several sizes too large if that was all he could access. They allowed a soldier to march extra miles without blisters. They meant a soldier's shoe didn't fly off when he kicked an innocent Jew in the stomach.

With every strap I sewed, I wished ill upon the wearer. I knew the other men in the factory felt the same, even if we didn't dare say so aloud. There were two dozen of us in Sala's factory, all young men, split roughly into three teams. The men at the tables behind us cut the leather into shape, then Chaim and I and a half a dozen other young men sewed the ends of one of the pieces into loops. Farther down the line, a team of eight punched holes and attached buckles and pins. Sala checked every single piece for quality before it shipped out.

Several hours passed as Chaim and I worked in silence. After more than a year in the factory, I no longer felt an ache in my back as I bent over the machine, and my hands were rough with calluses in all of the right places, so I could fall into a comfortable numbness and let my thoughts wander as I worked. It seemed like too much of a jump to move from finally learning Chaim's real name to asking if he had heard any reliable intelligence about what might be coming for the ghetto's residents, and so I decided I would leave it at the greeting for that day. Even so, when I shuffled into the cafeteria room at lunchtime, Chaim followed me and sat beside me. I nodded once to acknowledge him and then went back to my oatmeal.

THE WARSAW ORPHAN   43

When I left the factory that day, I checked my pocket for the soap, then began to walk toward the street vendor on Zamenhofa Street. I was so lost in thought it took me some time to notice the footsteps falling in time with my own. I glanced down at the worn boots beside me and realized it was Chaim. He seemed amused that I finally noticed him.

"What is it you need?" he asked me, and at my blank look, he gave me a patient smile. Chaim was a few inches shorter than me, but he had the kind of broad shoulders that suggested that, in better times, he might have been solid and muscular. His jet-black hair was always messy and seemed perpetually in need of a trim. My hair would no doubt have been in the same state but for my mother's determination that I keep it neat. I wondered if his parents were still alive.

"Something on the black market?" Chaim prompted. "Help with a problem? Or do you just need information?"

"I've been rude to you for over a year, and *this* is how you start a conversation with me?"

"You didn't finally acknowledge me out of the goodness of your heart. There are only three things people talk about now: the good old days, the utter wasteland of our current existence or the rare person…my favorite kind of person…" He paused, then gave me a quiet smile. "Ah, now this rare fellow wants to talk about the future. I know you aren't living in the past, because if you were, you'd be more cheerful." I grunted in agreement. It was fair to say I wasn't known for my sunny demeanor. "And I have a feeling you are also not the kind of person who is entirely consumed by our current reality, because *those* people complain much more than you do. That leads me to conclude that you tried to talk to me because you either need help and you have run out of other options, or you've heard the rumors that changes are coming and you want to know which version of this gossip is correct. Am I right?"

"Even if there were changes coming," I repeated, cautiously, "none of us would know what they were."

"Some of us do," he said and shrugged easily.

"What do you know?"

"They will, at some point, deport us to camps."

"I already heard that rumor," I muttered.

"It's not a rumor. It is simply the truth. And once we are there, they will kill us."

He said this without so much as a hint of emotion.

"My stepfather says that they will not kill us while we provide free labor. He has heard rumors that the Germans have built large factories at Treblinka and that each of us will have a job, plus much better living conditions."

Chaim barked a harsh laugh.

"Do you want to engage in fairy tales, or would you like me to be honest with you?"

"You know no more than I know. How could you?"

"I can't tell you how I know, but I can tell you *what* I know. In January, a man escaped the camp at Chełmno. He saw evidence that prisoners were being executed—hundreds of people at a time. He said it was a highly organized extermination program."

"How could they possibly kill so many people? Why would they bother to do so? Are we not starving to death quickly enough for them?" I muttered impatiently. I wanted to honor my mother and stepfather's request to find reliable information, but the very thought that there might be some truth to these rumors made my stomach ache. "No. It's absurd."

"What *did* you want today, Roman?" Chaim asked me. He stopped abruptly, and I realized it was because he needed to turn left, and I had begun to turn right. I looked at him one last time, mentally cataloged him as a fool who traded in fallacies and shook my head. There was no chance I'd pass the details of this conversation back to my family.

It turned out I'd only been interested in hearing a rebuttal to the rumors.

"I think you wanted to know what I knew, and you want to know because you want to save someone. A girlfriend, perhaps, or maybe your family."

"I told you. I don't want anything from you."

"Roman."

I glanced back at him impatiently.

"When you figure out what it is you want, ask me. I know people."

I sighed impatiently and continued on my way to the street vendor. There, I traded my miserable slip of soap for some turnip peels and a carrot top for my mother, and on my way home I made sure to avoid that quiet side street where I'd found the bread the night before.

"Good morning, my friend."

Chaim had begun greeting me this way every morning. He chatted almost incessantly through most workdays and then made a point of walking beside me on that first block after we left the workshop. I was gruff with him, even when I wasn't openly ignoring him, but he seemed undeterred. Having studiously avoided any kind of attachment to my workmates for so long, I thought I could continue to ignore Chaim's attempts to befriend me, but three weeks passed, and I'd become bafflingly fond of him.

"Good morning." I sighed, taking my seat at my machine.

"Did you sleep well?"

"Does anyone sleep well these days?"

"Do you live with your family?"

"Do you ever stop asking questions?" This question slipped out as sharp and flat rather than my usual gently gruff and surly tone. Chaim raised his heavy eyebrows at me. For a moment I thought I'd finally offended him enough for him to abandon his quest to befriend me. I was stunned to feel something like regret and then immediate relief when he chuckled and shook his head.

"Looks like my new friend has woken up on the wrong side of the bed."

Later that day, as we walked side by side on the first block away from the workshop, I gave in to a sudden impulse.

"Where do you live?" I asked him.

"Twarda Street."

It was almost as far from my apartment as I could walk within the walls, but I had nothing to trade for food that day and no plans beyond searching trash cans. Besides, Twarda Street was in the Little Ghetto where wealthier families lived, so an even better place for me to search. When we reached the end of the block, I turned left with him instead of right. Chaim didn't react, and we walked in silence for several blocks before he spoke to me in a murmur.

"My parents are in London. They went to visit my sister just before the invasion. I stayed in Warsaw because I had just started university, and besides, they were only going for a month. My mother didn't want to go. She was nervous Hitler was going to invade…but my sister had been very ill and she had a new baby, too, and in the end my parents had to choose between guarding me against a possible danger and helping my sister with an existing one. I worry about them, mostly because I received a few letters from Mother early on, and I know the guilt of leaving me behind is eating her from the inside. Even so, I'm glad they aren't here. I'm happy that they are safe."

"You talk a lot."

"And you, my friend, do not talk enough, and I don't know if you have noticed this, but you are unusually surly." I frowned at him, and he laughed. "Are you on your own, too?"

"If you are on your own, who were you living with? How have you survived?" I asked, ignoring his question.

"I am one of the lucky ones," Chaim said easily. "Some of my parents' friends took me in, and since I am the youngest member of the household, they let me sleep in the bathtub all by myself. I live like a king."

"And food? Money?"

"I took what I could when they moved us here. And I'm resourceful. I make do."

"What you said about Chełmno," I blurted, "is it true? Do you know any more?"

"Everything I told you is true."

"This isn't the first time my stepfather has heard rumors."

"I've also heard rumors that come to nothing so I understand why you are skeptical. But I'm certain of this information. I have mutual friends with the man who escaped Chełmno. It's true that what I've heard is secondhand, but it is only secondhand, and I trust the man who shared it with me." He dropped his voice. "If what you're really asking is what we *do* about all of this, I can help."

"I can't," I said.

"Don't you want to fight?"

"Of course I do," I said and abruptly stopped walking. Chaim turned back to face me, eyebrows high. "But I also have to protect the most important thing—the one thing I have left."

"Your family," he surmised.

"Exactly."

"I respect that," he said easily, then he motioned to the sidewalk and began walking again, as if I hadn't just refused to take the bait he'd dangled in front of me. "Come on, friend, keep up. If I'd known you were as slow at walking as you are at sewing, I'd never have allowed you to walk me home."

5

Emilia

ALMOST EVERYTHING ABOUT LIFE IN WARSAW WAS DIFFER-
ent to life in Trzebinia, but I only allowed myself to think about
those differences at night. It had been three years since my father's death, but I still clung to a memory of resting in my beautiful bedroom in my father's apartment at the back of the clinic
he owned. I remembered the soft pink curtains the mother I
never knew had crafted before my birth, the white-and-green
wallpaper and fluffy brown rug, and best of all…my father snor-
ing in his bed, right across the hall. I even missed the room I'd
had at Truda and Mateusz's beautiful, lush home—although I
never thought of it as mine until we had to leave it.

The apartment Uncle Piotr rented for us was quirky: most
of the rooms were on the third floor, but my room was on a
kind of half floor, up a flight of stairs and built into a small
attic space. No matter what I did, my bedroom always smelled
faintly of dust, and my woolen blanket was always musty. My
mattress was soft, but the blankets were scratchy, and the bomb-

ing raids in the early days of the war had damaged the roof of the building and the lancet window that illuminated my room. Uncle Piotr patched the ceiling and window frame when we moved in, but building supplies were not easy to come by. He had been forced to reuse mismatched bricks, and the mortar he packed them with was fortified with hay, which stuck out here and there. Sometimes I stared at that hay, wondering if, on the other side of the roof, rats were pulling at it. Maybe the roof would cave in on me, and the last thing I'd see would be those rats.

Despite my overactive imagination, I was relatively safe there, but every breath reminded me that I was not at home, and that thought would always be followed by worse ones—that home was gone forever, that I was the last surviving member of my real family. Sometimes, I'd wake in the night, and even before I remembered where I was, the scent of my bedroom would remind me that my new, permanent status was *lost*.

The sounds were different, too. The long-standing curfew in Trzebinia meant that our sleepy village became deathly calm at night…for the most part. Occasionally, there'd be shouting or shooting or other signs of trouble.

Warsaw was never quiet, not even at night. Between gunshots or crying or dogs barking, the constant soundtrack of noise kept me awake when we first arrived. I'd grown used to it, but the night before my fourteenth birthday, sleep completely eluded me.

It wasn't excitement keeping me awake; I knew what my birthday would bring. Uncle Piotr was taking a day off work, and he'd made vague promises about an exciting outing, but I knew exactly what he was planning because I'd overheard Truda and Mateusz discussing whether I should be allowed to go after the lies I'd told. That deception had only come to light the previous week, and their hurt was still fresh.

I wasn't excited about Uncle Piotr's planned trip to Krasiński

Square to join in Palm Sunday festivities. I had no idea what exactly these festivities would look like, but I knew that anything sanctioned by the Germans was not likely to be fun for us Poles. Even so, I found myself outraged at the idea that Truda and Mateusz might refuse me permission to participate.

My father used to say that people don't always make sense, and the older I got, the more I knew this to be true, even about myself. It seemed that the very act of Truda and Mateusz prohibiting an activity now had the power to make that activity unbelievably tempting to me. *That* troubling pattern was becoming quite clear.

So I tossed and I turned and I huffed and I groaned in frustration, and I thrashed my limbs against the mattress, irritated that I could not shut my mind down. Perhaps that's why it took a long time for the sound to register in a meaningful way. Exhausted but also wide-awake, I gradually noticed a new noise in the usual cacophony. Was it a kitten? I crawled out of bed and went to the window, excited by such a possibility. Of course, we couldn't keep a cat, but maybe if it was a stray on the rooftop, I could find a morsel of food and try to pet it. I carefully, gingerly opened the window. The sound was still muffled, but it did seem louder, although sadly, it no longer sounded like a cat. I paused, straining hard to identify both the sound and the direction of its origin, until it struck me: the sound was coming from Sara's spare bedroom, upstairs in her apartment, on the attic floor adjacent to my room.

I pulled the window closed and pressed my ear against the wall. When this had no effect, I stood staring at the tattered wallpaper for a long moment, listening as the muffled sound ebbed and waned.

My curiosity finally won out. My heart had never beaten so loudly as I edged along the hall, then stepped down one stair at a time, trying to will my footsteps into a lightness that wasn't physically possible. But it was so late, and the city was so noisy.

Uncle Piotr, Mateusz and Truda all slept on the lower floor, and
no one stirred. In the foyer, I slid our apartment key from its
hook and dropped it into my pocket, then I rummaged through
the hall table drawer as quietly as I could manage, seeking Sara's
spare key.

I held my breath as I pried open the front door, cursing the
whine of the hinges, and as soon as I stepped into the hallway,
I saw movement out of the corner of my eye. I reached for the
light switch, and the hanging bulbs in the hallway burst to
life—so bright for a second that it made me squint. But as my
eyes adjusted, I saw a figure moving swiftly toward the communal stairs: a young girl, my age or maybe younger. As she
reached the railing, she looked back at me, and for the briefest of moments, our eyes met. Hers were bright with a kind
of terror I'd only ever experienced once—the night I'd stared
into my dead brother's eyes and wondered how on earth I was
supposed to survive in a world that no longer made sense, the
night we fled Trzebinia.

"Are you okay—?" I started to whisper, but she was gone
before I'd finished the sentence. I heard the soft, rapid patter of
her footsteps as she ran down the stairs, followed by the door
of the lobby closing as she ran out into the street. Alone again,
I became aware of the mess in the hall. There were drips and
small puddles all along the floorboards, and a lingering scent—
something deeply unpleasant but that I couldn't quite put my
finger on. I glanced back at my door and bitterly regretted not
putting on my shoes. As I stepped farther out into the hallway
and my bare toes met the filthy water, I tried not to think about
the source. I wanted to convince myself that Sara was expe-
riencing some plumbing problems, but that didn't explain the
stranger in the stairwell. I wondered if I should just go home,
back to bed, to pretend I hadn't seen any of this. I dismissed that
thought in an instant. Whatever was going on, Sara would surely
be grateful to have my assistance with the cleanup, especially

if it extended all the way down to the front door. Mr. Wójcik on the second floor was a real stickler for keeping the communal areas clean, and Sara wouldn't want any trouble from him.

This thought reassured me that I was doing the right thing, and my footsteps became bolder. By the time I reached her door, I had convinced myself that rather than disobediently sneaking around our building in the middle of the night, I was simply doing the Christian thing by helping my neighbor.

"Sara?" I called softly as I unlocked her door and let myself inside. The smell from the hallway was much stronger here, so strong that when I breathed in, I unexpectedly gagged. Panicked, I pressed my fist to my mouth and looked around her room in alarm. I finally stopped pretending otherwise: if Sara were having plumbing issues, it was definitely her toilet, and my feet were covered in waste. "Sara?" I called again as I closed the door. Upstairs, I could hear the sound I had heard from my bedroom—only now that I was closer, it sounded nothing *at all* like a cat and exactly like a child sobbing.

A chill raced down my spine, and goose bumps prickled across my skin. The pounding of my heart became so intense I could hear my pulse thudding in my ears. I thought about turning around and creeping back across the hallway to burrow back into bed. But I couldn't put the pieces of the puzzle together. How exactly did the smell of sewage and the mess in the hall and the strange girl and the crying child all fit together?

I started up the stairs, following muddy footsteps. As I reached for the balustrade, my hand was shaking, but I pressed on. At the top, I paused at the door and pressed my ear against it. There, I heard the unmistakable sound of quiet speech. I couldn't make out the words, but I recognized at least two voices and thought I could detect the soothing cadence of Sara's. I drew in a deep breath, and then knocked quietly and called, "Sara?"

The voices stopped abruptly, and then in an artificially high tone Sara called back, "Elżbieta? Don't come in here!"

There were frantic sounds within her bedroom, and I knew I should obey her and walk away without opening the door. But desperate curiosity and an instinct I couldn't explain compelled me to push the bedroom door open. As I did, several things caught my attention: a heap of dank and muddy clothes, spreading a filthy puddle toward the rug beside Sara's spare bed, and Sara herself, her hands on the shoulders of a semidressed child as she shuffled her into the closet. Sara closed the door so fast that she barely missed catching the child's fingers. She stood with her back to the closet door, raised her chin high and crossed her arms over her chest.

"What are you doing here so late?" she demanded.

I stared at her, almost doubting my eyes for a second or two. It had all happened so fast. Had I really seen a child there? Surely not. Why would Sara have a child in the closet in her bedroom?

My gaze fell to the pile of muddy clothes, and I drew in a breath. As the scent of sewage hit my lungs again, I covered my nose and my mouth, then narrowed my eyes on her.

"Was that a child?"

"There is no child," she said abruptly, then took a step toward me. "You are dreaming. Go back to bed."

But the closet betrayed her, because from inside I heard a strangled, muffled sob. Sara met my gaze, almost pleading with me not to draw attention to it—which, of course, I immediately did.

"Let her out!" I exclaimed, stepping hastily toward her.

"She's fine," Sara said, sighing in resignation. "*They* are fine."

She turned and opened the door and dropped her voice, murmuring quietly in soothing, soft tones, as she shepherded four small children out of the closet. Two were completely naked, other than smears of mud and filth across their skin. One little boy was fully clothed, from a neat black cap on his head down to makeshift shoes of muddied hessian wrapped around his feet, tied tightly with wound twine. The last child, the little girl I'd heard crying, was barefoot, but she was still wearing a dress. I looked from the children to Sara and then back to the children again.

Until that very moment, I thought I had understood what it was to be afraid, but it suddenly occurred to me that there were depths of fear I had never imagined possible. These children—these emaciated, filthy children—looked as though they might drop dead from terror at any minute.

I rubbed my eyes, as if that would make the children disappear, but this was no hallucination. As tired and bewildered as I was, the smell in the room was so overwhelming it could not be denied.

"Are you going to stand there gawking, or are you going to fetch me some towels?" Sara asked me pointedly. My jaw flapped, and then I retreated and ran down the stairs, very nearly slipping on a puddle. I gathered towels from Sara's linen closet and returned to the bedroom, where I set them on the bed. Sara took one and crouched to gingerly, carefully wipe the filth from the face of the littlest girl, who was still weeping. Without looking at me, she said lightly, "Now, Elżbieta, you must go and draw me a bath. Make the water as hot as you can stand against your own skin. And we will need soap—there is a fresh packet under the sink in the kitchen. Take all of it into the bathroom, and then let yourself out, and go home and back to bed."

"I don't understand. Who are these children?"

"I'm babysitting for a friend."

"Why did you hide them in the closet, then? And why are they covered in…" For some reason, the word stuck in my throat. "Why are they so dirty?" Sara glanced back at me, her gaze expressionless. For a moment, I convinced myself that there was a perfectly logical explanation for all of this, and I was being obtuse. Just before Sara turned her attention back to the child, though, I caught a hint of panic in her gaze. "You're lying to me."

"It's just very complicated and—"

"I'm not a child."

Sara threw an amused smile over her shoulder.

"You're thirteen years old. You most definitely are a child."

"I'm fourteen tomorrow, Sara. And I'm mature for my age because everyone is mature for their age now."

"Well, isn't that the truth?" she said and sighed heavily, then she rose to stand and looked me right in the eyes. "My friend had an accident at home, and the children were caught up in the mess. It's very dangerous for children to be exposed to raw sewage like this, so she asked me to look after them until she cleans up. Any other questions?"

"Then, why hide them?"

"You startled me. That's all."

"I startled you, so you pushed four children into a tiny closet?" I said incredulously. Sara met my gaze boldly, almost daring me to challenge her further.

"It's late. I'm tired, and I wasn't thinking," she said, finally looking away to the little girl, who was gasping for air between each desperate sob. With a sigh, Sara bent and scooped the girl up and held her close, and she murmured quietly into her ear. She spoke so softly I couldn't identify the words, but one of the sounds registered and a shock wave of tension ran through my body.

Sara was speaking Yiddish to this child, and the impossible scene before me suddenly made some sense.

"Elżbieta, I need to soothe this little one and get these children clean, and you need to get to bed." The little girl rested her head against Sara's shoulder and stared at me. Her cheeks were hollow, and her red-rimmed eyes seemed artificially huge in her tiny face. Worst of all, the child's skin had a sickly gray-yellow tone to it, visible where Sara had wiped the mud from her face.

"What's wrong with her?" I whispered, taking an automatic step into the room. Sara closed her eyes briefly, then turned away to look down at the other children, who seemed frozen in complete and terrified silence. When she didn't respond, I prompted her again. "Sara?"

"She is unwell, but it is not the kind of unwell that comes from disease. It is a kind of unwell that comes from neglect. This little girl simply hasn't had enough to eat."

"We could get her…" I was ready to suggest Uncle Piotr could find food for us, maybe even to admit for the first time something I'd scarcely even admitted to myself up to that point: Uncle Piotr seemed to have an uncanny ability to get hard-to-find objects. Rarefied foods sometimes appeared in our kitchen, and more than once, I'd heard him on the telephone discussing objects I knew to be contraband, like crystal radios or identity papers, like the ones he'd found so quickly for me. But before I could say any of this, Sara interrupted.

"This is not something we can fix with one meal, Elżbieta. This little girl needs to go to a new home. They *all* need to go to new homes."

We stood in fraught silence for several more moments. I didn't want to say it, as if speaking the words aloud would somehow increase the danger we were all in.

"These are Jewish children, aren't they?" I whispered dully. I raised my gaze to Sara's. She swallowed, then forced a laugh.

"Of course not—"

"Sara," I said, my throat tightening. "Please do not lie to me. I'm not a fool."

Her tone, at last, grew impatient.

"These children have swum through a sewer to get here, Elżbieta. They are tired, and they are dirty and scared, and if I don't clean them, they will all die."

"Die?"

"There is typhus in the sewer," she said plainly. "There are typhus germs all over their little bodies, even as we stand here stating the obvious. I need to scrub these children clean, wash and dry their clothes, and then get them out of this apartment before sunrise. I do not have time to explain this to you—not right now anyway. You must leave me to my work, and then tomorrow we will talk, I promise."

"Let me help."

"If your family wakes up, they will notice you missing—"

"—and they'll step into the hallway, see a trail of festering sewage that leads to your door and check here first."

Sara winced.

"There is a mess in the hallway?"

"It's not nearly as bad as it is in here, but yes, there is a very obvious mess." Sara closed her eyes briefly, seeming momentarily defeated, and that's when I made my decision. "I'll draw the bath for you, then go clean the hallway."

Sara looked so exhausted in that moment that my heart ached for her. She opened her eyes and stared at me.

"Please," I added, "let me help. I can't sleep anyway."

"Fine," she said and sighed, then she bit her lip. "But you must be quiet out there. No one can hear you, because if someone comes out to see what's going on—"

"I'll tell them there was a problem with your toilet."

"Good girl. And start at my door, won't you? Work your way downstairs from here." She looked down to the child in her arms and then back to me, her gaze intense. "The sooner we hide where the trail ends, the better."

It took more than an hour to clean from Sara's apartment to the front door of our building. It wasn't a significant distance, but I had to move slowly in order to remain quiet. By the time I walked back upstairs, the floor was drying, and I paused in the hallway to survey my handiwork.

Truda had taught me well. I had done a good job, and this unexpected burst of late-night domestic activity was the most satisfying thing I had done in months. It wasn't the cleaning, it

was the simple fact that I had helped my friend and the knowledge that I was doing exactly what my brother and father would
have done.

When I let myself back in, Sara was sitting on the sofa, her
head in her hands. It was oppressively hot in her apartment
now, the stove on and the oven door propped open. The children's newly cleaned clothing hung in every conceivable space
to dry. As I set the mop and broom down, Sara looked up and
offered a weary smile.

"Where are the children?" I asked her uncertainly. Sara
pointed toward the stairs.

"Sleeping. And you, my friend, must take yourself into the
bathroom and wash your hands and your feet very carefully
with what's left of my soap." She rested her palms on her knees,
then pushed herself to her feet. "While you do that, I'm going
to make us some tea."

I scrubbed my skin so carefully that by the time I was finished, my hands and feet were red and raw. By the time I returned to the kitchen, Sara had two steaming mugs of tea on
her low-set coffee table. I thanked her quietly as I sat beside her.
She gave me a sad smile as she reached for her tea.

"I know you're curious, and I'd love to explain the whole,
complicated mess to you, but it would be far too dangerous. All
I can tell you is that a courier was taking these children somewhere safe. But there was an incident, and she had to quickly
find an alternative place."

"They were escaping from the Jewish Quarter, weren't they?"
I guessed. Sara didn't answer me, so I blew on the tea, then
tried to prompt her again. "I do know the Jewish Quarter has
been walled in."

"It may be forbidden to use the word *ghetto* in Warsaw now,
but in *this* apartment, we tell the truth. That's what it is, and
that's what we will call it." I was struck by a pang of guilt, because I had so often avoided the truth while I was in Sara's apart-

ment. And I'd heard Uncle Piotr and Mateusz discussing the Jewish Quarter and the rules about the word *ghetto*, but I hadn't thought much about why that rule would exist. "The Germans like to give off an air of civility. They want the world to think that they are the master race, smarter and more dignified than the rest of us. They also want to be able to disguise their cruelty with polite words. Instead of facing the truth of their own cruelty, they dress it up with airs and graces, as if using different words could change the reality of their evil deeds—" She seemed to catch herself, and she winced and shook her head, then sighed. "I am being careless now, but I am too tired to play the game. A group of sewer guides and couriers were escorting the children to a safe house, but the Germans were waiting at one of their exit points, and they arrested one of the guides. That guide will be tortured by the Gestapo, and she will inevitably give up some of the details of her rescue work. Most of the children were captured with her, but the other courier escaped with these four." She gestured upstairs. "She panicked and brought the children here, knowing that I would shelter them overnight."

"Should I not ask how she knows you?"

"You definitely should not."

"The children are so thin," I murmured, almost to myself.

"Yes." She pressed her palm against her chest and swallowed heavily. "It has been months—years even—since they ate properly, and there are no reserves left in them, no fat beneath the skin to keep them healthy, no vitality in their bodies. The Jewish rations are half our rations. *Half.* Think about how little you would have to eat without your uncle's extra supplies, and now imagine that was halved. Every single person on the other side of that wall is starving to death."

"Well...you told me there is typhus in the sewers," I said awkwardly. "And...the Germans say the Jews are walled off because they have typhus..." That's what the posters and signs around

the ghetto said anyway, and I knew that's what the Germans
wanted us to believe. The shameful truth was I hadn't thought
much about the wall or the Jewish people trapped inside it. I had
been entirely consumed with my own problems since we'd arrived in Warsaw. It hadn't occurred to me to think about those
who might have had even bigger problems.

"You really think the Jews are dirtier than we are?" Sara interrupted me, eyes flashing with fire, then she seemed to catch
herself. She drew in a deep breath, then she asked me carefully,
"Elżbieta. Does it matter to you that those children are Jewish?"

"You told me to wash my hands—"

"Because of the sewage! Not because the children are *Jewish*!"

She had never spoken to me so sharply, and I felt my face
flushing with shame. I was tired and anxious and now as nervous about Sara's disapproval as I was about the danger we were
all in with those children in her apartment.

"I...I know..."

I wanted to tell her then that I was really Emilia Slaska,
born of a family who loved their neighbors, Jewish, Catholic
or whatever they might happen to be. That my father had been
killed by the Germans right in front of my eyes, that my brother
Tomasz had died because of his efforts to help the Jews, that I'd
seen him in death, too.

Had I not so recently been caught breaking Mateusz and
Truda's rules, I might have told her that night, but as Truda
had warned, just because I liked Sara did not mean I should
trust her. I was tired, confused just trying to figure out if Sara
should be trusted now that I knew she had secrets of her own.

But then I remembered the stories I'd heard about the Germans—how they could be so incredibly crafty, and how they'd
sometimes go to great lengths to test loyalty and root out those
working against Hitler's goals. It struck me that even this complicated situation in Sara's apartment could be a ruse, set up to

determine whether or not I was a sympathizer to prohibited activities.

Mateusz had told me to be paranoid, and in that moment, I truly was—but I was also wary of the sharpness in Sara's gaze. All I could do was try to walk a fine line between maintaining her approval and saying and doing the things I knew I was supposed to do.

"You should not be hiding Jewish children in your apartment," I said with conviction, intending to convince her that I believed it, just in case she'd set all of this up to trap me. But Sara's eyebrows drew down, and her lips pursed. My answer displeased her immensely. Although I knew I'd done exactly what I was supposed to do, I hated that I had disappointed Sara. My cheeks grew hot, and I stood, suddenly desperate to retreat—away from the sick children and my dear friend who, it turned out, I didn't really know at all. "I know the Jews aren't dirty," I blurted, and I dropped my voice low. "I know they are just people, just as we are. My family had many Jewish friends back in…where we came from. But I am scared for you. It is so dangerous for you to have Jewish children in your home, even overnight."

"It is," Sara conceded slowly, then she added, "Did you know that I had a child, a son?"

My eyes widened. Sara had never once mentioned her life before the war.

"You were married?"

"I was. I don't speak about him because it hurts too much, but I think of him every day."

"What happened?"

"His name was Janusz. He was three years old. He had my smile, my husband's eyes… He was the best thing that ever happened to me. My mother was watching him that day—the very first day of bombing. I went to the hospital with my husband, who was a doctor, and we were tending to the wounded. Our apartment building was hit by a bomb, most likely within a few hours of me leaving. Mother's injuries were awful—she surely died instantly. My son, though…" She broke off, her voice trembling. Sara drew in a shaky breath, then sipped at her tea and finally cleared her throat. "I couldn't get back to our building because the roads were blocked, and the hospital was in such a state, and every time I tried to leave, someone would rush at me with another injured person and… I just kept telling myself that Janusz was with my mother and that they were certainly okay. But they weren't okay, and when I finally got back to the apartment two days later, I saw that the building was destroyed. I will never forget the sight of him. Janusz was lying beneath a small beam. When I lifted it off him, I saw that he was lying in a pool of his own blood. He'd scratched at the beam for so long that he had worn the skin away on his fingers."

"Oh, Sara…"

"The worst of it was that I *know* that part of Warsaw was flooded with people in the days he lay dying, because the building was on a major arterial road. Thousands of people walked right by him as they evacuated. Someone heard him crying— maybe many people did. I understand that the people who happened past were all rushing out of the city. I know that they were probably terrified and trying to save their own lives and their own families…but *no one stopped*. No one would put themselves at risk. And my baby died alone and terrified." The tears in her eyes spilled over. She let them roll down her cheeks, but she met my gaze, daring me to face the full force of her pain. "He always cried for me when he hurt himself, Elżbieta. In my heart, I know that he was crying and calling for me as he died. Maybe his very last thoughts were of the abandonment…wondering why I wasn't coming to help him."

"I am so sorry," I said because, as useless as the words were, they were surely better than the stunned silence I was tempted to sit in.

"To know that my son suffered and he was alone and no one did anything to help him has changed me. It has driven me not just to madness but beyond it. I make foolish decisions every day because I cannot rest my head on a pillow at night unless I've done everything in my power to help children like my son. *That* is why these children are here tonight. One day, I will likely die for a child like one of those precious souls upstairs, and I am at peace with that. I'm at peace telling you this story, even though just a minute ago, you made me wonder for the first time if you are the kind of person who would believe the German lies that the Jews are somehow *less* than anyone else."

"I don't believe that," I blurted, shaking my head desperately. Her disapproval was much more frightening than even death seemed to be in that moment. "I was scared. I *am* scared. I thought you were trying to trap me."

"Trap you?" she repeated, frowning.

"The Germans are so wily," I said, my throat tightening. I suddenly felt foolish to have doubted her. "I thought it might be a ruse. That if I didn't say or do the right thing, you'd turn me in."

Once again, Sara's expression softened.

"These are hard times. Knowing who to trust is never an exact science, not in a place like this, not when there is so much to be gained from betrayal. It is late, and I've had a long day— but so have you, and you need to go home to bed now."

I sat my now-empty teacup on her coffee table, then paused.

"Your husband," I said. "Where is he?"

She sighed sadly.

"They bombed the hospital, too. I was there at the time, but I was in the shelter in the basement and was uninjured. Wojciech was in surgery upstairs—he died instantly. I lost him the day after I lost Janusz and my mother. And now," she said shrugging, "now it's just me."

I looked around her apartment, suddenly realizing why I'd assumed she'd never married.

"You don't have any photos of them."

"All our photographs were in the apartment when the building was destroyed," she whispered.

I slipped back into my bed a few minutes later, Truda and Mateusz and Piotr none the wiser. I lay awake for hours, thinking about Sara and her loss and the wall around the Jewish Quarter and all of the people trapped within, wondering for the very first time about the other stories taking place in Warsaw while I had been so focused on my own.

6

Emilia

OUR APARTMENT BUILDING LAY IN WARSAW'S OLD TOWN, exactly in the middle between two definitive Warsaw landmarks—Krasiński Square to the west and the Vistula River to the east. The location of our neighborhood had been almost irrelevant to me until my fourteenth birthday, in part because I so rarely left the building—we could have lived on the moon for all I cared. I had passed but never visited Krasiński Square, and as Uncle Piotr led the way that morning, I was startled to see a fair looming before me. Street stalls and performers were scattered all around the square, but my gaze was drawn to two massive Ferris wheels towering over everything else. One was marked *out of order*, but the other was turning slowly while a long line of revelers waited for their turn in the spring sunshine.

It was a beautiful, jubilant sight—painted against a horrifying background. The unmistakable shape of a wall loomed just behind the merriment. At least ten feet tall, constructed from a chaotic mix of unmatched bricks, it was topped with a line of wound barbed wire. I stopped dead in my tracks as I recognized it, realizing that the buildings I could see beyond that wall were the rooftops of homes in the Jewish Quarter.

I had seen that wall before, from different angles, in different parts of the city. But I'd never seen it like this; it was as if the events of the night before had removed scales from my eyes. I tried not to gape as I gazed around the square. Hundreds of people were mingling, and almost every person was wearing clean clothes and a smile. My gaze flitted between the revelers and the wall.

"Come, then," Uncle Piotr said cheerfully. "What should we do first? Should we buy some flowers? And of course, we need to stop for food—sweets, perhaps? I *know* how you like candy. And—oh! We must take a trip around the Ferris wheel. Have you ever been on one? I have to say, it's a lot of fun."

I couldn't drag my eyes from the wall. I wanted to clutch at Uncle Piotr's arm and to point to it and to scream *Don't you see it? It's right there. What are all of these people doing out here in the sunshine having fun when there are children starving behind that wall right there?*

"What is this?" I asked him, through numb lips. Uncle Piotr frowned.

"What do you mean?" he prompted, then comprehension seemed to dawn. "Ah, we have kept you locked up in that apartment too long. This is Krasiński Square."

"But it's not always like this."

"No, your birthday falls on Palm Sunday this year. The Germans don't allow us much freedom to celebrate our faith, but every now and again, they do allow us a glimpse of joy." Uncle Piotr gave me a bright, radiant smile, and then he chuckled at what he was probably misinterpreting as delighted shock. "Come on, then, little one. Let's go have some fun."

I went along with it. I ignored the steady pull of the wall, and I walked from street stall to street stall, behind Uncle Piotr, who seemed determined to spoil me beyond even my wildest dreams. I laughed when I knew he was expecting me to laugh, and I even feigned impatience as we lined up for the Ferris wheel. As the line began to snake its way forward, I told myself the buzzing butterflies in my stomach represented excitement rather than anxiety.

I *was* nervous about the height—but not because I feared I would fall: I was nervous about what I might be able to see from way up there. The ride was close enough to the ghetto wall that it towered over it, and knowing that the Germans had sanctioned this festival, I couldn't help but wonder if it was intentional. I could easily imagine some commander delighting in the idea that the Jews trapped within the ghetto might see the huge wheel representing freedoms they had long lost. Life for those of us on the Aryan side was neither comfortable nor free, but I was starting to suspect that comfort and freedom might be highly relative terms.

When Uncle Piotr and I finally took our place in one of the gondolas, and the giant ride lurched to life, he suddenly placed his hand over mine. I looked into his eyes, expecting him to make some joke about holding his hand if I became too afraid, but instead, I saw that he was, for once, deadly serious.

"Please do something for me."

"Anything."

"Don't look that way, okay?" he said lightly, pointing toward the wall. "The ride is fun, but its location is unfortunate. Enjoy the views of the square and any other parts of the city you can see, but don't look over the wall."

I searched his gaze. Uncle Piotr, at least within the privacy of our home, had made no secret of the fact that he despised the Germans—but I had known plenty of other people who despised the Germans and still somehow managed to hate the Jews, or who even managed to *blame* the Jews for the occupation, through some convoluted logic I'd never quite understood.

It occurred to me on that ride that I simply could not bear it if Uncle Piotr revealed himself to be that kind of person, so I refused to give voice to the dozens of questions that immediately popped into my mind. I knew that at least when it came to me, Uncle Piotr had the best of intentions. I had been a stranger to him only months earlier, but I was now part of his family. He wanted to give me a glimmer of hope and, on my birthday, just a tiny glimpse of the childhood I should have been enjoying.

Try as I might to respect his wishes and to keep my eyes focused on our side of the wall, they were drawn back to the Jewish Quarter again and again. I didn't want Uncle Piotr to catch me looking, and he seemed determined to distract me with a constant commentary on the various landmarks we could see from the Ferris wheel, so I could only steal glimpses here and there.

I saw buildings, not so different from the ones on my side of the wall, but I could also see crowds of people on the street. *So many people.* I wanted to see those crowds as one mass—one entity I could turn my back on. I told myself I was just a child and that group of people was not my problem at all. I had enough problems, and besides, what could I do for them? I had nothing to offer the Jews trapped behind that wall.

But I couldn't shake the feeling that God was trying to tell me something, because the visual contrasts were a slap in the face. I saw the gray of the cobblestone streets, the black of the tar rooftops, the brown bricks and beige mortar. Even their clothes were dull.

But *my* side of the wall was a rainbow of color and life. The stalls around the Ferris wheel were bursting with the flowers of early spring—white snowdrops and yellow and purple crocuses, willow twigs with their yellow and white buds, all speckled beneath and around the vibrant green of new spring growth of mature trees. Women wore cornflower blue dresses, and the men wore crisp white shirts, and little old ladies carried umbrellas in shades of green and gold and pink.

As the ride stopped, and as Uncle Piotr stepped off our gondola and extended his hand to support me as I followed, there was a shout and the sound of a gunshot, and then a bloodcurdling scream of pain, and another gunshot, and then just a single heartbeat of utter stillness and silence.

And then, a split second later, everyone in Krasiński Square went right back to what they were doing. The ride operator encouraged us to enjoy our day. The street vendors went back to selling their wares. The revelers went back to enjoying the spring sunshine.

"I think it's time for some flowers, don't you?" Uncle Piotr asked me, his tone forcefully bright. He led me away from the ride to stop at a nearby flower peddler. While Uncle Piotr tried to draw my attention to various flowers, I turned away from him, back toward the Ferris wheel and beyond it.

I did not make the decision to walk toward the wall. But my fingertips soon touched the roughhewn bricks, and I closed my eyes for what surely must have only been a single moment. Sounds swam into focus, sounds of horses and carts against cobblestone, quiet conversations in Yiddish and Polish. I inhaled and caught just a hint of something oppressive. Was it death or sewage or some other hallmark of masses suffering?

I didn't decide to get involved in helping the Jews. No, it was decided for me, the minute I was born into a household that knew our Polish neighbors, regardless of religion or heritage, were an extension of our family. Perhaps I'd had valid reasons for my inaction before that moment: I was young, traumatized, lost, utterly *ignorant*. But children younger than I had been involved in both resistance and relief efforts, and I'd seen proof of that the previous night.

"Elżbieta!" I heard Piotr's frantic cry behind me, and when I turned to him, his eyes were wild. He took a hesitant step toward me, then stepped back, motioning frantically for me to come away from the wall. I startled out of my reverie and walked briskly back toward him, but I could still feel the rough brick beneath my palms, as if the shapes of the stone were imprinted into my skin.

"What were you thinking?" Piotr hissed under his breath, and when his hand caught my elbow, I felt that he was shaking. "What possible reason would you have for touching it? If a soldier had happened past, they would have assumed that you were trying to help someone get out or were throwing food over the top. You would have been shot. *You would have been shot!*"

He kept his voice low enough that the bystanders just a few feet away couldn't hear us, but there was no mistaking Uncle Piotr's fury and shock at what I had done. I apologized profusely and assured him I didn't know what I was doing, and then I promised him I would be more careful.

And all the while, in the back of my mind, I began planning my next steps.

"Sara," I called, as I let myself into her apartment later that evening. With a fat slice of a relatively indulgent poppy-seed cake in hand, I was ready to go to battle with my friend.

"In here, Elżbieta," she called back. "Come through, please."

I found Sara in her living room sitting beneath a lamp. She rested her knitting in its basket, then reached down beside the sofa.

"The birthday girl arrives," she announced playfully, as she lifted a small box and extended it toward me. I gasped in delight, then swapped the plate of cake for the box as I sat beside her. The box was surprisingly heavy, and I rattled it, trying to draw out the anticipation of what might be inside. I glanced at Sara and found her staring down at the cake, a look of glee in her eyes. She looked back at me, and we both laughed.

"Go on," she said.

"You, too," I said, nodding toward the cake.

Sara broke off a piece and popped it into her mouth, then moaned in sheer joy.

"Truda is a wonder," she said, her eyes alight. "How did she manage this miracle?"

Having eaten two slices of the cake already, I knew it wasn't all that extraordinary. It was dry and bland and, by prewar standards, barely deserved the title of *cake* at all. Even so, I understood the lengths Truda had gone to in order to make me a birthday cake, and I well appreciated how rare such a thing was. It had been a day of small miracles. Cake and cut flowers and candy and even a carnival ride, not to mention a calling from God.

"She has been skimming rations for a few weeks, plus..." I understood that a bond of trust between Sara and me existed only by circumstance. She had been forced to trust me the previous night and, as such, I now held her life in my hands. But if things were to progress as I planned, I now needed to demonstrate my trust in return. There was one obvious way to do so. Sara still thought that Truda and Mateusz were my real parents, but I had promised Mateusz that I would not betray that secret, and I intended to keep that promise. Instead, I had to share something else.

"Well, Uncle Piotr occasionally dabbles in the black market," I said conspiratorially.

"Ah," she said, but her tone was completely neutral. I scanned her face, expecting to see some kind of reaction, but instead, she pointed toward the gift. "Open it. I'm eager to see what you think."

I opened the box and drew in a sharp breath as I recognized the objects inside. There was charcoal and oil pastels and pencils and not one but *two* notebooks—more brand-new art supplies than I'd seen in years. Such a thing would have been impossible to procure in Trzebinia.

"You remembered," I whispered. I'd mentioned to Sara in passing that I loved to draw but that I hadn't done so in some time. The truth was I hadn't been able to bring myself to draw since Tomasz died. Drawing felt like the act of an innocent, childlike version of myself—a girl who had been lost forever with the last remaining member of my real family. But as I opened that gift from Sara, I knew immediately that I would not only use these precious items, I would *relish* using them. My fingers already itched to pick up the charcoal. "How did you do this?"

Sara gave me a wry smile.

"I, too, occasionally dabble in the black market."

She set the plate down on her coffee table, and I leaped from my seat to hug her.

"Thank you," I said, my throat feeling uncomfortably tight. I told myself that I must not cry, that the entire purpose of this visit was to convince Sara that I was adult enough to help her with her secret work. But in this kind gesture, I saw shades of my beloved Alina, who had always encouraged my artistic efforts, and I was almost overcome with relief and gratitude to find that someone in Warsaw finally understood me.

After a moment, though, I pulled myself together to start what I expected was going to be a difficult conversation. I extracted myself from her embrace, moved back to my chair and drew in a deep breath, but as I opened my mouth to ask her if I could help her, I lost my courage at the very last second. My gaze fell upon the half-eaten cake, and my tone was a little manic as I said, "Aren't you going to finish that?"

Sara laughed and patted her belly.

"I'm stuffed. I couldn't possibly. You should eat it for me so it doesn't spoil."

It was a lie, and an unconvincing lie at that—Sara was so selfless that she seemed determined to share even this rare treat. However, drawing attention to her lie would mean I would have nothing to talk about other than the thing I needed to talk about, and I was suddenly far too anxious to start that conversation, so I picked up the cake and began to toy with it. Then, recognizing that wasting food was an unforgivable crime in our present circumstances, I stuffed little pieces of cake into my mouth to prolong the silence.

This left me in the absurd position of being full for the first time in months, but still eating regardless. After just a few seconds of this, my conscience would not allow me to let the situation persist, and I thrust the plate back toward Sara as I blurted, "You really must eat it. And you really must let me help you."

Sara blinked at me.

"I told you, I'm full. Really I am. And do you want to help with the knitting? I would love—"

"Not the knitting." She avoided my eyes, and I drew a deep breath and prayed desperately to sound adult and confident as I said, "You know what I'm talking about."

"I'm afraid I really do not."

We sat there staring at one another in silent battle. For just a moment, I considered the possibility that I imagined the previous night. It had been so late…and it had seemed surreal…

"But…the children?" The words escaped my mouth as a question.

"What children?"

"You…there was a…" I pointed upstairs. "Last night, remember?"

"Last night we unwound this yarn. Then you went home."

"Yes…but…"

"Elżbieta, are you well?" Sara's tone took on a soothing, slightly scolding quality. She went forward and rested the back of her hand against my forehead. "Your cheeks are flushed. You must have had too much sun today. Piotr told me he was taking you to the square. Perhaps it is sunstroke. You really should get home and rest. You'll feel much better in the morning... less confused."

She'd almost convinced me, but there was something about her tone that was laden with a hidden depth of warning. My gaze narrowed on Sara's face as she removed her hand and sat back in her chair. I dropped my voice and spoke again in a rush.

"You had four Jewish children in your bedroom last night. I didn't dream it and I'm not confused. Sara, I am going to help you."

Frustration twisted Sara's features into a scowl. She stood abruptly and caught me by the elbow to drag me up the stairs toward the spare bedroom. Once inside, she slammed the door behind us, and she gripped my upper arms in both of her hands. I had never seen Sara look so fierce, and for a moment I was afraid.

"This isn't a game! Perhaps you have some fantasy of becoming a heroine here, but that is foolish, childish nonsense. You need to go home, back to your parents, and do exactly as I told you last night and pretend that nothing happened. You're a child yourself, Elżbieta. You are too young to get involved in messy business like this."

I frowned at that.

"How old was the courier? Or was she a guide? The girl I saw in the hallway, I mean," I said. A raspberry flush stole over Sara's cheeks.

"Her situation is very different from yours."

"Was she twelve? Thirteen?" I could see that I was close, if not correct, purely from the guilt on Sara's face. "Surely you can find some way for me to help?" I looked into her eyes and added bitterly, "I am sitting in that apartment all day, I cannot even go to school. The most interesting thing I've done in months has been looking at pictures of bodily organs with you! I am a wasted life, which makes me a wasted opportunity for you and your efforts. I could be doing something...anything.

Surely you understand how frustrating that is, given I understand what is at stake?"

"I sympathize with your situation, I really do," she said sadly,
her gaze softening. "But there is no safe way for me to involve
you. I hope you understand. I cannot betray your parents' trust,
and I really cannot betray your uncle. He is my friend, and he's
done so much for me over this past year. I know he would never
forgive me if I involved you in something like this."

"I cannot live like this," I exclaimed. "I cannot live in this
nice apartment, living off rations that can be skimmed for cake,
in a house that has money, and with my uncle who seems to be
able to get any luxury item we can dream of. Not while, just
a few blocks away, children are swimming through sewers to
avoid starving to death. And I cannot *believe* that you would
ask me to."

"Things are not so easy for you," Sara said calmly. "Truda
managed to skim enough flour for some cake, but you and I
both know that our rations are not generous. But for your uncle,
you would only be just getting by, too, and even with his help
your family is hardly living the high life."

"But we are still surviving," I whispered, as my eyes filled
with tears. "Sara, I can't bear it. Uncle Piotr took me to Krasiński
Square today, and I saw that wall, and I wanted to tear it down
with my bare hands. You must let me help because this feeling—" I pointed helplessly to my chest, trying to explain the
outrage that had been boiling away inside me since last night
"—it will destroy me if I don't use it to do some good. Besides,
this is *not* a choice between safety and danger. I'm probably already in danger!" I had said too much, and at her concerned
look, I hastily added, "Everyone in this city is. The German
cruelty can be so random."

"All the more reason you should keep to yourself, Elżbieta."
She seemed to suddenly deflate, her exhaustion from the previous night now written in the deep lines around her mouth

and in the gray bags beneath her eyes. "This is a very admirable desire, but it's impossible."

"Okay," I said, feigning sadness. I pulled away and made as if to leave the bedroom. "Well, do you have any suggestions?"

Sara gave me a blank look.

"Suggestions for...?"

"Who I should ask next?" At her frown, I added, "I don't know anyone else in Warsaw, so if you won't help I'll just go down to Miodowa Street, and I'll ask every passerby if they can connect me with the underground efforts to help the Jews..."

"Elżbieta!" she groaned in frustration.

"I mean it. If you won't find a way for me to help you, I *will* find someone else."

I could see that Sara was trying to maintain her irritation with me, but in that moment I saw the first glimmer of reluctant admiration in her eyes.

"You must let me think this through," she said, after a long and careful pause. "And you must understand that if I find something for you to do, it *cannot* be on the front lines. There is so much to be done, and all of it is heroic, but much of it is behind-the-scenes."

I had been entertaining fantasies of heroically carrying dying children through the sewers so this was somewhat disappointing, but I would take what I could get.

7

Roman

"I FEEL YOUR HATRED SOMETIMES, ROMAN. I WANT YOU TO know that I understand why you feel that way, and I forgive you for it."

Samuel had found himself with a free afternoon, and he and I had decided to call upon the street vendor on Zamenhofa Street, to thank her for her help over the past few weeks. She had saved vegetable scraps for us consistently since that first day I visited her, passing them to Dawidek or me when we came after work, but this was the first time Samuel had been able to speak with her personally. While they were hardly thriving, Mother and Eleonora were both alive, and I had a feeling that might not be the case but for those scraps.

Now, Samuel and I were returning to our apartment, running a little later than we should have and scurrying to make it back behind our door before the seven o'clock curfew. We had been walking in silence until Samuel's breathless statement. I looked at him in alarm. His expression was set in a stiff mask, and he stared ahead, as if he couldn't bear to look at me.

"Samuel, no! Why would you say such a thing?" I protested.

"We both know exactly why." He shrugged. "It is my fault you are here."

"It is *their* fault we are here," I said flatly.

"Yes and no."

We walked in silence again for almost a block while I tried to understand how to talk about this. It was not something he and I had addressed before—an unspoken truth that I did not even think about unless I could find no way to avoid it. As such, I hadn't collected or sorted my own thoughts on the matter, and now that Samuel had brought the murky issue from the shadows into the light, I was too confused to reply.

"Your mother wanted to flee," Samuel reminded me. "I convinced her to stay."

"You did what you thought was best."

"Then she wanted to get you false papers. She wanted you to go into hiding with your school friends. But I dismissed that idea, too. I was so sure we were best off staying together."

"I wouldn't have gone anyway, Samuel. The *only* blessing in our current situation is that we are together." We were still scurrying along the streets, both studiously avoiding eye contact. "I don't blame you for any of this," I said unevenly. "I could never blame you."

"You could have escaped, Roman. You don't deserve to be here."

"*No one* deserves to be here!" I exclaimed, stopping abruptly as my hands curled into fists. Samuel turned back to me, first to look around in alarm that I might have drawn attention to us, and then to give me a pained, miserable frown.

"I just meant..." Samuel, so wise and calm and hardly ever lost for words, trailed off. He raised his hands in defeat, then shrugged sadly. "I just meant to say that *you* could have avoided all of this. You could have hidden in plain sight outside of these walls."

For once, the ghetto seemed silent all around us. I stared at him, desperately trying to figure out both how to end the conversation and how to resolve it. I hated talking about this, almost as much as I hated that Samuel had been suffering from this incorrect assumption.

"It breaks my heart that you think I…" I drew in a sharp breath, then, almost squirming with awkwardness, I said, low and fast, "I love you. I do *hate*, but it's not directed at you. Never at you."

"You are my first son, Roman. You are the boy who taught me how to be a father. I love you, too."

My eyes were stinging with unshed tears. We were late, and we needed to run, but after a moment I'd been squirming through and desperate to end, I found a moment I was desperate to linger in. I wished I had the words to express so much to Samuel—how much he meant to me, how grateful I was to him—but my throat felt tight, and I knew that if I tried to say those things, I'd wind up weeping. Instead, I kept my gaze fixed on the pavement ahead of us as I admitted hoarsely, "I don't know how to keep going sometimes. This is all too much. I worry that I'm not strong enough."

"We just need to keep putting one foot in front of the other, son. When everything else has been taken from us, all we have left is each other, so we remain true to ourselves and look after one another." He cleared his throat. "What else is there to do? The bitterness would kill us, otherwise."

Bitterness. I tasted it on my tongue even as he said the word. That captured the toxic feelings in my gut perfectly, but the worst thing was Samuel was more correct than he knew.

The bitterness was killing me, and every day the poison became more potent.

* * *

My mother met Florian Abramczyk in a park on a hot summer's day when she was nineteen, and the way she told the story, she laughed in his face when he asked her out on a date. She was certain her parents would kill her for dating a Catholic boy, but Florian was charming and persuasive, and by the time she and her friends left the park that day, she'd agreed to meet him the following weekend.

Their romance bloomed over summer, and by the time her parents found out about Florian in early autumn, Mother was already besotted. But my grandparents were every bit as horrified as she had feared they would be, and they threatened to throw Mother out of the family home. The story goes that she broke up with Florian but fell into such a black mood that after several weeks, her friends convinced her to reconnect with him. My father proposed the minute he saw her again. They married soon after, and I was born twelve months after that.

My grandparents were livid right up until they held me in their arms, at which point all was forgiven, even if it was never forgotten.

I was four years old when Florian died after a short bout with what was probably stomach tumors. My memories of him faded with time, but I always knew the legend of him—mostly because, for years after his death, my mother spoke about him so often I took the threads of those stories and stitched for myself new memories of our family life together. Florian was strong and brave and handsome and *so* clever: a lawyer and a self-made man who had risen above his circumstances as an orphan and supported himself with part-time jobs even as he studied at university. His commitment to the Catholic faith was absolute— sick or well, busy or free, he never missed Mass or confession or finding some way to volunteer in support of his congregation at St. Kazimierz each week. Mother used to tell me that the most important things in Florian's life were her, me and anyone or anything associated with that church.

Florian died at twenty-five years old, just months after he had put a down payment on a house for us and just as his career began. It wasn't long before my mother and I were in dire financial straits. My grandparents tried to help, but my mother was also from a humble background. There was only so much they could do.

The only person in our lives who had the means to help us was Samuel. Mother and Samuel had been friends since childhood, and he'd been on the periphery of our family for as long as I could remember. When Florian first fell ill, Samuel had promised him that whatever happened, Mother and I would be cared for.

Samuel was a man of his word.

At first, I was comforted by the reliability of his visits. If Mother was sad, Samuel knew how to cheer her up. If she was worried, he knew how to ease her fears. If the pantry was empty, he would often visit with a box of food, and he'd always include sweets for me.

I had a front-row seat to the shifting tone of their relationship over time. At first, I was confused when their gazes began to linger or when Samuel was suddenly giggling like a child when my mother made little jokes intended to amuse me. One evening I found them sitting on the couch together holding hands as they listened to the wireless radio. I climbed up onto Mother's lap and pushed them apart so I could sit between them.

When I was six, my mother told me she and Samuel were going to marry. We moved into Samuel's apartment in the Jewish Quarter, but I continued to attend a Catholic school, and she and Samuel went out of their way to ensure I was still active in my father's congregation at St. Kazimierz, just as Florian had wanted.

Even once we were walled into the ghetto, I still periodi-

cally attended Mass—there were thousands of Jewish Catholics
trapped within the walls, and many still worshipped in one of
the three Catholic congregations that operated inside. And, back
when we were allowed, my family would observe the Jewish
holidays, and I'd join in those occasions, too. I *liked* the diver-
sity of our family life. I loved that my mother and Samuel had
chosen to honor Florian's wishes to raise me in his faith's tradition, but I loved the richness and the rhythms of Jewish culture and religion, too. I took Communion, but my *Kennkarte*
identity card was yellow and stamped with a *J* to indicate that
I was a Jewish man. I wore the compulsory Star of David armband on my arm with pride, not the shame the Germans would
have had me feel.

Samuel was right that Mother wanted us all to run before
the wall went up, and even once we were trapped, she argued
fiercely for me to try to escape on my own. If a German soldier
saw me walking down the street on the Aryan side of Warsaw,
they might never have looked twice, and even if they did, their
first likely action would be to check that I was circumcised. I
wasn't, simply because my mother and Florian had decided to
raise me in his faith's tradition, rather than hers.

But Samuel and I had been determined that I should stay
with the family, and even as conditions worsened within the
ghetto, I never regretted it. In one sense, I was a prisoner by
choice, perhaps out of stubborn pride, perhaps out of loyalty
to my family but, mostly, out of sheer terror at the thought of
being separated from them.

At the end of the day, *that* was my worst nightmare—not the
trials of the ghetto.

I would endure torture and starvation and even death if it
meant I could stay with my family. There was nothing more
important to me in the world.

8

Emilia

SARA INVITED TRUDA AND MATEUSZ FOR COFFEE AFTER supper one evening. My parents were exceedingly suspicious about this, even as we prepared to walk down the hallway to her apartment.

"I don't understand why she wants to meet with us," Truda muttered, shaking her head.

"She probably just wants to ease our minds about her friendship with Elżbieta. I don't think there is anything sinister about it." Mateusz shrugged.

"I'm glad that you're going to meet with her. She is a good friend to me," I said as innocently as I could because I knew exactly the reason for the invitation.

Just as Sara and I had planned the night before, my parents were soon seated around her dining room table, with steaming cups of genuine coffee cradled in their palms. Much of what passed for coffee in those days was a poor substitute—ground acorns or chicory or, when things were really tight, plain old wheat grains. But Sara had asked Uncle Piotr to procure some quality coffee beans, determined to make an occasion of the gathering.

"I wanted to meet with you to clear the air and to get to know you a little better," she began. "After all, Elżbieta is so dear to all of us, so we have something important in common. Besides, in these difficult times, new friends are always a blessing," Sara added quietly. Mateusz nodded and smiled, but Truda's eyes narrowed.

"We are pleased to get to know you better. Piotr speaks so highly of you."

The faintest of flushes stole over Sara's cheeks, and it struck me for the first time that she often blushed when Piotr's name came up. I tucked the observation away in the back of my mind, something to ponder later.

"He is a good friend. But I have to confess, I do have something to ask of you tonight. I'm not sure if you are aware that I work for the Department of Social Welfare and Public Health, for the Warsaw Council. We are very busy, with so many struggling and suffering. It is hard but noble work, managing and organizing a series of soup kitchens around the city. And I was thinking about Elżbieta here, and how clever she is and how it is such a waste to have a bright young mind sitting idle when there is so much to be done. So I spoke with my supervisor, and we wondered if perhaps Elżbieta would consider coming aboard our team in some capacity. After all, were it not for the occupation, she would be studying at high school right now. But it would not break any rules for her to undertake, say, an apprenticeship with my team." There was a stunned moment of silence as Truda and Mateusz glanced from Sara to me, and Truda's eyes narrowed further. Sara continued, undaunted. "There is no rule which says that bright young women cannot learn at work. I myself got my start through a nursing apprenticeship when I was not much older than Elżbieta is now. I know that she has perhaps not made the wisest choices of late due to her boredom, and I do trust that you know what is best for her. However, I wondered if, rather than punishing the behavior, you would consider some meaningful work as a strategy to address the root of it…a strategy to mitigate her boredom, perhaps."

"I don't think this is a good idea," Truda said firmly, her tone low and directed only to Mateusz.

He was watching me closely, thoughtfully, and then he turned to Sara and asked, "What exactly would Elżbieta be doing?"

"There is a mountain of paperwork on my desk that needs filing, for a start, and then maybe after that she can help answer the phones. If we clear the backlog, I thought I would have one of the typing-pool girls come in to show her how to use the typewriter so she can help me with my notes. There is much to be done from the safe confines of my office while she will be learning about public health and about how the city cares for our citizens. It's not quite the same as a nursing position, but it will lay a great foundation for her if she chooses to pursue nursing as a job once the war is over." Sara paused, then grimaced self-consciously. "I could really do with the help. The typing pool is so far behind. It's months before they get to my work, and often by the time they do I've forgotten what my scrawls were supposed to mean."

"That seems innocuous enough," Mateusz said, but he was still frowning. "Still, she would need to get to and from your office, and I don't like the idea of her traveling alone around the city."

"Actually, she would travel with me on the tram. There's no danger, provided she carries her papers. And I can assure you that working in my office would be every bit as safe as staying inside your apartment all day—perhaps even more so, because she would be less inclined to make mischief."

I'd have protested at the way they were speaking about me, but I wanted this so badly I could taste it. I had come to understand that my days at Sara's office would only marginally be more interesting than my days staring out the apartment window, but the idea of contributing to something bigger than myself had sparked an excitement in me that I hadn't known I was capable of feeling. If me typing would free up some of Sara's time to help the Jewish children, then I'd be the best typist she'd ever had.

"We will need to discuss this," Truda said stiffly. She watched me closely as she took a sip of her coffee, her gaze sharp.

"Of course," Sara said, her tone mild. She glanced at me, and then she added, "And, of course, I'll understand if this isn't right for Elżbieta. It was my friendship with your daughter that inspired this idea; however, there is a whole city of bright young women underutilized at the moment, so I can always find someone else to assist me. Now, that is enough of the business talk. Tell me about your home—you were originally from Morowice?"

We weren't from Morowice, but that was the story we'd decided to tell people when we arrived in Warsaw, and so Mateusz took it from there, providing Sara with our fictitious backstory. We stayed until the coffee was gone, but I sat in silence while the adults made small talk, and then I held my breath as I walked along the hallway with Truda and Mateusz, waiting for their reaction to Sara's proposal. As we slipped into the foyer of our own apartment, Mateusz gave me a look.

"Do you want to do it?"

"More than anything," I answered him honestly, and then I added, "I'm so bored. I know I don't deserve your trust after what I did, but I'll be so grateful if you let me do this."

He nodded, and I knew that he was ready to consent, just from the softening in his gaze. Truda was going to be a much harder sell, but I could only hope that Mateusz would convince her. She gave me a hard look and pointed to the stairs. "You should go to bed."

I wasn't even close to sleep when Mateusz pushed the door to my bedroom open half an hour later.

"Are you still awake?" he whispered.

"I am," I said, and I sat up expectantly.

"You may go to work with Sara."

"Really?"

"A smart girl like you deserves the chance to learn and to contribute. Just don't let us down."

Sara's office in the Warsaw City Hall was on the ground floor at the very back of the building, deep within a rabbit warren of offices bustling with social workers and public-health staff. Her team was entirely female and was presided over by the utterly terrifying Matylda Mazur. Matylda was less than five feet tall, but she somehow possessed a presence much larger than her diminutive stature. I had only just arrived at Sara's office when Matylda stepped inside and closed the door behind her.

"You," she greeted me, pointing her finger as if in accusation. "You caught Sara with Jewish children."

Her bluntness startled me. I had no idea what to say.

"She did," Sara answered for me. She was on the other side of the huge cherrywood desk, removing her hat to hang it on a hook on the wall. I could barely see Sara over the piles of paperwork on her desk. She had not exaggerated.

"So you know that there is more to our work than soup kitchens and welfare checks," Matylda continued, when I only managed to stare at her with my jaw open. "That means you are in our circle of trust now. You betray us, people will die. Do you understand that?"

"I do," I croaked, wide-eyed.

"Good. Now, we run more than a dozen soup kitchens across the city, and each one is constantly asking for more supplies. We don't have the budget to keep up with demand, and even if we did, we can't get the resources. Our phones ring constantly, so you can help us manage the constant requests, but I should warn you. You will become very accustomed to disappointing people in this job." Matylda looked at me expectantly. I nodded hastily.

"That's okay. I can talk on the phone."

"Good. Almost all of my team find themselves juggling two roles, and one of those roles is most definitely unsanctioned by the city. And even though you are aware of this, you must *never* speak about it outside this office, or even inside this office when the door is open—one *never* knows who is listening. Working alongside our team, you will inevitably overhear things, but Sara is determined that you not engage with that other side of our work, so mind your own business. Do you understand?"

"I do," I croaked again. "I mean, I will."

And then she was gone, bustling off to another office, slamming the door behind her. I looked at Sara, who hid a smile.

"That is our Matylda. You'll get used to her."

"She is terrifying."

"She is wonderful. She is simply obsessed with her mission."

"Since I am allowed to ask you about the other business when the door is closed," I said suddenly, "can you tell me what happened to the orphans, the ones at your apartment?"

Sara sat behind her desk and smiled sadly.

"I wish I could tell you otherwise, but we ran out of options, and they had to go back into the ghetto."

"No!" I gasped. I had thought about those children often since that night, but I had assumed they were somewhere safe, hopefully eating good food and growing well. The thought of them enduring the ordeal of traveling through the sewers only to be sent right back made my chest hurt.

"I know. It is very upsetting. The safe houses were compromised so there was just nowhere for them to go."

"Couldn't they have stayed with you?"

"No, Elżbieta. That would not have been safe for anyone.

We tried everything we could, but in the end, we really had no choice but to smuggle them back to the Jewish side of the wall."

"Will you try to get them out again?"

"Just as soon as we have somewhere for them to go, but that's going to take some time to organize. Now, enough of that. You have work to do. Come over here so I can explain what needs to be done."

I tried to make sense of the mess on Sara's desk. And the phone did ring constantly: by the end of that first day, I began to understand the scope of the need and the struggle on our side of the ghetto wall, as well. It felt good to help Sara out with those endless calls, even though Matylda was right—I was constantly deflecting impossible requests.

But still, the day flew by, and then several more like it, and soon Sara told me that she was going to be out of the office for several hours each day from then on.

"Probably no need to mention to your parents that I will not be with you in the office all of the time, but I really need to resume my normal work schedule. There will always be other social workers here, even if Matylda and I are out in the field."

"Where are you going?" I asked her.

"Matylda and I and some of the other nurses conduct public-health checks as part of our work. The Germans are particularly concerned about typhus, so they allow us to go to places where others cannot go."

"You go into the ghetto?" I asked, eyes wide.

"Yes. Six days a week."

"What do you do in there?"

"I check for typhus."

"But..."

"Jews are no more prone to typhus than anyone else. If you crowd any huge group of people into a tiny space and cut off access to running water and soap, you will get typhus."

"So...could you get it?"

"I have been inoculated against it."

"And can you help the Jews? Can you inoculate them?"

"We do what we can, Elżbieta. It is not much, but we do what we can."

I was completely fascinated with Sara's other work. Over the next few weeks, whenever the door was closed, I would bombard her with questions about the things she had seen and done. She was usually vague, but that didn't stop me asking.

I would meet Sara in the apartment lobby at seven in the morning, and then we would take the tram across town. We would work together in the office for an hour or more, and she would assign the administrative tasks for the day.

When I had first decided to press Sara to involve me in her work, I'd been entertaining much grander aspirations, but as time passed, I became grateful that what Sara had me doing was so much less dangerous. Every time I went home and sat at the kitchen table with Truda, she asked me about my day, and I gradually realized it was a blessing to be able to tell the truth. I still wanted to help the Jews—but my bravado had quickly faded away.

Matylda continued to terrify me. She had no time for pleasantries, and she was always moving. She would barge into Sara's office unannounced several times a day, usually to bark, "Where is Sara?"

I would squeak out an answer, and Matylda would growl and spin on her heel. I'd hear her barking at the poor woman in the next office, and sometimes in the office after that. After a while, I realized that when Matylda came looking for Sara, it was because she had found another family in desperate need of help—often another small child in need of a home. Sara was absolutely correct: the entire team was desperate and determined and devoted, but Matylda was obsessed.

"She has single-handedly rescued hundreds of children. It was she who organized my pass so that I could travel through the ghetto checkpoints, and often when I visit a family to see if I can help with the child, it is because she has heard of their circumstances. She even organized the entire network to care for the children we have rescued, and she keeps detailed records so that when the war is over, we can reunite children with their families. She is the brightest, bravest woman I have ever met, and I wish I could be half the person she is," Sara told me one day.

Despite Sara's obvious admiration for Matylda, I sensed that there was a tension to their relationship. More than once, I had heard Sara and Matylda arguing in whispers in the corridor or in Matylda's office, and sometimes during these heated arguments, I heard my name. Given Matylda's general lack of warmth toward me, I came to assume that she had allowed Sara to recruit me only reluctantly.

I made it a point to be as helpful as I could around the office, but this only seemed to increase the frequency and intensity of the squabbles.

Some days at the Warsaw Department of Social Welfare and Public Health were quiet. Some days were busy. Some days were inexplicably tense, like the day when Matylda stormed into Sara's office and dragged her out by her arm. When Sara returned to the office, she closed the door behind her, then hesitated just a second before she locked it.

"Are you all right?" I asked her.

"I just need a moment to myself."

If that was a hint for me to give her peace and quiet, I missed it.

"Is she angry with you today?"

"She's angry with the world." Sara sighed. She walked around the desk to take a seat, then linked her hands behind her head and leaned back, staring at the ceiling as she said almost absent-

mindedly, "One of our children was almost caught today with
her new family on this side of the wall."

"Oh, no!"

"It is very unfortunate. Do you remember the children in
my apartment that night?"

"Was it one of them?"

"No, but it is the same old problem, and the reason we sent
those children back. We can get the children *out* of the ghetto
through a variety of methods. None of them pretty, but we
have ways to do it. There are even people who help us secure
false papers for them, but that is only half the battle. There is a
Franciscan orphanage on Hoża Street which takes most of the
children when they are first rescued. The Sisters there help the
children remember that once they are out, they must only speak
Polish. Most are more accustomed to speaking Yiddish which,
of course, gives them away. Today, our little girl was speaking
Polish just fine, but something about her appearance tipped a
soldier off, and he asked her to recite her prayers."

"Her prayers?" I repeated, frowning.

"A Jewish child doesn't know Catholic prayers, does she?"

"Oh."

"The orphanage didn't have room for her so we moved her
directly into the home of a foster family. This little girl was out
and about with them but hadn't yet mastered her prayers. For-
tunately, the mother was quick enough on her feet to pretend
the child was simple and couldn't speak much."

"So why is Matylda angry?"

"She is frustrated, not angry. We have discussed educating
the children before they leave the ghetto, but…educating the
children is very time-consuming, and if we were to make sure
that every child knew all of their Catholic prayers before they
even left the ghetto, we would be saving many fewer children."
Sara closed her eyes, and her voice was thick with emotion as
she whispered, "Whenever we successfully rescue a child, I

don't sleep any better that night, because I know that there are thousands more waiting. We gradually try to expand our operation, but every new person we bring into our confidence is an immense risk. The weight of the world rests on Matylda's shoulders, especially now. There have been rumors for some time that those within the ghetto will soon be deported elsewhere, and more and more, we think the time is growing near."

"Where are they going to be taken?"

"No one knows for sure, but I know this much, Elżbieta... It won't be anywhere good."

9

Roman

CHAIM AND I MET AT THE END OF THE BLOCK EACH MORN-
ing to walk to our desk in the workshop together. We sat together at lunch. And sometimes, he walked me home.

"It's a long way out of your way," I pointed out to him the
first time he offered to keep me company. He shrugged.

"I have business at the youth center up the block from your
house," he admitted. "I stay at an apartment there sometimes.
So, it's no trouble to walk with you on the days when I am
going there anyway."

I made a point not to ask for details of this business, aware
that it was related to his activities in the underground. On the
days when he was going to his home in the Little Ghetto, I
would join him for the walk, and he always helped me check
the trash cans around the area for scraps of food.

It felt strange to have a friend again. Our friendship felt like
a daring risk, but I was gradually growing to trust Chaim, although it was true that despite the burgeoning friendship, our

conversation remained somewhat lopsided. He had an easy, affable air. I felt like I'd forgotten how to speak freely the way he did—sentences that flowed one after the other, words of all different shapes and sizes. Despite the disparity, we managed to squeeze conversation into the gaps around the noisy machines, swapping the parts of our history that felt safe enough to share. I couldn't figure Chaim out. He seemed so eager to make a new friend, and I wasn't sure if that was why he had taken the small opening of my initial greeting to firmly plant himself inside my life. But if he was lonely and desperate for company, why did he seem so much happier than I did? I felt so sorry for him. I couldn't imagine what it would be like to be imprisoned in the ghetto without my family, and I certainly couldn't imagine what it would be like to be thousands of miles away from my parents like he was.

I was working at my machine one day when I gradually became aware of a shock wave echoing through the factory. All up and down the neat row of sewing machines where my workmates sat, productivity was slowing as news was leaking from workstation to workstation. I watched as it made its way toward the table I shared with Chaim. But just as it reached the table behind us, Sala happened past, reminding us that we had a quota to meet for the Germans that day so we had to focus. Chaim and I resumed our work in silence while we waited for the opportunity to speak. When Sala finally continued down the line, pleading with his other employees to work faster, Chaim leaned back in his seat to speak to the boys who worked at the table behind us.

I learned about the deportations as though in slow motion, watching the comprehension dawn on my new friend's face. By the time he leaned forward to pass the rumor on to me, I was bracing myself for something horrific. In an environment like the ghetto, where shocks and horrors were a daily occurrence, I thought I was past that bracing fear that clenched your stomach, that made your palms sweat. I had become numb to it, or so I thought. All it took were four words, and the very thing I had been so frightened of for such a long time was right in front of me.

"The resettlements have begun."

"What?" I was immediately frozen in fear. "When?"

"This morning. People are being moved to the *Umschlag-platz*." The loading platform, on Stawki Street, just blocks from my apartment.

"How many people?" I asked breathlessly. I put my hands on the table as if to push myself back. "And who?"

Please be targeted. Please be targeted at someone other than us.

"Many thousands. And it seems random so far, mostly people in the street."

"Where are they taking us?"

"A camp, supposedly."

There was a dryness to the way that Chaim said *camp*. I remembered the rumor he had shared with me only a month or two before about mass executions at the camp at Chełmno. Panicking, I looked at the clock. I had hours left in my shift, but for a moment I thought about leaving my desk and running from the workshop. Perhaps I could sneak through the streets to check on my family.

"Roman," Sala called from the other side of the workshop. The machines fell quiet, but the clatter of panic in my mind was deafening. I realized that I was standing and had taken a step away from my desk. The entire workshop was staring at me. "Don't you leave, son. I know you're scared—we're all scared. But if you leave to check on your family, you'll probably get caught up in the deportation. Besides, if we don't meet this quota today, none of us will have jobs to come back to tomorrow. I need you to sit back down and get back to work."

I couldn't afford to lose my job. I sat back down at my desk, and even as my head spun and my hands shook, I got back to work.

★ ★ ★

That day, I did not amble home lazily with Chaim after my shift at the workshop. Instead, I ran. Most of my coworkers at the workshop did the same. We burst into the streets and scattered to sprint toward our homes. I gradually became aware that Chaim was right on my heels.

"You don't have to come," I panted. Chaim only shrugged. For once, he was the silent one.

When we finally reached my family's apartment, I hesitated on the doorstep and looked around the street for some sign that my family had survived the roundup. All I saw was incontrovertible evidence that even if the Germans really had taken thousands of us, hundreds of thousands more remained. The street was as busy as always. The usual collective of hungry children was begging across the road, a cluster of them sitting together wearing little more than rags, extending their cupped hands toward anyone hurrying past. Groups of people stood whispering in every conceivable space, and a few doors down an elderly woman was wailing and rocking on her doorstep. A middle-aged man sat at a makeshift table on the sidewalk opposite us, the table covered with kitchen utensils, and when people passed, he would lift a spoon and plead with them to buy it.

So only the usual horrors on Miła Street, but that meant nothing about what I would find inside my house. A wave of nausea crashed over me, and I leaned against the doorframe for a moment, too terrified to open the door in case I found the house empty—or, perhaps worse, still full except for the room I shared with Samuel and Mother and Dawidek and Eleonora. A heavy hand descended on my shoulder, and I looked back to Chaim, who offered me a sad smile.

"Do you want me to go in first?"

My first instinct was to refuse his offer. My family didn't know him, neither did our reluctant roommates. What would they make of this strange young man stepping into our living space? And yet the very thought of going inside alone was sickening, and so after a brief hesitation, I nodded. Chaim opened the door, and as soon as he did, I saw Dawidek. He was sitting on the floor with Judit and Laszlo's little girl, Anna. They were rolling a ball between them. From the doorstep, I stared at Dawidek until my vision blurred with unshed tears.

Even if the rest are gone, I can survive for him.

Because Dawidek had been spared, I could face whatever else waited for me in that apartment—maybe because *for* him I could be brave. As I followed Chaim into the apartment, he glanced back to ask, "Shall I go home?"

My mother came into view before I could answer. She was holding Eleonora and standing with Grandmother and Judit. When Mother saw me, she ran across the room and threw her spare arm around me as she wept into my shoulder.

"My baby. You are okay! We were so scared. They were letting those with work permits go, but you never know, do you?"

"Hush, Mother. I am okay. Is everyone okay here, too?" I looked around, then asked hesitantly, "Mrs. Kukliński…"

"She went to visit her cousin to see if he has news. We are all fine," she said unevenly, as she pressed her palm onto my cheek. "For now, we are fine. But what are we going to do? They say the deportations will continue."

"We will find a way," I told her, even though I didn't believe it. I glanced over my mother's shoulder and saw that Chaim had removed his hat and was now fumbling awkwardly with it in front of his chest. I extracted myself from my mother's embrace and extended my hand to shake his.

"Thank you, my friend" were the only words I could push past the lump in my throat, but I hoped that as Chaim looked into my eyes, he saw all the words I couldn't figure out how to say. *Thank you for being here. I don't know if I could have faced this alone. I'm so glad you are my friend.*

★ ★ ★

That night, Mother put Eleonora and Dawidek to bed, then came to join the rest of the adults in the living room, which had become a market for gossip. We were all hungry for information, but we were starving for hope.

"There were soldiers on the rooftops," Laszlo murmured. "They had their rifles pointed down at the street. I heard that they sealed the checkpoints to make sure that no one could escape. The Kapo were plucking people at random from the street at first, but the quota is very high—thousands per day, they say. My friend who lives on Stawki Street said that by lunchtime, Kapo were just pushing groups of people toward the platform. Some managed to talk their way out, but not many."

"All of this fuss for nothing," Mrs. Grobelny said suddenly. She spoke with the confidence of someone with an inside source. She had a cousin on the Jewish Council, and he provided her a constant supply of information, both correct and otherwise. I had come to realize that Mrs. Grobelny survived by believing what she wanted to believe. "They are only taking the very young orphans and the very old, and besides which, they are taking them to another work camp. It can't be any worse than here, so we have nothing to fear."

"If our ultimate end is a work camp, why would they take the very young and the very old first?" Grandfather asked her gruffly.

That gave Mrs. Grobelny pause, and for a moment her mouth hung open, but no sound came out. Then she raised her chin stubbornly. "Perhaps they are the easiest to move," she said.

Mr. Kukliński had spent the last of his family savings that day buying a German-issued work permit so that he could begin work in one of their factories. The cost of these permits had more than tripled overnight, but he was adamant that this was a good investment.

"My friend's brother said he heard that anyone with a job is exempt. Their families, too." He turned to his wife and took her hands in his. "You see? It is worth the cost, even if it means I have to move into the lodgings at the Schultz factory while you stay here."

He seemed to be determined to convince himself of this, and maybe that's why none of us pointed out the flaw in his logic. *Families couldn't possibly be exempt because the family was separated from the worker, and if the work permit was the one thing that would save them all, it would be with the worker. If families were exempt, the Germans must be trusting everyone's word, and if that were the case, Mr. Kukliński need not have parted with his entire savings to buy a work permit because he could have just lied about having one in the first place.*

"We must not let the children out of our sight," Grandmother said suddenly. "One thing we know for sure is that many children were taken today. If we are not with them, they will be taken without us, and I can't bear the idea—"

"We won't let them out of the apartment," Judit said firmly. "Between us, one of us can stay home at all times. We will make it work."

I sat beside Samuel, mirroring his posture. Our backs were to the wall, our knees tucked up close to our chins. Like my step-father, I watched all of this, but I didn't speak. His expression was completely blank, as if he were too shocked to contribute.

I just kept remembering how I had chosen to stay at the factory because it was the right thing to do. If I'd left, I would have let Sala down, and I would have lost my job. But staying was also the wrong thing to do because I had betrayed my own values: my family was all I had left, and I should have immediately gone to check on them.

I had to face the reality that I had absolutely no control over what came next, and that even if the exact same events unfolded the very next day, I would have to make the same tortured decision all over again.

When we finally said our good-nights and my family retreated to our own room, I was awake long after my parents. There was just enough light that I could watch them as they slept. I drank in the sight of the four of them, all too aware that I could no longer take for granted the simple peace of closing my eyes to rest, knowing they were safe.

"I'm so relieved that your family was okay," Chaim said, when he met me at the corner the next morning. I nodded curtly. He fell into step beside me, and then he dropped his voice. "But yesterday was the beginning of this, not the end. Do you understand that, my friend?"

"We don't know that for sure."

"But we do," he argued quietly. "*I* do."

I kept staring straight ahead, avoiding his gaze.

"Pigeon," I said suddenly, "do you know of anything I could do to keep them safe?"

"Do you have any money?" he asked, without hesitation.

"No. Nothing. But I need to save my family. Whatever it takes, I will do it."

"Roman," he said, sighing.

"Please," I whispered, voice thick. "I need to do something. I can't bear this anymore."

He hesitated.

"You've spoken about your brother, but you didn't mention that there was a new baby in your family, too. Your mother looks ill."

"It has been difficult to get enough food to keep her and the baby going," I admitted unevenly. "That is why I check the trash. Every day it is a new struggle."

"You know I sometimes go to the youth center. It is a huge facility, many hundreds of people there at any one time, but they have recently started a soup kitchen, too. I know one of the organizers, and he sometimes slips me a little extra food. Perhaps we can ask him if he can do the same for you."

"Thank you. And…the deportations?"

"The only people who are escaping this prison are those with reserves of wealth or extensive resources on the other side of the wall. But…"

"But?"

"There may be something we can do to help. Leave it with me. Leave it *all* with me. I'll see what I can find out."

10

Emilia

SARA RETURNED FROM HER VISIT TO THE GHETTO ONE DAY, hours earlier than expected, and she was obviously distressed. Her shoulders were slumped forward, and her gaze seemed fixed on the floor. She took her seat on her side of the desk and began to sort through paperwork, but I knew her routine well enough to know she wasn't doing anything productive. She was mindlessly going through the motions, and I knew her mind was entirely elsewhere.

"Bad day?" I asked after a while. She looked at me as if I'd materialized out of nowhere.

"Sorry, Elżbieta. I didn't even greet you."

"That's okay. You look...tired."

Tired was a polite word for how she looked. She was visibly wrecked, but she'd only share why when she was ready. To my surprise, her eyes filled with tears, and she looked back to the desk. I looked away, unsure of what I should do or say.

"I was going to evacuate a child last week," she whispered.

"He was four years old, and he had the cutest little smile you've ever seen. I sent his little brother out first. The little one was unwell, and I figured the older child could have some more time with his mama before…well, before. But today, I went back for the boy, and he was—" Sara broke off abruptly. She reached to retrieve a small handkerchief from her handbag, wiped her eyes and blew her nose, then finished weakly, "I was too late."

"He died?"

"He is gone."

The familiar sound of Matylda's heels against the hardwood floor in the hall grew louder, and I looked up to see her there, with a small folder in her arms.

"Those documents you asked for," she said quietly, but then she closed the door behind herself, and her carefully neutral expression slipped into one of desperate grief. "Oh, God, Sara. You've heard?"

"Yes. The little boy on Dzielna Street was deported this morning," Sara murmured.

After that, it was as if the two women forgot I was in the room. I sat in silence as they talked, shocked and bewildered by what I was hearing. Their words washed over me—words that should have made sense, but in context, they seemed impossible. *Roundup. Umschlagplatz. Thousands upon thousands. Loaded onto trains and then gone.*

"Andrzej said that it was mostly random today—anyone who appeared incapable of significant labor…those who don't have a work permit, the sick, the weak or infirm or elderly or…" Matylda's eyes filled with tears, and she shook her head fiercely. "The young. So many of those deported today were street children. They were easy to find and incapable of resistance."

Those last words hung in the air, and I tried to imagine what it all meant. I still knew so little about the ghetto. But I could tell by the gravity in Matylda's and Sara's voices that whatever happened that day was horrifying on a new level.

"Where did the trains take them?" I asked uncertainly.

"No one knows for sure yet," Matylda said abruptly. "But there have been rumors for some time that the Germans planned to deport all the Jews from the ghetto to execute them."

"What?" I whispered, looking to Sara frantically, hoping she'd protest this, but she simply looked to the floor. "All of them? But…"

"It is too terrible to believe, I know," Sara murmured.

"If the rumors are true, this will happen more and more," Matylda said. "We will go to rescue children and find that those children are already gone. What happened today was a nightmare, but it is going to be a daily nightmare, and you are fooling yourself if you do not believe it will escalate. And who knows how long they will allow us to use our permits to come and go? Sooner or later, they will seal the ghetto off completely—it is a miracle we've had access for this long. Mark my words, every risk we do not take now will be a stain upon our conscience for the rest of our lives. We need bolder action."

"What more can we do?" Sara asked unevenly. "There is so much to balance. We have exploited every excuse we can. Our team simply cannot make more trips past those checkpoints. It will arouse too much suspicion."

"Do you agree with me that every child counts?" Matylda asked Sara, her voice low and steady.

"You know I do!" Sara exclaimed.

"Do you?" Matylda pressed, then her gaze shifted to me.

"She is too young."

"Many of the couriers are even younger, and yet we rely on them every day."

"This is different! Elżbieta is…"

"Is what? Is not Jewish, so is not expendable?"

"How can you say that to me, after everything I've done?"

"It is one thing to risk your own life. I know that you would welcome death because it feels to you as though you have nothing left to live for. No, the greatest sacrifice for you would be to risk your friend. That's why I am asking you—how much do you want to help the children in the ghetto? Because you allow her to sit here with your busywork when she could be making a real difference in the field." Matylda raised her eyebrows at me. "Well, Elżbieta?"

"I don't understand what you want me to do," I said uncertainly.

"The couriers are already in danger," Sara blurted, pressing her palms down onto the desk and leaning forward, as if to convey the urgency of her argument. "Whether or not they are leading children through the sewer or sleeping in their beds in the ghetto, their fate is already sealed. It is different with Elżbieta. She is a child, and she is already safe."

"No one is safe in this country," Matylda said dismissively.

"I'm not a child. I'm fourteen," I started to protest, but my voice was weak and wavering. Sara waved her hand to silence me.

"I will not betray your parents by allowing you to join us in the field!"

"How noble of you," Matylda said bitterly. "You value the opinion of this Catholic couple more than the lives of potentially dozens of Jewish children."

"That is so unfair."

"You want me to smuggle children through the sewer?" I asked. Wasn't it exactly what I had wanted in the beginning? Now, the very thought of putting my life on the line for strangers left me feeling physically ill. I went weak with relief when Matylda shook her head.

"That would be a waste. You have more valuable skills that we could utilize. You are Catholic, no?"

"Yes."

"Do you know your prayers?"

"Of course I do."

"If you could spend a little time with each child, getting a head start on their Catholic lessons and practicing their Polish, perhaps we could shift at least a few more straight into foster homes to avoid the bottleneck in the convents."

"But I would still go into the ghetto with you?" I said uncertainly. Matylda nodded.

"With Sara, I think."

"But how?"

"My contact will issue you a permit. You will march right through the checkpoints. It is almost as safe for you as sitting at this desk."

"Don't lie to her, Matylda," Sara said fiercely. "If you're going to ask this of her, then at least tell her the truth." I looked to Sara in confusion, and her gaze pleaded with me. "Walking through those checkpoints will be the most terrifying moments of your life, Elżbieta. Every day brings new danger, especially now. And if our mission is ever discovered, you could be captured and tortured…even killed. I can't ask you to do this."

"Every other person who knows our real mission is contributing and active in the fight. Elżbieta here discovered your secret and proved she can be trusted."

"She is fourteen years old," Sara said defensively. "Besides, the work with the soup kitchens is important, too."

"Of course it is. But it is not urgent in the same way that thousands of children at risk of being murdered is urgent," Matylda said fiercely. Both women fell silent, and the only sound in the room was Matylda's ragged breathing. Her face was red, her eyes wild and her fists clenched against her thighs. She drew in another sharp breath, and then she said, "She could sit at the youth center, in the back room Andrzej uses for his meetings. You could accompany her in and out, but while you do your home visits, she could sit with children to help prepare them. Besides, could she not smuggle in just a handful of bread beneath her clothing that might keep a child going for a day or two more? Could we not fit her with one of your brassieres and have her smuggling more typhus vaccine in or, for God's sake, cyanide pills?"

"Cyanide pills?" I repeated, feeling the color drain from my face. "Why would the Jews want cyanide pills?"

"Sometimes, the only mercy one can offer is a quiet death," Matylda murmured. My stomach dropped as I considered this. My father had not died a quiet death. My brother had not died a quiet death. Would I have had the courage to help them achieve this, if I'd had the power? I pictured myself sneaking into the ghetto with Sara, my pockets stuffed with precious pills. My father and my brother would have been so proud.

"I'll do it," I announced.

"I knew you would," Matylda said, and she patted my hand, pleased. She glanced at Sara. "I'll organize the permit. Please find her some more suitable clothing to wear."

Matylda closed the door behind her, leaving Sara and me alone at the desk. I glanced across a stack of paperwork and found her staring at me, her eyes filled with tears.

"To do this would be to betray your parents and your uncle. To do this would be to betray their trust in me."

"What is the worse sin?" I asked her carefully. "Betraying their trust or allowing children to die?"

She pursed her lips, then shook her head in frustration.

"*You* will probably die if we do this. Do you understand that? To Matylda, it is a simple case of math because she has reduced the complex morality of what we do down to its most basic form. She would do anything to save more lives. There is no risk that is too great for her to take because she has nothing to lose. I am in the same boat—my family is already gone. I do this because when I am caught and when I am killed, there is no one left to grieve me. That is *not* the case with you! Even if you do survive, the things you would see inside that ghetto would haunt you for the rest of your life."

"I have seen the cruelty of the Germans with my own eyes," I said bitterly. "Nothing you could show me would surprise me."

"Darling child, I am sure your journey has not been easy, but there is a depth of suffering in the ghetto that even I did not realize was possible."

"Isn't that all the more reason that you should let me help?"

I could tell that Sara was still deeply disquieted by the idea, but in the end, she agreed to take me in with her. That afternoon, I received my first dose of the typhus vaccine, and Matylda contacted her friend to arrange my pass.

A week later, I left home at seven with Sara as I always did. We made our journey across Warsaw in silence, and then when we arrived at the offices, I followed her into Matylda's office.

As I often did, I wore my hair in a braid that day, but the first thing the women did was unwind the braid, leaving my long hair wavy. Matylda teased the hair at the front of my head and pinned it high above my crown, fanning the rest out around my shoulders. I had never worn makeup before and was so excited I could barely sit still as she drew around my eyes with a dark pencil and then filled in my eyebrows with a lighter shade. Finally, she painted my lips with a soft red lipstick, and Sara handed me a bag.

"Get changed in the bathroom," she said heavily. "And then we will go."

The outfit Sara had found for me was more grown-up than any of my clothing. There was a brassiere, with thick padding sewn into the cups, and a black-and-white polka-dotted shirt with large buttons down the front, paired with a neat gray skirt that fell to my knees, and a pair of flat leather shoes. I could barely believe the woman looking back at me in the mirror was really me. I looked several years older, but that wasn't the only transformation. I looked like a proper professional woman, like Sara or Matylda or any of the other social workers in the department. When I walked back into Matylda's office, she nodded in satisfaction.

"Perfect. You could easily pass for seventeen or eighteen. If anyone asks, you explain that you are Sara's apprentice. Understand?"

Sara stood reluctantly and slipped her bag over her shoulder, then took a step toward the door.

"Is there anything else I should know?" I asked them frantically. "Are you going to tell me what to say or do?"

"The main thing to remember is that when we are walking to and from the youth center, do not leave my side. Hold on to me if you must," Sara said and sighed. "It is very crowded in there—incredibly crowded. If you lose me, you will never find me again, so make sure you do not lose me."

"That's it?"

"When you get to the checkpoint, hold yourself with confidence," Matylda murmured. "The guards will check your papers and your permit. If you are confident, they will wave you through. You mustn't look nervous, and you must be very careful not to panic."

"Don't panic," I repeated, suddenly aware that my palms were beginning to sweat. I wiped them on the skirt Sara had given me. "Okay. What else?"

"Everything else you will have to see with your own eyes," Sara said flatly, then she glanced at Matylda one more time. "I hope to God you know what you're doing."

As we walked toward the checkpoint, I fixed my gaze on the sign above it. *Typhus Infection Area. Authorized Passage Only.* I had been nervous as Sara and I made our way there from the office, but it was quite a pleasant kind of anxiety; a mild adrenaline rush, combined with curiosity and excitement that I was finally—*finally*—about to do something brave. I wondered if my father and brother were looking down on me, chatting with the saints about the extraordinary young woman I had become. I wondered how Alina would react when I one day traveled to England to find her and told her about my courage.

"Get your pass ready," Sara said, dropping her voice. "And your papers."

My papers. I had them with me as I always did, but I so rarely left the apartment and I'd never had to show them. But in all of the excitement about my epidemic-control pass and this trip to the ghetto, I had completely forgotten that I was living under a false name, and that my identity papers were false identity papers. They looked realistic enough, but would they pass intense scrutiny? The worst thing was I had honored my parents' insistence that I not trust Sara with this information, and she had no idea that we were about to pass through a German checkpoint with false paperwork. I made a sound of pure panic in the back of my throat, and without breaking stride, Sara whispered under her breath, "Head high. Be confident. You insisted you could do this, and if you panic now, I swear to God I will throttle you."

I sent up a series of increasingly frantic prayers as I walked, but by the time we reached the checkpoint, my hand was shaking violently.

"Sara," one of the guards said, his voice warm in a way that made my stomach flip over unpleasantly. "You have brought a friend today."

"Good morning, Captain Fischer. This is my apprentice, Elżbieta," Sara said. She was polite but firm and surprisingly cool with the guard. "Elżbieta, show Captain Fischer your pass, please."

I moved to extend my hand, but then Sara snatched the pass and my papers from it and handed them to the guard.

"She looks nervous," he said mildly, glancing between my paperwork and my face. At this, my stomach dropped, and I felt the blood drain from my face. I couldn't believe I had already aroused suspicion. Suddenly, the guard barked out a laugh. "I'd be nervous, too, going in there with those filthy animals."

He handed the papers directly back to me, then turned his attention to Sara.

"Let me check your bag, Mrs. Wieczorek," he said, and Sara fixed a tight smile on her face and handed him her medical bag. He seemed to delight in delaying us, shifting through the contents of her bag piece by piece, checking every item, regardless of how innocuous it was. This whole process could have been completed in seconds—her bag was mostly empty—but somehow, Fischer drew it out, and given that my anxiety was already bending time, I soon felt as though we had been standing there for hours. Sara waited patiently, not so much as breaking a sweat. When he finally returned the bag, he turned his attention back to me.

"Will you be visiting us again?"

"She will," Sara answered for me.

"Let her speak, Sara," he said, taunting her almost playfully without breaking eye contact with me.

"I—" My voice was so hoarse that the word escaped as a squeak. I cleared my throat, then remembered Matylda's words. I raised my chin and squared my shoulders. "Yes, I will be, sir."

He waved us through, without another word. We walked a few feet past the checkpoint, and a sensory wave crashed over me. The scent of human waste and body odor and rotting flesh was so thick I could barely believe anyone could breathe it and survive. On the other side of the road, an elderly woman lay flat on her back. Her skin was yellow and gray, her mouth slack, her eyes closed. People stepped over her body as if it wasn't there.

"Eyes forward," Sara said briskly.

"But—"

"Keep your damned eyes forward."

I was seeing a whole new side to Sara: hard, focused and determined, her strength evident in every aspect of her posture and her expression. I had never before thought about the kind of courage and strength it must have taken her to risk her life every day, sometimes multiple times a day. Regardless, it immediately made sense to me that she would become hardened. To face the inhuman, one must become superhuman. I had wanted to be heroic, just like my brother, just like my father, just like Alina. As my eyes drifted back to that woman's corpse, I realized how foolish I had been and how utterly, horrifically out of my depth I was.

I was about to confront a level of suffering that could not be aided by any of my efforts, and no matter how successful my attempts were, it would never be enough. To achieve anything at all, I would now have to pass that checkpoint twice a day and look right into the eyes of people who were damned and knew it.

"I don't think I can do this."

The words were hoarse and uneven, and my stomach turned over as I said them. Sara grabbed my upper arm and pushed me backward, steering me around several people. She pushed me hard up against the glass door of an apartment, and it rattled with the impact.

"You have a pass," she hissed, her face close to mine. "You wanted to help. Now you have a moral obligation to follow through."

"What if I can't?"

At that, she pulled me away from the front of the building and pushed me to face the street. Sara's hands gripped my arm so tightly I knew I would bruise, and she shook me. She stood close behind me and whispered in my ear. "All of these people are going to die. Every child you can see right now is going to die. You are one of a handful of people who can do something for at least *one* of these children. I am telling you right now, Elżbieta—they are trapped here, but *you* can leave. I can march you right through the next checkpoint, and you can go home and pretend you were never foolish enough to insist that you could help us."

That sounded perfect. I stared at a passing child, and my conscience prickled at me. Sara released me, then turned me gently to face her.

"But if I do, I know that you will never live with yourself. Not now that you know."

I blinked at her, trying to shake off the fog of shock settling over me. Images flicked through my mind of that terrifying encounter with the guard, and I wondered if Sara's entry to the ghetto was *that* tense every single time.

"The guard," I blurted. "Do you know him? Did you know he would search your bag?"

"He is a vile sociopath," she said, releasing me. "He has taken a special interest in me, and I go to great lengths to avoid encounters with him. We rotate the checkpoints we use to enter and exit and generally I manage to avoid him, but every now and again, like today, I am unfortunate enough to meet him."

"Do you have anything in your bag that you shouldn't?"

"There is a hidden compartment in the bottom," she admitted. "Today, there is a loaf of bread and six vials of the typhus inoculation."

"I'm glad I didn't know that when we came in," I whispered, my stomach churning again. Sara sighed and pulled me close for a hug.

"Are you okay?" she asked me.

"Not really."

"Well, pull yourself together. We have work to do." She reached into her bag and withdrew two small fabric bands. It took me a moment to recognize the shape embroidered upon them, but when I did, my eyes widened.

"The Star of David?"

"Yes. When we come into the ghetto, we wear the armband."

"But we aren't Jewish."

"We wear it in solidarity with those who are. It shows that they can trust us."

She extended the armband toward me. I stared at it anxiously.

"What if the Germans see us wearing these?" I whispered.

"You are scared to wear it, aren't you? In case someone thinks you belong in here?" Sara asked me. I nodded, and she shrugged and pointed to the street behind us. "Good. It gives you a taste of how they must feel. Now, let's go."

11

Emilia

THE YOUTH CENTER WAS ON MIŁA STREET, A FEW BLOCKS
from the gate we entered, only a half-dozen blocks from the
apartment building Sara and I called home. As we walked
through the streets to reach the center, I struggled to keep tears
at bay. Little details jumped out at me, things I decided I would
need to paint or draw later to excise them from my consciousness. An elderly man holding a cup in one hand, holding his
wife's hand with the other, as they sat in the gutter and begged
for food. Two SS officers walking along calmly, blessedly on
the other side of the street, but then without provocation, they
knocked a man to the ground and kicked him unconscious.
The wall of a store, where posters might once have displayed
the day's specials, now displayed hundreds of slips of paper, new
ones pasted over old ones. As we moved closer, I felt a shiver
down my spine as I realized that each announced a death. The
sheer volume resulted in a macabre wallpaper so thick in places
it could have chipped off in solid clumps.

"Eyes forward," Sara kept saying, even as we reached the youth center. She opened the door for me, but my attention kept snagging on the long line of people waiting to reach the window where soup was being distributed. Eventually, she tugged at my arm and pulled me inside. I was startled by the size of the room. The facade of the building suggested this had once been a store, but the interior walls had been removed, opening the space across what would have been adjoining buildings. In the cavernous room that stretched across a city block, people of all ages were sitting around tables or milling in groups.

"This is a youth center?" I said, confused.

"It started as a youth center, but the organizers are no longer focused on one age or service. Every time I visit, they have added new support for the residents of the district, but the original name stuck."

Sara took my elbow and led me through the room. She greeted some people as we passed but did not stop until we had reached a smaller space at the very back of the building. This room was empty, except for some furniture and some books and a tall man and a small child.

"You made it," the man said, rising from a chair to approach us, a broad smile on his face.

"Andrzej," Sara said warmly, and she shook his hand, then motioned toward me. "This is our friend and your new teacher, Elżbieta."

"It is a pleasure to meet you," Andrzej said, and he motioned all around him. "Welcome to our youth center. We're so glad to have your help."

He reminded me a lot of Uncle Piotr, with his generous smile and his ruddy cheeks, but this man was half the breadth of Uncle Piotr.

"Andrzej is the coordinator of this youth center, and he is a great asset to our work," Sara murmured.

"You flatter me, Sara," he said, winking playfully at her.

"Nonsense."

"Elżbieta, we do a lot of good work here, but none more important than connecting families to Matylda and Sara and their team," Andrzej said, the smile in his eyes remaining even as he grew more serious.

"What else do you do?" I asked him.

"Well, we sometimes house people, and of course there is the soup kitchen, and we also quietly run a few classes here and there. We help families out wherever we can. Speaking of which, let me introduce you to someone."

Andrzej waved to the little boy sitting in the corner of the room, holding a book. When Andrzej indicated he should join us, the little boy scrambled to his feet and approached us, his book hanging loosely from his left hand.

"Elżbieta, this is Icchak. His parents are no longer with us, and he has been waiting for a place in an orphanage for a while. I have other groups of children coming later so that you can work with them together, but Icchak's situation is quite urgent so we thought you could start with him one-on-one."

"Icchak has no one," Sara said, her voice low as the boy approached us. "He has been living on the streets. On his own."

"On his own?" I repeated, looking between them in alarm, then back to Icchak. "How old are you?"

The child opened his mouth to speak, but before he could make a sound, Andrzej interjected.

"And remember, Icchak, when we speak to Miss Elżbieta, we use Polish, not Yiddish."

"I am six," Icchak said carefully as he raised his chin. "But I am very clever. I can learn fast."

"I'll bet you can," I whispered, blinking rapidly. *Six years old and all alone.*

"He's very excited to learn from you today," Andrzej said quietly.

I stared down at the little boy, and as he looked up at me with eyes shining with hope, the last of my nausea passed. I could almost feel my courage returning as I stared at him.

I could do this. I had to do this. Icchak needed me to help him, and even more than that, he trusted that I would.

"In that case, Icchak, we should get to work. Would you like to learn some prayers with me today?"

I spent most of the day in the youth center, sitting in the back room with Icchak, and then with a procession of other children. They were eager to please and quick to learn, but it would take multiple visits for each to become sufficiently confident with the prayers.

By the time Sara returned for me, I was exhausted—physically and emotionally spent, eager only to bathe and then roll into bed. It was a much longer walk to reach the gate we needed to leave through, but as Sara explained, carefully cycling through the checkpoints enabled the team to continue their work much longer than they had originally expected to. Tired or not, we had to walk, and so in silence, we made our way through the streets. I couldn't even collect my thoughts enough to explain to her how shocked I was by the things I had seen that day, but I had questions, and eventually I found my voice.

"What will happen to Icchak?"

"Children like Icchak are resourceful. If he wasn't, he wouldn't have survived this long. The sad reality is that there are plenty of adults here who are still alive because children like him have been sneaking onto the Aryan side and bringing back food since the beginning."

"Wait—so he knows how to get out?"

"He does."

"So why doesn't he—"

"In his case, getting him out is not the difficult part. When the time is right, we will tell him to squeeze through a hole in the wall or through a small tunnel and to meet us at a particular checkpoint." She sighed heavily. "No, the real challenge will be keeping him alive once he's out here."

"And how will we do that?"

"Matylda and I will plan his evacuation. Sometime in the next few weeks, we will move him into our network. Icchak is one of the lucky ones—the blond hair, the light eyes—his features are not typically Semitic, which makes things so much easier for us. If he learns his prayers and gets a new name and the right papers, he will pass easily on this side, although his new identity will have to be a female."

"Female?"

"It is the tradition of the Jewish faith to circumcise boys. If he is placed in a family as a boy and suspicions are aroused, a soldier might ask him to expose himself and then his secret will be revealed. So, for Icchak's sake, we will dress him as a girl and give him a girl's name."

"Does that work?" I asked hesitantly.

"It is not a perfect system, but it's the best we can do for some of these children. And what is the alternative? We must help him as much as we can and pray that he can do the rest."

I was suddenly overcome by embarrassment at the way I had panicked that morning.

"I'm sorry about…"

"No," Sara interrupted me, and she was back to the soft-hearted, calm friend I was so accustomed to. "I'm the one who should be sorry. I knew this was going to be too much, and I knew that you didn't understand what it would be like in here. But desperation makes us foolish, and I let Matylda talk me into this, even though I knew it was a bad idea. You see now, though, why she was so determined that you become involved. Even if you can teach some children while I visit other families, or once you are used to crossing the checkpoints, if you can smuggle in a tiny chunk of bread, just a little medicine here or there, you will have made a tremendous difference. I am sorry

I was so hard on you. The thought of what those in the Jewish Quarter are enduring is beyond reason. I'm frantic with desperation to do good."

"I will do better tomorrow."

Sara slipped her arm around my shoulders and hugged me.

"You did well enough today."

"What's that you're drawing?"

I was sitting at the kitchen table that night, drawing absentmindedly in the book that Sara had given me. I wasn't consciously trying to capture anything in that sketch, I was just trying to calm my frantic mind enough that I could turn in to sleep. When Uncle Piotr startled me out of my reverie, I looked down at the page.

"It's a child," I said. I had sketched a small child in tattered clothes—a close likeness to Icchak, except that I had yet to draw the face. Uncle Piotr sat opposite me and peered at the drawing.

"It's good."

"Thank you."

"Is it to be a happy sketch or sad sketch?"

"I don't know yet."

Uncle Piotr looked down at the paper again, then leaned forward and tapped against it with his fingertip.

"The way you have drawn the child's hand, it's missing something. It looks almost as though it should be holding a toy, don't you think?"

I realized then that I had drawn Icchak. His hand was empty, but my subconscious mind had probably intended to fill in the book he'd been looking at when I first saw him. Suddenly, though, I gave in to impulse, and I reached down and quickly placed a little doll in his hand instead.

"Why a doll?" Uncle Piotr asked.

"Maybe this child doesn't have parents," I said, my throat suddenly tight. I thought about Truda and Mateusz, who were in their bedroom reading, and I had a sudden urge to rush to them and tell them I loved them. But for their generosity, I'd have been alone like Icchak. "Maybe this child doesn't have anyone to hold him close at night. Maybe he would appreciate something to cuddle."

As I finished the toy, I could suddenly see the child's face in my mind. I shifted my hand to fill in the face, sketching Icchak's wide eyes and Cupid's-bow lips, curved into a faint smile. His eyes echoed his sadness, but his lips spoke of finding joy despite his circumstances.

"Wait here a moment," Uncle Piotr said, and he pushed back his chair and retreated to his room. When he returned a moment later, he had a small chunk of wood in his hand and an even smaller knife. I watched in silence as he began to whittle away at the wood.

"What are you making?" I asked him.

"Your toy," he told me, nodding toward the page. "Art is generous, you know. Each artwork has its own energy, but it is never self-contained. One piece can be inspired by another piece, and in turn it can inspire, too, and on and on. It's self-reproducing, each piece spreading a different kind of beauty or thought or lesson to each person who sees it."

In no time at all, Uncle Piotr had carved the rough shape of a small doll. He pushed it across the table toward me, and I lifted it thoughtfully.

"Your doll needs a face," I said. Uncle Piotr chuckled.

"That's your department, Elżbieta. I can whittle. I cannot draw."

"Do you have more wood?"

"Rough waste wood like that? Only a little, but I can access it easily enough."

I picked up my charcoal and sketched a quick face onto the doll, then turned it to show him. Uncle Piotr smiled.

"Would you like to do a little project with me?" I asked him.

"Perhaps."

"Could you make me more of these?"

Half an hour later, Truda and Mateusz emerged from the bedroom, amused as they looked at the table covered in wood shavings and tiny figurines.

"What's this?" Mateusz asked, picking one up. Truda also scooped up a doll.

"I thought Sara could distribute them to some of the children at her soup kitchens," I lied. "They have so little. I know they'd appreciate something to play with."

"You're going to give *naked* dolls to innocent children?" Truda said, then she clucked her tongue. I looked up at her, and she hid a smile. "We can't have that. I'll sew some clothes."

Sara was delighted with the dolls when I showed her the next morning. We had made half a dozen—each with a different face and a different outfit, hand-stitched by Truda from scraps of fabric around the apartment.

"I'm going to take some of these dolls to the children you met in my bedroom that night," Sara told me. "They are still in the ghetto, although we found room for most of them at the Korczak Orphanage. Still, they need to wait a little longer to be evacuated, which has been immensely disappointing for them. You would be amazed how much a small thing like this can cheer a child up."

This soon became the new rhythm of our days. Each night I would craft dolls with the adults in my family, giving us a shared task to bond over and a creative outlet which we all enjoyed. In the morning, I would lie to those very same adults and leave the house ostensibly to go to work with Sara, only I'd actually go to her offices at City Hall to change into other clothes and don makeup.

Soon I was marching through the checkpoint with a bag in hand, the bottom stuffed with a chunk of bread or forbidden medicines and as many dolls as I could fit. Sometimes I'd hand these out to the street children we passed on our way to the youth center, but mostly I saved them. Some of the children I was teaching were resistant to learning with me, and the lure of toys was a powerful motivator.

All day, I'd sit with children in the back room. Most of the time I was teaching them the basic tenets of the Catholic faith, but the older the child, the more in-depth this teaching had to be. The younger children thought it was all a game. The older children understood that this was life or death.

"This is God's work," I would whisper to myself, on the days when I felt like I'd be physically ill. And I *felt* that it was God's work during the good moments—when Sara announced Icchak's rescue had been a success and that he was settling into a new home with a family on a farm in the countryside, or when a particularly stubborn child would suddenly get it, and Sara would announce that child was ready to be evacuated, soon to be safe or at least saf*er*, and all because of me.

When there was no way to avoid it, I visited homes with Sara, usually if we were to walk past a particular family's home on our way to or from a checkpoint. While Matylda was focusing on the street children or going door-to-door trying to find children to evacuate, Sara was investigating referrals through Andrzej and his network at the youth center. In theory, this was much safer than Matylda's brute-force approach to finding new families to help, but it didn't feel safe. It didn't even feel like kindness. Helping make a plan to get the orphans from the Jewish area was one thing; visiting homes and looking into the eyes of desperate parents while we tried to convince them to let us take their children was another.

"I don't know how you do that every day," I whispered shakily after a mother and father told us in no uncertain terms to leave their apartment.

"Neither do I," she admitted, smiling ruefully. "Some days

I think I have reached the end of my tolerance, but other days I know that it is not for me to decide when enough is enough. Not while these people cannot simply opt out. The thought of that helps me carry on."

12

Roman

CHAIM INTRODUCED ME TO THE MANAGER OF THE YOUTH center, a social worker named Andrzej Neeman. Once Andrzej heard about my mother's situation, he proposed an agreement.

"You come here after your job and work in our kitchen— clean the pots and pans for me. If you work until just before curfew, I will give you a small ticket which your family can exchange for a portion of food the next day. You can do this up to four times a week, because I have to be fair to the others who need help. And it won't always be a hot meal—sometimes it will be vegetable scraps or some flour or oil, but I will always have something to offer her. Deal?"

"Yes. Please," I said, almost falling over myself in my haste to commit to this arrangement. I didn't mind the long days, especially when my mother assured me that the extra food was really making a difference.

"I'm making more milk," she said, beaming as Eleonora suckled at her breast. "I'm so proud of you for figuring out how to do this. My clever, clever son."

I couldn't see any difference in Eleonora's condition, but I took my mother's reassurance at face value. It felt good to be doing *something* to help, and my work with Andrzej gave me something positive to focus on each day, a welcome reprieve from the constant anxiety I felt about the deportations, which were now happening every day.

Thousands upon thousands of people marched through the streets to the *Umschlagplatz* with every sunrise now. Some volunteered after the Germans promised three kilograms of bread and a kilo of jam. And then posters appeared in the streets, instructing us to pack our belongings and our valuables, as we would need them when we resettled at the new, spacious camps. Some people believed this proved we were moving into a less cruel chapter of the occupation.

"I told you!" Samuel said, triumphant. "I told you the Germans would soften toward us. Maybe it is time that we volunteer."

Mother and I looked at him in disbelief.

"You cannot believe this is true," I said.

"We have no proof that it is not," he said, shrugging. "What if we are stubbornly staying here in hell, when we could be comfortable in a beautiful new camp at Treblinka?"

"No," Mother said flatly, in such a harsh tone that the conversation ended, and Samuel did not suggest it again.

It didn't matter what golden promises the Germans or the Kapo made us, people eventually saw through them, and within days of these efforts, volunteers stopped coming. But a certain number needed to be removed from the ghetto each day, and so the roundups became increasingly vicious. Sala's workshop was abuzz with horror stories of on-the-spot executions of those who resisted and of crowds stuck at the loading platform for up to twenty hours without food or water.

"It just doesn't seem right," I muttered to Chaim one day. "If they are really taking us to some luxurious camp so that we can work for them at Treblinka, why would they kill those who are hesitant to go or let us sit at the *Umschlagplatz* until we are half-dead, waiting for the transports?"

"You know my thoughts on the matter. If they were slaughtering Jews at Chełmno, they are slaughtering us at Treblinka, too."

It seemed that we were damned if we resisted and damned if we went. Thankfully my precious work permit meant I was relatively safe—as much as anyone within the ghetto was safe. But I had to make that walk home every afternoon, and it was harder and harder to convince myself to do it.

Now, I walked straight to the youth center, not even stopping at our apartment when I walked past it, and I worked until the very last second before curfew, sometimes much longer than Andrzej even needed me, and often every day of the week, even though I'd only get the meal ticket four of the days. And when Chaim discovered that we could access the roof above the youth center and then walk all the way along the block to my building, safely out of sight of the patrols, I began staying out with him, later and later and long past the curfew.

"Now you see where my nickname came from," he winked at me, as we sat on the rooftop one night. "I always liked to sit on rooftops. Up here, everything is better—it's never crowded or noisy, and the smell is dragged away by the wind. Up here, I feel closer to heaven."

"Who knew you were a poet?" I teased, and he threw a broken roof tile at me.

We would sit on the roof and talk for hours some nights, and then Chaim would climb down to sleep in Andrzej's apartment above the youth center, and I would climb across the rooftops, to drop through a window into the internal stairwell of my own building.

THE WARSAW ORPHAN 129

"Roman," Samuel scolded me one evening, when Mother had risen to use the bathroom and Dawidek and Eleonora were sleeping. "You said that you would only be working at the youth center four nights a week and only until the curfew. You are coming home later and later. You're never here when Dawidek is home, and he's missing you. Besides, your mother has been so worried about you."

"What I'm doing is perfectly safe," I muttered. "I'm just spending time with my friend. I'm not even out on the street."

"Mother misses you, Roman," Samuel said uneasily. "Maybe...you could please come home in time tomorrow night so that we could sit down for the meal together."

"You know I don't even eat here," I snapped. Samuel's eyebrows drew down.

"Do you *want* to eat here? You are entitled to your rations—"

"That's not what I meant!"

Defensiveness made our tiny bedroom suffocatingly small. There was nowhere to retreat, no way to sort through my complicated fears and anxieties. I knew that I was hurting my family, but I couldn't seem to help it. It seemed easier to push them away, to try to start the process of learning to live without them, to delay facing whether they were there or gone. I had no hope of finding the words to explain this to Samuel and Mother, so when she tried to start a conversation with me about my day, I pretended to go right to sleep.

But Samuel's words played on my mind the next day, so when I finished my shift at the workshop, I walked Chaim to the youth center, then doubled back and went home.

I paused at the door as I always did and let my imagination play out the worst-case scenario: that I would push the door open, and the apartment would be empty. My palms went sweaty, and my stomach churned, but I forced myself to open the door—only to find that everything was wrong.

There was a stranger sitting on the Grobelnys' sofa. Eleonora was on the woman's lap, and Dawidek was sitting stiffly beside her.

For weeks, I had feared coming home to find my parents missing, and it seemed that this had finally come to pass. I swept my gaze through the room. *This apartment was always crowded, so many of us lived here, but now there is just this stranger and the children and, my God, they are gone! My parents are really gone.* Blood began to pound through my body, fear and fury and grief somehow leaving me both weak and unnaturally strong. I could barely hold myself up, but I wanted to tear the world apart, and I was certain that I had it in me to do so.

"Who are you?" I demanded, and I looked around the room, eyes wild, my thoughts a torrent I could not slow or control. *This woman found my sister and brother on the street and somehow made her way here, but I have lost my parents to a camp at Treblinka that they will never come back from. I can't do this, Mother. I can't do it without you, Samuel. What am I going to do?*

The panic was immediate, and it quickly became vicious. If all I had left was my brother and my sister, I wanted this woman as far away from them as possible. I stormed across the room and snatched Eleonora out of the woman's arms. I barely noticed the baby's wail of protest. The stranger's presence consumed my focus, and she instantly became an undeserving target for all my fear and rage. Two voices inside me were battling for supremacy. The monster in my gut wanted to tear her limb from limb, to take out all my terror on her, because she was here staring blankly at me, and she was *in our home with my siblings.*

But the stranger was staring up at me with huge green eyes full of terror. This registered somewhere in the recesses of my mind, and I tried to convince myself to calm down, to talk rationally about this and to find out what was really going on. The Germans deserved my rage, but they were not in the room with me. This woman was, and the beast inside me won the battle. I shouted at her, raging so fiercely that I was trembling from head to toe.

"How did they get separated from the children? Did you see them taken? Did you even *try* to help them, or did you just watch them go?"

The door to our tiny bedroom flew open, and Samuel and my mother were there, both wide-eyed with shock. Behind them stood another woman, who pushed her way past them to stand between me and the woman on the couch.

"Don't you *dare* shout at her like that!" the older woman shouted right back at me, just as my mother crossed the room to take Eleonora from my arms. I scanned the room again, confused and trying to understand what was happening, trying to battle the flood of hot tears that threatened.

"Roman!" Samuel exclaimed. "What on earth are you doing?"

I didn't know what I was doing, and that was the problem. The red heat of my rage was fading into other emotions—shame and embarrassment and a sheer, bewildering humiliation, all so much louder than the relief I also felt. These strangers were staring at me, and the door from the kitchen flew open, and there was Judit and Mrs. Kukliński and even Mrs. Grobelny, and then from down near the bedrooms, my grandparents slowly came into view.

They were all still here. Every single one of them was still here. My knees buckled. The relief was overwhelming.

"I... The... I..."

"What is going on with you?" my mother asked sharply, cradling Eleonora to her. As my rage began to ebb, I noticed new details: my mother had been crying—her eyes were red-rimmed and puffy. Eleonora was crying, too, now, her pitiful cry ratcheting up, obviously startled by the loudness of my voice. Dawidek was staring up at me with visible horror, clutching the doll to his chest, and the growing audience of my reluctant housemates looked every bit as scared and confused as the stranger on the couch.

I looked to Samuel, hoping that he could give me some guidance, but found he was leaning against the doorjamb, his eyes closed, utterly dejected. Because of me?

"I thought you were gone," I said to my mother, and my voice broke. Mother's gaze softened, and she stepped forward to gently touch my upper arm.

"We were just talking to the social worker. She has come for a visit to discuss Eleonora and Dawidek. She wants to help us, Roman."

My gaze dropped to the woman on the couch, and now that I was calming down, I realized at last that she wasn't so much a woman as a girl, and she was close to tears. The older woman reached down and hooked her hand into the girl's elbow, pulling her to her feet. She addressed my mother with a firm, quiet tone.

"Think about it, Mr. and Mrs. Gorka. I'll call in again to see if you want to discuss it further."

As the older woman left, she shot me one last fierce look. The girl stared at the floor as she walked away. When the door closed behind them, I asked my parents, "Think about what? How are they trying to help?"

My mother looked to Dawidek, then forced a smile.

"It doesn't matter now. We can discuss it later."

13

Emilia

I WAS SHAKING AS WE LEFT THE GORKA APARTMENT. EVERY trip into the ghetto was new and upsetting in some way, but I had never physically feared for my safety before, not in the way that I just had.

"Are you okay?" Sara asked me as we walked. We had been running so late that day, and I was hungry and tired, and *all* I wanted to do was go home to my bed and cry. I clenched my teeth and nodded.

"Are we evacuating those children?"

Sara shook her head.

"It is a common story." She sighed heavily. "The mother was receptive, but the father wants to keep the family together. In that case, he seemed determined to convince himself that there is reason to hold on to hope here. Of all the places in the world, I never thought I would find an optimist in the Warsaw Ghetto."

"The baby—she was sick."

"The mother is not making enough milk, so the baby's development is stunted. And of course, it is a miracle that she has survived this far. If the Germans knew of her, they might have killed her already."

"What a wasted miracle," I muttered under my breath. "What good is it for God to grant a miracle to save a baby like that, only for her to starve to death?"

"Elżbieta, my darling, when one is standing in hell, it is best not to delve too deeply into theology," Sara said wryly. I could see her point. Every new block brought some new abomination against goodness. Where was God in all of that? I hadn't allowed myself to challenge my faith in this way, not since Tomasz had died. That day, I had promised myself I would never pray again. How could I believe in a loving God and the Blessed Mother if they would allow a good man like my brother to be killed for his kindness?

But the brief glimpse of a faithless life had terrified me. I felt like a ship without a rudder, and by the time the sun set that day, I was back to praying. Now, though, I wondered if that was foolish of me. If there was a God, could He not see what was happening in the ghetto? Or could He see but was powerless to intervene? Because the alternative was that He *could* see and He *could* intervene, but He was choosing inaction.

"Do you still pray?" I asked Sara uncertainly.

"I stopped praying when my son died. If there is a God, I want no part of His version of justice."

"I need to pray," I said, my voice small. I thought about my whispered prayers each night, and how certain I was that Tomasz and Father were with me in those moments.

"I'm jealous of you. I miss believing that there is some purpose and some sense to life," Sara said, sighing. "Maybe, tonight when you pray, you could send up a little prayer for me, too."

14

Roman

I FOUND MYSELF SITTING UP WITH MY PARENTS THAT NIGHT, watching as Dawidek fell asleep. I hadn't spoken a word since the women left. We had gone about our nightly routine, everyone eating in silence, the atmosphere strained and heavy. The sun was setting, so Samuel struck the carbide light. In the dim yellow glow, I watched Dawidek's eyes flutter closed, and as his eyelashes came to rest upon his cheeks, I felt an affection for him so strong it left me close to tears.

"The women are social workers from the Warsaw Council," my mother said quietly. "The young one is an apprentice. She was watching the children so Samuel and I could speak to the older nurse... Sara is her name."

"What can they do to help us?"

"They know one of your friends. Andrzej?"

"That is the manager at the youth center. He is the one who has been giving me the tokens for food."

"He sent the women, Roman. I believe your friend Chaim asked him to."

"I asked Chaim to help us find a way out. He said he knew someone that might be able to help, but I didn't realize… He must have passed on our address."

"Their visit was a shock, that's all. I wasn't prepared, and then you came in shouting and… I just wasn't expecting any of it." Mother tilted her head back to stare at the ceiling, and heavy tears trickled down her cheeks.

"I thought the Germans had taken you. I thought the girl on the sofa had found the children in the street by themselves," I whispered. "So the women wanted to help us?"

"They have been smuggling children from the ghetto and resettling them on the other side. Mostly with Catholic families or orphanages. The nurse said she could try to find a place for Eleonora and Dawidek." Mother searched my gaze, then her eyes dropped to the floor. "She said that Eleonora is severely malnourished. That's why she is so quiet."

I looked at my mother in alarm.

"Then, I will get you more food, Mother. There will be a way. Those women came in here today and asked you to hand over half our family?" I said incredulously. I was going to kill Pigeon the next time I saw him. I would tear him apart with my bare hands. I felt the tension returning to the muscles in my arms and shoulders, my body preparing for the fight.

"We said no," Samuel said abruptly. "Things will get better soon, at least the overcrowding will ease with the deportations. If there are less people, there will be more food and less disease. And…maybe the war will end. We could be free any day now. We have to stay together."

There it was: the glimmer of hope I'd been relying on him to find. Samuel's determination to paint such a positive picture had irritated me in the past, but that night, I needed it. I let the relief wash over me, until I saw my mother. The tears were still rolling down her cheeks, and she was staring at Eleonora with heartbreak written all over her face.

"Mother?" I said slowly, shaking my head. "Tell me you're not seriously considering this. You would send them away from us?" My voice rose almost hysterically, and my parents stared at me in alarm. I knew I needed to keep my voice down, not only because the house was full of people trying to sleep but also because right in that very tiny room with us my baby brother and sister were resting, and Dawidek would be up hours before the dawn because he still needed to work the corpse crew. But I just couldn't help myself.

"How can I not consider it?" Mother asked me fiercely. She waved toward the window, motioning toward the street. "What kind of life is this, Roman? What if there is a knock on the door one morning at dawn when the roundup begins, and they force us to leave? They have been doing that in some blocks, you know. They go from door to door, and they force everyone out! I will respect Samuel's wishes, but *I* wish I could say yes to those women. I would sleep like a baby at night if I knew *my* babies were on the other side of that wall. Safe together, with at least enough food in their tummies to keep them alive."

"We are doing just fine," I said flatly. My mother failed to stifle a sob.

"Just fine," she mocked. "Eleonora is half the size she should be. You may not know how a child should grow, but Eleonora is my third baby. Believe me when I tell you she is not *just fine.*"

"That's enough," Samuel said abruptly. "It does us no good to squabble or to dwell on these things. It was kind of your friend to try to help us, but we have told the women we cannot accept their offer, and that is the end of it. It is better for us to stay with the children so that we can be sure they are safe. Please thank Chaim for trying."

I wasn't sure how to be grateful to him for trying to set this up. I wasn't even sure how I'd calm myself down enough not to launch myself at him when I saw him the next day.

"Roman," my mother said suddenly. "Today…when I came into that room, I thought you were going to hurt that woman. Would you have?"

"Of course not," I said sharply. "Of course I wouldn't have hurt her. I just thought…" When I blinked, I was back in the living room, and I was so sure that my parents were gone all over again. I gave a full-body shudder, trying to shake the memory away. "I panicked. I thought she was a threat, I guess. I'm sorry."

"The girl—the young one," Samuel said slowly. "Perhaps it is her you owe an apology to."

I decided not to confront Chaim about the social worker visit during the workday. Instead, I put my head down, and I ignored his attempts at conversation. By lunchtime, he had given up, and we worked in silence for the rest of the day. But as we left that afternoon, I finally turned to him, and I said, "Two social workers visited my apartment yesterday."

"They are going to rescue the children?" Chaim looked so hopeful I felt a burst of pure irritation.

"Rescue them? They wanted to take them!" I said. He tilted his head and looked at me blankly.

"What did you think I meant when I told you I might know someone who could help?"

"Not *that*. I need to keep my family together, not break it apart."

"Roman, the only hope you have is to send the children away," he said, then he added gently, "To stay in the ghetto is to accept death."

"Samuel says things might get better," I said flatly. "With the deportations, things won't be so crowded and—"

"You are not foolish enough to believe any of that. If your

parents are not willing to send the children out, you should convince them."

My hands curled into fists at my side.

"You don't understand," I snapped. "If your family were here, you would understand that all we can do is stay together."

"You are a fool if you think it is better for your family to die together than for the children to be saved."

I grabbed Chaim's lapel and twisted it hard. Our faces were only inches apart, but he met my gaze unblinkingly.

"Who could protect the children better than we can?" I demanded. The red mist of rage was clouding my vision, and I could feel the anger rising throughout my body. My hands shook, my stomach churned. I wasn't sure how much longer I could control myself.

But this was Chaim. My friend. One of the only people I trusted. At this thought, I finally understood why his betrayal stung so much.

"Literally anyone on the other side of that wall can protect those children better than you," Chaim said, his voice low. "Here, you are powerless. Our days are numbered, Roman."

"You don't know that!"

"I *do* know that," he said, and he pushed me away impatiently. "We have heard nothing from the tens of thousands who have gone to Treblinka. No one has escaped to tell us it is safe, and there are those who went willingly for the Resistance, purely so that they could report back. Everyone who has stepped onto those trains is *dead*, Roman. Do you hear me? They are *dead*! Every last one of them!" My hands fell to my sides, and I stared at him in shock. His conviction was undeniable. "You and I? We are doomed. We will die at the hands of the Germans, if not in here, then at Treblinka. But the children...?" He shook his head at me, frustration flaring his nostrils. "Those children could survive if you and your parents would allow them to."

He shook himself off then and walked away from me, leaving me standing dumbfounded by the side of the road. But after only a few minutes, I continued toward the youth center for my shift in the kitchen.

Chaim was wrong. He simply had to be. The alternative was unthinkable.

Chaim and I continued to sit opposite one another all day, every day, but we no longer spoke. He attempted to start a conversation a few times, but I would only look at him sharply and continue with my work. No longer did he wait for me at the corner as we walked into the workshop, and although we both still walked to the youth center after our shifts sometimes, we no longer walked side by side, and the days of me staying out late with him were over.

"Are you okay?" Andrzej asked one evening. He was hovering beside me with his hands in his pockets, obviously open to the idea of a conversation. But I didn't want to vent, and I wasn't yet ready to feel better. Besides, Andrzej had sent the social workers. I needed him, and I needed his favor, but if he was willing to split my family up, I could no longer trust him.

"I'm fine," I snapped and went back to washing the pots and pans.

The next day, I was walking to my shift in the workshop when I noticed Chaim standing in our usual spot on the corner at the edge of the block. I intended to push past him and continue to our desk, but he reached out a hand to stop me.

"Don't—" I started to say, but he shook his head, and that's when I saw the expression in his eyes. "What is it?"

"Sala," he said, and his voice broke. His hand fell to his side, and he exhaled shakily. "Yesterday, after we left. He and his family were deported. The workshop is closed."

"When are you going to tell your family that you no longer have a job?" Chaim asked later that day as we stood in the kitchen at the youth center, side by side washing dishes. We'd been there all day, helping where we could to keep ourselves busy as we tried to digest the news that our boss and his family were gone.

"I won't tell them. They will only worry," I admitted. "What will you do for food?"

"The same as you," Chaim said, and he gave me a cheeky smile. "I'll beg what I can from Andrzej and supplement that with as many delicious scraps from the trash as I can find."

"We are a miserable pair," I said and sighed, handing him a pot to wipe.

"Hey, at least you're speaking to me again. Things aren't all bad."

The next day, I left my apartment at the usual time, determined that my parents would not know I no longer had a job. Chaim and I agreed to meet at the youth center, where we would try to speak to Andrzej and see if he could help us earn more food. I was daydreaming as I walked, until I looked up at a crossroad and saw Dawidek, walking right past me, sauntering in that jaunty way I was so familiar with, carrying the little doll the girl had given him when she came to try to take him away.

But Dawidek wasn't with his work crew, and he wasn't dressed in his own clothes. I had never before seen the outfit he was wearing. The trousers were pressed and clean, the shirt spotless, the ensemble far too nice for him to wear to his job. He was walking in a large group of children, but none of them were familiar to me, and that's when I finally realized that although that child looked just like my brother, it was just a coincidence. This was a group from one of the orphanages, maybe out for a morning walk.

Each child held a little bundle, tightly wrapped in cloth, and as the line of children stretched and stretched, I noticed that, every now and again, I would see one carrying a doll just like Dawidek's. Some of the children could not have been more than three or four years old, and these were usually walking with older children, their hands linked and swinging as they went.

I smiled to myself, and I stopped walking then, a few dozen feet back from the intersection. I leaned against the cold sand-stone wall of the building and watched. The children walked in obedient silence, but it wasn't a strained silence. I wondered where they were going. It wasn't as though the ghetto offered much in the way of amusement for young people. Once upon a time the sight of children in such finery would have suggested a trip to the synagogue, but, of course, those days were long past. But this was a sweet scene. A refreshing scene. I breathed in deeply, and I focused on the coolness of the morning air rather than the oppressive smell that always lingered.

I felt almost hopeful at the sight. There was something so pure about the way they looked around as they walked, taking in the streetscape of the ghetto as if they might spot something worthy of their interest. No wonder that one boy had reminded me of Dawidek. He wore the same expression of wonder some-times, despite everything he had seen and done.

I must have only watched the children for seconds before a group of Kapo and some Germans also passed, and the true con-text of the march became apparent. These children weren't just being taken on an outing for their amusement. They weren't flanked only by nurses and older children. They were under armed guard, and when I considered where they were coming from and where they were headed, a jolt of shock ran through my body.

They were walking to the Umschlagplatz.

Hundreds of children, marching happily toward their deaths. A burst of adrenaline overtook me, and I moved to run toward the children, but I took only a few steps before a man stepped in my way.

"Kid, don't do it," the stranger warned me, his voice low, desperate and hoarse. How quickly I had shifted from quiet amusement to this…burning, seething shock and horror and fury. It raced through my veins, urgent and determined, until I was vibrating with the force of it.

"I have to warn them," I said, pushing the man back so I could see the line of children. I considered the direction they were walking from and realized that this was probably the Korczak Orphanage, the largest orphanage in the ghetto, famous for its generous care and its immense size. There was still time… Maybe if I caused a scene I could—

"Kid," the man said, more urgently this time. "There is nothing we can do. Think this through, will you? So I let you run over there—you'll be shot, and the children will *see* you shot. They aren't scared right now. They don't know…" His voice broke. I looked up at him and saw that his eyes were shiny, despite the stubbornly high set of his chin. "Look how calm they are. Maybe they've been told they are going for a grand adventure. It's a mercy to let them walk out of this place in peace. No one benefits if they are scared."

"But it's not right," I said choking, looking back at the seemingly endless line of children.

"None of this is right, kid," the man said, and he pushed me abruptly back and shook his head. "Don't get shot in front of them. Don't let that be the last thing they see here."

I leaned back into the wall again, and this time, I counted the SS soldiers, supervising the Jewish police as they supervised the children, layer upon layer of oppression, as if children had any hope at all of resistance. And at the back, I saw the orphanage director, walking between two children, holding each child's hand tightly in his. His chin was high, his eyes clear and wide.

I hated the moment, and I hated the world, and most of all I hated those German bastards who would take hundreds of children and march them through the streets of a prison to load them onto a cattle car and—if Chaim was right—to execute them. Imprisoning us was one thing, starving us to death was

another, torturing us day by day for years… Maybe I had almost grown numb to those things. But the wholesale murder
of hundreds of children, in one monstrous act? I knew in theory that this had been happening and that children had been
rounded up every single day. But I hadn't seen it. On some
level, I hadn't believed it.

I suddenly realized that the street around me had cleared and
that the only people left outside were those who were being
marched away under armed guard. I swore under my breath
and pushed at several doors at street level, only to find them all
locked. Now my heart was racing with panic. I tried to clear
my head so that I could consider my options. The youth center
wasn't far, just ahead, the entrance on the opposite corner, but to
cross the road would be to draw too much attention to myself.

I ran to the next door and pushed at it frantically. It was
locked, too, but the latch was weak. I pulled back, and with
all my strength rammed my shoulder into it. The door gave,
and I ran inside, then pressed an armchair up against the door
to close it.

The apartment was empty, and I tried not to think too much
about who might have owned the furniture and clothing I saw
scattered around, and I told myself to not even *think* about looting it…but, of course, that's where my thoughts went. I could
get several days' food for some of these items, even if they
weren't mine.

Not now, Roman. Think of it later.

I felt a bizarre need to watch those children for as long as I
could, to try to catalog them so that someone—*anyone*—remembered after they were gone that they had been here. I ran
up a set of stairs and found an empty bedroom which faced the
crossroad. Hiding behind a curtain in a stranger's abandoned
apartment, I wept, sobs racking my body in a way that I hadn't
wept since I was a child.

When the last child had walked out of view, I wiped my

eyes on the curtain and looked out to the street, trying to assess whether it was safe for me to return to the youth center. I could see it from my vantage point. The doors were closed, and the usual groups of people waiting outside for food were nowhere to be seen.

I looked toward the roof, thinking about the times I had sat up there with Chaim, chatting and even laughing, as if we were normal teenagers enjoying a normal night in our normal lives.

My gaze dropped, and I suddenly found myself staring into the apartment above the youth center—Andrzej's home. There were people standing at the window staring out at the cross street just as I had been doing.

Among the crowd of unfamiliar faces I saw her—the girl I had found sitting with Dawidek and Eleonora when I came home from work that day. She was looking down at the street, tears rolling down her cheeks, her red-rimmed eyes full of fear and fury, just as I was certain mine were.

But that expression on her face was familiar to me because I'd seen it before. I'd *caused* it. This realization hit me like a punch to the gut, and I suddenly understood that Samuel was right. My actions mattered, big and small. If something I did had put that same fear and sadness into that girl's eyes as this monstrous scene, I needed to make things right.

At the youth center that afternoon, I found a scrap of paper in a bookshelf, and I sat alone at a table to write a note. It took me several attempts, and I was tearing at the paper between each one, so that the remnant became smaller and smaller.

Sorry didn't seem enough. I had to rip myself open, to make myself vulnerable. It was the only way she would understand that I meant the apology.

I know I frightened you last week, and I would like to ask your forgiveness. It is no excuse, but I thought for a moment that my family had been taken, and I lost my head. The truth is, I have been doing that a lot lately. I don't know how to cope with everything that is happening around me, but I do not want to be the kind of man who would put fear in the eyes of a woman the way I did to you that day, even while the world is this out of control.

I am very sorry. Thank you for trying to help my family. I have decided to try to convince my parents that they should have another conversation with you and your friend. If you visit our home again, I will be grateful for the opportunity to apologize to you in person.

I folded the paper and approached Andrzej. Maybe the girl was still upstairs in his apartment; maybe she was somewhere in the building. It was such a chaotic space, it was entirely possible I'd missed her leaving. In any case, I was too ashamed to look her in the eye so I didn't ask for her.

"Did you organize for the social workers to visit my house?"

"Yes," he said cautiously. "I understood that your family wanted help. I know that you declined the offer, but—"

"We shouldn't have," I blurted, throat tightening as I thought of the orphans that morning. "I'm going to convince my parents to reconsider. And, please, could you give this note to the girl? I scared her, and I want to apologize."

He took the note and slipped it into his pocket.

"It takes strength to apologize, Roman."

"I don't know about that," I muttered. I certainly didn't feel strong.

"And it takes wisdom to understand that in our current circumstances, every day may be our last, and we cannot let grievances remain unresolved. She'll be back tomorrow, and I'll be sure that Elżbieta gets your note."

"We need to send the children away."

I waited until Dawidek and Eleonora were asleep before I spoke to my parents. The carbide light was off, and we were all lying in the darkness. My parents didn't react, and I wondered if I had waited too late to speak up: despite everything,

Samuel still slept like the dead. After a moment, though, my mother rolled toward me.

"Why do you say that?"

I thought I could tell them about the orphanage children without weeping, but I was wrong. By the time I finished explaining what I'd seen, my face was wet with tears, and my mother and Samuel had risen from their mattress to sit on either side of me. It was hot that night, and the air was still and sticky, but I was so desperate for comfort that I sank into their embrace.

"We keep hoping things will get better," I croaked when I'd finished sharing the story. "We keep assuming things are going to get better. Things just keep getting worse, and every time I think things can't get any worse, they do. We have an opportunity to free Dawidek and Eleonora from all of this. We have an opportunity to save them from whatever lies after the *Umschlagplatz*." I turned my head to the right and sought Samuel's eyes in the darkness. My voice broke as I whispered, "Please, Samuel. Please let them go."

"We need to stay together as a family," Samuel whispered. He slid his arm around my shoulders, and he squeezed gently. "We can still look after one another."

"Are you so sure of your optimism that you would gamble Eleonora's life on it?" my mother asked him bitterly. She shifted away from me, just a little, and angled herself to stare past me to Samuel. "Roman is right. Even if it is a work farm at Treblinka—even if it is another camp with more food and fresh air—it is still a *camp*. Our children do not belong in prison! Those social workers would place the children in a family."

"You said you agreed with me," he said, after a pause. "We talked about this last week after they left. You agreed with me. What changed?"

"I didn't agree with you. I could just see that there was no point arguing with you," my mother snapped. "All of my energy is going to surviving, Samuel. Every thought, every emotion, it is all just to get through one more day—to drag the children through one more day of this hell. I keep trying to conserve my energy for making milk, but she's fading anyway." I could hear the tears in Mother's voice, and my own eyes were still wet with tears. I reached down, and my mother took my hand.

"Sending the children with the social workers is a risk," she conceded hoarsely, "but you are right, Roman. Keeping them with us is even riskier."

"Do you realize that if we send them away we may never see them again?" Samuel whispered desperately. "Our children are all we have to live for. If they go, how do we go on?"

When Mother spoke again, her voice was strong.

"We go on in the knowledge that we have done the only thing we *could* do to give the children a fighting chance."

15

Emilia

NO DAY IN THE GHETTO WAS A GOOD DAY, BUT THAT DAY, the day the orphans left, that was the worst of the worst.

We had only just arrived when the shocked whisper ran through the youth center of the procession marching down Smocza Street. Sara and Andrzej suggested we shelter in his apartment in case trouble came knocking at the center, too, but that also gave me a front-row seat to watch the children go.

The dolls. They had my dolls. The children were carrying my dolls.

As soon as the roundups were over, Sara suggested we go. I pulled myself together long enough for us to leave the ghetto and return to our office at City Hall. But the minute Sara and I were behind closed doors, I collapsed in a heap, slumped over her desk. Matylda joined us after a while. We all sat around in Sara's office, she and Matylda in a state of shock, me completely overwhelmed.

"I was so sure the children were safe there. It is the most famous orphanage in all of Poland. I thought they'd never go near it," Matylda whispered. She was dry-eyed, but deathly pale.

"We could have done something," I blurted. "Couldn't we? Should we have? Maybe someone else helped them. There were still blocks and blocks to walk before they reached the loading platform. Maybe something happened…maybe someone intervened. Maybe they are okay. Besides, there was nothing we could do. Right?"

But the women had fallen silent again, staring into space. I so desperately wanted someone to tell me that it was okay. I wanted someone to absolve me.

After a while, Matylda left but returned with a bottle of vodka. She poured three glasses and pushed the smallest in front of me.

"Matylda," Sara scolded her, "how will I explain drunk Elżbieta to her parents?"

"Perhaps tell them that she watched two hundred children marched to their deaths today," Matylda said sharply, and then she sighed. "Sara, we cannot expect her to assume adult responsibilities without any adult comforts."

Vodka tasted like poison to me, but I picked it up and sipped it gingerly. Sara downed hers in one gulp, and then rested her elbows on the table and covered her face with her hands.

"Sometimes, I still feel like this is all a nightmare. Isn't it crazy?" I said, again desperate to fill the miserable silence in the room. "After all of these years, this is our normal now, but it doesn't feel normal. And sometimes when I wake, for the first few seconds I forget. I forget everything we've lost. I forget that there is very little hope for us, and I just exist. I love those moments. On a day like today, though, I can't help but wonder if I will ever have a moment of blissful ignorance again. When you have seen these things, things so horrific that you cannot help but become hardened to them, how can you just go back to existing again? Even if the war ended tomorrow, I feel like I would be broken for the rest of my life, and in ways that I can't even understand, let alone explain."

"I hope the children didn't suffer," Sara said, almost to herself. "They obviously weren't afraid, at least not the little ones. I hope that right until the very last minute, they thought they were going somewhere wonderful—"

Her voice broke, and then she started to cry. That set off a chain reaction around the table. Soon even Matylda was weeping.

I wasn't the only person in that room left feeling broken by what we had seen that day. The sound of those women weeping validated my deep, uncompromising grief.

The next day, I did not meet Sara in the lobby to catch the tram at seven o'clock. Instead, I lay in bed, curled up in a little ball, thinking about the children walking with their dolls. I'd barely slept because the image of that line of children just kept marching through my head, an endless circle of lost hope and life.

"Elżbieta, I know you're unwell, but you must try to eat so you can keep your strength up," Truda said, bringing me a plate of soup at lunchtime. "Sara called from your office. She said that they are missing you very much and that they are hoping you will be back there to work tomorrow."

"Perhaps," I said dully. "I'm not hungry. Could I eat it later?"

I stayed in bed all day. This was something I had not had the luxury of doing after my father's death, and certainly not after my brother died. In some way, I had some grieving to catch up on, and as I lay in bed on that rainy day, I luxuriated in it. Just after seven o'clock my door opened, and Sara stepped into my room. She closed the door quietly, then sat on the edge of my bed.

"You are sulking," she said. "I understand why. I did my share of pouting last night, too."

"I am *grieving*."

"There were two hundred children in that orphanage."

"Did they survive?" I asked, suddenly so hopeful that I sat up. Sara winced.

"Darling, no…" She shook her head. "No one knows for sure what lies beyond the train, but they definitely went on the train, and they aren't coming back. Listen, I need you to understand there were two hundred children in the orphanage. That they are lost is an immense tragedy, but think about the scale of this, Elżbieta. There are maybe fifty thousand *more* children in that ghetto tonight. We could not save the two hundred, but there will be others, and every life we save is a life that counts. You need to come back to work tomorrow."

"I can't," I said, sinking back into the pillow. "I'm sorry, Sara. I just can't."

"I know we ask a lot of you, and you are but a child yourself. I know it is too much, but when I think of what the children in the ghetto are being forced to endure… Well, when I consider that, I don't feel guilty about the things we ask of you. Besides, you are within our circle of trust, and it is a *very* small circle—every part counts. And besides all of that?"

She reached into her pocket and withdrew a small note that was folded tightly. She reached for my hand and pressed it into my palm.

"Do you remember the Gorka children last week? The sick baby, the young boy?"

"The angry brother," I said hesitantly, and she nodded. I shuddered, and tears filled my eyes. "Sara, I am not strong enough to keep doing this. I thought I was, but I was wrong. I can't."

Sara picked the note up out of my palm and unfolded it, then rested it back in my hands.

"The Gorka children are not lost. In fact, Matylda has found a foster mother for the baby—a woman who has lost a child of her own and who has milk and food and can help that tiny babe recover. But the only way that mother connects with that baby is if we continue to do our work."

"You can facilitate that without me," I whispered. "I don't even help you with that side of things."

"You will see, Elżbieta. What you do is just as important as the work I do, and I cannot let you give up like this. I will see you tomorrow morning in the lobby."

"No," I protested, but she rose, kissed my forehead and murmured, "Darling, read the damned note," and then she left.

I stared down at the paper in my hand. The words were written in a firm, blocky fashion; even the handwriting looked to be simmering with rage. Even so, there was no denying the immense humility it had taken him to write me, and I could sense genuine remorse in the words. I pictured his little sister, and I remembered how empty her gaze had been.

Empty like my brother's eyes after his death.

I suddenly understood the rage I had seen in Roman Gorka. I thought about that young man, trapped within the ghetto walls all but doomed, and yet still committed enough to goodness to make amends. There was nothing he could do to help his family other than convince his parents to let their children go.

But there was something I could do. I could pull myself together and go back into that ghetto to teach his little brother the Catholic prayers. I climbed out of bed and went to have dinner with my family.

"Are you feeling better?" Mateusz asked, ruffling my hair as he moved to take his seat.

"I am," I murmured.

"Should we make some dolls later?" Uncle Piotr asked cheerfully. I shuddered involuntarily, thinking of the dolls in the hands of those children.

"I'm still tired," I forced myself to say. "I'll have an early night."

The dolls had been a pure idea—an innocent gesture to benefit innocent children. Even so, I knew I would never sit with my family to draw faces onto those figures again.

Maybe I could force myself to return to the ghetto, but I would have to learn how to stop bringing the ghetto home with me or I'd never survive.

I was always nervous to do house visits, but Sara insisted we call on the Gorka family on our way home the next day, to tell them the news about the placement she'd found for baby Eleonora.

"Thank you for coming back," Maja said, offering us a shy smile as she let us into the apartment.

The last time we visited, the other families in the apartment had been occupied with tasks in the kitchen and courtyard. Today, there were people everywhere, and I was struck by the thought of all these people trying to live in this tiny space. An elderly woman sat on a cushion on the floor, watching as three children squabbled over a little ball. Two frail and elderly men were reading, and through the open kitchen door I saw two middle-aged women sitting at the table, talking.

I reached into the hidden compartment of my bag but found I only had two dolls. I sighed and withdrew my hand, but just then, Sara reached into her own bag.

"I need to empty the compartment in my bag," she murmured, shuffling around in it, then handing me a chunk of bread and three dolls. I took the gifts across the room to the children and crouched to their level.

"Hello," I said. "Would you like a gift?"

I broke the bread up into three pieces, and the children immediately took their share and stuffed it into their mouths.

"Thank you, lady," the little boy said, around a mouthful of food.

"And look." I handed them each a doll. "From me and my friend."

Their gazes were wide with wonder. The smallest child lifted the doll to her mouth as if to eat it, and the twin girl laughed and pulled it away, murmuring to her in Yiddish. The toddler seemed to get the idea after that, and she copied the other children, holding the doll against her chest.

Baby Eleonora was lying on a blanket, staring up at the ceiling not far from where I sat with the other children. Maja picked her up and cuddled her close, then led the way into a bedroom.

"Our friends have returned," Maja told her husband, as she closed the door behind us. Samuel was lying on a mattress on the floor, reading. He set the book down and looked at me, his dark gaze expressionless.

"We have concerns," he greeted us, closing the book. "Maja and I appreciate very much your kind offer, but we can only do this if we know that we can find our children when the war is over."

"My team is careful to audit the placements of our children. My supervisor keeps a strict record of who has been placed where. It is of utmost importance that we find the children when the war is over so that families can be made whole again. We are also financially supporting the host families as much as we can. Your children will be well cared for."

"We don't have any money," Maja said, her face falling. Sara gave her a sympathetic smile.

"Very few Jewish families have money now. No, we're trying to find other ways to fund our operation."

"So where would they go? Our Eleonora and Dawidek?" Samuel asked.

I knew this next conversation was going to be delicate. Dawidek didn't seem to be home that morning, but I had seen him on our last visit, and I knew his placement represented a significant challenge. Dawidek had beautiful, deep brown eyes with dark eyelashes and a thatch of almost-black hair. He looked nothing like his much-fairer brother. In fact, Dawidek looked exactly as I imagined his father would have decades ago.

We couldn't place him in an orphanage even for an instant: his appearance was too classically Jewish, and beyond that, he was tall and, although emaciated, his bone structure was too broad for him to pass as a female child. We would never be able to hide him in plain sight. He was going to need a family who could truly hide him indefinitely. Finding a safe place like this was going to take some time, and I wondered how Sara would explain this to the family. I expected her to tread lightly, to carefully explain the difficulties, but instead she said bluntly, "We cannot place them together. I'm sorry."

Maja's hand covered her mouth in shock.

"You will separate them? But you can't! They will need each other—"

"We must," Sara said gently. "Eleonora needs to go to a home where she can be breastfed. We know a foster mother who can do this. In fact, she lost her own daughter only a few weeks ago—even in her grief, though, she is determined to help another child, and she has gone to great lengths to ensure that her milk does not dry up. Even more than that, the woman's husband is a physician. Eleonora would be in good hands there. She will have lots of space and fresh air and good food and a spacious house. She will be able to leave freely because her foster mother's neighbors do not know that her own baby has died. Eleonora will have a new name, but she will have a genuine birth and baptismal certificate. I cannot even tell you how lucky we are. It is as though the stars have aligned."

"That sounds wonderful," Maja whispered, looking down at her baby, but when she looked back to us, her gaze was full of fear. "But Dawidek. What about Dawidek?"

"He is going to be much more difficult to place. That family simply cannot take him. It would arouse too much suspicion. It pains me to say this, but you must understand that Dawidek's appearance would give him away, regardless of where we place him. His rescue will not be so simple. We really must think this through and work to find somewhere he can be safely housed. But Eleonora is a much simpler and much more urgent rescue. Mrs. Gorka, you know as well as I do that she needs proper nourishment immediately. Besides which, every day you hide her here is another day of risk to you all."

"If they cannot go together, they will stay with us," Samuel said, shaking his head. "I thank you both for your time—"

"Mr. Gorka, please," I blurted. "Please let us place your children. You must have heard the rumors. You must know where the trains are going—"

"I won't separate my family because of rumors! And—"

"Samuel," Maja pleaded. The man's composure wavered. Tears filled his eyes, and he wrapped his arms around his waist and began to rock gently, back and forth.

"No, Maja," he choked. "I can't."

"We need to let them go. We need to let *her* go. It is the only way she will survive."

"How can you ask me to do this?" he whispered. "There must be something more we can do here, some way to get you more food, to help you make more milk—"

"If there was a way, we would have thought of it already. We have to let her go."

"I can't." The man choked on a sob as he shook his head. "Maja, I cannot do this."

"Then, I will do it for us," the woman said, and she raised her chin stubbornly. She looked at Sara. "What happens next?"

Samuel wept in the corner, curled in a ball, a sound so raw and empty it left me bereft. Maja was dry-eyed, though, as she helped Sara prepare the baby to leave, dressing her in her best outfit, wiping clean her tiny hands and face as she whispered gently in Yiddish.

I had never seen this part of the process because Sara had taken great care to leave me out of it. But Eleonora was so ill and so weak, and given the situation, the sooner she was settled with her foster family, the better for everyone. And soon enough, Sara indicated that I should follow her to the other side of the room to give Maja and the baby a moment alone together.

Sara reached into the hidden base of her bag and removed the false bottom, and I did the same with my bag. She passed me her collection of secret medicines—just a few sad vials marked with ink, all of which I hid in the base of my bag. But Sara kept one bottle, resting it on the floor beside her feet as she scribbled onto a piece of paper to calculate a dosage.

"Sedative is hard to come by," she murmured, as she drew the liquid from the bottle into a metal syringe. "Every single drop counts, and it is easy to give a child too much, which can make her stop breathing. It is better to give too little than too much—but it means we will have to hurry through the gates before she wakes. She will sleep for only one hour. We were supposed to use one of the farther gates today, but we are short on time, so we're just going to have to hope that Captain Fischer doesn't happen to be at the gates on Muranowska Street."

"If he is?" I whispered, stricken at the thought. Whenever we saw Fischer, he inevitably stopped us and riffled through our bags, delighting in inconveniencing us. He'd never found the hidden compartments, but then again, neither one of us had ever had anything even close to the weight of a child in there. "And will she be able to get air in the bag?"

Sara showed me a tiny flap on the corner of the hidden compartment.

"I will leave this open while she's in there."

"Sara, if Fischer is on the gate—"

"We will cross that bridge if we come to it."

Maja was rocking the baby, singing gently to her as Sara ad-
ministered the needle. The baby barely reacted to the pinch, but
within seconds, her little eyes fluttered closed. Sara took a piece
of muslin cloth and stretched it out on the mattress and Maja
gently rested her sleeping child on it. She arranged Eleonora's
limbs this way and that, and then kissed her on the forehead.
Samuel composed himself momentarily, then stepped forward
to press a kiss to her cheek. His voice was hoarse as he whispered to the baby, and I didn't need to speak Yiddish to know
he was saying goodbye.

I knew Matylda kept meticulous records so that the children could be reunited with their parents after the war, but I
also knew that the chances of Maja and Samuel surviving were
slim. I was so relieved to be with Sara. She was calm and composed. As soon as Samuel stepped away from the baby, Sara took
his place, wrapping the baby up tightly and efficiently, leaving
just a gap in the cloth around her mouth and nose, then lifting
Eleonora to gently rest in the bottom of the bag.

"This is safe?" Maja choked, finally close to tears.

"I have done this many times," Sara murmured. "The bag
is designed for this. Elżbieta, a hand?" I stepped closer, and she
dropped her voice to just loud enough for me to hear her say
"We need to do this quickly. Help me, please."

I helped her rearrange her medical supplies back on top of
the baby, and then Sara straightened.

"We will return to discuss Dawidek as soon as we figure
out where he can be safe," she said, and then she stepped toward the door.

I moved to follow, but Maja caught my arm. "Please take
good care of her," she whispered, through her tears. "She deserves the best kind of life."

I didn't know why she was saying this to *me*. My role in that
moment was just to follow Sara. I didn't even know how to re-

spond, so I squeezed Maja's hand, then said awkwardly, "We will make sure she is cared for."

"Thank you. Thank you for helping us."

I thought of the note Roman had sent and wished I had taken the time to write a reply. Most likely I'd be training Dawidek at some point, but I didn't want to wait. Time was so precious in this place.

"Could you please tell Roman that I forgive him? He wrote me a note, apologizing for what happened here last week… I'd appreciate it if you could let him know that I received it."

"He is a good boy. I'm so glad he apologized."

I nodded sadly, then had to go. Sara was already on the street.

"Come," she hissed when I finally stepped outside. "The sooner we are out, the sooner *she* is out. Faster footsteps, please, Elżbieta."

I had been in and out of the ghetto dozens of times, often enough that I no longer felt terrified every second of each journey. But that day, with that tiny baby in the bottom of Sara's medical bag, my anxiety was as high as it had ever been. We walked briskly, heading to the gate on Muranowska Street, not engaging in conversation. There was no distracting us from the reality of what we had just seen and what we were currently doing.

But as we turned a corner around the last building before the gate, Sara stopped abruptly. I almost ran into her back, and she hissed under her breath, "Stop. *Stop.*"

I came to a shuddering halt and pressed myself against the side of the building. My heart was racing so hard and so fast, I could feel black at the edges of my vision. I had to remind myself to breathe slow and deep. If I passed out, I'd be a liability and a distraction, and the baby could die.

There was movement near my feet, and I was startled to see that Sara had lowered the bag onto the ground and was slowly pushing it back toward me with her heels. I reached out and pulled it along the sidewalk, back toward my feet.

"Give me your bag," Sara whispered.

"My bag? But why—"

"There is a line at the checkpoint," she whispered to me from around the corner. "Fischer is there. He has seen me so if I turn back it will look suspicious, and he may follow me. You will have to go on your own."

My heart lurched as I looked between my bag and Sara's bag.

"What do I do?" I whispered frantically, as I pushed my bag along the ground toward her.

"There isn't much time. She shouldn't be in there much longer. Walk to the gate at Krasiński Square, then go to the tram stop on Muranowska."

"By *myself*?" I choked, but she had already stepped away from the corner. The line had moved on.

Sara's bag was heavier than expected, but even so, far too light to contain a human being. The minute I lifted it off the ground, my stomach heaved. I was out of my depth and utterly terrified. Yes, I had been in the ghetto dozens of times, but I'd never so much as passed through the gates alone.

Now there I was, not just on my own, but entirely responsible for the rescue of an unwell infant.

Everything slowed until I could hear my heartbeat in my ears. When I dragged in a breath through my nose, trying to calm myself down, I was acutely aware of the scent of death and suffering in the air. I thought about how clear and fresh the air was on the other side, and I thought about how much that baby needed that air, but I was frozen in panic and fear.

I can't do this. I'm not strong enough. I'm not brave enough. I am a child playing an adult's game.

I turned the corner and found an alleyway. It wasn't deserted; nowhere in the ghetto was ever deserted. But the alley

was home to only a few children on their own and an emaciated man sleeping under his coat.

I sank down onto the cobblestones and stared at the medical bag.

I could take the baby back to her parents. I knew that this
could be an entirely reasonable thing to do. Sara and I could
try again tomorrow. I tried to convince myself that if I did this,
she would be proud of me for thinking so sensibly about the
situation, when *she* was obviously not: she had likely panicked
when she saw Fischer, and that was why she hadn't thought to
suggest this.

Or maybe I could just take the baby back to the youth center.
Andrzej would help. Maybe there was a tunnel I could crawl
through with the medical bag. That would save me from going
through the checkpoint on my own.

But we had used precious sedative, and I knew how hard
that was to come by. Besides, could I really expect that family
to say goodbye to their precious daughter a second time? Sara
had told me *exactly* what to do. I was just too scared to follow
her instructions.

Tears threatened, but I blinked them away because I knew if
I let even one out, I would dissolve into sobs. Instead, I drew
in some deep breaths and began to pray.

*God. Please. Help me know what to do. Tomasz, if you can hear me,
I need you to intercede for me. Father, if you're listening, please help me.*

Just bringing my family to mind was enough. I knew that my
father would have scooped up that bag and marched through
the checkpoint with his head held high. Tomasz would have,
too. Courage was in my blood. I had inherited it at my birth,
and I had learned it from their legacy.

I just had to reach inside deep enough to access it.

I carefully lifted the bag as I rose, and I made my way to the
Krasiński gates. I checked my pocket to ensure that I had my
paperwork. I made a point to avoid eye contact with those who

passed, in case some desperate soul had the idea to try to steal my bag. I stared at the ground as my footsteps fell rhythmically.

They will ask why I am here alone. Who in their right mind would allow a fourteen-year-old to perform epidemic control on her own? All it will take will be for the soldier to question me, and I will burst into tears. My hands are so sweaty, what if I drop the bag? What if the baby is already dead? What if I'm caught and tortured? I would give the whole game up. I wouldn't have the strength to keep Sara's and Matylda's secrets. I can barely keep my own.

The checkpoint was ahead. A tradesman passed through as I approached. The guards checked his papers but barely acknowledged him. They were standing side by side at the gate, one of them smoking. I withdrew my papers and offered them to one of the guards, just as I might have done if Sara was with me.

I waited for him to ask why I was alone. I waited for him to inspect the bag. I waited to be caught, exposed, executed—just like my father, just like my brother. How swiftly would death come? Would I feel the bullet as it entered my skull? Would I hear the gunshot? Or would the first I knew of it be my entrance to heaven, and if that were the case, would I be greeted by my father and brother? Would they be proud of me for trying to help this baby or disappointed that I'd failed?

"Miss?" the soldier prompted sharply. My breakfast was a solid lump in my throat, ready to escape.

"Yes?"

He gave me a pointed look. They had waved me through, but I was so caught up in my terror, I was frozen. I nodded curtly, seriously and sensibly as I imagined any adult would, and I began my march up the road.

My next challenge was finding the tram stop, and this was more complicated than I expected it to be. Which *one* was I supposed to take, and where was it? I was disoriented in my panic, and I had no idea which direction I should walk. It seemed unsafe to ask for directions. Just then, I felt it—the tiniest rolling movement from within the medical bag.

Eleonora was waking up. A baby was about to start wailing from the bottom of my bag.

I broke out in a cold sweat, conscious of random German soldiers patrolling the street and of unsympathetic Poles. I looked around, desperate to find some familiar landmark, and that's when I realized which side of the ghetto we were on.

My home—Sara's home—our building was only two blocks away.

I let myself into the lobby and started up the stairs toward the third floor and apartment entrances. The rolling movement from within the bag was coming constantly now as Eleonora squirmed, and I thought maybe I had heard a little cry of protest. My hands were so sweaty I had to keep wiping them on my skirt.

I had no way to explain to Truda why I was dressed in Sara's clothes. No way to explain why I was wearing makeup. But there was no alternative—I had to go into our apartment to get Sara's spare key. As I sat the bag down on the floor outside of our apartment, I prayed again.

Please. I need another miracle, just a tiny one this time. Please let Truda be in her bedroom resting or in the kitchen making such a racket that she doesn't hear the front door.

The door swung open, and I peered cautiously inside, finding the apartment still and at least the living areas blessedly empty. My hands were shaking violently as I swiped the spare key, collected the bag from the hall and let myself into Sara's apartment.

I locked the door behind me, set the bag on Sara's sofa and rushed to remove the false bottom. Eleonora Gorka's big brown eyes stared back at me. She blinked at the light, then gave a miserable, feeble cry.

I leaned away from the bag just as I was sick all over Sara's carpet, but there was no time to stop to clean my mess or even feel relief. We weren't safe yet. I still had to figure out what to do next.

I lifted the baby and went to Sara's sewing kit to retrieve a thimble. I filled it with water from the tap and lifted it to Eleonora's lips. She protested furiously at first, and I hushed her gently, grateful in some sad way that in her weakened state, her cries were weak, too. When I had at least moistened her lips, I carried her with me to the phone, and I called the switchboard and asked for Matylda's office.

"Hello?"

"Matylda," I blurted when the line was connected, suddenly panicking all over again. But I knew that no one in the team ever disclosed the details of their covert operations on the phone. The phone lines were not secure, switchboard operators eavesdropped all the time. I tried to think about the little games I had heard the women of the department playing when they called the orphanages. They made small talk, and in the small talk they would often disclose details in code to help the Sisters at the orphanage know when children were arriving and how they would be dressed.

But that system only worked because people on both sides of the phone knew the game.

"Elżbieta," Matylda said cautiously, "how are you today?"

"Sara and I were doing an epidemic check today when I became ill," I began slowly. "She went on without me, but I just wanted to call the office to let you all know that I had to come home. I have Sara's medical bag, and I know that she will be looking for it."

"Thank you for letting me know, Elżbieta," Matylda said. I had no idea if she had caught on until she added mildly, "Now, do you think it would be more convenient to leave the bag in Sara's apartment, or should I send someone to collect it?"

"Well, Sara will need it quite urgently," I said. "You know

how she relies on her medical bag. But she probably doesn't realize that I came home sick. She was walking to a tram stop after her typhus check to go back to the office, and she may be waiting there for me now. I was just so dizzy I couldn't find my bearings."

"Do you know what, Elżbieta?" Matylda said suddenly. "It is such a lovely afternoon. I think I'll come and collect the bag myself. By the way, I have a feeling it was the Muranowski Square stop she was using today. Does that ring a bell?"

"It was!" I exclaimed, feeling suddenly stupid that I'd forgotten. "Do you think I should go there now to find her?"

"No, that's fine. You just rest. I will go past the tram stop on the way to pick up the bag just in case Sara is there waiting for you. I'll see you in half an hour."

As I hung up the phone, relief washed over me, and my thoughts began to calm. I finally noticed the sour smell throughout Sara's apartment: Eleonora had soiled herself in the bag, and my vomit was all over the carpet. I found a towel in Sara's linen closet and tried to clean the baby as best I could, then I repeated this process on the carpet.

When this was done, I sank onto the sofa and stared at the baby. She was sleeping again, her breathing rhythmic and easy. I touched my fingertip to her cheek, just where I'd seen her father press a kiss.

I rose from the couch, retrieved some paper from Sara's desk and poured my terror and relief and confusion and courage onto it, capturing a sketch of the baby in black-and-white, concrete images, on paper where the world made sense.

16

Roman

MY MOTHER WAS SITTING ON THE FRONT STAIRS TO THE apartment when I arrived home that evening. She was drawn and pale but dry-eyed. It was rare to see her outside of the apartment since her pregnancy had become visible, and while I was relieved to not have to wonder if anyone was inside, I was immediately wary at the sight of her.

"Roman," she said quietly, then patted the space on the stair beside her. "Sit with me."

I did, and for a moment, we sat in silence watching the street. The children across the road were begging again. I noticed that the elderly man and woman I'd often seen on the doorstep across the road were gone. Were they *gone* or just indoors?

"Before you go in, there is something I need you to know."

I glanced at my mother, startled at the severity of her tone.

"Mother, you're scaring me."

"Everyone is fine," she assured me. "I sent Eleonora with the social workers today. They are taking her to a family in the village, away from the city. Her new father is a doctor, and her new mother lost a baby a few weeks ago. They have breast milk and papers and love to spare. Eleonora will slip into the family, and no one will even know any different."

I could not believe that we were discussing this in such a dispassionate fashion. I stared at my mother, trying to understand how, mingled with the strain and the desperate grief on her face, I could also see joy. Mother wasn't just grieving. She was also deeply relieved. We had all done everything we could to make Eleonora well, but it truly was best for her to be elsewhere. Even aside from the deportations, this was necessary, plain and simple.

"I'm so sorry, Mother."

"I miss her already, Roman, but I'll rest tonight in a way that I haven't rested since I realized I was pregnant," she whispered, blinking away tears. I reached for her hand and squeezed it, hard. "I want you to know that I'm going to do everything I can to get you and Dawidek out of here. I trust Samuel, and I love him. He believes that there is good in people, despite all the evidence we can see with our eyes. But we cannot sit idly by anymore and wait to be rounded up. We need to escape, and although it will probably be impossible for me and Samuel to go with you, there is surely a way we can get you children out of here."

I could not bear to think about being away from her and Samuel. Not yet anyway. Besides, before we could even think about trying to find a way for me to evacuate, we had to help my brother.

"Dawidek must be our highest priority."

"It is not so simple for him. His hair, his eyes… Plus, he will need to learn to speak in Polish all of the time, and you know he defaults to Yiddish…" Mother sighed. "It is my fault. It was easy to let his Polish slip here. We need to insist he speak Polish only now, to help him remember."

"I can do that."

"I know you can," Mother said softly.

"So…" I cleared my throat, feeling myself flush with shame again as I thought about that girl and the fear in her eyes when I lost my temper the previous week. "Was it the same social worker? The same apprentice?"

"Her name is Elżbieta. She left a message for you. She said to tell you that she forgives you. You wrote her a note to apologize?"

I grunted and shrugged. My mother touched the back of her hand to my cheek, and I looked at her hesitantly.

"You are a good person, Roman."

"You always say that to me," I said uneasily. "I just feel so much, and I don't always know how to make the right decisions."

She dropped her hand, then jabbed her forefinger against my chest.

"You, my son, get lost in your mind sometimes. But your heart is pure, and when you listen to it, I see who you really are. A good person. Like your father. Both of your fathers."

I caught her hand in mine, and I squeezed it gently.

"Like my mother," I murmured. Her eyes filled with tears again, and she gave me a sad smile.

"I don't know about that. But I know this much—watching you grow into a man has been one of the best parts of my life. I wish Florian could see you now. He would be as proud of you as I am."

The emotion in her eyes had grown to be too much for me. I shifted on the stair, then motioned to the door behind us.

"Should we go inside?"

"Now that I no longer need the extra food, can you come straight home from your workshop job? To spend time with Dawidek…to practice his Polish?"

"Of course," I said. Her request had solved an immediate

problem for me. Now I could work in the youth center kitchen during the day and use the tickets I earned for food for myself.

My mother nodded and said quietly, "Go in and get started with Dawidek. I'll be in soon. I just want to enjoy the afternoon light."

As I stood, I looked up and down the street. I saw very little to enjoy: so much suffering, overcrowding, pain. But I also saw the way golden rays of light squeezed between the buildings, falling onto the street. I saw a hint of blue sky overhead. Two children across the road were playfully wrestling, and every now and again a smile would break on their filthy faces.

And then I saw my mother, her shawl pulled tightly around her shoulders, her dark hair in a bun behind her head, her eyes closed, tears running down her cheeks and a sad smile on her lips.

In my mother's face, I saw courage and a selflessness I could barely fathom. I wanted to record the image of her like that in my memory forever. She had never seemed more beautiful to me.

Andrzej waved for us to join him at a desk near the kitchen when Chaim and I arrived the next morning.

"Remember that young apprentice social worker?" he began excitedly. "She saved your sister's life yesterday. There was some trouble, and she was separated from her boss but somehow managed to get your sister through a checkpoint on her own. The team are all abuzz. Do you know she is only fourteen years old?"

"A fourteen-year-old social worker?" I said, eyebrows lifting.

"Seems to be the case," he said. I didn't know what to say, but Andrzej motioned toward one of the rooms at the back of the communal space. "She's here working with some children in the back room. I thought you might like to speak with her."

I let myself into the room and found Elżbieta sitting on the floor with three children in a semicircle in front of her. She looked up as I entered, and I saw surprise and recognition in her eyes. But I waved to indicate she should continue what she was doing with the children, and I wandered to the bookshelves at the back of the room. I listened as she chanted prayers with the children, the words as familiar to me as my own name. I helped myself to a seat at a table a few feet away, and I skimmed a novel. After a while, she dismissed the children and approached me.

"Hello," she said quietly, coming to stand near me. "Thank you for the note."

I looked at her then, really seeing her for the first time. My gaze skipped over her green eyes, rimmed in some dark smudge, and the wavy blond hair that fanned out around her shoulders, the front strands caught in a high roll above her forehead.

"Are you really only fourteen?" I blurted. Her eyebrows lifted in surprise, then she nodded silently and took the seat opposite me. "I heard about what you did for my sister. Thank you."

"I'm glad she is okay."

"Has she made it to her new family?"

"I don't know," Elżbieta admitted apologetically. "I only see a tiny piece of the big picture. It is safer that way in case I'm compromised. But when I passed her on to my supervisor yesterday, they were immediately taking her to her new home. I think she is probably stuffed full of healthy milk, sleeping deeply in a fluffy, warm bed, in a house that is as safe as any house in Poland could be right now."

I smiled in spite of myself, but the smile faded when I looked at Elżbieta's eyes and remembered the first time we met.

"I'm sorry for the way I behaved at my house that day," I said, my chest tight. "I'm so ashamed to think that you did something so wonderful for my family after I scared you like that."

"I understand."

"I saw the orphans being deported," I said suddenly, unthinkingly. She sat back in her chair and pressed her hand to her chest, her gaze dropping to the table. "I was hiding in a building across the street. I saw you crying upstairs in Andrzej's apartments." I wasn't sure why I was so desperate to bring it up, just that I needed her to know that I had seen it, too. I wished I could admit to her that I, too, had wept.

"It was very upsetting," she whispered, still staring at the table.

"Why do you come to help us?"

"What I do is not enough, and it is nothing in the scheme of things." She was so wrong, and I wanted to argue with her, but before I could, she blurted, "I wanted to stop coming in after I saw those orphans taken. I was *going* to stop coming. Did you see that some were carrying little dolls?"

"I saw them. You gave some to the children in my apartment, too."

"My family and I made those dolls. When I saw the orphans walking with them, I felt like they were taking a part of me with them. I know that is a selfish thing to say. Their deportation is not about me, but I'm telling you this because you said in your note that you felt ashamed, and I feel ashamed, too. I wish I were braver or stronger or clever enough to figure out how to help more people."

"There is so little left to live for. So little hope," I said, staring at the table between us. "You didn't just carry a bag yesterday, and you didn't just carry a baby. You gave my family hope. You gave us the chance that something of us will survive after all of this. For that, I will forever be in your debt."

She was silent, and it took me a few moments to gather the courage to look up and meet her gaze again. When I did, there were tears running down her cheeks.

"I'm sorry I've upset you," I whispered, stricken. She shook her head and gave me a wobbly smile, then wiped her tears, smudging black makeup over her cheek.

"Don't be. Thank you for saying that."

I began to rise, feeling heat in my face. "I should let you get back to your—" I stopped as she reached out and touched the table between us with her fingertips. I looked to her hand, then back to her face. She was staring at me intently.

"I need to wait for Andrzej to send more children through. Will you sit a while and keep me company?"

A new pattern emerged from the monotony of my days over the following weeks. I would leave early in the morning, allowing my family to think that I was still working with Sala, but making a beeline for the youth center, where I would spend time in the communal hall, reading or chatting with Chaim, and then I would spend time in the kitchen working. Some days, I joined the long queue in front of the youth center, hoping to receive a serving of soup.

And most days, when I saw that Elżbieta was free for a moment between her classes, I would visit her. I would always ask her for news of Eleonora, and she would always tell me that there was none. She would ask me how my day was, and I would tell her that it was fine, even though the truth was nowhere near that simple. And then, quite often, I would scurry away like a startled mouse, unsure of what else to talk about.

I was drawn to her, but I wasn't sure why. I got the sense that she liked when I visited, even though I never really knew what to say. It occurred to me that I could offer to help her teach the children their prayers, but then I would need to explain why I knew the Catholic prayers, and the whole subject was inevitably awkward. Whenever anyone found out I was Catholic, they always asked why I didn't try to escape. Especially since Eleonora had been rescued, thoughts of being separated from my family were too much to take.

"You seem to be visiting the back room a lot, but you never stay very long," Chaim teased me, after several days of this. I felt my cheeks warm, and I shrugged.

"She is a nice girl. She has done a lot for my family."

"So you stick your head into the room, say hello, then run away?"

"I don't know how to talk to her," I admitted awkwardly.

"Listen, my friend, it is true that you are far from a strong conversationalist," Chaim said and grinned, and I glared at him. "But if there is one thing I know about you, it is that you know how to listen. Why don't you ask her about herself?"

The next day, I approached Elżbieta's room with a new weapon in my conversational arsenal. I greeted her as I always did, then sat opposite her at a desk and asked, "Who do you live with?"

"I live with my parents and my uncle."

"No siblings?"

A shadow crossed her face before she shook her head.

"Have you always lived in Warsaw?"

"No, I lived in… Morowice until earlier this year, when we moved here for my father's work," she said slowly, but then she seemed to warm up to the topic. "That's why we are living with my uncle—he rented an apartment for us to share. It is not far from here, on the other side of Krasiński Square, on Miodowa Street, just up from Tepper Palace."

"I know that street," I said. "Nice homes."

"Oh, yes, it's a nice home. The top half floor where I sleep was damaged in the bombing, but my uncle has patched it up pretty well—all you can see from the outside now is that the bricks don't match and my window is damaged."

"What exactly does a half floor look like?"

"There's a bedroom built into the attic. That's where Sara's spare room is, too, so I like to say I have a whole floor to my-self—" She broke off, suddenly blanching as she looked around the room. "Oh."

"It's okay," I said. It was awkward for me, too, but I didn't want her to stop, so I added, "I know people outside the ghetto still have their own space. You don't need to be embarrassed. Do you like living there?"

"I do," she said, then she added quietly, "But I miss my old house. I miss my old bedroom."

"I'm still in the same apartment I've lived in since I was six, but I know exactly how that feels."

Chaim was a genius. It turned out that all I had to do was give Elżbieta the slightest prompt, and she could talk all day long. Now, I would sit up at night and think of questions to ask her the next day. What was life like on the Aryan side? Did she like music? What books did she like to read? I found her endlessly fascinating, and more than that, I found her company soothing. It was as though for those brief minutes I spent with her each day, the rage inside me eased, and I was close to content. I sometimes thought that if I could just stay in that room with her forever, life would almost be bearable.

"What do you want to do when the war is over?" I asked her one day.

"Well, in a fantasy world where Poland is not just freed but restored to its former glory, I would go back to school, then on to university and maybe one day become an artist. However, in the real world, my work with Sara is supposed to act as some kind of nursing apprenticeship, so I think it is most likely that I will end up working as a nurse. What about you?"

"When I was young, I wanted to be a lawyer like my father," I said. "In fact, I wanted to be a lawyer before I even understood what a lawyer really was."

"There are many kinds of lawyers. Would you be the kind of lawyer who draws up dull paperwork or the kind who fights for justice?"

"As fascinating as dull paperwork sounds," I said wryly, "I think I would be the latter. My mother tells me that I had a strong sense of justice from a very young age."

"Is that still true?"

The question caught me off guard.

"I think I still believe in justice, but it is impossible to fight for it under these conditions."

"Do you really believe that?"

"I promised my stepfather that I would never get involved with the underground," I said abruptly. I thought about Chaim, my closest friend. He had alluded to his meetings, and I assumed that much of his connection to the Resistance came about via that very youth center, particularly via Andrzej. But beyond those assumptions, I knew nothing about what he was involved in or what the endgame was. I was curious, but it was safer to remain in the dark.

"When I found out what life was like in these walls, I thought I would die if I didn't do something to help," Elżbieta said quietly. She thumped her fist against her chest and leaned forward to look into my eyes. "Working with Sara has been taxing and frightening, but I'm glad to do it. I don't know if I could have lived with myself if I had ignored the urge to do something."

"It isn't that simple for me," I said impatiently.

"I didn't mean to tell you how you should live your life," she said quickly. "I just sense so much anger and frustration in you."

"Do you wonder why?" I said, barking a harsh laugh, waving my hands like a fool.

"It's a righteous anger," she murmured. "It just needs an outlet."

"I want to tear this damned place apart. But we are *powerless*, and it is pointless."

"Maybe playing a part in the Resistance isn't even about winning a battle," Elżbieta said, after a pause. "Maybe it's just about being true to your values. About standing up for the things you believe and those you love, even if you know you can't win."

She had almost echoed Samuel's words but made the opposite argument.

"I should go see if the kitchen needs me," I muttered, excusing myself. Hours later, I was cutting potatoes in the kitchen when I felt a gentle tap on my shoulder, and I turned to find Elżbieta behind me.

"I'm sorry if I offended you earlier."

"You didn't," I said. She hadn't offended me, but she had unsettled me, and I'd thought of nothing else since our conversation. Without a word, she tucked a folded piece of paper into the pocket on my shirt, then smiled quietly and walked away.

I dried my hands on a piece of cloth and unfolded the paper. She had drawn the shape of a fist, painfully clenched, and underneath she had written *There are many ways to fight, but striving for justice is always worth the battle.*

The deportations continued to escalate, with people being removed at a staggering rate. The Germans were chipping away at us in individual strikes and in broad, sweeping attacks to clear entire buildings or streets. Sometimes, they would block both ends of a road and then go from door to door and room to room, dragging every single resident out into the street to march them to the trains. I drew some relief at this approach: given I spent all day at the youth center just down the block from my home, I figured I'd at least be deported with my family.

Sometimes the deportations were random, and sometimes they were highly targeted. Only one thing remained consistent: the threat seemed closer with every passing sunrise. Chaim hunkered down at the youth center for his so-called business several nights in a row, only to return to the Little Ghetto to discover his entire building was empty. The children who begged in the gutter opposite my apartment were caught in a roundup while they were wandering the streets looking for food. Mother went to the street vendor on Zamenhofa Street to see if she was willing to barter food for some of Eleonora's old clothes, only to find her gone.

Each night, when I returned to my apartment, I would stand at the door, and I would hold my breath until I heard a sound from inside. One day, I opened the door to find my parents and grandparents with Dawidek and the Kuklińskis seated around the living room, visibly distressed.

"What is it?" I asked uneasily.

"The Grobelnys," Mother whispered. "They were caught in a roundup at the market. I told her to leave Estera here with me, but you know how she was—so anxious to keep the little girl with her after losing her other children. Oh, God—that poor baby."

"We don't know where the trains lead. They might be fine," Samuel said, but his reassurances now sounded weak, as if even he didn't believe them.

I continued to visit Elżbieta in her little classroom each day, a brief reprieve from the endless tension. I got to know Sara a little, too, and made an attempt at a strategic friendship. I intuited that Elżbieta had little say in the order that children were evacuated, but it was evident that Sara had more power.

"Dawidek is still waiting to be evacuated," I would remind her, whenever I saw her coming or going from dropping off Elżbieta at the center.

"We are working as fast as we can, Roman. We are trying to find somewhere safe for him—but the longer the war drags on, the harder it is to find safe refuge, especially for a child with your brother's coloring. I am sorry this is taking so long."

"I'll check in with you tomorrow," I would say, and she would give me a sad smile and continue on her way.

Late in August, I noticed that Chaim's easy smile came less and less often, and there were new lines of strain around his eyes. I wondered if I were imagining things, but when I heard him snap at one of the boys in the kitchen, I knew something was wrong.

"Let's take a walk," I suggested. He shrugged, then smiled reluctantly when I led him toward the rooftop. "Well, you are the Pigeon, after all. I thought you might be comforted by your natural habitat."

We stretched out on the roof in the sunshine, side by side, looking up at the cloudless late-summer sky.

"I don't know how to ask you what's wrong," I admitted.

"Once upon a time, you wouldn't have even tried," he remarked.

That much was true. Having at least made some attempt to prompt a discussion, I left it for a while but eventually asked quietly, "Is there anything I can do?"

"You could join us." He hadn't asked me so directly for a long time. My eyebrows lifted. "We are mobilizing, preparing to fight."

"Who is this *we* you speak of?"

"Andrzej and I are members of the Jewish Combat Organization," he said quietly. It was the first time he had shared the details with me, but I had heard of *Żydowska Organizacja Bojowa* and suspected he was organizing with them.

"Is this why you are so quiet?" I asked him. "Is an uprising coming?"

I held my breath while I waited for his answer. My heart raced at the thought of my friends attempting to take on the might of the German army—such a rebellion was doomed to fail.

"Will you fight with us?" Chaim asked me quietly.

"You know Samuel would never forgive me..."

"Roman," he said, his voice strained, "do you believe that we will be deported?"

"It seems inevitable," I said.

"Don't you want to know what awaits us?"

"Do you know?" I turned to him in surprise. "Has someone come back to report?"

But I knew the minute I looked at him that whatever he had

to tell me did not involve wide-open spaces or meaningful work or food and running water or comfortable accommodations. I sank back down, unable to face the grief and fear in his eyes.

"Do you *want to know*?" he asked again.

Mother had told me that even if the news was bad, she would prefer to know. Lying on that rooftop with Chaim, I was reminded that my mother was much more courageous than I could ever be. Even now that I had the chance to know what our fates were, I couldn't bear to hear it said aloud.

"You don't need to tell me," I whispered, staring up at the bright blue sky. "I can see it in your eyes."

When we finally returned downstairs, I walked into the back room, interrupting Elżbieta as she worked with a group of children.

"Just give me a few moments," she said quietly to the children and then approached me, concern in her gaze. "What has happened? What do you need?" I stared at her for a long, fraught moment, trying to absorb her goodness. *Life is still good. Life is still worth living. See, there is still beauty and goodness in the world.*

"I just wanted to see you before you left," I admitted, and then I started to turn away, but she caught my hand. When I glanced back at her, she threw her arms around me, embracing me in the softest, sweetest hug I had ever had.

When Elżbieta released me, she squeezed my forearm, then nodded, as if in that wordless interaction, she had said everything she needed to say.

17

Roman
20 September, 1942

AUTUMN WAS GRADUALLY TAKING HOLD, EACH DAY A LITTLE cooler than the one before. That afternoon, I ran the length of the block from the youth center to my home in pelting rain, thinking about the coming winter and all the desperate tactics we'd need to employ to survive the cold. I was shivering by the time I reached the apartment, so focused on the weather and my drenched coat and hair that I forgot to brace myself on the doorstep.

The apartment had been so crowded and so bustling with activity for so long. There were days when I thought I would go insane if I couldn't find a moment of peace, when I thought the sheer stench of so many people living in that confined space was going to suffocate me. But then I threw our front door open, and instead of noise and smell and crowding, I found complete silence.

Often, when men face their doom, it is their mother they

cry for. But that day, it wasn't my mother I called for, it was my brother.

"Dawidek?" I whispered hoarsely. The rain was still bucketing down, but I could not bring myself to step inside. To do so was to confirm that my very worst fears had come to pass. To search each room and to find only emptiness would break me altogether.

No, better to stay in the cold and the rain.

"Dawidek?" I called again, my voice shaking. I held on to the doorframe, craning my neck to look inside, unable to convince myself to step across the threshold into the apartment. My voice echoed back at me. I waited, holding my breath in case my brother called back, in case his voice was quiet because he was hiding. I called him again, then again, then I sat on the front step, my feet flat against the floor, my elbows resting against my knees. I sat slumped, barely able to hold myself up.

I thought about taking myself to the *Umschlagplatz*. People sat there for hours sometimes. Maybe my family was still there, at the very first stop in their journey. If so, I could join them. And even if I failed to find them, I might be executed just wandering the streets after curfew. I had feared that possibility for so long, but that day, I was sure death would be a mercy.

I just couldn't risk it until I was sure, and I couldn't be sure until I moved into the apartment. The rain came down harder as darkness replaced the late-evening light. I was in such a sharp state of shock that time somehow both stretched and condensed.

"Roman?"

A warm hand descended on my shoulder, and I turned back toward the street to find Chaim behind me.

"They aren't answering," I said numbly. "I've called out to them, but they aren't answering. Why aren't they answering?"

"My friend, let's go inside. The curfew passed some time ago. If you're found out here…"

"Why are you here?"

"Andrzej just heard some of the buildings in this street were cleared this afternoon. We thought we should check on you."

I was too shocked to feel the pain, too confused to grasp the magnitude of my loss. All I could think about was Dawidek.

"Tell me the truth," I said stiffly, resisting Chaim's attempts to shift me into the apartment. I scrambled to my feet and pushed him away, fiercely and furiously as if all of this were his fault, and on the slippery concrete he stumbled. He landed hard against the balustrade and gripped it with his hands twisted behind his hips, but his gaze did not leave mine. I raised my voice at him.

"I should have let you tell me on the rooftop, but I am a coward. Tell me now. What comes after the *Umschlagplatz*?"

He grasped my shoulder in his hand and turned me toward the door.

"I have never lied to you, and I never will. But I am not going to stand here and watch you get shot, so *go inside*."

Chaim insisted I change out of my wet clothes before we talked. By now, perhaps some of the shock was wearing off, because I was becoming aware of the cold. I was shaking so hard that my teeth chattered, and I couldn't feel my toes.

It took several attempts to get undressed, not just because of the cold and my shaking hands but because I couldn't bring myself to look at the closet where my family's clothes hung. If they were untouched, then my family had been taken without warning. But if they were disturbed, they knew that they were about to be taken and they might have even packed, which was somehow more brutal. I wondered how my mother must have felt. I wondered if Samuel had forced his unlikely positivity upon them, even as he was forced from his home. Then I started to think about Dawidek, and my composure completely crumbled.

By the time I left the bedroom, I was weeping. I ran through the apartment, a man possessed, and found Chaim in the kitchen. He sat at the table, the lamp lit in front of him.

"Tell me what you know," I said. He hesitated, and I wiped my eyes with my sleeve, then I slammed my fist into the door-jamb. "Tell me!"

"Roman, you didn't want to know," he reminded me gently.

I choked on a sob, then through my tears tried to explain.

"I need to know now. Tell me, *please.*"

"What good can come of me telling you this?"

"I need to be able to picture it," I choked. Chaim sighed heavily and pushed the plate of our oatmeal rations toward me. I looked in disbelief—I couldn't imagine ever wanting to eat again, but especially not *this* food. It belonged to my family and our roommates. If I ate our food and they returned home, they would go hungry.

"Eat," he said flatly. "Eat, and I will tell you."

I sat at the table and picked up a spoon, then shoveled some of the sludge into my mouth. My stomach revolted at the taste and the texture, but I forced myself to swallow. Satisfied, Chaim nodded.

"A young man escaped last month and brought news back to us at the ŻOB," he said. "The trains go first to Małkinia, and from there divert on a track to a platform that has been built in the forest. An orchestra plays on the platform to welcome the trains—they play beautiful Yiddish songs, and some of the people sing at the top of their lungs as they depart the trains. There is a sign there welcoming the travelers, advising them that they have arrived at a transit camp, telling them to hand over their goods for disinfection. They swap their belongings for a receipt, and then they are led to a bathhouse, where the women and children are separated from the men. Everything is clean and organized. There is nice soap, lots of towels. Your family surely felt very safe, probably even relieved to have such a nice facility for bathing after the filth of the ghetto."

As he spoke, I closed my eyes and pictured the scene laid out before me. I wanted to draw comfort from his story, but his tone did not match his words. The picture he painted was not menacing, and it certainly wasn't sad. But Chaim spoke like a man delivering the worst possible news. I opened my eyes to find his gaze had dropped, and he was staring at the plate of food between us.

"And then?"

"There are two mercies in this. The first is that right until the very last minute, the travelers likely believe they are at a transit camp. The signage, the orchestra, the clean bathhouse— it is so much more than people are expecting, so most of the deportees are calm and relieved. And the other mercy is that when…when it happens, it happens fast, my friend. Within an hour or two of arriving."

"*It?* Say it. What is *it* that happens fast? Are they shot inside the bathhouse?" I was crying again, tears rolling down my cheeks, too distressed and distraught to even be embarrassed.

"There are tanks," he whispered thickly. "When our man escaped into the forest, he heard tank engines running, but the tanks weren't moving. He hid in the forest, then later saw prisoners dragging bodies from the bathhouse. We believe the Jews are being suffocated by the tank exhaust fumes in the bathhouse and then buried in mass graves in the forest."

"But there are hundreds of thousands of us gone now. Surely they can't have murdered them all?"

I sounded like Samuel, and recognizing his words in my mouth made me sob all the harder. Chaim tilted his head back to stare at the ceiling but said nothing. I wanted to argue with him, to bargain with him, to do whatever it took for him to admit that there was no truth behind the story. But I knew in my heart of hearts that the time for self-delusion had passed.

"How sure are you?" I managed after a while.

Chaim lifted his chin and looked me right in the eye.

"Sure enough that I'm telling you not to hold on to hope, my friend. False hope will only hurt you. It's time for you to grieve."

"Grieving is what you do when those you love are lost to you. They have not been lost to me," I said in disgust, weeping. "They have been *taken* from me. There is a difference."

Hours later, we had moved only as far as the living room floor. I couldn't bring myself to return to the bedroom, but every soft space in the apartment had once been someone's bed, so I couldn't bear to sit there, either. We sat on the floor, backs against a wall, and we had been sitting in silence for some time.

"I'm not going to grieve them," I said eventually.

"You can't *not* grieve them, Roman," he said softly. "That isn't something you can choose not to do."

"You're wrong. I am going to channel every bit of my rage and my loss into action. You have to tell me how I can help with your rebellion."

"Are you sure you don't want to take a few days before we talk about this?" he asked hesitantly. "I've given you so many opportunities to get involved over these past few months… It was obvious that you didn't want to be a part of what we are doing."

"I had to protect my family," I said. "Now I have nothing left to lose."

18

Emilia

SARA WAS WAITING IN THE HALLWAY WHEN I OPENED THE
front door to my apartment on Monday morning. The minute
I saw her there, I knew something had gone horribly wrong.
She motioned silently for me follow her back into her apartment
and as soon as the door closed, I asked, "What is it?"

"I'm so sorry, Elżbieta. Roman's entire family was deported
yesterday."

"But we didn't get Dawidek out yet," I whispered, instantly
dizzy with shock.

"No," she said, sighing. "No, we didn't."

"Roman is gone?"

"No," Sara said carefully. "Matylda spoke with Andrzej.
Roman was at the youth center when his building was cleared."

I wanted to feel relief that he was alive, but I knew instantly
that Roman would not be relieved. I had become so fond of him
over our visits, and if there was one thing I was sure of, it was
that Roman Gorka had been living and breathing for his family.

"He won't survive," I said miserably. "He won't survive without them."

"This roundup yesterday was different—so much larger than the daily roundups over these last few months. It sounds as though many of the young people left behind are planning to take up arms," Sara murmured.

"He promised his stepfather that he would not join the Resistance," I said, exhaling a shaky breath. "But with his stepfather gone…"

"It is horrifying to be the only remaining member of a family," Sara said quietly. "I suspect he will try to fight with the other young men. I know exactly how desolate it feels to want to burn the world down because you have nothing left to lose."

"So do I," I whispered unthinkingly, and Sara gave me an odd look. I startled, realizing belatedly what I had done.

"I'm going to heat some water for tea," she said slowly. "Perhaps you should think about whether you want me to ignore that statement or whether you would prefer to explain it."

"…so we left Trzebinia, and we went to Lodz, but of course Uncle Piotr was actually here starting his new business, so then we came here and found him, and the rest you already know."

"So you are potentially wanted by the Germans, but you have been showing them your identity card every day for months," Sara said, frowning.

"Oh, no. Uncle Piotr bought these papers for me. My real name is Emilia Slaska, not Elżbieta Rabinek."

Sara closed her eyes as if she were in pain.

"So you mean to tell me that you have been walking into the ghetto with a *false* identity card every day for months."

"I didn't think about how risky that was before I agreed," I admitted weakly. "And then once we made it through once, I figured it was safe enough. Uncle Piotr seems to have a lot of friends who can pull strings. I knew the card *looked* genuine."

"Oh, he has a lot of friends who can pull strings, all right," Sara muttered, shaking her head. "You do understand what this means? Now that I know, I can't possibly take you back in."

"What? But—"

"Elżbieta—*Emilia*—I'm as desperate as you to make every visit count. But had I known this, I would never have allowed you to come. This isn't even about you, it's about the entire operation. I know that you mean well, but you put us all at risk."

"But… I also showed them my epidemic-control pass to get in, and that's not real, either."

"It *is* real—Matylda has those passes issued by an ally on the City Council, but he is a real doctor, and his responsibility really is epidemic control. We would never try to go through the checkpoints with a false pass. If we were ever found out, they would shut us down."

"Matylda will tell you," I said, raising my chin stubbornly. Right from the beginning, Sara had been more cautious than Matylda, so I was confident that once she knew the truth, Matylda would be undeterred. "She will make you see sense. I have been going in and out of the ghetto for months without any problems. It is no riskier now."

We made our way into the City Hall offices, and after swapping commiserations at the news of the roundups, Sara explained to Matylda the truth about my identity card. I watched her face grow red as Sara spoke, and her gaze was sharp on my face.

"Do you understand how foolish you have been?"

"I'm sorry," I whispered, casting my gaze downward. But then I fished in my pocket for the card and held it out toward them. "But you can see it looks real. It is as close to real as it could be. There is no new risk—"

"Do you know how many children we have rescued, Elżbieta?"

"No," I said hesitantly.

"I haven't counted for some time, but the last time I sat down and tallied the names, it was over two thousand."

"That is amazing."

"It is. But you need to understand that we have moved those thousands of children out of the ghetto only to move them *into* our care. We are still supporting most of them financially, still helping their new families hide when necessary. Sometimes we provide them with food or other essential supplies. You have seen one part of the operation, but the broader picture is an immense machine, and the reason we have been able to coordinate on this scale is that, while we take risks, we do not take foolish risks. Allowing you to visit the ghetto would be a foolish risk. Sara...myself...all of the other social workers who visit the ghetto have genuine identity cards and blemish-free histories. If anyone becomes suspicious and they try to dig into our pasts, they won't see any red flags. But it would take very little time to realize that your identity card does not match a baptismal record or even a birth certificate. That would raise questions which could expose us all."

"But, Matylda—"

"Do you still want to help?"

"I do. Of course I do! Now more than ever," I said vehemently.

"And you will do whatever it takes?"

"Anything you ask of me, I promise."

"Good," she said, nodding curtly. "Then, go home to your family, and let us get back to work."

I tried so hard to change their minds, but it was quickly obvious that neither Matylda nor Sara was willing to allow me to continue to work with the operation. Sara took me home on the tram.

"What will I tell Truda and Mateusz?"

"I'm going to handle that for you," she said quietly. "I'm

going to tell Truda that the City Council is laying off staff and that we no longer have the resources to supervise you."

While she sat at the kitchen table to deliver the news to Truda, I went to my room and opened the top drawer of my bedside table. I riffled through the scraps of paper until I found one I had drawn weeks earlier.

I stared down at the sketch of baby Eleonora. I had thought about giving this to Roman or to Maja and Samuel, but the image was imperfect. I had drawn it in such a state of distress that it was far from my best work. At the time, I had stuffed it into my drawer, unable to bear looking at it. Now, though, looking at the sketch with fresh eyes, those minor imperfections were difficult to spot.

When Sara was preparing to leave, I walked her to the door and handed her the sketch.

"Please explain to him why I'm not there?" I asked her.

She gave me a sad look, then pulled me into a hug.

After Sara was gone, it struck me that I would never see the inside of the ghetto walls again. I felt a confused sense of relief. I would not miss how sick with fear I felt every time I passed through the checkpoints or miss coming face-to-face with the undeniable horrors of the ghetto environment.

But I was also struck by an overwhelming sense of sadness. I'd grown so fond of Roman Gorka. The thought of never seeing him again—of never even having the chance to say goodbye—was heartbreaking.

19

Roman
18 April, 1943

IN THE SEVEN MONTHS SINCE I LOST MY FAMILY, I HAD gained a whole network of brothers and sisters with one goal in common: a dignified death.

Nobody knew why the deportations stopped the previous September. The day after my parents were taken, the Jewish police and their families were deported, and then, for a while, the roundups just stopped. Those months of sudden quiet were eerie for us left behind, and they were a serious tactical error for the Germans. Those of us left behind all knew exactly where the trains led, and when the Germans announced another round of deportations in January, their calls for voluntary *resettlement*, as they called it, were ignored. They attempted a forced roundup, but a small group of ŻOB fighters mounted an offensive. This caught the Germans off guard, and within a few days, they abandoned attempts to deport us. They also stopped providing our rations.

I couldn't bear to think about how close my family had come

to escaping the last deportation. Sometimes that seemed brutally unfair; at other times, as food became even scarcer, it seemed like a mercy. Even Sara and her team could no longer gain access, the Germans now being past the point of pretending they were interested in keeping us healthy.

But instead of accepting our lot, those of us left behind had been encouraged by the ŻOB's ability to stun the Germans in January, and we mobilized, turning the inevitability of our deaths into action, turning our rage and our pain into organization.

I joined Chaim and Andrzej in the ŻOB, and I spent every waking minute of the previous seven months preparing to take some measure of revenge. Chaim and I now lived in the apartment opposite the youth center, in the same place I had sheltered on the day the orphans left. We spent little time there other than to sleep because we worked day and night to prepare ourselves, and the ghetto, for all-out war.

We built bunkers and dug tunnels beneath buildings and constructed barricades on rooftops. With a little help from the Polish Home Army, we smuggled weapons into the ghetto through the sewers and stockpiled them at strategic points, ready for when conflict began. I discovered my job in Sala's workshop had given me a particular tolerance for repetitive tasks, and I'd put this to good use in a makeshift factory, developing crude incendiary devices. Others in my unit struggled with the smell of the chemicals, complaining of headaches and burning eyes, but I relished the discomfort. Every time I packed a bottle for use against the Germans, I focused on my mother's face or on particular memories of Samuel or Dawidek. I poured my longing and my rage into each and every bottle.

For two years before their deaths, I had been terrified of my anger—but once they were gone, I reveled in it. I taped two images to the wall beside my bed. One was the clenched fist Elżbieta had drawn for me—the words beneath it now my driving mantra: *There are many ways to fight, but striving for justice is always worth the battle.* The other image was the extraordinary sketch Sara had given me the day she told me that Elżbieta was unable to return to the ghetto.

Eleonora. The last piece of our family, out there in the world but lost to me, other than the sketch.

"But why can't Elżbieta visit anymore?" I'd said, feeling this new blow land hard, even as I was still submerged in the foggy depths of grief.

"Her family situation has become complicated" was all Sara would tell me.

"Could you take her a note from me?"

"I don't think that would be a good idea."

So that was that. All I had left of both Elżbieta and Eleonora was the sketch, and sometimes, late at night when I lay in bed, I would stare at it and wonder what they were both doing on the other side of the wall, while I was trapped in what was left of the ghetto, waiting for the Germans to make the first move to kick off our rebellion.

On the eve of Passover, Andrzej announced that he'd planned a Seder meal for our ŻOB unit.

"You'll be amazed at the lengths I've gone to," he said. Chaim slapped him on the back playfully.

"I'll be amazed if you've gone to any lengths at all, given you've been working twenty hours a day organizing for the rebellion," he chuckled.

"It's going to be a real occasion, Chaim. I've got a beautiful white tablecloth and some candles. I baked matzo this morning, and I found a bottle of wine *and* even an egg," Andrzej informed him smugly, but then he sobered. "I know it's not perfect, but given the circumstances, it's important. We will pause, and we will be together to reflect on the journey from slavery to freedom."

But by late afternoon, word had spread through the ghetto that a deportation was planned for the following morning.

"Four o'clock," Chaim told us, recounting the story he had heard from another ŻOB unit a few blocks away. "They know we are planning to rebel, although I hope to God they don't know how organized we are."

"They won't expect it," I murmured. I stood, finding myself unable to be still. "If they had any idea what we've planned, they'd have intervened months ago."

"Seder will have to wait," Andrzej said sensibly, as if it would merely be postponed until after we'd finished rebelling. But I knew, and he knew, that not one of us expected to make it out alive.

Our freedom from slavery was coming, but it would not come in this life. If we died with courage, we would die free, even confined within the ghetto walls. I was at last ready to fight for justice, although I knew I could not win.

The ghetto had become a quieter place, but it had never before been silent. Now we all sat and waited, and the anticipation was unbearable. It was so quiet and I was so on edge I heard movement from blocks away when it began just at four in the morning.

Our unit sat on the rooftop above the youth center, asking questions with our eyes because we were too afraid to whisper them with our mouths. We soon heard the sounds of men below shuffling into formation, but it was nothing like the bold goose steps we were expecting, and for hours we sat in confused silence, watching shadows shifting on the streets below us.

It wasn't until a messenger approached at dawn that we learned what was happening. The first wave of Germans had crept into the ghetto individually, assuming they could sneak in unnoticed to assess our preparedness.

"What do we do?" I asked Andrzej, my fingers itching to pick up the rifle he'd given me.

"We wait," he whispered back. "When the time is right, we'll know."

As the sun rose, a wave of tanks rolled through the streets, marking the end of the eerily silent overnight standoff. Behind the armored vehicles, still more German soldiers marched in tightly closed formations through the deserted streets of the ghetto.

This was what I'd expected. These footsteps fell heavily, the sound of their boots strident against the cobblestone street. I peered through a gap in the rooftop barricade and felt my entire body tense at the assured expressions on the soldiers' faces. It was evident they thought they had won, that because we had allowed them to assemble without so much as a shot fired, we had given up before we began. The soldiers were barely scanning their surroundings as they marched.

I had reached a place beyond fear, a place where all that mattered was my values. Life in the ghetto had broken down the last of my hopes and dreams, and I was conscious of being free of the pressure to find a way to survive. I wanted only to die with honor, perhaps even avenge my family as I went. If anything, I was relieved that the moment had now come and that it would all be over soon.

Our unit remained on the rooftop, waiting for the signal that it was time to act. In the meantime, at the intersection where I had watched children from the orphanage walk toward their deaths, the Germans had set up a command center, unaware that they were entirely surrounded.

At last, a signal came from a ŻOB leader hidden at ground level. There was an immediate eruption of violence, improvised incendiary devices flying from every direction, gunshots raining down from apartment windows up and down the surrounding blocks. Unprotected German soldiers on the street were dropping like flies. A Molotov cocktail hit a tank right in the turret, and I peered between the gaps in a barricade, watching as the tank caught fire, then exploded.

"I hope that was one of the bottles I assembled," I cried, after the explosion rang out. Chaim slapped my back in support. He was impatient after the long night of anticipation, visibly itching to join the skirmishes on the street.

"Can we go?" he asked Andrzej, who shook his head.

"Patience, Pigeon. This is a marathon, not a sprint."

German soldiers and commanders were desperately trying to retreat, but other ŻOB units closer than ours were anticipating this, blocking their escape. Still, we waited on the rooftop. After hours of this, only a handful of Germans remained alive, cowering behind mattresses they retrieved from a ground-floor apartment. Andrzej took Chaim on a scouting mission, leaving me with the rest of our unit. When they returned, Chaim was grinning.

"If we move to the next barricade farther along the street, we will be able to take them out."

"Remember, boys," Andrzej said suddenly, scanning the gazes of the twelve men in our unit. "No matter what happens, make sure they don't take you alive."

We all nodded our understanding. This was something we had discussed at length in the planning. It was a practical principle—if we were taken alive, we'd suffer torture until our deaths anyway—but it was also a reflection of our goal. Andrzej grimaced as he always did as he delivered the final part of his instructions from the ŻOB leadership.

"And the orders remain that if somehow you escape the ghetto and find refuge on the Aryan side, lie low and prepare for the broader citywide Uprising. Try to connect with the *Szare Szeregi*." The Polish Boy Scouts, known as the Gray Ranks. We had learned that they were organizing in preparation for a broader Uprising. Chaim snorted and rolled his eyes, just as I had known he would.

"None of us are getting out of here alive," he said.

"I just hope that we are each lucky enough to achieve a dignified death," I said, and there were murmurs of agreement from the rest of our unit.

Most of us who had trained and prepared for the rebellion felt the same. We had no expectation that any of us would escape the ghetto. There was no chance a ragtag bunch of skeletal men and women with a handful of makeshift weapons could ever overcome the might of the German forces. We harbored no secret dreams of saving our own lives or even saving the lives of the women and children and elderly folk still trapped within the walls.

No, the goal of the rebellion was simple: we wanted only to die with dignity. We wanted to achieve something like revenge and to leave this life with courage.

"This year we are slaves. Next year may we all be free," Andrzej murmured, just as he might have recited from the Haggadah. I'd heard those words every year at Passover, but they had never resonated with me the way they did that night.

As we adjusted our positioning on the rooftop, I saw the wisdom in Andrzej's decision to have us lie low. The Germans positioned themselves so they had cover from our fighters in the buildings, but they didn't know we had a station on the rooftop. Chaim and I positioned ourselves behind one barricade, with Andrzej and the others just a few feet ahead of us. Crouching low behind the roofline, adrenaline coursed through my body. I looked down, and my hands were shaking violently, but I wasn't scared. It was anticipation.

Soon, Dawidek. Soon I will avenge your death.

"Look between the gap in the barricade, boys. Do you see

them?" Andrzej hissed. When we nodded yes, he said, "Take the pair on the far side of the road."

"You take the one on the left," Chaim murmured. "I'll get the one on the right."

I had trained for months for this moment, and now, habit took over. My hands steadied as I raised my rifle and lined the sights up. When Andrzej gave the signal to fire, I pulled the trigger without hesitation. My target fell immediately. It took Chaim several attempts, but soon his fell, too. Within a few minutes, the street was completely silent. Blood drained from the corpses on the street, running down between the cobble-stones, dripping into the sewers.

There was no time for us to pause, to reflect upon what we had done. We could hear the drone of planes coming near, the first wave of the bombing raids we expected, and so our unit fell into step behind Andrzej as we retreated.

"How do you feel?" I asked Chaim, as we ran down the stairs toward the basement.

"Alive," he said, and I knew exactly what he meant. For so long we had endured an oppression that felt insurmountable. It felt *good* to see German blood in the streets, but it wasn't enough for me, and that was curious.

I had expected that the minute I fired that gun, I would feel relief, but the reality wasn't nearly as simple. Frustration and fury and aggression charged through my body, locking the muscles in my arms and setting my teeth on edge.

They had to pay. *I* would make them pay.

By two o'clock that day, the Germans had entirely retreated from the ghetto. We lost only a handful of men and buildings in the bombing raid, but all in all, the first day of our rebellion had deeply embarrassed the Germans. To me, that made it an unexpected and resounding success.

20

Emilia

"CAN YOU BELIEVE IT? THE JEWS ARE FIGHTING BACK!"

It seemed as though the whole city was abuzz. I was on a tram with Uncle Piotr, the morning after we awoke to sounds of gunfire and explosions from the other side of the wall. As the violence continued into a second day, I couldn't bear listening to it for another minute. I'd prayed so many rosaries the day before, my fingers were sore, and I'd tried covering my ears with a pillow, but the sounds pierced it. Truda was impatient with my fretting, and Mateusz had gone to work, so I'd pleaded with Uncle Piotr to take me on an outing.

"The Ferris wheels are set up at Krasiński Square again," he suggested. I stared at him in disbelief.

"But the Jews are rebelling on the other side of that wall!"

"I know. But there are plenty on this side of the wall who are curious to peer over the top—those who enjoy seeing the Jews humiliate the Germans, and then of course there are those who enjoy seeing the remaining Jews suffer." Piotr sighed, but then he brightened. "But we could ride the Ferris wheel and just look at the sights on our side of the wall. That was fun last time we did it, no?"

"Anything but that," I said flatly. "Take me as far away from the Jewish Quarter as you can."

In the seven months since I'd lost my supposed job, my world had shrunk all the way back down to the size of the apartment, and all that kept me sane was evenings with Uncle Piotr and Sara. They had obviously grown close, and although Sara assured me they were just friends, I saw the way they looked at one another. I decided it was adorable to watch old people falling in love, and when I told Uncle Piotr this, he reminded me in no uncertain terms that they were both only just forty, which hardly counted as *old*.

In any case, Uncle Piotr agreed to take me out to a café on the other side of the city. Now, on the tram, I realized my mistake. I could no longer hear the gunshots, but I could hear the incredulous whispers of our fellow countrymen. As the passengers on the tram got on and off, snippets of conversation bombarded me.

"Why now?" one man asked his traveling companion. "I heard it's almost empty in there, that most of them have been moved to labor camps out of the city where conditions are less crowded. If they had it in them to fight back, why wait until now, when the Germans are trying to help them move to more comfortable accommodations?"

I looked at Uncle Piotr, who was reading his newspaper, apparently unperturbed by the comments behind us. I clenched my hands into fists so tight that my fingernails dug into the soft skin of my palms. I focused on the pain hoping it would drown out the sounds of the conversation.

I told myself that it was entirely possible these men had no idea about what life was like behind the wall, and I tried to remind myself that they, too, had probably suffered under the occupation.

"I heard this fighting is not about conditions at all, but that the Jews are concerned they will no longer be able to make money in the work camps. You know how Jews love their money."

"I'm sorry, Uncle Piotr," I whispered urgently.

"What for?" he asked me, startled.

I spun around and faced the men, and I hissed, "The walled district has been a cruel prison since it was established, and those left inside know they aren't being removed to a work camp but to an extermination camp. You should be ashamed of yourselves."

The entire tram fell silent. I looked around, frantically checking to see if there were any soldiers on board—not that this was our only threat. We had no way of knowing how many civilians on the tram would be eager to turn us in.

Uncle Piotr rose silently, took my arm, and all but dragged me to the door. The tram pulled to a stop, and we stepped off. As the tram continued on its journey, Uncle Piotr gave a frustrated sigh.

"I don't need to tell you how stupid what you just did—"

"I know," I snapped, shaking his hand off my arm. "I *know*. But did you hear what they were saying? How could you *stand* that?"

"It achieves nothing to speak up. Do you really think anything you said will make them question their beliefs? It changed nothing, and you put yourself *and me* in grave danger."

"So you sit in silence and let them speak that nonsense about innocent people," I said as I crossed my arms over my chest.

"Yes," he exclaimed, throwing his hands up in frustration, but then he paused. "You seem awfully sure about the conditions in the walled district for one who has never been there."

"I've heard things," I muttered, avoiding his gaze.

"Elżbieta, you only ever speak to the four of us. It wasn't your parents or me filling your head with this nonsense." His frown grew deeper, but then his eyes widened. "Wait. Sara didn't tell you these things?"

"What would Sara know about the Jewish area?" I said lightly, aware that not even Piotr knew about her epidemic-control pass.

"So where did this come from, then?"

"I found an underground newspaper in the courtyard one day," I lied. "I threw it away as soon as I read it, but it made perfect sense."

"You can only look out for yourself in a time like this," Uncle Piotr said quietly. "Find ways to survive...find ways to thrive. You can do nothing for the people in the Jewish area, and you can do nothing to change the minds of those who aren't sympathetic to whatever the Jews' plight truly is. Worry about yourself—your family. That's the best thing you can do."

"Have you given this lecture to Sara?" I asked him.

He sighed, then muttered, "I've tried to. It doesn't go down well."

That night, with the sound of gunfire still echoing in the distance, I sat alone with Sara in her apartment and told her about the conversation on the tram and Uncle Piotr's comments.

"It was foolish of me, I know," I said. "I lost my temper. I just couldn't bear it, after the things I've seen and the stories we heard."

"I know, Elżbieta," she said quietly. "There is a whole city who would much rather turn a blind eye to the suffering behind the wall, and sometimes that is very difficult to bear. I tell myself that it is enough that history will harshly judge those who did not act, but I *know* in my heart that it is not enough. I wish I could drag some of these people into the ghetto and force them to look into the eyes of the people we have seen. You understand the problem, don't you? Bystanders have allowed themselves to be convinced that the Jews are not like us, and as soon as you convince someone that a group of people is not human, they will allow you to treat them as badly as you wish. If those men on the tram or your uncle had the chance to see the humanity of those caught behind the wall, they would never stand for it."

"Uncle Piotr disappoints me maybe most of all," I admitted.

"He is a complicated man with complicated principles, that's for sure," Sara muttered. I peered at her thoughtfully, then finally gave voice to a question I'd been pondering for some time.

"Do you love him?"

"I could," she said, after a pause. "But I, too, am a complicated woman with complicated principles, and unfortunately, our principles make us incompatible. That's why we are only friends."

We both jumped in fright as the windows rattled with an explosion in the distance.

"What do you think will happen to the partisans in the ghetto?" I asked her, my voice small as I thought of Andrzej and Roman.

"It will be a bloodbath." Sara's eyes filled with tears. "I'll be surprised if they last another day. But they will go down with dignity and with honor. I am proud of them for that, and you should be, too."

21

Roman

FOR DAYS, THE GERMANS TRIED TO GAIN A FOOTHOLD IN the ghetto. With every new sunrise, I told myself that I had finally reached the day I would die. This ever-present reminder of my imminent mortality was enough to drive me through some sleepless nights and shifts in the incendiary-bottle factory that sometimes lasted more than twenty-four hours. If I wasn't packing bottles with chemicals, I was with my unit, skipping along rooftops and defending homes or shepherding families between the basement bunkers. Only when I was too exhausted to continue would I finally retreat to a bunker to sleep the deep, dreamless sleep of those who are too tired to play in their rest.

I could not keep the days straight. Sleep deprivation and the constant, adrenaline-fueled panic of combat played games with my mind. When Andrzej pointed out that two weeks had passed since Passover, I protested.

"Surely not."

Chaim was sitting beside me cleaning his rifle. He flashed a tired grin.

"Doesn't time fly when you're having fun?"

The Ghetto Uprising may have been more successful than we'd anticipated, but it didn't feel glorious or triumphant. For the first few days, it was satisfying to push back, and I certainly enjoyed knowing how humiliating our success was for the Germans. There were moments when I was fighting with my unit or scouting with Chaim when I felt freedom was almost within my grasp, but I couldn't quite reach it. I expected to reach a distinct point when I would feel I avenged my people, but as the body count grew, peace continued to elude me. What would it take? Did I need to kill a particular number of men? Or did I need to kill in a particular way?

Chaim and I led dozens of families into the massive basement bunkers we had built, and with each new group, I stared into the eyes of mothers and fathers and children and grandparents who had suffered unbearable trauma and who had been treated with unfathomable hatred. Worse still, these innocent people were living out the last days of their lives. And as we managed to rally and hold the Germans at bay for more hours or more days or even weeks, the ghetto was now cut off from the outside world. We had been starving before, but now, even the trickle of smuggled food that kept us alive was gone. We had no long-term plan, no endgame in mind. We knew from the outset that we didn't need one.

"You're a surly bastard, Gorka, but you're one of the smartest men I've ever met. I don't know how I would have survived the last year without you," Chaim said one night. We were lying in the darkness of a bunker, both too wound up to sleep.

"Same," I said gruffly. He chuckled and rolled toward me.

"If the war ended tomorrow and you were free, what would you do?"

I'd asked Elżbieta that same question once. That conversation led to our discussion about justice, and I'd thought about that time and time again over the months since, every time I looked at the fist she'd drawn for me.

"I'd still fight for justice," I said. "I'd fight until we were all free and equal. There's no greater cause to live for."

"I'd rob a bank, find a beautiful girlfriend and buy myself a castle in Scotland," Chaim said wistfully.

"You two really need to get some sleep," Andrzej grumbled, as he stood from his position on the floor beside me and moved to the other side of the room to avoid our laughter.

Predictably, the Germans did not take well to our rebellion, and in the face of continual failure, they began to shift their methods. We were faster in the streets, and we had fortified homes into bunkers, but even bunkers cannot withstand fire, so when the bombing and the bullets failed, it was fire the Germans resorted to.

Now they were burning entire blocks, setting each building on fire, then waiting at the exits to shoot those who tried to flee. Families who were safely hidden in their bunkers were now trapped, suffocating in the heat and the smoke. The air in the ghetto had long been filled with the scent of rotting corpses, but now the black, choking smoke became so pervasive there was no escaping it. My headaches from the incendiary-bottle factory were nothing compared to the headaches from the smoke. Entire city blocks were consumed by fire, and the sounds of explosions and screaming and crying and gunshots echoed day and night.

I thought I had lived through hell on earth, but as we began to lose the battle, I realized I had been wrong: there were still more depths for humanity to sink to, still more suffering to be endured. I had hardened myself to survive in the ghetto through those years, but no human could harden themselves against the things that I had seen in recent weeks. More than once, I saw a family leap to their deaths from a burning building, only to be shot before they even reached the ground. I saw burns and wounds and infections that would have terrified the most experienced doctor. I picked through the burned ruins looking for food or survivors, only to find the innocent who had perished in the flames.

"I can't stop thinking about the people trapped in the bunkers," Chaim said one morning. The strain was visible on all our faces, particularly as we began to lose ground, and it became even harder to sleep. Chaim developed a nasty, hacking cough that he just could not shake. "To die as the building above them burns. It is so cruel."

"I can't let myself think about it," I said flatly. "Please, don't talk about it."

"I can't believe we're still alive," he murmured, then he glanced at me and said suddenly, "Roman, I hope you escape somehow."

"Escape?" I repeated, then I laughed bitterly. "From the first day of this rebellion I have been waiting to die. Now, I'm starting to hope for it."

We kept fighting, even as ammunition ran low and as we ran out of materials for crafting our crude explosives. We kept fighting even after it became undeniably apparent that we had no hope of battling their fires. With so few bullets left and so few options for defending ourselves, the streets were completely still during the day. My unit hunkered down in the back room of the youth center, taking turns sleeping while one of us kept watch at the front door and another by the alleyway. We knew that when the Germans decided to burn our building down, we would be powerless to resist them, and that would be the end. We kept watch not to save ourselves, but so we could fight to the very end.

At night, we ran through the streets like rats, patrolling whatever block we were sent to, trying to inflict damage upon the Germans with our desperately limited resources. One by one, each member of my unit succumbed, until Andrzej, Chaim and I were the only surviving members. By that stage, we hadn't had contact from the other units for days.

From the rooftops, we could see that the Germans were circling closer to the few large bunkers that remained, hunting out survivors with dogs and machines that detected sounds underground. They had interrupted our city water supply, and we had entirely run out of food. The once-vibrant streets of the Jewish Quarter were now a hellscape of rubble and death. The end was finally near.

"We have done our ancestors proud," Andrzej said. "Do you know how long it has been, Roman?" That I kept losing track of days and weeks had been a source of unending amusement to him and Chaim, even throughout the horror.

"Two weeks?"

"It was two weeks the last time I asked you this question," he chuckled. "Do you want to guess again?"

"I was hoping we'd hold out for three days."

"And we made it to twenty-seven," he said, and then his voice cracked as he murmured, "I'm not sure there has ever been a group of men and women as courageous or as resourceful as we have been. We will go down in history as heroes."

"Will we?" I said, too tired to laugh.

"You doubt this?"

"Do I doubt that we are heroes? Yes. How can we be heroes when we lost the battle?"

"To the very end, Roman, we have stood for our values. We have had courage and conviction. We have stood up for what was right. That is what makes us heroes."

"Even if that is true, you seem to forget that there is no one left to write the history of what happened here. The Germans will surely win the war, and even if they don't, none of *us* are making it out alive. The Poles on the other side of the wall will have no clue about how fiercely we fought or about any of our small triumphs." I sighed heavily, then shook my head, pushing my overgrown hair out of my eyes. "No, Andrzej. History will not remember us, let alone remember us as heroes."

"There's that sunny disposition we all know and love," Chaim said mildly, and he playfully threw a bottle cap in my direction. I swatted it away.

We didn't talk about why this felt like a goodbye. We didn't have to. We had completely run out of ammunition, other than a single grenade Chaim had found in the coat of a dead ŻOB soldier. The three of us were going to try to make our way to Franciszkańska Street, where we hoped there was another unit hiding in a bunker, but we had no idea what we'd find even if we made it there, and it was an almost impossible journey. The streets were again rife with German patrols, becoming ever-bolder as our attacks against them faded. Andrzej hoped the patrols would slow once the sun went down, but night came, and German soldiers just kept rolling through.

"I miss the days when we could run along the rooftops," Chaim said.

"Of course you do. You're our Pigeon," Andrzej said, but he sounded exhausted, and the playful tone had faded from his voice. "But smoldering rubble doesn't have a rooftop, and that's all that lies ahead of us. We're going to have to walk on the street."

We tied scraps of fabric around what was left of our shoes, hoping it would muffle our heels against the cobblestones, and then we moved to the street. As tired and as weak as I was, I could not allow myself to breathe as heavily as I wanted to, because even the sound of our breathing could give us away. Shallow breathing left me faint, and I wondered if I would just pass out, if that would be the end of me.

The sound of an engine turning over sounded up ahead. Suddenly, the street was lit with headlights. A shot was fired, then another and another. It was dark other than the headlight, and I was momentarily blinded. My whole body jolted as a white-hot, searing pain exploded in my right arm. The next bullet would surely do the job. I didn't even tense as I waited for it. Instead, I exhaled, feeling the tension of anticipation leaving my body at long last.

Here it is. Peace. Peace at last.

But I'd survived for so long. Self-preservation had become a habit.

"This way! There's a manhole in the alleyway," I heard Andrzej hiss, and then Chaim, who was just to my left against the wall, disappeared from view. I followed them, blinded by pain and shock, holding on to my consciousness by a thread. More gunshots sounded, and then, just ahead of me, Andrzej stumbled and fell face-first to the ground. The headlight from the car flashed over him as I approached, and I saw that it was a clean shot—right through his skull.

There was no time to react and no time to grieve. Chaim was still running, and I was stumbling after him into the dark alley. The headlights hadn't followed us, but we weren't out of danger yet. Voices and laughter sounded behind us, echoing off the walls in the alley.

The Germans had us cornered. A chill ran down my spine as the seconds began to stretch. No gunshots now meant they intended to toy with us or, worse still, to capture and torture us.

"Your grenade," I reminded Chaim. He kept running, and I kept following, trying so desperately to keep up. Our time was upon us, and after everything we had been through, it seemed fitting that we would face the afterlife together.

There were boots on the ground behind us—thick, hard boots, so different from the sounds of our worn shoes.

I'm coming, Mother. Samuel, I'm coming. Andrzej, pour me a vodka. We will toast the success of these past weeks.

But Chaim stopped suddenly, and then I heard him groan as he lifted the manhole cover.

"You first," he said urgently. I hesitated, and he grabbed me, his hands rough. He shifted the fingers of my left hand to press my palm over the wound on my right, then shoved me into the manhole, down into the sewer. My feet found a platform, but it was a small space—not even tall enough for me to crouch, so instead I stretched out horizontally. My eyes watered with the stench, and below me I heard running water.

Suddenly, Chaim's face was above me. It was dark, but I could just make out the shape of his teeth against the grime on his face.

"Don't waste it," was all that he said, and then he looked away.

"Don't waste—" I started to protest, but Chaim pulled the manhole cover back into place. I tried to reach to stop him, to pull him down into safety with me, but my hand reached only the concrete of the underside of the alleyway. I couldn't figure out how to pull myself up any higher. The pain in my arm was overwhelming, and my thoughts were growing fuzzy.

As the manhole dropped back into place, I heard Chaim taunting the soldiers. He was using himself as bait, making sure the Germans following us were all close enough that the grenade would take them all out, just to be sure they couldn't follow me into the sewer.

"No," I cried weakly, clawing uselessly at the underside of the alleyway with my good hand. "Please, Chaim, don't do this. I need you—"

The soldiers were right above me now, close enough that I could hear them talking to Chaim. I heard his final, triumphant burst of laughter. This was Chaim's whole-body laugh, and I'd seen it a million times by then, so I could picture him up there in the alley, head thrown back, mouth open wide, his whole body shaking with the joy of it.

Before his laughter had even faded, an explosion burst above me, and I passed out.

★ ★ ★

When I woke, everything hurt, from my head all the way down to my toes. I was hot and dizzy even before I sat up, and there was movement at the other end of the platform. As I reoriented myself, I realized the squeaking, scurrying sound could only be rats. I kicked them away furiously and tried to gain my bearings. Once I had, I wished I could pass out again.

The explosion above me, the bullet in my arm, the hellscape of the weeks that had passed, and everyone else was dead.

I thought about dropping down into the sewer to let the filth wash me away. Then I imagined lying there and letting nature take its course. The wound in my arm would inevitably become infected, and given how weak I was, it surely wouldn't take long for an infection to finish the job the Germans had started.

But I hadn't fought for so long and so hard to die an impotent death. I forced myself to find the manhole—feeling the ceiling above me with the fingertips of my left hand, and then struggling, I managed to push the cover away onto the surface of the alleyway. As I struggled to rise, the odor of blood and gunpowder overtook the reek of the sewer.

Chaim's blood. Why had he saved me?

It was dark now. I squinted, trying to find the shape of the truck, but it was gone, and the street was still and silent.

It took several attempts to drag myself out of the sewer. My injured arm wasn't strong enough to bear my weight, and my left arm wasn't strong enough to pull my entire body out on its own. But staying in the sewer wasn't an option. I was going to die being useful, or at the very least facing the enemy with courage.

I was grateful for the darkness when I finally found myself aboveground again. The alleyway was a mess of bodies and body parts, and some of that mess was Chaim. I stifled a sob and forced myself to start walking, shivering now, hot and cold in alternate measures. Even as I left the alley, I was becoming confused about where I was and what my options were.

I had walked the streets of the ghetto more times than I could count, but the landscape had changed in the past twenty-eight days. Every building was burned or demolished, and the landmarks I'd once used to navigate were all gone. I decided to try to find Franciszkańska Street to locate the other bunker, just as Andrzej and Chaim had planned.

I was at the wall before I even knew I was near it, and that's when I realized how lost I was. I'd walked in the wrong direction and had accidentally stumbled my way to the Krasiński Square side, all the way at the wrong end of the ghetto. I groaned, furious with myself, and moved to turn away.

But as I did, my gaze snagged on a small pile of rubble. I hesitated but ultimately walked toward it, thinking I could shelter behind it to gather my thoughts and make a new plan. Only when I stepped around the rubble did I realize that a burned-out building had collapsed, and part of its structure had fallen onto the wall—leaving a small gap.

I approached it cautiously, bracing myself for the sounds of gunfire from the other side. I paused, listening intently. When I heard no movement, I held my breath and peered through the gap to find Krasiński Square in all of its glory, completely, shockingly deserted.

I sank back onto the ground, leaning against the wall, breathing heavily as I tried to clear my foggy mind to make sense of this.

Chaim is dead. Andrzej is dead. But I'm alive. Chaim saved me. Why did he save me?

Why the hell isn't a German soldier waiting on the other side of this wall with a machine gun?

As my heart rate slowed, the scenario before me finally began to make sense. Of course the Germans weren't rushing to repair or even to guard the wall. There was barely anyone left, and very few who were well enough to escape.

Maybe I could just walk right out of there. But if I left the ghetto, where would I go? Everyone I cared about was dead. Everyone who cared about *me* was dead.

Elżbieta.

Her face flashed before me, along with a memory of conversations we'd shared in the back room of the youth center. I knew she lived on Miodowa Street, and she'd described her apartment in such detail that I was certain I could find it. Sara lived there, too, and she was a nurse. They *knew* people. People who could help me.

I leaned against the wall, and I looked into the square, then I looked back to the ghetto. Escape had been so unlikely I hadn't even thought to daydream about the possibility, but there I stood, swiveling my view between two clear paths: life to the east across Krasiński Square or death.

I slipped through the wall and into the square, and then I started to run. The burst of energy surprised me, and it wasn't until I was clear across the square that I realized what was fueling it.

Hope.

It had been such a long time since I'd felt it that I didn't recognize the emotion. By some twist of fate through the generous act of the best friend I'd ever had, I had not only survived but bumbled my way onto the other side.

I found the building easily enough. It was exactly as Elżbieta had described: three and a half stories tall, with clumsy patching on the top floor.

After years trapped within the ghetto, I didn't know if there was a curfew in the broader city, but the streets were deserted so I had to assume there was. But at the height of summer, the days in Warsaw were so long and the sky was beginning to brighten, so I knew it was probably close to four in the morning.

I scooped up a pebble from the garden bed outside her apartment building, and threw it toward one of the two peaked windows on that top floor. It missed by miles, so I tried again, and then again. On the fourth attempt, the rock hit the window and clattered down to the pavement. There was no sign of movement.

And worse still, the early rays of sunlight were beginning to breach the sky.

Any moment now, the city would awaken. Workers would take to the streets, and Germans would begin their morning patrols. I hadn't bathed properly in years. I was bleeding profusely, my shirt soaked in blood both front and back. My hair was wild and my beard scruffy. I could not have looked more conspicuous if I'd tried.

I walked to the door that led to the street, pushed it open and stepped inside, drew in a deep breath, and mounted the stairs. By the time I reached the third floor, I was struggling to breathe. Here I found two doors, and I *thought* Elżbieta had said one was her apartment and one was Sara's, but that conversation had been seven months earlier, and I was so dizzy I could barely stand.

I went to the first door and thumped against it with my strong hand. After a few moments, it opened, just a crack. A man stood there, staring at me through wire-framed glasses.

"Yes?"

"Is this… Does Elżbieta live here?" I asked the man, stepping back, conscious of the stench of my body.

"Who are you?"

"I am her friend," I said. His gaze skipped down my body, then back to my face. "I'm…" My vision was fading. I clutched the doorframe, then realizing that wasn't going to be enough,

I tried to guide myself safely to the floor. But the man pushed the door open, and just as I crumpled, I felt his hands slide beneath my arms to catch me.

22

Emilia

ROMAN WAS ON OUR SOFA, UNCONSCIOUS, LYING SAND-wiched between hastily laid towels and a layer of blankets. When Uncle Piotr came to get me, I smelled the boy on the couch before I saw him.

He was gaunt when I'd known him, but Roman was all but skeletal now. His beard was wiry and patchy, and his hair was overgrown and matted. The banging on our door had woken us all up, but Uncle Piotr insisted we hide in our rooms as he went to investigate. Roman was limp and out cold. I could have fainted myself when I recognized him.

I'd grieved him during the weeks of the Uprising. Every time I heard a gunshot or an explosion, I wondered if that was the one that had taken his life. Not for a second had it occurred to me that he might survive.

As I stared at Roman on the couch, my family stared at me. I didn't dare to meet anyone's gaze. I could feel their confusion, their fear and their anger. We were all at risk now, and it was my fault. But I was almost as confused as they were. How had Roman known where to find me? Despite the risk, I was glad that he had. I was happy and relieved, even if his presence in our apartment complicated everything.

"We will talk later about this," Truda said suddenly. I glanced hesitantly at her and saw only confusion and alarm in her face. "For now, we have to help him. He is bleeding from a wound in his arm, and I think he's dehydrated—look at his lips."

I did and saw that his lips were bone dry; from the corners of his mouth, cracks disappeared beneath the hair of his beard.

"He asked for you before he fainted." Uncle Piotr hesitated, then said carefully, "Does Sara know him, too?"

"Yes."

"Please go across and wake her up," Truda murmured. "I'll get some supplies."

As I crept across to Sara's apartment, I thought about the night I caught her with the orphans in her spare room. I felt a painful clench in my chest as I always did when those children came to mind. I had taught myself by then to think about the positives. Those children, like all others who had wound up in the orphanage, were likely lost—but others had been saved. Icchak had been saved. Eleonora had been saved.

Roman was injured. Roman was in my apartment, and my whole family was in danger. But Roman was *alive*. It was a miracle—there was no other explanation. Maybe the many prayers I'd offered for him over those weeks had worked.

"Sara?" I knocked cautiously on her bedroom door and heard her stir. "I'm sorry to wake you, but there's an emergency."

She was at the door in seconds, sleep rumpled and alarmed. "Elżbieta? What is it?"

"Roman. He's here, but he's injured."

"Here?"

"In our apartment. He's unconscious."

"How did he find us?"

"I don't know," I admitted. Sara slipped back into her room, but only to pull a dressing gown over her nightgown and to scoop up her medical bag from beside her bed.

"I hope you realize what this means. We're going to have to tell your parents the truth."

"I know."

"They're going to kill me," she said, sighing. "Piotr is going to kill me."

"Me, too."

In silence now, we slipped back across the hall and into my own apartment. The entire room had been rearranged. The coffee table was pushed closer to the sofa, and a bucket of soapy water and some towels rested on top. Beside this was a glass of water and a spoon. Our armchairs were moved out of the way, over toward a window, giving Sara space to work.

"I tried to give him some water," Truda explained, motioning toward the spoon.

"I'll need scissors," Sara said briskly, as she dropped to her knees beside Roman and tenderly pushed the hair back from his forehead. She paused, then her voice was thick with tears as she whispered, "You poor boy. What have you seen and done in these weeks?"

Sara once told me that I would need to pray for her because she no longer had it in her to do so. Watching her tend to Roman now, I took it upon myself to pray harder than I had ever prayed in my life, asking for her to be granted the wisdom to help him, asking for protection for our whole family while Roman was in our home.

While I prayed, it occurred to me how proud I was to be a part of this family—a transplant, but a lucky one. I had been ripped from one family that cared for those around them and placed in another. For all of his bluster, it didn't seem to occur to Uncle Piotr, or even Truda and Mateusz, that we could turn

Roman away. I knew that all across Poland, there were other families who would have reacted very differently. Even those who cared may not have cared enough to take the risk. Others would have immediately called the Gestapo.

Truda returned with a pair of scissors, and Sara used them to cut the scrap of filthy fabric of Roman's shirt, exposing a gaping wound on his upper arm.

"He has been shot," she said, then she clucked her tongue. "This is a bad wound, and it seems that he's been through the sewers. He needs a surgeon."

She paused for a moment, then began firing off orders.

"Elżbieta, bring everything to the bathroom—the soapy water, the towels, the scissors. Get me more towels, too. Line the bath with them. Mateusz, when she finishes, carry him in and lay him in the bath. Truda, the water is a good start but we're going to need more than that to rehydrate him—get some sugar and salt and bring it all to the bathroom."

"And me?" Uncle Piotr prompted her. Sara looked up at him.

"Get dressed," she said, in a tone that left no room for argument. "You're going to fetch the surgeon."

Our bathroom was small, and we wouldn't all fit. Sara asked me to assist her, but Truda insisted that she do it. I didn't argue. Truda knew nothing of the things I had seen in the ghetto and probably thought I'd be shocked by the wound.

She and Sara got to work, sponging Roman's body, trying to clean what they could of the wound, spooning water into his mouth and trying to rouse him enough to swallow it at regular intervals. Every now and again, I would hear Roman cry out, and inevitably I would hear Sara and Truda frantically hushing him.

We were lucky that our apartment building was small and that the closest adjoining apartment was Sara's. We were also unlucky in that there were four other apartments on the floors beneath us. It wouldn't take much for the sound to travel down.

Mateusz and I waited in the hallway outside the bathroom. We had closed the door to contain the noise, but the silence in the hallway was tense.

"You are going to have some explaining to do," he said, after a while.

"I know," I muttered.

"We need to get him help and then get him out of here. Then you and I and Truda are going to sit down to talk."

"I know."

"How do you even know—" he started to say, and then he broke off, drew in a deep breath.

"I had to do something," I blurted. Mateusz closed his eyes, as if the words caused him physical pain. "I couldn't do much, but an opportunity arose, and I took it, because once I knew what was happening, I had to do something. I could not have lived with myself if I hadn't."

"What *was* it you did?" he asked, his gaze pained. "Who is this man? How does he know where we live?"

"I…"

My eyes stung, and then tears began to roll down my cheeks. I could do nothing to stop them. Knowing that the time was coming when Truda and Mateusz would know the extent of my deception left me sick with anxiety.

The door opened, and Sara and Truda appeared, each drying their hands with a towel. Sara was pale and her gaze serious. I wiped at my eyes with the back of my hand.

"How is he?" I croaked.

"The bullet is lodged deeply in his arm. I think it may have hit the bone so there's nothing more I can do until the surgeon arrives. Roman has lost a lot of blood, and that is even more dangerous than it would have been because he is desperately dehydrated and so malnourished." She drew in a deep breath and then looked at me. "Elżbieta, you are going to stay with him and continue to encourage him to drink the salt and sugar mixture I have made. Spoon the water into his mouth, then massage his throat to encourage him to swallow. He needs to rehydrate. This is our priority."

"Are you leaving?" I asked her anxiously. She shook her head, then looked at Mateusz and Truda.

"No. But your parents deserve an explanation. I take full responsibility for this, so it should be me who provides it."

"Come," Truda said and sighed. "I'll make us some coffee."

Roman lay limp in the bathtub. He was covered by a blanket, except for his right arm which rested upon it, the wound oozing through bandages. He was cleaner than I had ever seen him. His head was resting on a folded towel, his face tilted toward me, his eyes closed and his mouth slack.

"I'm so glad you're alive," I said as I sat on the floor beside the bath and took the spoon. "I missed our conversations." I drew in a deep breath, then stared at his wan face as I whispered, "I missed *you.*"

Somewhere else in the apartment, the adults talked, and all I could do was wait for the ax to fall. I knew that upon hearing what Sara had to say, Truda and Mateusz would want to raise their voices—except that they couldn't, in case they roused one of the neighbors. Even though shouting was off the table, I was soon to face a maelstrom of disappointment and anger, and there was nothing I could do to stop it.

"You simply must wake up," I murmured to Roman as I dripped the water into his mouth, then cupped his chin in my hand to tilt his head back. I did this time and time again, although I felt I was achieving little. Water always dribbled out the corners of his mouth, then ran down his beard to soak into the towel. Still, I had nothing else to do other than sit and listen to the muffled voices. At one stage, I heard the volume of

Truda's voice rise sharply, and my efforts to coax the unconscious boy in the bathtub to drink redoubled. "Please wake up
and drink for me."

When the glass was empty, I sank onto the cold tiles and
covered my face with my hands. I sat like that for a long time,
until my bottom had become numb. When I stretched my legs
out in front of me, trying to dispel the pins and needles, Roman
suddenly stirred. His eyelids fluttered, and so I rolled onto my
knees and took his uninjured hand in mine.

"Elżbieta?" he whispered, prying his eyes open with visible
difficulty.

"I'm here," I said. The glass was empty, so I hastily refilled
it with water from the tap. "You're badly dehydrated. Can you
take some sips of this?"

Roman winced as he sat up. He drank the entire glass greed-
ily, then sank back onto the towels. The pallor of his skin, already pale, turned a sickly shade of gray, and he gave me a
panicked look.

"I think I'm going to—"

I reached for the bucket just in time, as what water he had
managed to swallow was violently ejected from his body. The
sound of his retching drew Sara from the kitchen.

"You're awake," she said, delighted, then dismayed when she
saw the bucket. "The surgeon is coming shortly, and he will
rehydrate you through injection. Until then, we just need you
to take small sips of the mixture. Elżbieta, go and ask Truda to
make some more."

I almost protested. I was nervous to face my adoptive parents.
But Sara seemed unconcerned, taking Roman's pulse and wiping his brow with a cool cloth, and so I sighed and scrambled
to my feet. When I stepped into the kitchen, Truda and Mateusz were embracing. I cleared my throat.

"Sara needs more supplies for the hydration mixture."

Mateusz released Truda, and now both of their gazes were

upon me. I couldn't read their expressions, but I dropped my gaze, feeling their disappointment.

"Do you remember the day that my father died?" I asked them, my voice small.

"Of course," Mateusz said.

"Can you imagine a world where Alina brought me to your house and you walked past us and closed the door, refusing to help me?"

"Never," Truda said fiercely.

I forced myself to meet their gazes again. My stomach was alive with butterflies.

"I thought I could be a heroine. I could do something remarkable to honor my family legacy. I was thinking about myself, mostly, but I was also so desperate to do something. If I hadn't found some way to help at least a little, I wouldn't have honored the example you set for me when you took me in or the examples my father and Tomasz set, or even Alina." My voice broke, and tears filled my eyes. "You raised me in a family of courage. And I know I should not have lied to you, and I know I have done the wrong thing. But I had to balance my own conscience as a child of God with my responsibilities and respect for you as my parents. Please forgive me."

Mateusz crossed the room and embraced me in a bear hug so tight that his arms shook around me. He kissed the top of my head and then held on to my upper arms as he looked straight into my eyes.

"We will need to speak about this more later, once your friend has been moved on," he said, his eyes shiny, but I could already tell that he would forgive me for the deception, sooner or later. Truda was going to be a much harder sell. On the other side of the room, she stared at me through narrowed eyes, her arms crossed over her chest.

"I'm going to have nightmares for the rest of my life about you going into that place, Emilia," she said, her tone curt. My real name sounded strange on her lips. "Later, when all of this is over, I'm going to throttle you for lying to us, and I'm going to shout at you for taking such foolish risks. In the meantime…" she puffed out a long breath, then turned and picked up the sugar bowl "…come over here and get what Sara has asked for."

23

Roman

I HAD NO CONCEPT OF WHETHER IT WAS DAY OR NIGHT, but this was a very different blur from the one I had lived through in the ghetto. I drifted along on a sea of pain and sickness, never quite sure if I was awake or hallucinating. A strange man came and went several times, leaving me only with the impression that I had met him before, maybe several times, but I could never quite grasp his name or why he was there. I was vaguely aware of injections in my good arm and then a period of blinding, white-hot pain in my right arm and of suffocating—desperately gasping for air, but someone's hand was over my mouth.

Then maybe I woke for a while, but soon came a fever, and I drifted on a sea of delirium for still more time. Chaim came to visit me, sitting on the end of the bed, cracking jokes and smiling that broad smile I had become so fond of. Later, Andrzej came by, and after him, my whole family. My friends had been vibrant, full of color and life, but as my mother sat on the end of the bed, I saw her in blurred black-and-white, like a photograph. Dawidek held her hand, and although I could hear them murmuring to one another in Yiddish, they didn't speak to me, despite my desperate efforts to get their attention. Samuel waited out of reach by the door until he came and touched my cheek.

"I'm proud of you," he said, but then he, too, was gone.

There were ferocious dreams, too—German soldiers chasing me through a sewer, rotting corpses all around me and a hunger that turned my body inside out. And then sleep—a confused sleep, because I was so exhausted that even as I began to recover, I could barely keep my eyes open for more than minutes at a time. Elżbieta or Sara or the strangers in the apartment would rouse me and spoon-feed me broth or water, and then I would sleep again.

When the storm passed, I woke properly, to golden sunlight filtering through a gauze curtain in an open window, in a room I was vaguely familiar with, only this was the first time I viewed it through clear eyes. I was lying in a bed of clean linen and a soft mattress, wearing clothes finer than any I'd worn since we moved to the ghetto. I sat up gingerly and felt my right arm with the fingers of my left. Heavy bandages and a splint protected the wound, but even so, the light pressure was enough to make me gasp. The fingers on my right hand were swollen and red, but I had a vague memory that at one point, my entire right arm had been in a much worse state.

I felt so weak that I knew not to get out of bed, although I was desperate to relieve myself, and that's when another memory struck me: Sara and Elżbieta's mother, each helping me to use a pan. Humiliation heated my cheeks, and I wasn't sure how I would face them. I didn't have to wonder long because there were footsteps outside my door, and then Sara was there.

"You're awake!" she exclaimed, as she pushed the door open with her back, while precariously balancing a tray on her forearms. The aroma of soup filled the air, and my stomach rumbled.

"I'm feeling much better. I don't know how I'm going to repay you for this."

"You are going to repay me by getting better," she said pointedly, and then she set the tray on the table beside my bed and surveyed me closely. The heat on my cheeks intensified. "Yes, you look so much better. Now we just have to build you up a little."

"How long have I been here?"

"A little over two weeks. You've been very ill, Roman. You turned a corner while the surgeon and I were trying to figure out how we could amputate your arm." I looked at her in alarm, and she gave me a weak smile. "At that point, my friend, it appeared it was your arm or your life. You must have heard us speaking and rallied your body's defenses against the infection."

I looked down at my hand again and tentatively attempted to move my fingers. Pain immediately burst along my upper arm, and I groaned involuntarily with the force of it. Sara gave me a sympathetic look.

"The bone in your arm was damaged when the bullet hit you. It will heal, but it will take some time. You will have to be patient and treat yourself well while you recover. And speaking of that, it is time for soup. Can you manage it yourself, or do you want me to help?"

"I'll manage," I said, as my stomach rumbled again, loudly this time. Sara propped an extra pillow behind my back, then rested the tray of food across my lap. Two rolls and a bowl laden with vegetables, swimming in a thick broth. My vision blurred. "I haven't eaten a meal like this for years."

"I've been trying to build your strength while you've been ill," Sara said gently. "It will take your stomach some time to get used to substantial meals again. I'm sure you're hungry; however, you need to take a few bites, then rest. And then, we will repeat. I will reheat that soup a hundred times if I need to.

It is much better for you to graze all day than to eat too much too quickly and be ill again."

I awkwardly scooped the spoon into the soup, then lifted it to my mouth. It was so good—salty and rich and satisfying. I closed my eyes and gave a groan of satisfaction. Beside me, Sara chuckled.

"I'm not known for my culinary skills," she said wryly. "It's nice to have my cooking so appreciated."

"This is delicious. Incredible," I said, but her words were ringing in my ears: I could feel my body wanting to race through the dish, wanting to devour it all in one sitting. But it would have been a crime to waste such delicious food, and so I resisted the temptation to gorge on it. After a few mouthfuls, I reluctantly motioned toward the tray. "This is the best meal I have ever eaten, but I think I should leave it there for now."

"Good," Sara said, satisfied. "Yes, you truly are on the mend at last." She shifted the tray back onto the table beside the bed and then surveyed me with her gaze. "I imagine that when you escaped, you had something in mind for your future?"

I cast my eyes downward, suddenly ashamed.

"I'm grateful for your help but also so sorry to have put you in danger."

"There is no need to apologize. I'm only relieved that you're alive. But..." She cleared her throat, linked the fingers of her hands and rested them on her lap. "Roman, this is a very delicate conversation, and I know that you are still weak, but we do need to discuss it. I have been helping you with your toileting and bathing over these weeks, and I couldn't help but notice that you are not circumcised."

I had survived years in the ghetto and the violence and a bloody uprising that had taken almost everyone I loved—only to die from embarrassment as this kind woman discussed my body.

"My father was Catholic," I mumbled, unable to meet her

gaze. "He died when I was young, but he and my mother had decided to raise me in his faith. So…"

"It makes no difference to me, except that it means you have easier options for what happens next. Piotr has contacts—he can get you false identity papers."

"I don't have any money."

"You don't need to worry about that."

"Why?"

Her gaze was brimming with pity.

"Simply because it is still the case that sometimes people are good."

I looked away, eyes stinging with unshed tears, but Sara gently placed her hand on my good arm.

"Stay with me. We can tell people that you are my cousin, you've come from out of town after you were injured in a farming accident. This will make sense because people know I am a nurse, and it will explain the comings and goings of the surgeon, should anyone have noticed him. It will mean that you can go about your life. Once you are well, we may even be able to find a job for you."

"I don't understand why you would do this for me."

"Young Elżbieta has been trying to convince me that it is a miracle you survived, but I don't believe in miracles. And after all you have seen and done, I suspect that you don't, either. I can't help but wonder if your survival is not a testament to the strength of your spirit and your resourcefulness. Whatever happens next with this war and the occupation, this nation is going to need strong, resourceful young people like you. You and I don't know each other well, but I hope that you know I will do whatever it takes to help protect the younger generation of this nation. They are—*you* are our future."

"I'll find a job," I promised. "I'll pay you back for everything."

"You'll pay me back by resting and getting well."

★ ★ ★

Elżbieta came to visit me later in the day. She was carrying a pile of books so high, she had to stretch her neck to look over it.

"You're awake!" she said cheerfully. "I could barely believe it when Sara told me. How are you feeling? How's your arm? Have you had enough to eat? I brought you some books, but I wasn't sure what you liked so I brought you a little collection. You'll be bored, and you need to rest, and you told me that you used to like to read at school, and you wanted to be a lawyer, so then I doubled the pile."

Finally finished talking, she set the books down on the table beside my bed and gave me a radiant smile. She looked so different, and it took me a moment to figure out why. When she had visited us in the ghetto, her hair was worn around her shoulders, pinned at her crown to lift into a smooth pompadour above her forehead. Now, her eyes seemed lighter and brighter, her hair was braided, and she was dressed in a light floral dress, rather than the professional skirts and blouses I had seen her wearing at the youth center.

"Did you always talk this much?" I asked. A flush swept over her cheeks.

"Sorry. I'm excited."

"Don't apologize. This is wonderful," I said, laughing in spite of myself. I, too, was excited to see her, glad for the company and the opportunity to thank her, but now that I had seen those books, I was excited for her to leave so I could read. It had been years since I had read a book for the first time. I cautiously reached to pick one up and was surprised to find it was a Bible.

"Sara…she mentioned that you're actually Catholic," Elżbieta muttered, the flush intensifying.

"I'm not really any one thing," I admitted, staring at the book. "My mother was Jewish. My father Catholic."

"Why didn't you tell us?"

I looked up at her and frowned.

"Tell you that I'm not really any one thing?"

"Well, I just mean why didn't you tell us that you weren't Jewish," Elżbieta clarified.

"But I *am* Jewish. My mother was Jewish, and I'm her son."

"I…" She cleared her throat. "I think you know what I mean, Roman."

"Would it have made any difference?"

"Not to me," she said firmly, but then she winced. "But…we may have been able to help you try to escape if we had known that you would pass on this side of the wall."

I sat for a moment, trying to figure out how to explain, and then I pointed to my injured arm.

"You were there the first morning, when I came here, weren't you?"

"Yes."

"You saw my blood."

"Yes."

"If you saw my mother's blood, it would have looked the same. Her blood is in my veins, and her blood is Jewish blood. To the Germans, this was enough for them to decide that I was worthless. But I know that if there are any good parts in me at all, they came from my mother. To deny her heritage is to deny my heritage, and I would rather die than do that," I said, then I shifted awkwardly. "But my father and my mother decided I would be raised Catholic. I went to a Catholic high school. I take Communion and I go to confession. So I am comfortable with Catholic identity papers. But if the only way to get those papers would have been to leave my family behind? I would have faced death proudly before I considered it."

Elżbieta listened, watching me intently, and then nodded. "I respect that."

"God, it is so good to see you," I said, and then I laughed in spite of myself. "I was so sad when you stopped visiting us."

"It's a long story," she said, looking away. "Maybe I will bore you with it another day."

"What have you been doing now that your work in the ghetto has finished?"

"Reading. Knitting. Cooking. Drawing. And repeat," she said with a sigh. "Your arrival was quite a shock, and I'm stuck on this floor until my parents learn to trust me again, especially since the ghetto rebellion. The Germans seem paranoid that the rest of us Poles will be inspired by your battle and try to fight back, too. So they are coming down on us harder than ever, and my parents don't let me out of their sight. But I'm actually relieved that they know the truth. It was hard lying to them."

"Why did you help us?"

"Every role model I have ever had in my life would have done the same," she said and shrugged. "Besides, I don't know how other Christians can sit by and look the other way. My conscience would have been unbearable if I hadn't at least tried to help."

When I yawned, a soft smile covered her face.

"You need to rest."

"You'll come back and see me?"

"I can't think of anything I'd like more."

And she left, leaving a sweetness in the air and a brightness in the room. And it struck me that living next door to Elżbieta indefinitely was not going to be unpleasant at all.

24

Emilia

WITH FALSE IDENTITY PAPERS COURTESY OF UNCLE PIOTR'S mystical network, Roman was a freer man than he'd been in years. These days, it was only his health that kept him prisoner.

Just as he'd seem to improve and begin moving slowly around Sara's apartment, he'd suffer a setback. Several times, the infection in his arm appeared to clear and the wound healed over, then swelled again overnight. With his new set of papers, he might have been able to visit a hospital, but Sara decided it was better to avoid any questions about how he got the wound. So every time his infection flared up, she would call one of her doctor friends to perform another agonizing debridement to clean out the wound. And while Sara tried to build his gut up slowly to handle consistent food, several times he was stricken with bouts of violent vomiting or diarrhea, and then he was all the way back to sipping spoonfuls of broth.

"Why is this taking so long?" I asked Sara one day, when I

visited to find Roman was once again in bed, resting after a night of intense illness.

"He came to us very near death, Elżbieta," she said gently. "A person does not recover from that kind of physical trauma overnight." Her face grew sad, and she added carefully, "Nor the mental trauma. Just remember that."

I could sense how frustrating it was for him to have freedom within his grasp, only to be held at bay by his own body. Roman was never one to complain, and at times it was hard to even get him to acknowledge his pain.

"How are you feeling today?" I'd ask him, even when he was positively green or Sara told me that he'd been awake all night in pain.

"Just fine," he'd always say and shrug.

But for all of the challenges, those months became a magical interlude for me. The war raged on outside Sara's apartment, but inside her spare room—the room that was now Roman's room, right on the other side of my wall—all was quiet, except for the beating of my heart and the quiet rhythm of our chatter.

"You're *so* smart," I said, shaking my head as he told me about how he'd been unable to sleep the night before, so he'd read through one of Sara's nursing handbooks. Now, he was full of all sorts of information about how the typhus inoculations worked and why soap was so useful for preventing the spread of disease. He seemed to possess an uncanny ability to absorb information, even if he'd only read it once.

"You're smart, too," he said.

"Not *book*-smart like that."

"Well, I was good at school."

"When did you finish?"

"I was thirteen when they stopped us from going to school, but I was finishing tenth grade."

My eyes widened.

"You *are* book-smart."

"I skipped some grades," he said, shrugging, as if it was nothing, then asked, "How about you? When did you finish?"

"Fourth grade," I muttered, flushing. "Mama tried to homeschool me after that. She did her best, but she'd had a limited education, so she really wasn't able to teach me." I still called Truda and Mateusz by their real names, but Roman had no idea they weren't my real parents, so whenever he was around, I forced myself to remember to call them *Mama* and *Papa* instead.

"How did you learn to draw like you do?"

"I was bored back at our old house. There wasn't much to do, but Mama and her sister gave me paper to draw," I said, then I asked him hesitantly, "Would you like to see some more of my drawings?"

I'd collected dozens of them over the year since Sara gave me those notebooks, mostly sketches in charcoal. I fetched the pile and held my breath as Roman flicked through them.

"Most of these are of the ghetto," he commented.

"I know. That's why I couldn't show anyone else."

He studied a rough sketch I'd made of the youth center building, tracing his finger over the lines of the doors.

"This building was still there when I left, but most of the rest of the ghetto had been burned down."

"I think they finished the job while you were recovering," I told him hesitantly. He looked at me in surprise. "It's *all* rubble now, all of the blocks of the ghetto. There's nothing left, not even the wall in most parts. Even the Great Synagogue is gone. The SS blew it up...punishment for the Uprising."

"I'm still glad we did it," he said.

"What was it like?" I asked him softly. Roman looked at the paper again.

"I thought it would feel cleansing to avenge my family. To avenge the suffering. But it wasn't enough." He touched the sketch again, then asked, "Why did you draw so much of the ghetto? It was hardly a scenic landscape."

Roman shuffled through another paper, another scene from the streets he'd been confined to for years. This time, I'd drawn a body on a sidewalk, the woman's arm stretched out above her head, reaching toward help that would never come.

"You expected that vengeance would be cleansing," I replied quietly. "I think when I draw, I'm looking for the same thing. You know sometimes when your thoughts are so cloudy you can't make sense of them? That's when I draw. I can usually find a way to let things go if I just draw what I'm thinking about. When I'm really overwhelmed, I pray and I draw."

"How do you know how to capture it?" he asked and pointed to the shading around the woman's face. "How do you know how thick the line should be? How do you know where to put the shadow?"

"I *feel* it," I said, leaning forward to trace a line just beneath his finger. "There's an endless dance between the shadow and the light…the way the shadows shift as the light shifts, illuminating different parts of a thing, bringing different pieces into focus. Capturing an image like this is feeling that dance in my bones and pouring it onto the paper."

He looked at me, his gaze thoughtful.

"You are so lucky to have such a talent. But you're also lucky to have an outlet."

"What's your outlet?"

He shrugged. "I guess I have to figure that out, now."

Now that our bedrooms were separated only by a thin wall, I sometimes heard his nightmares. He would cry out in anguish, and I'd startle awake, heart racing at the thought of his suffering. Usually, I would think about slipping out of bed to go to him, but I never did. Instead, I'd lie in bed and pray for him. Often, if the shouting went on for a while, I'd hear the creak of the stairs as Sara went to check on him.

The more time I spent with Roman, the more fretful Truda and Mateusz became about the propriety of it all.

"Keep the door open. Don't sit on the bed with him. Don't *touch* him," Truda would always instruct me when I was heading down the hall. Mateusz, too, found plenty to worry about.

"Please don't tell him the truth about yourself," he said.

"We can trust him," I said lightly. "He can't exactly leave the house just yet anyway—he's too weak—but even if he could, I know he would never betray me."

"We were only going to tell Piotr, remember? And now Sara knows, and then you widen the circle to Roman, and where does it end? We may as well paint your real name on the side of the building."

"But it's been more than a year," I said impatiently. "No one is even looking for me!"

"You don't know that. And maybe no one is looking for you because you have slipped off the radar. Let's say your friend recovers, and he goes out into the world again. He is a loose cannon, Emilia." Mateusz sighed. "Do you really believe he will lie low once he is well? He will find trouble because there is so much trouble in his heart. If he gets mixed up in the underground again, if he is captured and tortured, he cannot betray your secret if he doesn't know it. Promise me, or we will have to keep you two apart."

He left me no choice. I sighed impatiently but gave him my word. My time with Roman meant too much to me to risk it.

25

Roman

"IT'S TOO RISKY. YOU CANNOT BE SERIOUS ABOUT HIM living here forever."

I was in my room reading one of Sara's novels when the words floated up the stairs from her living area. It was late—long after I'd normally be asleep, but the book engrossed me, and I was feeling a little stronger. I had closed my door most of the way, but the latch hadn't caught, and it swung open just a little. I'd noticed that as it happened, but I'd been too lazy to get up to shut it again. Now, I closed the book and sat up, frowning as I strained to listen.

"Oh, you are uncomfortable with risk when it suits you?" Sara hissed. "I *knew* this was going to be a problem when I had to nag you to get his new papers. There is no money to be made from him, so now you are concerned about risk."

I slipped out of bed and walked slowly to the door so I could hear better. She was speaking to Piotr, and they both sounded frustrated.

"Sara, I am worried about you," Piotr said. "He is Jewish. This—"

"He is a *Catholic* boy who had a Jewish *family*," she snapped.

"You know that, to the Germans, there is no difference."

"It doesn't matter to me anyway. This is *my* home, and he will stay here."

"And if you are caught? If he is caught?"

"If I am caught for *this* small thing, I will just be relieved I haven't been caught for everything else I am mixed up in."

"I still can't believe you took her into that place," Piotr said suddenly, abruptly.

"This again? You know I had no idea about her papers. You didn't tell me."

"*You* didn't tell *me* you were sneaking into the bloody ghetto and taking her with you!"

"It is so fascinating to me that you have taken *that* child into your heart in such a generous way with no benefit to yourself, and yet the very idea of me doing the same for Roman is driving you crazy."

There was a stiff silence, then Piotr muttered, "As soon as they came here, I loved her. That's why I'm protective of her. I always wanted children and regretted that fatherhood had never happened for me. God has given me a second chance to know what it feels like to love someone like that. That's exactly why I'm so frustrated with you for taking these risks with her life."

"You take risks every day," Sara scoffed.

"That is my business. It's how I am earning money to support them all."

"Piotr, we both know that you could wind up your business, as you call it, here and take them back to Lodz tomorrow, and you could all still live comfortably."

"It's not a crime to make money."

"You chastise me for taking risks, even while you exploit the vulnerable!"

"There is money to be made in this war, Sara," he said impatiently. The whole conversation had the tone of one they had thrashed out a thousand times, a conversation they both sounded exhausted by. "I am saving a nest egg for us so that when it's all over, we can have a good life."

Sara groaned in frustration.

"I've told you I won't marry you. Not while you're mixed up in this *other* business."

"You won't marry me because you are stubborn and independent." Piotr's tone softened as he tried to cajole her, but Sara wasn't having it.

"No," she said abruptly. "I won't marry you because my first husband was a good man—a man with compassion and empathy and values. To tie myself to a man like *you* would dishonor his memory. Get out. Get out!"

I heard the door slam and then the slide and click of the door locking. Sara's footsteps were heavy as she crossed the apartment to her room, and then I heard her door close, too.

"What does your uncle do for work?" I asked Elżbieta the next day. I was finally making consistent strides with my health and had graduated to spending my days downstairs in Sara's apartment. I was relieved about this. I'd been so desperate for company that I hadn't mentioned it to Elżbieta, but it didn't seem right to be lying in my bed, talking to the prettiest girl I knew for hours on end.

"He and my father both inherited textile factories from their father. Uncle Piotr's factory is in Lodz, and he has a manager who is running it for him because he came to Warsaw to start some new kind of business. I'm not really clear on the details— he's just told me he's a *broker*, whatever that means. He also seems to be able to get his hands on *anything*, like your new papers," Elżbieta said easily.

"It's a legitimate business?" I asked her hesitantly.

"Legitimate?" she said and frowned. "What do you mean?"

"It doesn't matter."

"He does sometimes dip into the black market. Everyone does."

"I know. But he's not... I mean his business isn't entirely the black market. Right?"

Her eyebrows shot up. She blinked, then frowned again.

"I don't think so. But..." She cleared her throat. "I guess that would explain a few things. Sara has hinted to me that she cares for him, but their values don't exactly line up. I thought she was just obsessed with her work, maybe reluctant to tell him about what she was really doing." She shrugged, seemingly at ease again. "Well, even if he does run his business on the black market, I'm sure it's helping people. He certainly helped you with your papers, right?"

"And...yours?" I said. Elżbieta's eyebrows knit.

"What?"

"I heard Sara arguing with him. She mentioned something about your papers, too."

Elżbieta looked at the coffee table between us, then swallowed.

"Please don't ask me. I promised my parents I wouldn't tell you. I've already broken so many promises to them. I need to keep one."

I was stung by this. I thought Truda and Mateusz liked me. Even so, I forced a smile and a nod.

"We all have our secrets in war, don't we?" I said, as lightly as I could.

"Isn't that the truth?" she said with a sigh.

A new thought struck me, and I questioned her urgently. "Just tell me—are you in danger?"

She shrugged and gave me a half smile.

"Not nearly as much as you are."

But I could see that she really wasn't ready to talk to me

about whatever secrets she was keeping, and so, reluctantly, I let the matter drop.

"Okay," I said quietly. "I won't ask you again."

"Thank you."

I scanned my gaze over her delicate features, those sparkling green eyes and that golden hair I wanted so badly to touch one day. I thought about how it would feel to lift my hand to reach for her, to take some of those wavy strands and rub them between my fingers. Her hair looked soft, and sometimes when she breezed past me, I'd catch a hint of her scent on the air. She was my closest friend, wriggling her way to an emotional intimacy with me in a way that not even Chaim had ever done. But more than that, she was a distraction and an escape.

When I was alone, sometimes I became lost in my thoughts—in the swirling violence of everything I'd seen and done and in the reality that my work was not yet done. My body was forcing me to rest, but once it recovered, I had to find a way to get back to the fight.

But when I was alone with Elżbieta, I often found myself lost in different kinds of thoughts: of how good it felt to talk to her, to grow closer to her. Of how easy our friendship was, and a sense of wonder that while I was focused on her, I often slipped into an accidental kind of peace. I was most confused about that. I had so much left to do in that war, and I knew I was likely to lose my life in battle.

But when I was with Elżbieta, I wanted to pretend I lived in a different world—a world where I had a future.

26

Roman
25 July, 1944

I DIDN'T KNOW THE CODE NAME OF THE SCOUT WHO knocked on my door at dawn. Sara answered it, then knocked on my door to rouse me.

"Scout mail is here for you, Pigeon," she called playfully through my door.

I rolled out of bed and, in my haste to get to the front door, almost stumbled on the stairs. Sara was supportive when I had joined the *Szare Szeregi* ten months earlier, even if she remained amused by some of our conventions—like our code names, which we used religiously. I'd been mildly amused by the code names, too, at first, until my Scoutmaster instructed me to choose a name for myself.

"Pigeon," I had said. And all of a sudden, using a code name seemed like an honor.

When I reached the landing, I found a child standing in the hallway outside our apartment. He couldn't have been more than twelve years old. He was wearing tattered clothing, but I had no way to tell if he was in costume or genuinely living as a street rat.

"W hour. Tonight, five o'clock," the child said, but he was already shifting from foot to foot, eager to run to his next task.

"Are you sure you have that right?" I asked him, frowning. I had been expecting this, anticipating it even, but I'd been told to expect W hour to be at sunrise. Five in the evening made little sense.

"That is the message. Five o'clock tonight. Do you confirm receipt and understanding?"

When I nodded, the boy ran down the hallway and disappeared into the stairwell, continuing on to his next home. I knew that young *Zawisza* Scouts like him would be running all over the city that day, couriers from junior Scouting units across the city, spreading this message to thousands of soldiers and auxiliary workers.

W hour was another code name—*W* for the Polish word *wybuch*, meaning *outbreak*. This signified the start of Operation Tempest. The Polish Home Army, known as *Armia Krajowa*—the AK—had planned an extensive series of anti-German uprisings, aimed at seizing control of Warsaw. The planning had been underway for months, but the execution was on hold until the AK leadership identified just the right moment. We needed the Germans distracted, fortifying their territory against the advancing Soviet Red Army, but we had to move before the Red Army seized control.

I was nervous about the Soviets, concerned that as the footing of the war shifted and the Germans began to lose power, all this meant was that we would be caught between two very powerful and untrustworthy enemies. But I was a simple foot soldier, a member of the Boy Scouts' senior division—the Assault Group, the *Grupy Szturmowe*. Like all other Boy Scouts seventeen and over, I had spent the last ten months in combat training preparing for this Uprising, and just like that messenger boy, all I needed to do were the specific tasks I was ordered to do. I had to trust that the plan was in the hands of those who could see the bigger picture.

When I came downstairs, Sara was dressed for work, sitting at the kitchen table with her coffee.

"Today?" she asked. The Uprising was an open secret across the city—some intelligence chatter suggested even the Germans knew it was coming, although they had no idea how extensive it would be. I drew a fierce and constant pride that the actions of my Jewish brothers and sisters had inspired and motivated the rest of the city to mimic them.

"I thought we would have more time. Another few days, maybe weeks. We aren't exactly ready..." I exhaled, tension across my shoulders. My troop would be fighting with the AK Wigry Battalion, and we would be stationed just a few blocks from the apartment. We were short on weapons, but the weapons we did have were stashed across the city. They would not be easy to retrieve quickly without drawing attention.

"Be safe," Sara begged, as she came around the table to embrace me.

"I will do my best," I promised, which wasn't a lie. I was more than ready to die for Poland—every single time I met with my squad, I repeated our oath: *I pledge to you that I shall serve with the Gray Ranks, safeguard the secrets of the organization, obey orders and not hesitate to sacrifice my life.*

I meant those words with all my heart, but I also intended to make my life count. Wasn't that exactly what Chaim had told me to do? *Don't waste it* had been his final words—his dying words. Here, a second chance loomed for me to die for my country, too, in a way that would mean something. If we could just take Warsaw back, it would bolster the spirits of the rest of the nation.

That didn't mean I wasn't scared. I felt sick at the thought of returning to combat—memories of the Ghetto Uprising were fresh on my mind, even twelve months after it ended. Adren-aline was already coursing through my body, and as I stared down at Sara, I felt a filial affection that made me wish I could stay, to shelter in the apartment and keep her safe.

"You be safe, too," I said. "Please." I hesitated, then added, "I wish you would go to Lodz with Piotr." Theirs was an ever-unstable relationship. I'd catch them embracing on the sofa one day, but by the next, they'd barely be speaking, and I under-stood the tension. They obviously cared deeply for one another, but their priorities were out of sync. Piotr saw the war as an opportunity to grow his wealth; Sara saw the occupation as a humanitarian tragedy and believed she had a moral obligation to help in any way she could.

But with whispers of the citywide Uprising looming, even Piotr was ready to hunker down. He decided to pause his black-market business and take Truda, Mateusz and Elżbieta to shel-ter at his apartment in Lodz. Elżbieta was predictably frustrated by this because she wanted to stay and help. I was only relieved the matter was out of her hands, and I desperately wished Sara would join them.

"I won't think of running away," Sara said abruptly. "I'm going to skip work and go to the Church of Our Lady," she said, referring to an iconic church just around the corner from our apartment. "The Sisters from the convent over on Hoża Street have evacuated their orphanage in case things get rough. Those left behind are going to operate a makeshift clinic in the base-ment. I know the nuns from the good work they've done with Jewish children over the years so I'm going to help. When you or your friends need assistance, that's where you'll find me."

I kissed the top of her head, then turned to leave but hesitated at the doorway. Matylda had been arrested six months earlier. For a whole month, whenever there was a knock at the door, Sara and I would hold our breath, expecting it was the Gestapo. Instead, the announcement came that Matylda had been executed, with no explanation of charges, and not a single member of the team beyond her so much as interviewed. The loss hit Sara hard, especially as she settled into the reality that she had now assumed both Matylda's senior position with the City of Warsaw…and her unofficial position, as the sole gatekeeper of the identity of over 2,500 Jewish children, scattered across Poland in orphanages and private homes. In the aftermath of Matylda's death, I'd asked Sara about my sister.

"Matylda left a record, and we've placed it somewhere for safekeeping. It's not easy for me to access," she had said, her gaze sad. "When the war is over, I'll hand it on to Jewish leaders, and they'll be able to reunite children with their families… where that's possible. Eleonora's new identity is safely hidden there, and until the war ends, it's best we leave all of those records untouched."

I trusted her, but everything had changed in the months since that conversation. I now understood that for me the war could end as early as five o'clock that evening. I didn't want to die without any word of my sister, so as I lingered in the doorway, I drew in a deep breath and asked again.

"Sara?"

"Yes?"

"Can you tell me anything about Eleonora?"

"I thought you would ask again, so I did look her up." Sara smiled, then said gently, "Eleonora is doing well. She and her new family are safe at Częstochowa."

My eyes burned with tears of gratitude.

"Thank you, Sara. Truly. For everything."

Sara's eyes filled with tears, too, and we stared at each other, an ocean of unspoken words between us.

"Go!" she said suddenly, waving me off as a tear trickled down her cheek. "Do what you need to do."

I crossed the hallway and thumped on Elżbieta's door. Uncle Piotr answered, rubbing his eyes blearily.

"Son," he said, frowning. He had warmed to me over time and had gradually come to accept my presence in Sara's apartment. He even procured some handguns for my troop, although we paid a hefty price for the favor.

"It's happening, Piotr. You need to get them out of the city by five o'clock today."

"I see," Piotr said and sighed. "So soon? I have things to finish…"

"Well, I will tell the AK that they need to wait, so you can finish making your money before they free our city," I said dryly. Piotr shot me a look. "I have to go, but is Elżbieta awake?"

"I doubt that," he said.

"I hate to ask…"

"Come in." Piotr sighed, shifting out of the doorway. He walked toward the kitchen, stopping only to stick his head into the stairwell that led to Elżbieta's room to call, "Elżbieta! You have an early-morning visitor." Then he muttered something about coffee and shuffled toward the kitchen.

I helped myself to a chair in the sitting room, but soon Elżbieta appeared, pulling a dressing gown over her pajamas. Her hair was up in a bonnet, and her face was puffy with sleep. My heart contracted painfully at the sight of her.

If anything could have been enough to make me want to survive the war, Elżbieta Rabinek was it. I loved her fiercely, even though I had never told her as much. It would not have been fair. To tell her I loved her would have meant promising a future, and I knew that we could never share one. She and I spent so much time together over that year—hours upon hours of playful conversation and in-depth philosophical chats. She liked to lie on the floor of Sara's sitting room to draw while I read, and I liked just being in the same room as her. The Uprising was always going to be difficult on our friendship, and I tried my best to prepare her for that.

"I don't want to go to Lodz," she told me flatly as she entered the room. "I want to stay here. The Girl Scouts have auxiliary units. I know they do. Help me find a contact today. They are surely going to need help." From the kitchen, I heard Uncle Piotr sigh heavily at this.

"Elżbieta," I said softly. "This is not your battle." Her eyes flashed fire.

"Is this not a battle for Polish sovereignty? Am I not Polish?" she said incredulously.

"You are, and Poland is going to need brilliant, creative souls like yours to rebuild."

"And yours," she said, frowning at me. I first realized how far gone I was when I caught myself thinking about how adorable her frowns were. "I hate it when you talk like this, as if you're already dead."

"I just came to say goodbye," I said, my throat tight. Between the Rabineks in apartment 6 and Sara in apartment 5, the top floor of this building had become my home because it contained my new family. Leaving was harder than I had anticipated, but I had to do it—my troop, my city and my nation were counting on me. I rose and took a step toward Elżbieta.

"Go to Lodz," I said quietly. "Be safe and be well."

"Come with us," she whispered. We'd had that conversation, too, several times in the weeks that had passed.

"You know I can't."

She closed the gap between us and flung her arms around my waist, pulling me close. I luxuriated in her embrace just for a moment, but then I gently unwrapped her arms and stepped away.

"Tell your parents I said thank-you and goodbye," I whispered unevenly, as the tears began to pour down her cheeks.

"Tell them yourself when we see you again," she said flatly. I nodded, then walked toward the door.

"Bye, Piotr," I called.

"Goodbye, son. Do us proud."

When I reached the door, Elżbieta called out quietly. "Roman?"

I spun to look at her one last time. She was standing with one arm wrapped around her waist, her pale face wet with tears. She lifted her free hand to her lips, pressed a kiss against it and blew it toward me.

I pretended to catch it, then tuck it into my pocket, and then I left, as quickly as I could, before my resolve weakened.

By eight that morning, I reached our headquarters on Długa Street. We would be attempting to seize control of the Śródmieście district—essentially, the area around the Old Town district, including Miodowa Street.

I was the youngest member of my squad of twenty-one: everyone else was eighteen or older, but I was also the only member who'd seen active combat. As we prepared for the Uprising to begin, I felt like the cynical old man of the group. My squadmates were in a jovial mood, inspired at the thought of what lay ahead.

"I'm going to kill so many Germans, I'll be notorious across the Reich. They will train their young soldiers to beware the mighty Sword," one of the squad members announced. Sword looked like he was about thirteen years old. He was clean-shaven and baby-faced and skinny as a twig. The only evidence that he really was twenty years old was that he was at least a foot taller than I, extraordinarily tall even for an adult.

"I'm going to kill one for every member of my family who has died," Vodka declared.

"Can you even count that high?" Tank mocked him playfully.

"I will take off my socks so that I can count on my toes, just to be sure."

"You think it is going to feel good to kill them, don't you?" I said mildly. I had just finished lifting a wooden crate full of ammunition into place, and their lighthearted chatter irritated me to the point that I was writhing inside. The boys all turned to me, probably startled to hear me speak. I had made a determined effort to avoid friendship with any one of them. I wasn't about to make the same mistake I'd made with Chaim.

"It will," Tank said flatly. "My mother bled to death in front of me, Pigeon. It's going to feel damned good to get revenge."

"I have news for you: it won't *feel good*. You won't feel vindicated. There is no justice in this war, only more pain. And if I have to listen to you idiots laughing about this for one more minute this afternoon, I don't know how I will stop myself from shooting you myself," I snapped.

"Pigeon," our commander, Needle, called to me, his tone flat. He pointed to a spot by his feet. "Over here. Now." I glared at the young men, then walked to the commander.

"Sir."

"They are idiots, and they are naive, but they are excited. When the shooting starts, that excitement is going to disappear in a heartbeat, and they are going to realize how out of their depth they are. You don't need to hasten that, Pigeon. When the time comes, you and I will need to be there to refocus them. Until then, let them enjoy their last hours of innocence. They will never get to feel like this again."

"Yes, sir."

"At ease, Pigeon."

He had a point, but it was still almost more than I could take to listen to the boys as they laughed away the last few hours before the worst afternoon of their life.

We didn't make it to five o'clock. One of the other squads in our battalion was transporting weaponry in the back of a cart on Nowomiejska Street, just a block away from our headquarters, when they were stopped by a German patrol. Just after one o'clock, a volley of gunshots from the street left the headquarters in stunned and panicked silence.

"Armbands on!" our commander shouted, and we all reached into our pockets for the red-and-white armbands that signified we were fighting with the Polish side. As I ran from the doorway, training my rifle at the surrounding buildings, I thought about Elżbieta.

I'm doing this for you. For our country, so that you can be free.

As my feet hit the cobblestones on Długa Street, I cast my gaze back toward our building on Miodowa Street and whispered a prayer for Elżbieta and her family. I could only hope that they had left the city early.

27

Emilia

UNCLE PIOTR PREPARED DETAILED, CAREFUL PLANS FOR our escape to Lodz. Truda, Mateusz and I were to stay home to pack while he attended one last business meeting.

"Do we really need to do this?" I asked, as he stood in the hallway, donning his hat. He checked himself in the mirror, then shot me a wink.

"It's an important meeting, Elżbieta."

"I wasn't talking about your meeting, Uncle Piotr. I was talking about Lodz."

I'd gradually come to terms with the news that kindly, jovial Uncle Piotr was also something of a wartime vulture, snapping up precious black-market commodities and reselling them for as much money as the market would allow. I tried, on more than one occasion, to challenge the ethics of this, but he saw me as a little girl with no important opinions of her own.

"We could stay and see if we can contribute. Roman knows

people in the AK, and Sara knows doctors and nurses. I'm sure if we were to stay we could—"

"Elżbieta," Truda said sharply. I turned to look at her, and she pursed her lips. "We are most definitely leaving, and, Piotr, we should leave as soon as we can. Do you really need to do this deal first? Why must we cut it so close?"

"I will be back at three o'clock with a driver and a car. The insurgents will rise at five. That is eight hours away! There is plenty of time for us to clear the city," he said firmly, then he winked and tapped me on the nose. "You're going to love Lodz. My apartment is twice the size of this place, and the restaurants are fantastic."

I wasn't interested in a palatial apartment or restaurants. My heart was heavy, and I was so conflicted about leaving both the city and Roman.

Over our year as neighbors, our relationship had never evolved beyond friendship, although at times, I had the sense that we were skating on the edge of something more. Our eyes would lock in a way that was fascinating and delicious. On more than one occasion, I found myself just staring at him, thinking about his hazel eyes or the way his hair fell into neat curls around his head. I was drawn to him—not just emotionally but also physically. I wondered how it would feel to rest my head on his chest, to listen to his heartbeat, to breathe in his scent. Sometimes at night, I'd lie in bed, and I'd lift my hand to touch the wall between us, comforted that he was on the other side.

But for all of the ways I was drawn to him, something held me back. It was a glimpse of darkness that I understood, even as I feared it. He was relentlessly driven, barely out of bed after his recovery before he was out looking for a contact in the Gray Ranks.

"Maybe you should give it more time," I'd said to Roman, and he'd shaken his head, as if I was crazy to suggest such a thing.

"There is an uprising coming! I need to contribute. I can't waste this second chance."

"I'm not saying you shouldn't fight. It's just that if you are stronger, you can contribute more."

"Or I can rest in bed until I die of old age, and if everyone else opts to do the same, Poland will never be free. No one is coming to save us, Elżbieta."

Other times, he would speak about his martyrdom with a glint in his eye that I came to understand was longing. It seemed Roman wasn't just willing to sacrifice his life for our country, he was determined to.

"Aren't you afraid to die?" I asked him hesitantly one day.

"I already know death," he said, shrugging. "I've been so close to it, I could feel it. I know how it smells, I know the rhythm of it. Whatever lies on the other side, almost everyone I've ever loved is already there waiting for me. Why would I be afraid?"

I once described his anger as righteous anger, and I still understood that to be true. But I wondered where this darkness would lead, and I was nervous to link myself to someone who seemed so determined to destroy himself. I had closely watched Sara's relationship with Piotr over that year, and I knew she refused to make a commitment because there was an obvious disconnect in what mattered most to each of them.

I drew inspiration from that. I had a sense that I was connected to Roman in some way that was predestined, but even so, I controlled how fast and how deep that connection would grow. If I were honest with myself, deep down I *wanted* a future with him, but even when our gazes lingered or when our hands almost brushed or our conversation skirted the edge of how we felt about one another, I could not bring myself to cross that line. Roman, too, seemed reticent. I saw the way he stared back at me, and I was quite certain he felt something beyond friendship, too.

Whatever had been going on between us that year, neither one of us opted to confront it directly. And now, all I could do was pray for him, and I intended to do that with all of my might.

The first gunshots rang out just after one o'clock. They weren't in the immediate vicinity but somewhere in the blocks around us, loud enough to be startling. At Mateusz's shocked command, Truda and I joined him flat against the floor.

"It's not on our block," he told us, peering up at the window, as if we could see anything from the carpet on the third floor. "But stay low. Stray bullets can be unpredictable."

"But it's too early," I protested. "They said it would start at five…"

"Something has gone wrong already," Truda said, gnawing her lip. "My God. Piotr is out there. And Sara! She will be at work downtown."

"Sara was going to skip work to set up the field hospital at the church," Mateusz reminded her. "And Piotr is smart and a survivor. He will be fine."

"What do we do?" I whispered, looking up at the window. Above us, birds had scattered at the gunfire and were soaring in a cloudless sky. If I could block my ears, it could have been a perfect summer day—the perfect day for a car ride to Lodz.

"We don't have a choice," Mateusz said with a sigh. "Piotr was bringing the car back from his contact in Żoliborz, so we can't exactly go without him." Another volley of gunfire sounded. Mateusz winced. "Besides, now is obviously not the time to cross the city."

We sweated through an anxious hour on the floor of the apartment, listening to distant shouts and sporadic gunfire. Mateusz insisted we stay low, but when the shrill ring of the phone rang out, he crawled into the hallway to answer it. When he returned, his expression was grim.

"It was Piotr. He says there is early fighting in the Żoliborz district, too. He is going to stay there for now and try to get back if the situation calms down."

"And if it doesn't?" Truda asked.

"There are too many variables to make a plan, my love. Piotr suggested we stay here unless it becomes unsafe. He has spoken to some of the insurgents, and they tell him they are confident they will have a citywide stronghold within a few days, at which point the Red Army has agreed to back them up. God willing, the city should be safely in Polish hands in just a few days."

"So we will be in the city for the Uprising, after all," Truda said, sighing. She glanced at me. "You got your wish."

"I didn't want to be stuck on the floor of our apartment while the city fought around us," I muttered.

"At least the three of us are all together," Mateusz said suddenly, but he sounded nervous, and his gaze kept skipping toward the window. I reached across and put my hand over his and smiled.

"That is a silver lining," I said quietly.

"We'll just keep our heads down," Truda announced. "We'll just stay inside, lie low and wait for the drama to pass."

By nightfall on the first day, gunfire was rising in every direction, and other sounds came with it: shouts of pain and cries of fear, the whine of air-raid sirens, then the roar of planes overhead sporadically and explosions that rattled the windows. Whenever we heard a plane or an air-raid siren, we would run down the stairs to the basement to cower in the bomb shelter with the other residents of our building. The all clear would sound, and we would run back up the flights of stairs to our apartment all over again.

My thoughts were very much with the missing members of our extended family—especially with Roman. I was mindful of Uncle Piotr and Sara, too, and I kept them in my prayers, but I had the feeling that those two had the sense to run from conflict if it erupted around them. I knew with absolute certainty that regardless of how hot the battle was, Roman would run toward it.

On the third day, sounds of victory came from the street below us, and when I crept to the window, I saw AK soldiers and civilians walking freely along the road, waving banners with the vibrant red and white of the Polish flag.

"Can we join them?" I asked, but Mateusz pursed his lips.

"Not yet. Stay away from the window."

And so, for one more day, we maintained our life in limbo, eating as little as we could to stretch our supplies, staying low to the floor. I was more frustrated than scared by then, hearing the sounds of jubilation from down the street, while we seemed to be in a self-inflicted siege.

On the fourth day, the front door opened just after dawn, and Uncle Piotr was there, larger-than-life as he always had been, laughing at our tears of relief.

"All of this fuss for nothing," he said and chuckled. "I'm a survivor—you should all know that by now. The street fighting was intense down there in Żoliborz, so it seemed safer to hunker down. And would you believe it—I happened upon some weapons while I was there and sold them for a tidy profit."

Even Mateusz's nostrils flared at this, but I was too relieved to focus on Piotr's commercial exploits. Instead, I asked him, "How did you get back?"

"I came across some wonderful soldiers, and they were happy to exchange safe passage for some money. There are pockets under Polish control all over the city—my girl, it is glorious!" He looked at us, confused. "But wait—why are you three hiding up here when the streets are safer than they have been in years?"

"I'm not sure, Piotr," Mateusz said, glancing warily at the window. "There is so much we don't know."

"I wasn't sure how all of this was going to unfold, brother. You know that. But the scenes I have just witnessed—Polish flags flying proudly on the street, Polish soldiers in command at last! I feel like this is how it begins… This is the beginning of the end! Now let us go and find some good food and vodka to celebrate."

"Wait a minute," Truda said abruptly. "The plan was for us to go to Lodz. We agreed it would be safer to get out of Warsaw. Things are going well for the insurgents now, but there's no guarantee that's going to continue. Shouldn't we try to get out?"

Piotr shook his head.

"The AK has strongholds all over the place, but they aren't connected yet. We control pockets of the city, rather than a safe corridor we could use to get out. We are stuck here for now, Truda, but you'll see, it's going to be okay. We just need to give it a few days, and you'll see."

A few days stretched into a week. I didn't see Sara—Mateusz insisted I stay inside just in case of trouble—but Piotr went to the church basement occasionally to check on her.

"It's unpleasant down there," he told me, grimacing.

"Unpleasant?" I repeated.

"Blood, injuries…nasty business. But you know Sara. She's in her element with that kind of thing. She's fine."

"Did you see Roman?" I asked hesitantly. He shook his head.

"No, and Sara hasn't seen him, either, but we've heard news of his battalion. Most of this district is under AK control. You should be proud of him."

"I am," I said, "but I'm also worried."

"Well, his headquarters are right near the church. If things get hectic and we haven't heard from him, I'll wander down and ask around for you, okay?"

"I could come with you?"

Uncle Piotr smiled. "Let's just see how the next few days go."

Although the strongholds closest to us had not fallen, it was obvious something was changing in the districts beyond. Aerial bombing was increasing, and we made frantic trips up and down the stairs every time the air-raid siren sounded—now several times every day and night. From the first week of August, explosions constantly rang out, and I noticed a different kind of gunfire. It was sustained and constant—like dozens of machine guns firing, and sometimes all at once. For twenty-four hours, it seemed either our side or theirs was firing without a break. There were so many gunshots, the sounds all blended together until there was a general, awful hum echoing out across the city.

"What could it be?" I asked at breakfast. The jubilation in the streets had faded to nothing, and around our breakfast table, a confused, strained silence had fallen.

"Maybe it isn't even shooting," Truda suggested. "How could they be shooting so much? It sounds like the whole German army is firing at once. It could be some new machine they have invented."

"No," Mateusz said, shaking his head. "I think it is gunshots."

"I have an idea," Uncle Piotr announced, and then he left the apartment, returning after an hour with a wireless radio in his arms. These had been illegal in the city for some time, although plenty of people defied this order. Piotr turned the device on, and we crowded around it, listening as he tuned across various stations. First we found a Soviet station, broadcasting from their stronghold to the east of Warsaw, promising that relief was coming soon and encouraging the citizens of Warsaw to fight to push the Germans out.

"Could the noise be the Soviets?" I asked.

"No, it is coming from the west, not the east," Piotr murmured. He twisted the dials and this time found an underground AK station. There was a general update with a mixed bag of news—some areas lost, others gained—but the headline news made my blood run cold.

"…Germans are going from home to home in Wola, dragging civilians of all ages to the street and executing them in retribution for the Uprising. Heavy casualties are reported, with massive piles of bodies in streets around the district. Reconnaissance reports suggest tens of thousands of civilians may already be dead. Particularly heavy losses are reported at the railway embankment on Górczewska Street and factories on Wolska Street…"

"They're only a few kilometers away from us," Mateusz whispered.

Piotr reached forward and snapped the volume button off, the action so sharp and violent that it startled me. When I looked to his face, I found him ashen, and he was staring at *me* in horror.

"We should have left when we had the chance!" Truda exclaimed, pushing back her chair, her features twisted with rage. She slammed her fist down onto the table. "You just had to do one last deal, didn't you? What will your *zloty* benefit us now, when the Germans are going from door to door *murdering* us and we are trapped here?"

"God," Piotr said, choking, "what have I done?"

"What are we going to do?" I asked uneasily.

"We are trapped," Mateusz said, scrubbing a hand down his face. "There is nothing we can do. We have no choice but to stay here. They are still a few kilometers away, and there is a firm AK stronghold between Wola and Śródmieście, so we have time. And you heard the Soviet station. They are coming. We just have to hold on."

By the time the sun set that night, I had been listening to constant gunfire for thirty-six hours, and now I imagined I could hear screaming, too. Unable to sleep, I crept into the dining room and found Uncle Piotr sitting at the table in darkness, nursing a bottle of vodka. Even as I approached, I could tell that he was quite drunk. I sat opposite him, and he lifted the bottle to his lips and gulped at it, then dropped it heavily onto the table.

"Is there anything we can do?" I asked him.

"I have let you down."

"Uncle Piotr, I'm not interested in looking back. It's done now," I said. "I just want to know if there is anything we can do to get out."

"The AK are using the sewers as a transport route, but it is risky and supposedly only to be used by soldiers. I am going to make inquiries, okay? I'm going to see if I can find you a way out."

"Thank you."

"If we can get to the outskirts of the city, we can make our way down to Lodz, even if we have to walk. It is just over a hundred kilometers. We could do it."

"We could."

"I am worried about your young friend, you know," Piotr said, then he sniffed miserably. "If the Germans are slaughtering tens of thousands of civilians, they will not hesitate to execute the AK if they capture them. Even the boys, like Roman."

"I know," I whispered, feeling a pinch in my chest.

"When I was younger, I thought that life was fair. I thought that maybe each person was allotted a degree of suffering, but once they endured it, life would be easy. Now I know it is random, and that if there is any intention to life at all, it leans toward cruelty."

I'd never seen Uncle Piotr so flat, his demeanor so bleak. As worried as I was, I felt compelled to present some optimism.

"Life can still be good, Uncle Piotr."

"There are unexpected blessings, that's for sure. Take you, for example. Your spirit has brought me much joy, and it was most unexpected."

"Thank you. And...likewise."

"For these past two years, I have loved Sara, and she has rejected me time and time again because I am selfish and greedy." I didn't know what to say to that. I stared at him in the darkness, watching as he stared down at the bottle on the table. "I wish I'd listened to her. I wish I'd changed to be a better man so we could be together. I just kept thinking that in life, there were winners and losers, and I felt sure this would be true even in war. I wanted to be a winner. I told myself that she would wait and that when I made bucketloads of money, I would turn over a new leaf, and we'd be married."

"You still could..." I offered helplessly.

"I want to. I just keep thinking about your young friend and how, if there were a quota for suffering, he would have met it some time ago, and yet still he suffers."

"It's not fair."

"He is a good man, Emilia. Sara sees in him what she wishes she saw in me."

"You can change. Can't you?"

"I want to do something for Roman. Do you remember when we were supposed to go to Lodz, and you so desperately did not want to go?"

"Of course," I whispered, laughing weakly. "That was only two weeks ago."

"It feels like longer."

"It does."

"I should have insisted he come with us. I should have told him that he had already proved himself a hero and that he owed this country nothing. Do you know that I watched them march into the ghetto?"

"His family?" I said, startled.

"Probably. I don't know. I watched thousands of Jews walk past me on the street as the Germans marched them in, and I told myself all kinds of reasons that it was going to be okay and why I shouldn't get involved. Now I wonder...if I were a better man, would Sara have told me the truth about what she was really doing during those months? From time to time, she would ask me for papers or food, but I had no idea the extent of it. If I knew, would I have done something? If an opportunity had presented itself to me, could I have been courageous enough to take a stand? To risk my life, the way you did?"

"Uncle Piotr," I whispered, and I reached across to put my hand on his. He sniffed again and then wiped the back of his other hand across the bottom of his nose. In the moonlight, I saw the shine of tears and snot, and my stomach contracted. "You aren't perfect, but you *are* a good man. Most likely, you saved me and Mateusz and Truda."

"Sure," he said bitterly. "When my brother comes to me for help, I agree. Then I trap him and his family in a city as it begins to collapse around him." He removed his hand from mine to scrub it over his face. "You should go to bed. It's late."

"Are you going to be okay?" I asked him uneasily.

"I am going to atone for my sins," he announced, then he sighed heavily. "I just don't know how. But I'm going to find a way to do something good for your friend, and then I'm going to get you and your parents out of the city before it is too late."

The next few days, Piotr was constantly in motion. He was in and out of the apartment, visiting his friends all over our district, trying to find a safe passage past the AK barricades that were keeping us safe and through the German-held parts of the city.

"I promise you, I'll get you out of the city," he kept saying. "I know I let you down, but I'm going to make up for it. I promise."

"I know," I would say, feeling uncomfortable with his desperate contrition.

"I'm going to convince Roman to come with us. And Sara. I don't know how, but I'm going to find a way."

And then he was gone again, trying to find a sewer guide who would take us and a way to line up transport so we wouldn't have to walk to Lodz.

Our district had been within an AK stronghold almost from the beginning, but the conflict came in waves, and the borders were constantly shifting. The AK would fight back and gain ground, then the Germans would crush it and slaughter untold civilians and destroy entire buildings, as if to reinforce the point. From the safe harbor of our apartment, I could see columns of smoke rising here and there. Rooftops I could see one day gone by the next.

I was increasingly aware of a sense of doom creeping in. Even if Piotr could find someone to take us through the sewers, our chances of escape were slim. When Mateusz or Truda had ventured out for food over the weeks of the Uprising, they'd brought back increasingly awful stories of Germans dropping grenades down manholes onto groups of people below or welding shut the manhole covers to eliminate previously safe routes. I couldn't believe our best bet for survival was to wade through raw sewage, praying that grenades didn't fall onto our heads and hoping that the exit hadn't been sealed before we reached it.

On Sunday the thirteenth of August, Uncle Piotr came flying into the house in a flurry of excitement. He squeezed me in a bear hug, then announced triumphantly, "I figured it out! It's going to cost almost all of the money I have left in the city, but don't worry—we are going to be okay."

"What's the plan?" Mateusz asked him.

"I'll tell you on the way, brother. We need to speak with Sara, and we need to visit Roman—hopefully he will be at his battalion headquarters." Uncle Piotr pointed to Truda, then to me. "Pack lightly. One small bag, that's all. Nothing that can't be washed. We will be going through the sewers for at least part of the journey. When we get to Lodz, we will stay at my apartment. It's so much nicer than this dump anyway, and I have plenty of money stacked away there. Once we are safe, I will replace everything you have lost, I promise, and we will live like kings."

28

Roman

TWO WEEKS INTO THE UPRISING AND OUR SQUAD OF twenty-one had been reduced to six. Those left no longer boasted or celebrated. They were doing whatever they could just to make it through to another sunrise.

Sword seemed to have taken it upon himself to become my partner. It wasn't that he clung to me so much as followed me around—keeping a safe distance from danger whenever possible, allowing me to handle any conflict we encountered. We didn't have nearly enough weapons, which wasn't a bad thing for Sword. He shook violently whenever we encountered German soldiers, and at one point I found him rocking in the corner of the bunk room, whispering, "I didn't think it would be like this" over and over again. I did not want to feel sorry for him—after all, I had warned him—but there was something so boyish about Sword.

"When is help coming?" he kept asking Needle.

"We should get enforcements from the Red Army today. We just have to hold the line," Needle said over and over again.

And then another day would pass with more bloodshed and more casualties and more injuries and no sign of reinforcement or relief. The excuses began to wear thin: talk of the Soviets waiting for a strategic break in battle made sense at first, then less day by day, until it made *no* sense. Then, we heard Soviet announcers on their radio channels indicating they were waiting for reinforcements themselves, and for the briefest moment, we were reassured that there was a plan, after all. But then an AK squad brought reports of thousands of Red Army soldiers and vehicles sitting idly on the opposite bank of the Vistula River, watching the city burn.

I was again fighting a battle that could not be won. This city-wide uprising was better resourced than the narrow uprising in the ghetto, but in so many ways it was the same old story: wake up, take a life, try to find food, take another life, try to get some sleep. Try not to die.

Words floated by me that in another lifetime would have demanded my full attention: a massacre just blocks from us in the district of Wola, Germans looting the Radium Institute before assaulting and ultimately murdering patients and staff, civilian buildings sealed before residents were burned alive. But in the heat of battle, I didn't have time to digest any of this because every day brought a new battle just to stay alive. Even if it was hopeless, I would once again default to fighting to my very last breath. This was the only existence I knew.

At one point amid the chaos, I carried a wounded soldier to the makeshift hospital in the basement of the church and found Sara. There was no time for small talk. She gave me unexpectedly bad news without preamble.

"The Rabinek family are still here."

"But they were leaving," I said, shaking my head. "No, I told them about the W hour! They knew this was coming—"

"Piotr delayed their trip," she said bitterly. "And, of course, the fighting broke out early. They are hiding in the apartment, but Piotr tells me he is working on a way for them to escape..." She drew in a deep breath. "He also tells me that he wants you to go with them."

"I couldn't, even if I wanted to," I told her, frowning. "Desertion is punishable by death. I can't walk away. I have to make..." I pictured Chaim, staring down at me as he pushed me into the sewer. *Don't waste it.* "I have to make this count."

"I told Piotr that I didn't think you would leave, but he is quite determined. Please don't be surprised if he comes for you."

I sighed, irritated. I had neither the time nor the patience for whatever Piotr was cooking up.

"I have to get back to it. Please be well. You've heard about the massacre at Wola?"

"I have indeed."

"Sara, if you get the chance to leave with him—"

"I am considering it."

I looked at her in surprise.

"You are?"

"I am tired, Roman," she said, waving her hand around the basement hospital. "Look at this. And for what? Will it free our homeland? Does anyone benefit? It is more death, more pain. I just need to *breathe* again."

I was relieved by this. That Sara and Elżbieta would soon be safe was the first good news I'd had in weeks.

I kissed her on the cheek.

"Stay safe."

"You, too."

Another Wigry squad captured an unusual German tank early on Sunday morning, and the entire headquarters was abuzz with excitement, as if this one act could turn the entire Uprising around. I was so irritated by this that although I was on shift, ready to be sent back into the field, I waited in the bunks to avoid the seemingly irrational celebrations. My eyes were closed, but my mind was racing, cycling through images of the previous days' conflict.

"Pigeon." I hadn't heard Sword approach, but he was right beside the bed, almost within arm's reach, as he always seemed to be.

"What?" I said, irritably.

"There are people asking for you out front."

I wasn't surprised to find Piotr and Mateusz standing in front of the headquarters. Piotr seemed to be vibrating with a manic excitement, but Mateusz had his hands in his pockets and was staring at the ground.

"Come with us," Piotr greeted me quietly. "We'll leave at dawn. We'll be in Lodz by tomorrow night."

"I wish I could," I said truthfully. Escaping to Lodz with Elżbieta and her family seemed like some fantastic dream. "But I can't. I made a vow to fight to the death if that is what it takes to free Poland, and I mean to keep it."

A cheer went up along the street, and we all turned to see the cause of it. I immediately recognized the odd vehicle moving slowly down Długa Street as the famed and unusual tank. I had never seen such a vehicle: it was armored like a normal tank but low to the ground and missing its turret. Someone had fixed a Polish flag to a pole on the front, and the vehicle was surrounded by people—children riding on its flat top, others scrambling to touch it, as if contact could somehow bestow them good fortune.

"What good does it do for bright young men such as yourself to sacrifice themselves in a losing battle?" Piotr asked.

"I have to believe it means something," I said, pursing my lips. "If not, then I've lost almost every friend I've ever had for nothing."

"These are hard questions," Mateusz conceded. "But not

questions you can solve in the heat of war, Roman. Step away from it. Come with us."

"Why? Why do you even want me to?" I asked, frowning. "Your family has been so good to me, right from the beginning. Why?"

"I'm a flawed man," Piotr said, "but…"

Whatever he said then was drowned out by the roar of the engine as the tank rumbled past, moving to the barricade at the end of the street. We all turned to follow it with our eyes as it continued along the way, waiting for the sound to pass so we could talk again. But the crowd on the street was growing by the second. Families were running together, pouring onto the street from apartment buildings nearby, and soldiers were filing out of my battalion headquarters.

"What is it doing?" Piotr asked.

"The tank?" I said, jarred by the abrupt conversational shift. "It's a victory lap, I think."

At the bottom of the street, the tank stopped at one of our makeshift barricades, almost two meters high, made of furniture from nearby apartments. The crowd surged to help dismantle it so the tank could proceed. In the thick throng of people, the vehicle disappeared from our view. All I could see was the Polish flag, fixed to a pole at the front of the vehicle, blowing gently in the breeze.

"A crowd should not be gathering like this," Piotr muttered to himself, shaking his head. "It's not safe! What if the Germans fire a shell into the neighborhood? What if a plane goes overhead and sees how many people are on the street?"

"Hey, Pigeon!" Sword called, looking more animated than I'd seen him in weeks as he ran from the headquarters behind me and started off toward the tank. "Come and see?"

I shook my head just as Piotr stepped toward Sword.

"Hey, kid," he called. "Come here. Go back inside, and get your commander to clear the street."

"I'm sorry," Sword shouted above the roar of the crowd, motioning toward his ear. "What did you say?"

Piotr and Sword closed the distance, and as they chatted a few meters away from us, I turned to Mateusz. He looked exhausted, as if Piotr's sudden exuberance was as tiring for him as combat had been for me. Mateusz was tucked behind a pillar, his back to the stone, his legs crossed at the ankles and angled toward the front door of my barracks.

"What's gotten into Piotr?" I asked him. "He's not usually so community-minded."

"Conscience," Mateusz said and sighed, tilting his face toward the sky as he exhaled heavily. "He is blaming himself for going off to do a deal when we were supposed to evacuate. I think hearing about the people at Wola and thinking of how vulnerable we all are has driven him slightly mad. He is determined to convince you to come with us—"

I'd seen explosions plenty of times, but this was something altogether different. There came a flash of white light so bright I was rendered momentarily blind, and immediately after, a burst of sound so loud it took my hearing, too. After this came the force of it—a shock wave fierce enough to knock me from my feet and onto the sidewalk.

I didn't lose consciousness. If only I had. Instead, I was literally shell-shocked—prone on the cobblestone road, unsure if I were dead or alive. Even when my sight returned and my hearing began to fade back in, the street was completely silent, and I thought perhaps I had permanently lost some of my hearing. I scrambled to my knees and turned toward the tank—to find it gone, and the buildings around it, and the children and the revelers and the soldiers. All gone. What was left was a mess so catastrophic and horrifying I couldn't comprehend the scale of it.

I was drenched in blood and knew it couldn't all be mine, but some of it had to be, because I was gradually becoming aware of pain in my face. I lifted my hand to my cheek and could feel that it was damaged: from my hairline down to my chin, the right side of my face was grazed or burned or embedded with shrapnel. I had no idea what the actual injury was. All I knew was that it was *agonizing*.

Hands were on my shoulders. There was a ringing in my ears, and my mind felt foggy, as if I weren't quite awake. I turned, and there was Mateusz, covered in blood and debris. I scanned him, looking for injuries, but found only a small wound on his neck. His lips were moving, but I couldn't make out the words.

"Piotr," I think I said, trying to turn back to where the tank had been.

Mateusz shook my shoulders to regain my attention and mouthed a single word.

Gone.

I turned again toward the tank, and this time I saw Piotr's body—damaged beyond any possibility of survival, flat on his face on the pavement. But Sword was alive, leaning against a wall. I scrambled to my feet with Mateusz's help and shuffled toward him, feeling the ground tilt wildly as my ears tried to adjust from the trauma.

Sword was all but hysterical, staring down at his foot, which had been impaled by a sharp chunk of concrete. My hearing was returning by degrees, but I wished I could stop that recovery, because now I could hear desperate cries and the wailing of those searching for their friends and comrades and loved ones.

"Mateusz," I said, or maybe I shouted. I saw Mateusz's lips move again, but I couldn't hear his words. I leaned closer and tried to speak louder. "You need to take my friend to Sara. He needs help."

Mateusz pointed to my face, then gently touched his forefinger to my chest.

So do you, his lips said. I wanted to stay to help, but my pain felt worse by the second.

"I think I'm going to pass out," I said.

Mateusz slid one arm around Sword, the other around me, then led us toward the basement hospital down the block.

29

Emilia

UNCLE PIOTR AND MATEUSZ HAD BEEN GONE FOR LESS than an hour when an explosion seemed to rock the entire city. Explosions were common—but not like this. It was so loud I felt the sound in my chest, and the glass in the kitchen window shattered. All the pots fell from the hooks above the stove.

"What was that?" I whispered from the floor of the apartment, where I had thrown myself. Truda was on the floor, too, opposite me, and we stared at each other. I knew that we were both thinking the exact same thing.

Piotr. Mateusz. Roman. Sara.

The city was bizarrely quiet for minutes after the explosion— even the now-familiar sound of gunfire seemed to stop. Curiosity won out over fear, and eventually I crawled to the living room window, but the street below gave nothing away. It was only deserted, our neighbors apparently too scared to go outside.

Twenty minutes later, a frantic thumping sounded at our door.

"I'll get it," I said, but Truda shot me a look.

"Sit down," she said impatiently and made her way over. I followed her anyway.

When she threw the door open there was a child there, a little girl no more than eleven or twelve. She was wearing a red-and-white armband and a tattered and filthy Scouts uniform.

"Mrs. Rabinek," she panted, leaning against the wall as she caught her breath. Truda nodded slowly. "I have news from the hospital at the church on Długa Street."

The girl handed Truda a note, drew in one final, deep breath, then ran off down the hallway. It struck me that the couriers for the Gray Ranks were everywhere through the Uprising—always running to the next job, more efficient and discreet than the phone system had been in the years since the occupation began.

"The explosion we heard," Truda said, leaning against the wall as if her knees were weak, staring down at the folded note in her hand. "I thought it perhaps came from Długa Street."

"Read it," I pressed. She continued to stare down at her hands, so I snatched it from her and read the note aloud. *Truda, come to the hospital. Bring Elżbieta. I am fine. Love, Mateusz.*

Truda was not fast, not even at the best of times, and this was not the best of times. I was virtually dragging her by the time we made our way to the convent, and the closer we got, the more disturbing the scenes around us became. People ran to and from the basement—carrying empty stretchers away, carrying bloodied bodies on stretchers as they returned. Men, women and children sat on the road, most weeping, almost all of them splattered if not covered in blood.

I stopped a few times to ask what had happened, but the people who had been near to the explosion seemed deafened by it or maybe so traumatized that they could not yet explain what they had survived.

When we finally reached the convent, the scene of chaos was almost beyond comprehension. The smell of blood and the dust was so strong that I covered my mouth with my hands, trying to suppress the urge to gag. The only way I could tell who was staff and who was a patient was by whether or not they were running. Everyone, staff or otherwise, was covered in blood, and there weren't nearly enough beds, so plenty of injured people were standing or sitting on the floor.

"Mateusz? Mateusz Rabinek?" Truda and I asked every person who rushed past us, but most either shook their heads or didn't acknowledge us at all. My heart was racing, and my stomach was churning, and soon I began to shake and suddenly I couldn't breathe. Truda's hands gripped my shoulders and shook me to catch my attention.

"Listen. You need to hold yourself together until we find him, then I will get you out of here, you understand me?" she hissed, her face close to mine. "We find Mateusz, then we leave and you can fall to pieces. I'll pick you up and put you back together, I promise. *Just not yet.*"

I blinked at her but then shook myself and nodded. We continued to make our way through the basement, but now I kept my eyes on Truda's back, and then, out of the din of urgent conversations between the staff and the crying and gasping and moaning, I heard a voice I knew all too well.

"Truda," I said urgently, and she spun around to me. I pointed to a bed to our left, where Roman was arguing.

"I need to get back! I need to go back and help! Let me up!"

He was sitting shirtless on a stretcher, arguing with Mateusz, who was literally holding him in place. An extraordinarily tall young man was sobbing in pain at the other end of the stretcher, clutching his mangled foot. As we got closer to Roman, I couldn't suppress a gasp of horror. It looked as though someone had thrown a burning blanket over his face and neck. Scraps of melted fabric were embedded in his blistered skin, some within millimeters of his eye. The hair on that entire side of his head was singed, as was what was left of his beard.

I had never seen an injury so visually confronting. My emotions ran so high I couldn't separate them—revulsion and fear and love and concern all joined together, and I was overwhelmed by their combined force. I wanted to run and embrace him but also run away so I could pretend this hadn't happened. Truda grabbed my hand and began to tug me toward the bed.

"Mateusz, you don't understand," Roman said, his features twisted not with pain but frustration. "I have to get back—my squad is there. Some of them on the balcony. I didn't see where they went. I have to see if I can find Piotr."

"I already told you. Piotr is dead! You are in shock and confused. The last place you should be is out on the streets," Mateusz exclaimed, frustration leaving the words curt and blunt.

I didn't realize I had made a sound until Mateusz and Roman looked over at us. I saw Mateusz's face fall, and he released Roman to take a step toward me, grief and regret all over his face.

"I'm sorry," he blurted. "Forgive me, I didn't know you were there. There was an explosion and…"

"Is he really gone?" Truda whispered.

"I'm sorry," Mateusz said again, and he pulled me into his arms and held me tight against him, then pulled Truda in behind me, so we embraced in a collective hug. "I'm so sorry."

"I didn't hear planes," I whispered numbly. "Was it a shell?"

"No. The AK captured a tank. It seems the Germans rigged it with explosives. I'm sorry," Mateusz whispered again, and now he released Truda to cup my face and stare down at me. "Listen to me, Emilia. I need you to talk to Roman. He is in terrible shock, and he needs to see a doctor, but because his injury is not critical, it may be some time before he is treated. You need to convince him to stay here. He is beyond rational, and I cannot get through to him."

Roman was arguing with a nurse now—the skin along the burn an awful, inflamed red and gray, the rest of his face red

30

Roman

I HAD LOST ANY SEMBLANCE OF STABILITY, AND I HAD NO idea how to regain my footing. I was confused and disoriented, but even so, absolutely determined to leave the basement hospital. I needed to check on what was left of my squad, to find a rifle and then to exact revenge.

It wasn't just the horror of the explosion, it was Piotr—yet another person I'd come to care about, lost again to the damned war and mindlessness of German cruelty. His loss tipped me over some invisible threshold, and I was abandoned to a rage so pure I felt no hope of coming back from it.

Elżbieta had long been my safe space, and she had a reliably calming effect on me over the two years I had known her, but when I saw her approaching me, I wanted to sweep her out of my way: she was just another barrier between me and the battle.

This thought gave me pause. My anger had frightened and hurt her the first time we met, and I had promised myself I would never allow that to happen again.

"Please stay," she choked out as she came near. "Please. I am scared for you. It's not safe out there."

"That's exactly why I have to go," I said helplessly. It was taking all of my strength to keep fury from my voice. *You're not angry with her. Don't take it out on her. Do not make her afraid. She deserves better than that from you.*

"But you cannot deny that this is a losing battle." Her voice broke, and her big green eyes were shining with tears. She was pleading with me, not just with her words, but with her hands, her soft palms resting against the uninjured skin of my bare chest, her left hand flat above my heart.

"But you didn't see," I said in frustration. "You didn't see what they have done in that street. Your uncle is *dead*, Elżbieta! He's dead!"

"I know. I can't even think about that yet, but I will. Right now all I can think is that I cannot bear to lose you, too. Do you understand that?"

"I do, but—"

"Then, *stay*. Just until a doctor can look you over." She lifted her left hand, gently touching the undamaged skin on my face, her gaze full of sadness. "Roman, it's bad. You must be in so much pain. Please let them help you."

"I can't," I said, and I shook my head. "I'll be fine. I really will."

Her face fell, and I wanted so badly to see the approval and pride and admiration that I had grown used to seeing when she looked at me. I reached for her other hand and gently shifted it off my shoulder. I had known intense pain before, but this time the skin on my neck and my arm and even the side of my face felt like it was still on fire. It was maddening, but I wouldn't let it stop me.

I couldn't stop. Not until Poland was free.

I moved to rise from the stretcher just as Elżbieta slammed her hand at the edge of the burn on my neck. When I howled in shock and pain, she pushed me back down, leaving me limp on the stretcher. She shifted her hand away from the wound to rest it on my shoulder as she brought her face close to mine. Her eyes were fierce, burning with a fury and determination that I had never seen in her.

"I'm not letting you go until you listen to me, damn you," she hissed. "The time will come for you to fight again, but for now you need to rest and wait for a doctor to see you. You cannot make a difference if you are dead."

"You don't understand," I snapped, shaking her hands from my shoulder, this time the movement not nearly as gentle as the first time I'd done it. She was ruthless, and while a part of me admired that, I knew she didn't understand my rage or the urgency. How could she? "They murdered my *family*—"

"I've lost my family, too."

I couldn't hide my irritation. I knew her loss was raw and new, but it hardly compared to mine. I slid my legs away from Sword, who was still crying like a baby at the other end of the stretcher, and rested my feet on the floor, ready to stand.

"I know you and Piotr were close—"

"No. My *real* family." Elżbieta drew in a deep breath, then gave me a miserable look. "You knew I had secrets." All of the fight drained out of me. I sank back onto the stretcher, and between the pain in my face and the pain in my heart, I was finally silent and still. "My real name is Emilia Slaska. They executed my father in front of me just after the invasion. They executed my brother because he was helping Jews. That's why I am living under this identity, in case someone is looking for me because of his work. His girlfriend—my *best* friend—had to flee, and she is probably in England. My mother died giving birth to me." Her voice shook, and her gaze grew hard. "I have *no one*, Roman, other than Truda and Mateusz now. You are not the only person in Poland who has lost everyone who mattered to them."

I sank farther back, numb with shock all over again. I couldn't tear my eyes off her: the pain in her gaze was so vivid and so breathtaking, I wanted to weep for her. She was telling me this to shock me, in a last-ditch effort to convince me to stay. For a moment, the tactic worked. I was ready to ignore the war, to pull her into my arms and to keep her safe from any more pain.

"Why didn't you tell me?" I asked her.

"I wanted to, but Truda could see *this* in you," she said, smiling sadly. "She knew you would run straight back to the underground in some fashion. She was worried that if you knew, you might give me up if you were interrogated."

"I never would," I whispered, staring into her eyes. "I would die before I betrayed you."

"You're my best friend, Roman," she murmured, then she bit her lip and glanced at me hesitantly. "When I see the future— when I see *my* future—I see you. Do you understand that?"

"If we don't fight, there is no future."

"So you would have me go out there to join in combat, too?"

The very idea of it filled me with panic. She was tough and strong, but I couldn't bear the thought of Elżbieta seeing the things I had seen during combat.

"Of course not!"

"The reason you don't want me to go out and take up arms is that you care about me. How can you not understand that I feel exactly the same about you?" She huffed out a frustrated breath, then snapped, "You *stupid* man. Do you not understand that what I feel for you is more than friendship?"

I sucked in a breath, and she did, too, as if she hadn't meant to say the words.

"Don't say it," I said, dropping my voice low. "It's better that you don't say it, because when I'm gone you'll—"

"I love you," she interrupted me, eyes flashing fire. "Don't you dare talk to me about *when you're gone*. I need you to survive, and I need you to survive for *me*."

I took her hand, and I held it to my uninjured cheek. Her words made me fly, but the knowledge that I was about to break her heart left me sick with guilt.

"I love you, too," I said. Maybe I had known it all along, right from those early days when I couldn't stay away from that back room at the youth center.

Over her shoulder, Truda and Mateusz came into focus. They were both in tears, heads close and eyes locked, comforting one another and making a plan for what came next. *That* was the kind of connection Elżbieta and I shared, or could have shared, if the world were different.

"When the war is over, we could be together," she whispered. "We could have a family, build a home. You could study—become a lawyer like your father. I could paint and keep the house and raise our children. We would have a big family, and our house would never be quiet, and it would never be still, but we would love it that way. The noise would remind us that we were alive. The noise would remind us that we had survived. Can you see it?"

"I can," I whispered. I wanted the picture she painted so badly it hurt my chest to think about it, because that wasn't what lay ahead of me, and as much as I wished that things were different, I couldn't ignore the reality. The Red Army was sitting on the banks of the Vistula, but it was increasingly evident that they would come no farther. The insurrection was all but doomed. There would be no happy ending for Elżbieta and me because there would be no happy ending for our nation.

"Stay," she said. "Stay for me."

"I wish I could," I said, my voice breaking. "Elżbieta—Emilia—I wish I could."

I sat up and this time she didn't try to stop me. Instead, she dropped her hand to her lap, and her head lolled forward as if she were too disappointed to hold it up.

"Elżbieta," I whispered, stricken by the pain in her gaze. I

reached to cup her cheek in my hand, the most intimate touch
we had ever shared, but one that felt so natural. She slowly
raised her gaze to mine.

"I am so scared for you," she said.

"You don't need to be."

"You are kidding yourself if you think that you can survive
out there. You are so badly injured...so reckless with your life,"
she said sharply, but then her voice trailed off to a pained whisper as she added, "You are so reckless with my heart, Roman."

I leaned toward her, then carefully brushed my lips against
hers. I had never kissed a girl before, and during one of those
lazy chats in Sara's apartment as I recovered, Elżbieta had told
me that she had never kissed a boy. That first kiss we shared
was over in an instant, but it set a fire in my chest and in my
heart that would sustain me to the end.

"If you really won't stay, then you have to promise me that
you will guard your life as if it were mine," Emilia said, touching my skin near the injured side of my neck again, this time
with utmost gentleness. I rested my hand over hers. "Promise
me. Say you'll guard your life as if it were mine."

I hesitated only for a moment. Staring into her eyes, being
close to her, it seemed that I was powerless to refuse her, even
when she was asking for the impossible.

"I promise. I'll guard my life as if it were yours."

She nodded, but then her eyes filled with tears.

"Please don't go, Roman. Please."

I kissed her again, softly and sweetly, but then I walked away.
I left her crying in the basement hospital, and I ignored the
protests of her parents and the medical staff as I walked back
into the street.

31

Emilia

I CRIED SO MUCH THAT NIGHT THAT MY EYES WERE PAIN-fully swollen by the time I woke up. My throat was raw as if I had been screaming in my sleep. When I made my way to the kitchen, I found Truda and Mateusz already dressed, sitting at the table in silence, nursing cups of tea. They, too, looked emotionally exhausted.

We hadn't talked about Uncle Piotr's death—each of us trapped in our own prison of grief. Speaking aloud might have made the pain worse, and I was scared of the conversation we would have to have after that one—the conversation about what we would do next.

But the sun had risen on our first day without Uncle Piotr, and we could only put off that conversation for so long. Mateusz rose and silently made me a cup of tea. I joined them at the table.

"Can we still leave the city?" I asked, my voice husky. I had felt a range of emotions over the course of the war—few of them good—but I had never really felt hopelessness like this before.

We'd lost Uncle Piotr, Roman seemed to be on a suicide mission, and the city was closing in around us.

"I'm afraid it's complicated," Truda said. "Piotr organized safe passage, but we have no idea how or what the details were."

I looked to Mateusz.

"He was going to tell you…"

"He was distracted…so animated," Mateusz said, his voice thick with tears. "He was determined to convince Roman to join us. He felt he had let you down. He wanted to make it up to you…to put something right for Roman, too."

"I can't believe he's gone."

"Neither can we." Truda sighed, rubbing her forehead wearily. "But that also brings us to our other problem, Emilia. Piotr told Mateusz that the guides and vehicles he organized were going to cost almost all the money he had on hand, and we have no idea where that money is. I searched his room last night and even the basement. We have only a few hundred *zloty*, and we are guessing that we need tens of thousands."

"So we are trapped?"

"I have heard the Germans stopped the slaughter in Wola," Mateusz said carefully. "They are taking prisoners now, not—" He broke off, then cleared his throat. "I'm trying to say that we won't be… I mean, it's likely that…"

"When this district falls, and it inevitably will fall, we will surrender and hope for the best," Truda interrupted him. I nodded slowly, digesting this.

"And in the meantime?"

"As long as we have food and water, we simply have to stay put."

Our district was entirely out of food within weeks, and tens of thousands would have starved to death but for the AK taking control of a brewery on Ceglana Street. They distributed bags of barley to civilians in the blocks around our street every day, and people would use their coffee grinders to turn the barley into a powder they could boil. It would form a thin paste that came to be known as *pluj-zupa*: spit soup.

We were lucky. When Truda searched Uncle Piotr's room for money, she found a cache of beans and powdered milk under his bed. We shared our bounty only with Sara, who visited every few days for food and rest. When she came the first time, we wept together for Piotr and for Roman, too.

"Have you seen him?" I asked her, and she nodded.

"He came in to have the wound cleaned."

"Is it infected?"

"It's not too bad. It's going to leave an awful scar."

"If he survives."

She sighed heavily and nodded. "If he survives."

Each day had me swinging between the terror of the situation and sheer, monotonous boredom. I couldn't focus enough to read, besides which, I had already read every book I could get my hands on.

Desperation led me to start a new project. I collected my pencils and charcoal and then stripped the artwork from my bedroom wall. I moved furniture so that I had one gloriously blank wall, and then I considered it a canvas. I sat by the window to stare out at the streetscape, watching to catch the details that defined those days in Old Town. The elderly lady who hung her washing on a string along her windowsill. The window garden that a young mother grew herbs and flowers in last summer. The window in that abandoned apartment that had been cracked ever since I arrived in Warsaw. And the beautiful, ornate buildings—neat rows of homes that had mostly been built in the twelfth century and that had survived hundreds of years of ups and downs of life.

Down on the street, parents were just doing the best they could for their children. Elderly residents would sit on the doorsteps and tell anyone who passed that the city was brave and strong and that for all Poland had endured in its history, it could survive this, too. The AK fighters passed in their tattered uniforms, increasingly worn, but still there and still fighting.

I drew it all. I spent hours a day on the mural, until my fingers or back cramped. Every single morning, I picked up my pencils, and I continued to work. I *had* to—I was compelled to capture every detail of Warsaw that I could, while I could.

I could see from the rooftop that other parts of the city were on fire, and I couldn't shake the feeling that I was watching the last days of a city's life. Who knew how many of us would survive the war? Who knew how many of us would survive the Uprising?

But we mattered, and our city mattered, and I wanted to record it all—even if the building was destined to be destroyed.

Those agonizing weeks during the Uprising confirmed that art is not always for the viewer. Sometimes the very act of creating can mean salvation for the artist.

Summer had turned to autumn, and the taps no longer worked. We were going to the bathroom directly into drains, and we were surviving on rainwater, but even God seemed determined to bring the Uprising to an end, because it hadn't rained in days. The barley at the brewery was running out, and the civilians in the blocks around us were increasingly panicked. Worse still, the AK had run out of ammunition. The city was dying.

Soldiers were going from door to door, warning us that the capitulation agreement had been drafted.

"The agreement says that Warsaw will be cleared of civilians," a soldier told us. "I'm sorry, but you'll have to go, or they'll take you. But don't worry, the agreement also says that civilians will be treated well."

"But where will they take us?" Truda asked.

"First to a transit camp in Pruszków. Be prepared with your

bags tomorrow morning, then come out onto the street when
they call for you."

Later that afternoon, there was a knock at our door, and Sara
was there. The past weeks had taken a toll. She was visibly exhausted, but it was her hands I noticed most. The skin of her
hands and arms was filthy, and her fingernails were chipped
and black with dirt. I was curious, but when she saw me staring at the dirt, she simply shook her head.

"I just came back to tidy up a few things," she said quietly.
"And I wanted to say goodbye."

"We will surrender tomorrow anyway," Mateusz said. "Why
don't you wait here? Come with us."

"No, I have patients at the hospital who are relying on me,
and I should stay with the Sisters. They are anxious about sur-
rendering, and I think I can support them." She pulled Mateusz
and Truda close for a hug, then turned to embrace me. "I'm
proud of you, Elżbieta."

"Don't make me cry," I said unevenly.

She hugged me again.

"Have you seen him?" I asked her, one last time.

"Not for a few days."

"Be safe," I said, blinking away tears.

"When all of this is over, wherever I end up, I'll come home
to Warsaw. I have unfinished work here."

"I'll find you," I promised, and then she was gone.

The next morning at four o'clock, the Germans were on our
street with blaring loudspeakers, announcing that we all needed
to be prepared for evacuation at nine. I was wide-awake and had
been up long enough to pack a small bag of clothes for whatever journey lay ahead. I was sitting on the floor opposite my
mural, trying to record every detail to memory.

Just before we were due to leave, I scooped up my pencils,
ran to the wall and added two final figures to the mural. The

first was a girl with wavy blond hair and green eyes, and she stared lovingly into the eyes of a boy with chocolate curls and hazel eyes...a boy dressed in a Boy Scouts uniform.

32

Roman

DEFEAT WAS INEVITABLE, BUT THAT MADE IT NO LESS painful. Considering that we had prepared to fight for one to three days and managed to last sixty-three, ours was a proud failure—but a failure, nonetheless. We lost tens of thousands of fighters, including thousands of children fighting with the Gray Ranks. By the time we were told to stand down on the sixty-third day, Sword and I were the last two members of our squad.

I had seen and done things in those sixty-three days that I had never been prepared for, but when the capitulation agreement was formalized and we turned ourselves in to the Germans, I found myself in completely unexpected and uncharted territory. I was now a prisoner of war.

As we walked through the city under close German guard, I saw civilians being marched this way and that, flanked closely by triumphant and often mocking German soldiers. I couldn't bring myself to look at the civilians as we walked. We had done our best, but we had failed them. Likewise, I tried hard not to notice the destruction of the city. We passed dozens of buildings that were reduced to smoldering rubble and dozens more that were freshly ablaze. As punishment for our decision to rebel, our homes, our libraries, our monuments and our infrastructure would be reduced to dust. It wasn't enough that they had taken our people and our homes: they were going to take what was left of our culture. It was miserable, but I kept my spirits up by thinking not of what we had lost but of what I *had* achieved.

Against all odds, I had survived, and I had done so for Emilia Slaska. I had learned how to suppress the instinct to throw myself unthinkingly into every battle. I had learned to pause and to ask myself, *How can I be smart here? How can I guard my life as I would guard hers, just as I promised her I would?*

Between that small shift in my thinking and a whole lot of luck, I had made it to the end of the Uprising.

Over the weeks since the explosion, I had fought off several minor infections, even running on little food and almost no water. My face was a mess—the scarring was going to be horrific—but the pain was gradually easing.

Sword was not so lucky. Shiny pink skin had grown over the wound in his foot, but the bones beneath were visibly deformed, and he was in constant pain. He learned how to bear weight on it, but this left him with a significant limp. I had retrieved a pair of boots and thick woolen socks from the body of a dead German soldier for him, but I had a sickening feeling that if we were ever to receive proper medical attention, he would need to have the foot amputated for any chance of a pain-free life.

Perhaps I would have been less sympathetic to his plight had I not discovered his secret in the weeks since the tank bomb exploded. Sword's real name was Kacper Kamiński, and rather than being twenty years old as he had told us when he enlisted, he had just turned fifteen.

"Why did you lie?" I asked. "You could have still served."

The fifteen-year-old Gray Ranks had served in the Combat School, conducting minor sabotage and reconnaissance, rather than engaging in active combat like the older boys.

"I had visions of being a hero, and people always assumed I was older than I was because of my height," he said and barked a harsh laugh. "I felt lucky to be able to pass as an adult, so I did."

"And your parents?"

"I told them I joined the Boy Scouts. I didn't tell them that we were preparing for a violent uprising," he added miserably. "Our home was in Żoliborz. I haven't seen or heard from them since the night before the Uprising. They probably think I'm dead. Maybe they are dead."

After that, I had little choice but to take him under my wing. And now that we were marching toward an unknown destination as prisoners of war, I knew my protective duties had only just begun.

We marched for a full day until we reached a transit camp. That night, we were served a meal—muddy broth with vegetable scraps floating on top—and then led to a hall and told to sleep on the floor, without blankets. This led to some confusion among the other soldiers.

"But the capitulation agreement says they will honor the terms of the Geneva Convention," I heard someone say. "We're supposed to have meals of comparable quality and quantity to the German soldiers. We're supposed to be housed in safe and comfortable conditions."

"Are you going to complain that our caviar is running late, or shall I?" I said sarcastically.

"But they have to treat us with dignity! We may be enemies, but we are still human."

I ignored them after that, rolling over impatiently and trying to get comfortable enough to sleep. Beside me, Kacper asked quietly, "You saw active combat in the ghetto. I remember Needle saying so."

"Yes."

"You are Jewish?"

"It's complicated," I said heavily, too tired to explain.

"I heard it was bad in the ghetto."

"*Bad* doesn't even begin to cover it."

"Worse than the city uprising?"

"It was a different kind of hell."

"Do you think they will kill us?"

"If they were going to, they would have already done so. They will want to use us for labor." I wasn't sure I believed this myself after everything I'd seen, but I remembered how those words from Samuel's lips had once brought me comfort. There wasn't much else I could do for the kid other than offer him hope, even if it was false hope.

"If we have to walk again tomorrow, I don't think I'll be able to go as far." I noticed that in the last hour of our march, he had been stumbling with almost every step.

"I will help as much as I can," I told him, but as tired as I was, I couldn't sleep as I worried about my promise. I knew from painful experience how dangerous it was to assume the Germans would take pity on any one of us, and I hoped I could think quickly enough to help Kacper.

When we woke and were led straight to a nearby train station, I could feel Kacper's relief, but I didn't feel it for myself. The sight of those boxcars filled me with visceral dread, and as we waited our turn to board, I trembled from head to toe.

"Roman?" Kacper prompted when the line surged forward, but I didn't move.

"I can't get onto that train," I whispered. Images played before my eyes. Samuel, pulling himself up onto the bed of the carriage, then helping Mother up, too. Dawidek, one hand in each of theirs. The train winding to Treblinka and the beautiful platform with the orchestra and the welcoming signage—all a facade hiding fields of death.

I felt a rough shove from behind, and I stumbled forward, my hands colliding with the edge of the carriage. I looked back in irritation to see Kacper behind me.

"Come on, soldier," he said, with bravado I could see he didn't feel, because his gaze was full of fear. "You haven't come this far to give up now."

It occurred to me that if I refused to board the train, I'd probably be shot, and this kid would be all on his own. He knew that just the same as I did, which was why he was so terrified.

I sighed and scrambled up onto the platform, then turned to help haul him up, too.

33

Emilia

March 1945

"SOVIET TROOPS HAVE ENTERED THE OUTSKIRTS OF THE city," Mateusz announced. He set a basket of vegetables onto the counter, the goods from his trip to the market in Lodz. I'd been washing the dishes from breakfast and froze at his announcement, my hands stilling in the soapy dishwater. The click-clack of Truda's knitting needles at the kitchen table slowed behind me, then stopped.

After our march from Warsaw, we had joined tens of thousands of other Varsovian civilians in cramped and crowded conditions at a transit camp at Pruszków, and we languished there for two very long weeks, searching unsuccessfully for Sara and Roman. We eventually discovered that Roman was likely taken to one of any number of POW camps, but we had no clue what Sara's fate had been. We heard stories that some civilians were released into the countryside on strict instructions not to return to Warsaw, and others were sent to Germany for forced-labor assignments, and yet others were sent to concentration camps.

On the fifteenth day in the camp, Mateusz was finally called to a meeting with a German administrator to find out what our designation would be. He left that meeting without a single *zloty* to his name, but he managed to secure us release into the countryside.

The next day, we showed our papers at the gate, and then over the following three days we walked the hundred and twenty kilometers to the outskirts of Lodz. We found Uncle Piotr's apartment occupied by a German commander and his wife, so Mateusz took us to Piotr's factory. The vast space wasn't remotely homey, but we commandeered the front office for our temporary home. Mateusz sold bits and pieces of what was left in the factory to buy essentials, including mattresses and blankets and wood for a fire, and we stretched the rest of the money for food. We suffered through a very uncomfortable winter like that—but we survived.

And now, this news. In some ways, it was the news we had been waiting for. It was also the news we had been dreading.

"There are Polish flags in the street," Mateusz continued. "Some are celebrating."

We were aware of the advancing Russian troops for some time. Change was in the air. It had begun when the Germans came to the factory in November and requisitioned all heavy equipment, packing it onto trains to be taken into Germany. Then at the start of January, German soldiers began fleeing the city like rats abandoning a sinking ship. When Mateusz heard the last of the Germans were gone, he raced to Uncle Piotr's apartment, only to find it had already been looted. Even the windows had been stolen from their frames.

Just the previous week, we heard the Red Army had taken command of what was left of Warsaw. By all accounts, the entire city had been reduced to dust, but I struggled to imagine it, and because of that, I struggled to believe it.

I felt the instability of it all in my bones. So some were celebrating and waving Polish flags in the air, but I knew others would be cowering in their homes, well aware that the advance of Soviet troops meant that we were not yet liberated. It was unclear whether the Red Army's presence was going to be a mercy or an even greater torture.

I withdrew my hands from the water and wiped them on my apron. Truda was crying. Mateusz watched us both, his expression guarded.

"Whatever comes next," he said quietly, "we will manage."

"How much more do you think we can take, Mateusz?" Truda whispered unevenly.

"God will not give us more than we can handle," he said gently.

"Tell that to the Jews," I muttered.

"I'm scared," said Truda.

"Me, too," I said.

"We have made it this far," Mateusz said. "Against the odds, despite everything we have been through. We are still alive, and we are still together. The world is watching the Soviets. Maybe they will allow the government-in-exile to return so that we can rebuild."

"If that were their plan, they would never have sat on the banks of the Vistula and watched the Uprising fail," Truda said, wiping at her eyes. She raised her chin, then drew in a deep breath through her nose. "But you are right. We have a lot to be thankful for, and sulking will do us no good. It certainly won't tell us what to do next."

"We need to go back to Warsaw," I said.

"We have shelter here. We have *some* resources here."

"We need to find Sara and Roman. They'll be looking for us, and I know they'll both go back to Warsaw."

"Emilia," Truda chided, raising her eyes to heaven, "you will be the death of us. I hope you realize this."

"I hate that you think that," I muttered, shooting her a glare.

"What Truda means is that sometimes it's okay to wait and see how situations unfold," Mateusz said softly. "Let's say you convinced us, and we left Lodz today to return to Warsaw. Let's assume we could somehow find some transport. We would be on the road riding *against* the incoming Soviet troops. We would return to a city that by all accounts has been destroyed. And what for? So that we can struggle to find shelter? Food? Water? Right now we have a roof over our heads, food, water, a sewer that works, and coming into spring it's going to be more and more comfortable here."

"But our friends—" I started to protest.

Truda interrupted me. "If they have beaten the odds and survived the last four months, then they will survive another few weeks while we wait to see how this unfolds."

"If I were the one lost—"

"If you were the one lost, things would be different. But you are safe here with us, and we are safe here together. I'm sorry, Emilia, but Truda is right. Now is not the time to move—we should stay here and wait to see what happens."

Much to my frustration, that's exactly what we did. We remained in the empty shell of Uncle Piotr's warehouse, waiting for news, each day seemingly stretching longer than the last, my parents waiting for some impossible sign that a return to Warsaw was safe. It seemed obvious that Warsaw probably was *not* safe. That didn't mean we should stay away forever. Lodz was probably unsafe, too, now that Red Army soldiers could be seen on just about every block.

Soon enough, we heard stories about Soviet soldiers helping themselves to Polish property just as the Germans had done, and then came stories about beatings and imprisonments. One day, Truda returned from a trip to the market, visibly shaken.

"I won't go alone again," she announced fiercely, then she turned her gaze on me. "And, Emilia, you aren't to go anywhere alone, either, do you hear me? Don't you ever leave those doors again unless Mateusz is with you."

"What has you so shaken, my love?" Mateusz frowned. "Did something happen?"

"The woman who sold me the eggs…she told me not to wander alone. She said that in one household just a few blocks from here, three generations have been attacked since the Soviets came in January," Truda blurted, cheeks flushing.

"Attacked? More beatings?" I said, confused as to why she was so distressed by this, given we had been hearing such stories for weeks by then.

"No…not beatings," she said impatiently, then she muttered, "Attacks on *women*, Emilia. She said there is a village to the east where *every* woman was…" She paused, struggling to find a word, then finally sighed and said helplessly, "…violated. Even the elderly, even the young. These soldiers are different to the Germans. There are new dangers in these streets now for us women."

"We will be more careful," Mateusz said immediately. "Whenever we need to take a trip to the market, I'll be sure to come with you."

"Or is it even more reason to go back to Warsaw, given Lodz is probably no safer than our home?" I suggested.

"Not yet, Emilia." Truda sighed, shooting me a fierce look.

"Just a little longer," Mateusz assured me.

I would have to wait, but that didn't mean I had to wait patiently.

Sometimes, it felt like the walls of that little makeshift home were closing in on me, and on those days, Mateusz would invite me to walk to the market with him to pick up food. He seemed to use those walks to distract me when Truda and I were bickering. My seventeenth birthday was a day like that. I had wondered if they would surprise me on my birthday with news that we were returning to Warsaw, and when they didn't, I was disappointed and frustrated.

"It's been two *months*!" I had exclaimed. "How much longer will we wait?"

"You're seventeen years old now," Truda had snapped. "It's time for you to stop acting like a child. We are doing the best we—"

"Let's go to the market," Mateusz had interrupted. Truda fell silent. I crossed my arms over my chest and frowned at him, and he gave me a hopeful smile. "Come on, Emilia. Get your things. Let's get you some fresh fruit for your birthday lunch."

"You just need to be patient," he said, as we walked toward the market. A breeze was blowing, but it wasn't icy, and I was grateful that spring was coming. Spring meant better produce at the market and the return of sleep that wasn't disrupted by frozen limbs. We'd made do in the factory over the winter but had been far from comfortable in the coldest weather. "I know that for all of your strengths and talents, patience is not high on the list."

"Neither is holding my tongue," I muttered.

"I am well aware of that," he chuckled. "And the funny thing is Truda has the exact same problem. Have you noticed?"

I sighed. "Yes. I know."

"Can you give her a little grace, Emilia? I want you to think about her situation. You can be so selfless sometimes—rushing into danger if there is a chance you might help someone, and this is half the reason I have so many gray hairs. But the reason for the rest of my gray hairs is Truda. The last few years have been so hard on her. She is courageous and strong, but beneath it all, she is heartbroken, too. You and I are all she has left, and yet you constantly argue that we should gamble with your life, forgetting that asking her to do so means gambling with the most precious thing in hers."

I had been excited to go to the market, for the chance of fresh air and perhaps a conversation with someone new, but I was so chastened by this comment that I fell quiet as we walked the stalls. Mateusz gleefully showed me the first of the new-season apples, but I could summon only the weakest smile, despite having not eaten fruit for months over the winter. He began to haggle with the stall owner over the price, and I browsed the produce nearby, thinking about Truda.

She and I butted heads, but I loved her, and I was grateful to her. I had to find a way to be less of a burden to her and to show my gratitude.

I don't know how I lost him. I was distracted, and the market was crowded with others taking advantage of the improved weather. After a few minutes it occurred to me that I had probably wandered a little too far, and I turned and walked back to the apple stall—but by then, Mateusz was gone.

I scanned the crowd, waited a few moments, then approached the stall owner.

"Did you see which way my father went? He was the tall man with the cap and the beard. He was haggling with you over the price of your apples."

"I remember him. He told me that today is your birthday. Was that a trick?"

I laughed.

"No, it is my birthday."

"Well, in that case," the seller handed me a bright red apple, "happy birthday."

"Thank you!" I said, delighted. I took a bite, and the fresh, crisp taste flooded my mouth. "Oh, that is good."

"I know," the vendor said and chuckled. "He went that way."

He pointed back in the direction I'd just come from. I supposed it was possible that we had passed one another without realizing it, so I thanked the man and walked back the way I'd come. This time, I looked carefully, but when I reached the entrance, Mateusz was still nowhere to be found.

For the first time, I felt truly vulnerable. This was exactly the kind of scenario we'd resolved to avoid as word of the Red Army cruelty had spread through the city. As a young woman walking alone, I was vulnerable to all manner of dangers.

In the absence of any alternative, though, I began to walk back toward the factory.

I would always remember strange details from that day. I walked fast because I wanted to find Mateusz as quickly as I could, but I did not run because I knew not to draw attention to myself. The breeze picked up a little and my hair was down, so it kept blowing into my face and sticking in my mouth. I walked past a bakery, and the scent of bread was in the air, making my stomach rumble. I hoped that Mateusz had apples waiting for me, even though I could still taste the first one on my lips.

I was wearing flat leather lace-up shoes that Sara had given me when I was working in the department office. The shoes were tan, but I was wearing blue socks, which I knew didn't exactly match, but I was making do with the clothes I'd brought from Warsaw. The blue socks had a tiny hole over my left pinky toe that I had been meaning to darn, but I couldn't be bothered to mend it. I was always putting that kind of thing off, and it drove Truda crazy.

I was wearing a gray skirt that was a little too big for me. As I walked, the waistband kept slipping down, and I had to keep pulling it up. I was wearing a white blouse beneath a scooped-neck gray wool sweater. I loved that sweater, even though it always itched a little.

Someone called out behind me, Soviet words I didn't understand, but it didn't matter because my heart sank anyway. Mateusz wasn't sure what the rules were about papers now that the Soviets were in charge: we had been waiting for propaganda posters to appear on the walls to tell us what was expected. For so long, papers had been the difference between life and death so I still carried mine religiously. As I turned toward the voice, I reached into the pocket of my skirt to grasp my identity card.

It was three Soviet soldiers—a young one, maybe twenty-five, flanked by two older ones. The one on the left was overweight, his belly hanging over his belt, his cheeks a deep red, his nose bulbous and bumpy. The one on the right was the oldest. All of the men were clean-shaven.

They were walking steadily toward me. They looked angry, but it was a different kind of anger, one I didn't know how to interpret, and I felt frightened.

I stopped looking at their faces, and instead looked at their khaki jackets and pants and the red patches on their shoulders and the tan of their belts and their high black boots. Soon, they were close enough to speak without shouting. Soon, they were close enough that I could smell vodka coming off them in waves. Drunk and fat in the middle of the afternoon, in a city and a nation that had been starving for years.

"Do you know how long I have been away from my wife?" the man with a bulbous nose said. His Polish was stilted, his accent thick, but he wanted to make sure I understood. I took a step back, but only one. I did not try to run. "Three years," he said, his nostrils flaring. "Three years I have been fighting for this wasteland of a nation. Now we have freed you bastards, and the time has come for you to thank us."

People must have seen them drag me into the alleyway. I thought about those people. I didn't blame them for their inaction. The Germans trained us to pay no attention, and besides which, the Soviets had guns and knives and entitlement and rage. We had risen and failed, time and time again, and even when liberation came, we were only liberated to face more violence.

We had nothing left. I had nothing left. Those moments on the cobblestones were the lowest of my life. I burrowed deep inside myself, to a place I never knew existed, and I stayed there until it was over.

I lay bleeding and bruised on the cold cobblestones of the alley, and I was exhausted as if I had been running for days or years. My limbs shook with shock and cold. I had been sur- rounded by hatred for years, but this time, it was forced inside of me. I was scared, and I wanted to run, but I could not find the energy to get up. I barely had the energy to roll over, to vomit onto the street. Some of my hair fell into my mouth as I did, and it tasted of someone else's sweat.

I gagged again, and this time my whole body seemed to contract. The urge to vomit echoed from my toes to my hair.

"Come on, darling," a woman's voice whispered into my ear, and gentle hands touched my back. "We need to get you out of here. My husband is going to carry you. You're safe now." She paused, then repeated the words, slower and firm. "You are safe now."

More hands were on my body, and I was blind in my terror. *No more. No more!* I panicked, thrashing wildly, but the woman's gentle voice came again.

"This is Wiktor. This is my husband. He will not hurt you, darling. We are trying to take you somewhere safe."

I tried to focus on my breath, to calm myself so that I could regain control. This man was huge, just as big as the others, and if he wanted to hurt me, there was nothing I could do. Despite my best efforts, I was hyperventilating.

"Breathe now. You're going to be okay," the woman said, gently stroking my hair back from my face. I closed my eyes and wondered if this was all a nightmare. The edges of reality blurred as if I were dreaming, but not even in my worst night- mares had I had a dream like this.

They carried me up a flight of stairs, and then a door closed. I had no idea where I was nor who I was with. The man gently laid me on a sofa, and the woman covered me with something soft. Then, a wet cloth was against my forehead, and a glass was against my lips. *Vodka, no.* The taste of it made me gag. The glass was gone, then back again, only this time it was water. I took a sip, then collapsed back onto the sofa.

"Where is your home, darling?" the woman asked. Where *was* my home? It was a good question. It was also a logical one, I just didn't know how to answer it. At first I couldn't remember where I lived, and even once I did, I didn't know how to explain it.

"In a factory. We are staying in my uncle's factory."

"With your parents?"

"Yes."

"Do you remember which factory? My husband will go and get them."

I tried to explain it—describing the offices inside, where I had spent most of my time. This was no help at all, and I was starting to shake violently by then—tremors running throughout my body. The woman gently pressed me back down and rested the washcloth over my eyes.

"Rest now. We will find your parents soon."

I wanted to go to sleep and to never wake up. As soon as I closed my eyes, I saw them again—three Soviet soldiers, walking past a bakery, walking toward me with hate in their eyes. I sat up, wild with fear all over again.

"What if they come back?" I said, and at last my eyes filled with tears. I looked to the woman, but for the first time, I really saw her. She had fat silver curls beneath a brightly colored scarf and deep hazel eyes brimming with compassion.

"They won't come back," she promised, and then she pointed across the room. I watched as her husband dropped a chair by the door and sat heavily upon it. Beside the chair, a long rifle leaned against the wall. The man leaned forward and picked it up, resting it on his lap as he watched the door. "And even if they do, they won't get anywhere near you."

★ ★ ★

Maybe I slept, or maybe I just fell into that deep dissociative state I'd fallen into during the assault. Time passed, and for a while I wasn't cognizant of the pain…but when I roused again, it was the pain that I noticed first. From my thighs to my waist, I felt raw and bruised.

Although I could deduce the basic mechanics of what had happened to me, I had blocked out most of the assault, and some of my injuries made no sense. My left eye was swollen shut. My right upper arm and shoulder throbbed. My right heel felt bruised.

"What's your name, darling?"

"Emilia."

"Are you ready for some water, Emilia? Some food, perhaps?"

The silver-haired woman was still sitting beside me. Her husband was still at the door, reading by the electric light that hung from the ceiling, his rifle still in hand. I looked around the apartment for the first time and realized that I was in an upper-class home.

"Some water, please," I whispered. My voice was hoarse. I couldn't remember screaming, but maybe I had. My lips were cracked, and when the woman lifted the glass to my mouth, the water stung a little.

"Some vodka?" she suggested. I thought I would vomit again at the thought of it. I pressed my hand to my mouth and shook my head hastily.

"Have you thought about how we might find your parents?"

"The factory…" I said again, helplessly. My mind was a little clearer, and this time I at least thought to say, "My uncle owned it, Piotr Rabinek. It was a textiles factory. A large factory. It is maybe fifteen blocks from the market."

"In the industrial district," the man by the door said gruffly, and he glanced over his shoulder, met my eyes and then awkwardly looked away. I felt my face flush with shame. Had this kindly old couple *seen* it happen? Did they think it was my fault?

Oh, God. Was it my fault?

Had I done something to attract the attention of those soldiers? I should never have left the market. I should not have been walking alone.

"Can you tell us anything else about the factory?" the woman pressed again. "There are a lot of factories in the industrial district. My husband will go and look for your parents, but you need to give us something else to go on."

"There are red geraniums in a huge planter under the awning at the front near the offices. My father says there were also white ones there once, but they had to destroy them because..." The flag. The Polish flag was red and white. The Germans would never have allowed a patriotic display like that.

"Is it a large awning?" the old man asked, without looking in my direction. "And is there a row of oak trees along the front?"

"Yes! The oak trees..."

He sat the rifle beside the door, then slowly and carefully rose.

"Lock the door behind me, Maria. I know the place."

After he left, Maria helped me to the bathroom to wash up. I stared into the blackened mirror, and a stranger stared back. My lips were swollen, and I couldn't figure out how that had happened because none of the men had tried to kiss me. Then I remembered a hand over my mouth at one point and struggling to breathe through my nose, but my nose was blocked because I'd been crying, and I had thought for a while that I was going to suffocate.

My eye was swollen shut, bruised green and deep purple, yellowed around the edges. My underpants were gone. I couldn't remember them being removed. There was blood all over the back of my skirt—*so much blood*, as if I'd been caught off guard by my monthly courses. My thighs were bruised just as badly as my eye. I tried to use the toilet, but my urine stung and burned. It was easier to hold it.

I walked back to the mirror and tried to look at myself again, but this time there was so much shame in my eyes that I couldn't bear to see it. I gingerly washed my face with water and limped back out to Maria. I found her setting up a little table beside my sofa. Milky tea and a bowl of chicken soup.

"Thank you, but I can't eat," I told her.

"Sit," she said firmly, and when I did, she dipped a spoon into the soup and lifted it to my mouth. I ate it, too weak to protest.

"It's happened to a lot of us, you know," she said. "There was a strange mercy in the German disdain for us. They were happy to kill us and torture us and starve us to death, but they didn't see us as human, so they were at least less inclined to rape us." *Rape.* I hadn't let myself think the word. Now, though, it sat in the forefront of my mind, and I considered it from several angles. *The soldiers raped me. I was raped by the soldiers. I have been raped. This morning I was someone who had never been raped. I can never say that again. I am changed by this. Am I ruined by this?* Oblivious to my inner monologue, Maria continued softly, "But these Soviets are different. Some of their commanders have encouraged them to do it. They say the men need sex because they have been away from their wives for too long. They tell them they are entitled to it, and who bears the cost of that? *Us.*" She sighed and shook her head. "Again, it is the Poles who must suffer. As if this country hasn't been through enough."

Rape. I was raped. Lots of my countrywomen have been raped, too. Do they also wish they were dead? Will there be a whole generation of Polish women who will find themselves unable to look in a mirror because the shame is too great?

"This may be hard to believe right now, but you will be okay."

I didn't reply. I couldn't. She had been so kind to me, and I didn't want to tell her that I already knew she was wrong.

★ ★ ★

There was a tap at the door an hour later. Maria grabbed the rifle before I even had time to react. There was something so reassuring about that pint-size woman approaching the door with a rifle in her hand, as if she could take on the whole Soviet army.

"Who is it?" she demanded.

"It's me," Wiktor said gruffly, then a little lighter, "Please don't shoot me, dear."

Maria unlocked the door, and then Wiktor and Truda and Mateusz all rushed inside. I thought I would feel better when I saw them, but I didn't. All I felt was shame and guilt, especially when I saw that Truda was crying, and even Mateusz's eyes were red-rimmed.

"I'm sorry," I blurted. My lips were so swollen that the word sounded distorted. "I'm so sorry. I lost you in the market and then when I couldn't find you, I tried to walk home and—"

"Don't," Mateusz gasped, visibly horrified. "It's my fault. I should have waited longer for you, I looked for a little while and then I... I thought I would find you walking home but..." He blinked, and a tear trickled onto his cheek. He swiped it away so quickly I thought I might have imagined it. He and Truda sat on either side of me, but I couldn't look at them. I covered my face with my hands and began to sob.

"I'm so sorry. I'm so sorry."

We were all saying it—them to me, me to them, and the worst thing was none of us had anything to be sorry for at all.

34

Emilia

MATEUSZ AND TRUDA WERE THE KIND OF PEOPLE WHO ordinarily had no tolerance for self-pity, but in the weeks that followed, they seemed bewildered about how to help me and opted to give me space, which allowed me to wallow. I spent days in bed, physically recovering from the trauma, emotionally retreating into a kind of coma. I ate when Truda forced me to. I couldn't bring myself to look in the mirror in the small bathroom we shared, and so I had taken to covering it with a towel when I went in to use the toilet. I couldn't imagine ever feeling an emotion like joy again. At one point, I spent a whole afternoon trying to remember the steps between amusement and laughter.

It was as if those soldiers had reached inside me and removed my soul, leaving behind a broken shell. My bruises and my wounds slowly healed, but I still viewed the world through a haze of sadness and confusion. Once upon a time I had been so interested and concerned about the Soviet occupation and what it would mean for my nation. Now, I couldn't bear to see that uniform, so I didn't leave the factory at all. And I couldn't bear to hear them spoken about, so I avoided conversation. I couldn't focus to read. Mateusz had purchased a wireless radio, and one day, the Lodz station played the Polish national anthem. Prior to the attack, this would have brought me tears of happiness and pride. Instead, even at the lowest volume, the music seemed too loud, and it hurt my ears. Neither Truda nor Mateusz raised a protest when I got up and simply turned it off.

Days ran into one another. It might have been less than a week; it might have been months. One evening, I was lying in bed staring at the ceiling when Truda and Mateusz approached me.

"Emilia, we need to go back to Warsaw."

Not so long ago, those words would have sounded like music. But I couldn't bear music now, and the thought of facing Sara and Roman filled me with dread. I missed him desperately, but I couldn't imagine even looking Roman in the eye. I shook my head.

"I can't."

"We must," Truda said firmly. "We need to find word of our friends, and besides, sooner or later, industry will begin to rebuild, and someone is going to help themselves to this factory. We need to build a proper home, and there are grants for those who return to the city."

"Grants?"

"Five hundred *zloty* each," she said. I gave her a blank look, and she conceded, "I know. It is not a lot, but it will help with the cost of finding food and shelter even if the damage is as bad as people say. Besides, Emilia…we are slowly but surely running out of things to sell here at the factory. Soon we'll have no money and no way to earn more. We really have no choice but for Mateusz to try to find work, and there will be plenty of work in a city that needs to rebuild."

"No. I can't."

"Don't you want to leave this city, Emilia?" Truda asked me gently.

I stared at her. Truda's gentle side was a novelty, but not one I enjoyed. I missed brash Truda, honest and authentic Truda, the version of Truda I had always butted heads with. This careful woman was a stranger to me.

"I won't go," I said flatly. I wanted to enrage her. Instead, she just looked away.

"Okay, sweetheart," Mateusz said softly, and they both rose. But just a few steps from my bed, Truda hesitated, then returned to sit beside me.

"I don't know how to help you," she admitted, then she looked at me again, and this time there was deeper concern in her eyes. "I'm going to be honest with you, Emilia. We *need* Sara. She can help you recover, and I think we will—" She broke off, then cleared her throat and stared at the floor as she said weakly, "We just need Sara."

"She probably isn't even alive," I said bitterly. "She's probably dead. Or in a camp somewhere."

"We have to at least try to find her. And Roman, too."

"I don't want to see him," I said angrily. Her eyes widened in surprise, and I felt my face flush beet red. God, the shame was overwhelming. How was I ever going to learn to live with the shame? "I don't—I can't. I don't want either one of them to see me."

"Emilia," she whispered, gently touching my forearm. "Surely you know that you have nothing to be ashamed of."

"You don't know that. You weren't even there."

She drew in a sharp breath, then her hands tightened around my wrist.

"I wasn't there for you, and I will never forgive myself for that. But I'm here now, and I insist that you explain yourself to me—how could you possibly blame yourself?"

Her voice shook, with fury or frustration, I wasn't exactly sure why. But her rage felt good anyway, and I let it wash over me, as if it was directed at me.

"I didn't run," I whispered numbly.

"And what else?" she demanded harshly, shaking my hand as she spoke.

"I didn't cry out for help."

"And?"

"I didn't even try to... I just let them... I just... I didn't even try to fight back."

Now Truda released my wrist, but she did so only so that she could catch my shoulders in her hands, and she stared into my eyes, her face flushed with frustration and anger.

"If you had run, they would have shot you. If you had cried out, they would have shot you. If you had fought, they would have shot you. You were powerless against those men. You didn't *allow* them to do anything. You didn't invite them to do anything. Nothing you did or didn't do could have changed what happened to you. It was a combination of bad luck and bad men. I won't hear you speak like that again, and I won't sit back and let you blame yourself. Where is the Emilia who has always driven me crazy because she was ready to charge into the fight? You need to fight the shame, because on the other side of the fight there is pride and there is healing." She shook me gently, but when I still could not look at her, her tone grew sharper. "Do you hear me? We are going to Warsaw. We are going to find Sara and Roman. And you, my girl, are going to grow strong again and become the young woman who has always inspired and terrified me with her spirit. I will *not* allow those Soviet bastards to steal that spirit from you, Emilia. It has cost us too much to keep you alive only to lose you to their cruelty."

We sat in ragged silence for a very long time. Truda eventually released me, but only so that she could slide her arm around my shoulders and pull me close. My eyes were dry, but my heart was racing. I would need to process Truda's words. I would need to turn them over in my mind and consider them, to parse each word and determine what was truth and what I could ignore. I needed time—so much time—and my parents were forcing me to move, and by the sounds of things, they meant for us to do so immediately. Elsewhere in the factory, I could hear Mateusz packing up. Preparing us for the journey.

"I don't want to walk back to Warsaw," I whispered eventually. My body had healed, but I remembered Mateusz warning me in the early days that if we were to return to Warsaw, we would be making the trip against an advancing wave of Red Army soldiers. I couldn't imagine how I would convince myself to walk for over one hundred kilometers against a tide of men in *that* uniform.

"Mateusz is going to pay someone to take us. Probably in a horse or cart, maybe even in a truck. It will take only a few hours, and then you'll be home."

"And what if our building is gone?"

"Home isn't a building, Emilia," she scolded me gently. "*Your* home was never a building. It wasn't even the city. Home is family. And you were right all along. Our best chance of finding our family is in Warsaw."

Mateusz found a kindly if opportunistic farmer who owned a rusted but functional truck. In exchange for most of our remaining money, the farmer drove us the hundred kilometers back to Warsaw. When the truck began to slow, I thought perhaps we were lost.

The whispers and rumors we'd managed to hear in Lodz warned us that Warsaw was in ruin, but I didn't really understand what that meant until we approached. The Germans had gone from building to building and block to block, burning and demolishing almost every structure.

"I can't take you any farther," the farmer said hesitantly. I could see why. The road was covered in rubble—huge slabs of concrete and partial brick walls, scattered with smashed glass and thick dust. We had left the city in early October. There had been some damage then, mostly from incendiary devices and fires, but this destruction was all I could see for miles.

"There's nothing left," I whispered numbly.

"There are some buildings," Mateusz said, trying to sound hopeful, but he was entirely unconvincing. He sounded more confused and devastated than optimistic.

"This was a bad idea," I said. "I know that you did this because you thought it would cheer me up, but there is nothing here for us. How would we ever find Roman and Sara, even if they are alive? How would we even find our old building?"

"We have to make it work," Truda said flatly, and she opened the creaky door and slipped out of the truck. I looked at her incredulously.

"Truda, *how*?"

"Get out of the truck, Emilia," she said, pursing her lips.

Beside me, Mateusz and the farmer exchanged quiet farewells, then Mateusz cleared his throat.

"We really should get going. It is going to be quite the walk across the city."

"If we stay here, where will we even sleep tonight?" I asked, frustrated, then added sarcastically, "Do you think we will find a hotel? Maybe an empty mansion we can squat in?"

"We must find Sara. Roman, too. Remember? It was all we could talk about before—" Truda broke off abruptly, eyes widening in realization as if the mere mention of the attack was going to traumatize me further. This enraged me. I felt my face heating.

"Before *what*?" I said.

Truda's gaze dropped to the road. "We have to find them. Just because it's hard doesn't mean we shouldn't do it. That sounds like something you would have said to me, once upon a time."

Mateusz gently nudged me toward the door, and I sighed impatiently and shuffled across. I didn't want to do this. I didn't want to return to Lodz, either, but the thought of becoming vagrants living on the streets of a city that had been destroyed was much more unappealing. Still, I could tell Truda was determined, and I wasn't exactly sure how to counter such a thing. Especially in the state I was in.

I hesitated for another moment, trying to figure it all out, and Truda's patience finally wore thin. She planted her hands on her hips and leaned forward to hiss at me. "We *need* Sara. I do not know how to explain it to you yet, so I am asking you to trust me. There is a very good reason we need to be back in the city, so get out of the car, and let's *go*."

I slipped out of the car, planted my shoes in the crushed-concrete dust and glass that covered the entire street and took a reluctant step forward.

"Good," Truda said, satisfied. She pointed at the back of the truck. "Get your bag. The sooner we start walking, the sooner we will find somewhere to rest tonight."

Mateusz took my bag from the back of the truck and tossed it to me. I caught it, shot them both a resentful glare and set off toward the city.

Six hours later, we stood in stunned silence at the front of what used to be our building. It had fared somewhat better than many of the others we had passed, but it was still severely damaged. Sara's apartment was gone—I assumed a bomb had taken it out. Her side of our entire floor and the floor below us had just disappeared, leaving a gaping hole.

Our apartment was still there, but there were no windows, and there had been a fire on the ground floor. The one small blessing was that there were no corpses visible in the rubble around our apartment. I spent much of the trip stopping to gag, composing myself, then repeating the process all over again just steps down the road. Winter preserved the corpses, but spring had arrived, and they were finally beginning to rot.

We had seen dozens of other people on the road as we crossed Warsaw, at least half of them walking back out of the city, having decided they would prefer to go back to wherever they'd come from. But I didn't have the energy to fight with Truda and Mateusz. I barely had the energy to stand.

"So what do we do now?" I asked them. Truda wiped at her eye, dislodging an errant tear, but we were so dirty and dusty by then that the tear had turned to mud, and she managed to leave only a gray streak of it across her temple. The daylight was starting to fade.

"I'm going to go see how structurally sound the building is," Mateusz announced.

"You're no engineer." I sighed.

He shrugged. "I'll check that the doorframes are still somewhat square. Check that the stairs still have integrity. Check that I can even *get* to the top floors. Then I'll come back and get you girls, okay?"

"And if it's not safe?" I asked him.

He didn't answer. Instead, Mateusz walked through the smashed door and into the lobby. I saw him check the door to the courtyard, but he quickly abandoned that and walked up the stairs.

"Maybe there is still food in the pantry," I said hopefully.

"Unlikely," Truda said abruptly, then she waved her arms around us. "Do you really think there will be anything of value left anywhere when the city looks like this?"

"*I* wanted to go back to Lodz," I reminded her. She pursed her lips but didn't say anything.

After about ten minutes, we saw Mateusz coming back down

the stairs. He stuck his head out the front door, then waved to us to enter. As we approached, he smiled.

"The hallway is very damaged, but outside of that, the building hasn't fared too badly. The windows are all smashed, and some of the furniture has been broken, but our old beds are still there, and once we clean them off, they'll be fine to sleep on. It looks like the rest of the building was looted, but the looters didn't go to the top few floors. Best of all, Mr. Wójcik is still on the second floor and he's been collecting rainwater. He will give us enough for tonight, and tomorrow I'll walk to the river for more. Sound okay?"

"And food?" Truda asked.

"There's still cans under Piotr's bed," he said, then he beamed. "See? We're lucky."

"Lucky," I said and snorted, pushing past him to make my way upstairs. The gaping hallway and the void where Sara's apartment had been gave me shivers, so I quickly slipped into our apartment. As soon as I did, my gaze landed on the stairwell that led to my bedroom. I climbed the stairs two at a time, then rushed across the room to the wall opposite the window. I dusted it with my palm, wiping down the whole wall to free the mural from beneath the film.

The city was gone, but my mural was still there—capturing a moment that felt like it had been frozen a lifetime ago. I sank onto the floor by the couple I'd drawn at the last minute and then reached out to trace the boy with the tip of my finger. My characters were strangers now, but they were strangers I was immensely jealous of.

For dinner that night, we warmed up canned beans over a fire Mateusz built out of wood he had salvaged from the rubble on the road. Up high in our apartment, the stench of the city was not so bad, and I managed to keep my food down. Truda had done her best to shake the dust and chunks of debris out of our bedding, and they set my bed up in their old room, right beside their mattress. I wanted to protest and remind them that I was not a child, but I felt far from safe anywhere, and I was shaken by the chaos in Warsaw. We had seen no shortage of Soviet soldiers as we crossed the city, and I didn't want to be alone.

As soon as we finished eating, I excused myself and climbed into bed, and as I lay staring up at the ceiling in the fading spring light, it occurred to me that when I had lived in this household, I had prayed every night. I hadn't said a single prayer since the attack, but now, for the first time, I closed my eyes and offered one up.

Thank you for sparing our apartment. Please look after Roman and Sara. Please let them be happy and healthy and safe.

"She seems worse, not better," I heard Mateusz say. I opened my eyes, suddenly racked by guilt at the concern in his voice.

"We need to find Sara."

"You really think Sara can help her in some way that we can't?"

"I know she can."

"Why?"

"She knows things about…" Truda cleared her throat "…about women." There was a longer pause, then Truda's voice dropped further as she admitted, "I don't even know how to talk to her about this."

"Tomorrow, I'll start scouring the city. If she's here, I'll find her. But have you thought about what we'll do if she's not here? I hate to say this, but there's a very real possibility Sara didn't even make it out of Warsaw alive."

I rolled over then and covered my head with a spare pillow.

For the next few days, Truda and I worked from morning to night, trying to restore order to our apartment. We only left to walk the short distance to the banks of the Vistula River, filling buckets with water for cleaning. Mateusz made the same journey with us each morning, filling an additional bucket for drinking water. Then he would leave and be gone all day. He registered us for the grant the city was offering those who returned, and then he started looking for Sara and for a job.

As the days passed, I found a comfort in the city that I hadn't expected. Such a thing seemed impossible when we had first returned, but as I settled into life among the ruins, I began to see signs of recovery. They were only baby steps: a family returning here, a determined old woman raising hens on a patch of crushed cobblestones there, a man collecting bricks from the street and stacking them up on the sidewalk, doing what he could to clear rubble so that vehicles could move freely again. But each of these things seemed important, and I gradually stopped focusing on what was gone and started focusing on new signs of life. It made me feel strangely hopeful.

I was sitting in an empty window staring out at the street watching all of this, when a sudden thought struck me.

"Truda?" I called, climbing down from the sill and dusting myself off.

"Yes? What is it? Is something wrong? Are you okay?"

She blew in from the kitchen, flustered. Sometimes, I felt nothing at all; other times, I felt everything at once. In that moment, I felt an irritation so strong it could have knocked me over. It occurred to me that in the twelve weeks since the attack, I hadn't had a moment alone. Strength surged through me.

If Warsaw could recover, so could I.

"I'm going to get fresh air."

"Fresh air?" she repeated skeptically, and her gaze skipped to the gaping hole I had just been sitting in.

"I want to go see what's left of the courtyard," I admitted. Her gaze softened, and she wiped her hands on her apron, then began to remove it.

"Okay, let's—"

"Truda," I interrupted her gently. She looked at me hesitantly. "I want to go by myself."

"Oh," she said.

"It's safe. I'm just walking down the stairs."

"But…it's a mess down there. The rubble…" She gave me a bewildered look. "What do you even want to do down there?"

"I don't know. I just feel like going for a walk."

"I don't think this is a good idea, Emilia."

"If you're really concerned about me, you can stick your head out into the hallway and look down at me through the gap where Sara's apartment used to be," I said wryly. Truda sighed.

"Go on, then. But don't be too long."

Downstairs, I pushed at the back door carefully and, when it didn't budge, pressed my shoulder into it and applied more force.

"What are you doing there, Elżbieta?" Mr. Wójcik called from above.

"I'm trying to get into the courtyard, Mr. Wójcik," I called back. "The door is stuck."

"Give me a few minutes, and I'll come help you."

After a while, he limped slowly down the stairs with a tool-box in one hand. He set it on the floor beside the door and rummaged around until he found a chisel. I watched him tinker with the lock for several minutes, cursing and muttering. Just as I was about to give up, he gave a shout of triumph, and the door sprang open.

"There," he said, nodding in satisfaction. He peered out into the courtyard, then winced. "That mess isn't going to be as easy to fix, is it?"

"Thanks, Mr. Wójcik." I drew in a deep breath, then climbed over the rubble that partly blocked the doorway. Just as I reached the other side, the clouds parted, and the courtyard was suddenly flooded with golden spring light. I surveyed it all, seeing both the way it used to be and the way it was now. My gaze fell upon the apple tree. One half of it was healthy branches covered in fresh, new growth and pretty white blossoms. The other half was singed, but even so, green buds were emerging here and there.

The courtyard had never been an elaborate garden, but it had been ours. As I looked around the wasteland, I felt a pang of grief in my chest, then a surge of determination.

If every citizen of Warsaw had a part to play in our rebuilding, then I surely had a part to play, too, and I could start with this. Smashed glass, china, twisted metal and singed bits of wood, furniture and clothing, and torn scraps of fabric littered the courtyard. Maybe I couldn't move it all, but if I shifted a little every day, I could eventually make this space usable.

I made my way over the rubble and toward the apple tree. I sat with my back against it and looked up at our broken building and the glorious blue sky beyond it. I closed my eyes and I breathed in the sweetness of the blossoms. I was glad to be alive, and it was the first time since the attack I'd felt that way.

After a while, I rested my hands on the dirt to push myself up, and my palm collided with an unexpectedly smooth, cold object, partially uncovered in the soil beneath the tree. I rolled onto my knees and scraped the dirt around it until I could lift it.

The glass jar was filthy, but as I rubbed it to remove the dirt, I recognized scraps of cigarette papers inside. Hundreds or maybe even thousands of pieces, each neatly folded into squares.

I unscrewed the lid of the glass jar, wiped my hands on my shirt, then withdrew and unfolded a piece of paper. In Matylda's distinctive script, it read:

Ala Skibińska
Rescued 7 July, 1942
Taken to Franciskan Orphanage, Hoża Street
Placed with Walter and Zenobia Buliński, Szydłowiec

I carefully refolded the paper, then opened several more. Each piece was a trail of bread crumbs, designed to lead a Jewish child home. I remembered that final night before we were captured, when Sara had come to say goodbye and I'd been so fixated on her dirty fingernails. Now, it made perfect sense. She'd been burying Matylda's records in case the apartment was damaged.

The city had been destroyed—almost every building ruined, most of them beyond repair. But the apple tree had survived, and this fragile glass jar was completely undamaged. It was a miracle.

I considered taking the jar back up to our apartment, but my intense distrust of the Red Army dissuaded me. Instead, I deepened the hole beneath the apple tree. I buried the jar again and carefully covered it with soft black dirt, then covered that with rubble. I knew I would find it again—when I could find Sara, she would pass these records on to the Jewish authorities. The nuns at the convent could help, too. Some of the children we rescued might even still be there—

And that's when it hit me. If Sara had been captured, she probably would have been released by now, and she would inevitably have made her way back to Warsaw. And if she had nowhere else to stay, I knew a group of women who would not have thought twice before taking her in.

The next day, Truda and Mateusz insisted on walking with me to find the orphanage on Hoża Street.

"The convent might not be there anymore," Truda warned. "And even if it is, Sara might not be there."

"I know," I said. "I just want to see for myself."

"What will we do with the jar if we can't find her?" Mateusz asked.

"Leave it where it is," I said firmly. "Until we know who we can trust."

I knew that churches all across the city had been destroyed, but somehow in my heart I felt certain that if God had saved

that glass jar, he would have saved the women who helped Matylda and Sara fill it. We finally turned the corner onto Hoża
Street, and my knees went weak with relief. The facade and
roof of the orphanage were still standing.

"I knew it," I cried, then ran ahead, feeling something like
excitement for the first time in months. There were Sisters out
front, handing out bread to passersby. I didn't recognize any of
them, but when they saw me, they offered me a loaf of bread
anyway. I waved it away. "Is Sara here? Sara Wieczorek?"

The Sister motioned to the door behind her.

"I think she is in the kitchen preparing lunch."

I ran through the door, almost colliding with a nun coming
the other way. With tears in my eyes, I asked her for directions
to the kitchen. Truda and Mateusz followed closely behind.

Sara was sitting at the kitchen table, chopping vegetables with
a young nun. When I burst through the door, she looked up,
startled, and then she dropped the knife and leaped to her feet
with an exclamation of joy.

"You're alive!" she gasped, and then her gaze landed on Truda
and Mateusz behind me. "You're all alive, my God!"

I threw myself into her arms, then I began to weep across her
chest. She embraced me, murmuring reassurances into my hair,
immediately offering me comfort. Those around her shifted
away so that Sara could take her seat on the bench again and
pull me across her lap like an infant. I was crying so hard I
couldn't even hear the conversation between her and Truda and
Mateusz. War had forced me to become an adult far too soon,
but back in Sara's arms, I was a child. Grief and pain and fear
poured out of me, a torrent of tears that I was powerless to stop.

"Let it out, Emilia," she whispered, rubbing my back. "That's
it, sweetheart. You just let it all out. Everything is going to be
fine."

The busy kitchen gradually emptied, until only Mateusz and
Truda and Sara and I were left behind. Truda busied herself

making us all cups of coffee, and Mateusz handed me his hand-kerchief.

"Our clever girl found your jar in the courtyard last night," he told Sara.

She looked at me in surprise, then she asked hesitantly, "Is it..."

"It is intact!" I told her. "Under the apple tree."

"Yes!" She beamed. She clasped her hands against her chest and exhaled with visible relief. "When I first came back to Warsaw I went past the apartment building, but I couldn't get the courtyard door open."

"The lock was damaged," I told her. "Mr. Wójcik had to help me unstick it."

"What did you do with the jar?" Sara asked me.

"I buried it. A little deeper because it was exposed. And I have covered it with rubble. It's safe there unless you want me to bring it here."

"Thank you, Emilia." She smiled sadly. "I'll need to speak to some people—to try to figure out who in the Jewish community has survived...who can help us sort through those records. I'm not sure how many families can be restored, but the process will not be easy—the sooner we start, the better."

The four of us ate lunch in the dining hall, catching up on the months that had passed since the Uprising. Sara told us that at the transit camp in Pruszków, she was told she'd be sent to a concentration camp.

"So they loaded me onto the train, and I thought I haven't come this far to die in a godforsaken camp. Some of the women in my carriage figured out how to get the door open, and in the middle of the night, we waited for the train to slow for a corner and then jumped off it."

"Where did you land?" I asked her, eyes wide.

"In a puddle, Emilia," she chuckled. "I hid in the woods for a while, then I was lucky enough to find a farmer and his wife who let me stay with them in exchange for some labor on their farm. I've only been back in Warsaw a few weeks."

When we finished eating, Truda asked me to take the empty plates back to the kitchen, and when I returned, Sara stood, her expression grave.

"Come on, my friend," she said quietly. "Let's take a walk to my room."

I knew instantly that Truda and Mateusz had told her about the attack in Lodz. I glared at them, and they avoided my gaze.

"No," I said, shaking my head. "Let's just stay here and enjoy being together again. We don't need to talk about anything in private."

Undeterred, Sara gently slid her arm through mine. I sighed impatiently and let her lead me from the dining hall.

"Truda thought you might want to talk with me," Sara said quietly, as she sat upon her bed. I stood stubbornly at the door as she patted the space beside her.

"I *don't* need to talk about it," I said, looking away. "But thank you."

"Emilia, they are very worried about you."

"I'm starting to feel better," I said truthfully. "Today has been the best day I can remember for a long time."

"It's been a good day for me, too. I'm so happy to see you again," Sara said and smiled, but then her smile faded, and she cleared her throat. "There's something else, Emilia. How do you feel? Physically?"

"I'm better," I said quickly. "I really don't—"

"Sweetheart," Sara said softly. I looked at her, then looked away. "Truda is concerned that you may be pregnant."

My gaze flew back to hers.

"What? No! Why would she—"

But I realized then that I hadn't had my courses since the attack. I sank onto the bed. Suddenly, Truda's insistence that we return to Warsaw made a lot more sense. Truda, with her near phobia about frank discussions of human biology, would not have been comfortable broaching this possibility with me, let alone figuring out what to *do* about such a scenario.

"I can't," I blurted, shaking my head in fear. "I can't be…"

I couldn't even bring myself to say the word. Surely I would have known if…

"Can I examine you?" Sara asked gently. "It was three months ago, yes? Late March?" I nodded stiffly. She had me lie on the mattress, and she pressed her fingers on my abdomen. After a moment, her hand stilled on my belly. "Do you remember when we talked about my nursing textbook? Do you remember when I told you that we can measure the fundal height of the uterus to determine the gestation of a pregnancy?"

"Please, no," I whispered. My lips felt numb. Sara touched a spot on my lower stomach.

"I can feel the top of your uterus here. That means that most likely you are around twelve weeks pregnant."

"I want it out of me," I said, sitting up and pushing her hands away. I was shaking, trembling in a way that I hadn't since the day of the attack. I wanted to tear my stomach open with my fingernails. I felt as violated as I had lying on the cobblestones that day.

"Sweetheart, there is nothing I can do. You will have to do—"

"You have to find someone that can help me," I pleaded. "There has to be someone in the city who can… There has to be some way to stop it. I can't— You can't—"

Sara's hands gripped my shoulders, and she stared into my eyes.

"Emilia, you are strong. You have made it this far. You can do this."

"I can't," I whimpered. "This is too much. It's all been bad, but this is too much." A new thought struck me, and I pressed my hands over my mouth, feeling my lunch in the back of my throat. "People will know, Sara! People will *see*! What will they say?" I started to cry at last, feeling the shame rise all over again. "I don't know what's worse...that people might think I am a whore, or that people will know that I'm not."

"We will find somewhere for you to go," she said calmly. "Somewhere safe. The Sisters will help us... You can shelter somewhere until the birth, and then you can start afresh. No one will even know."

"I can't do this," I said again, sobs coming in earnest again now. "Please, Sara. Help me. There has to be a way to stop it."

"You and I have been through a lot, Emilia. That's how I know that you *can* do this."

By the time we left the orphanage that day, new plans were in place. I'd be moving to a Franciscan convent in Marki. The Sisters would take me in until the baby was born.

"And then what?" I asked Sara numbly.

"Then we will find someone to adopt the baby, and you can move back to Warsaw with Truda and Mateusz to figure out what comes next."

35

Roman

IT HAD BEEN ALMOST SIX MONTHS SINCE THE UPRISING HAD failed. I marked the days with tiny notches on the wooden frame of my bunk in the dormitory at the Stalag XIII-D POW Camp, on the Nazi-party rally grounds in Nuremberg.

"I don't understand why you're in such good spirits," Kacper muttered. This startled a burst of laughter from me.

"No one has *ever* said those words to me before."

He and the other Polish prisoners were shocked by the dirty barracks, the broken windows as well as the lack of heating, the worn mattresses and the bedbugs. Some protested at the pits we used for outhouses or the troughs of cold water we were provided for bathing. To those prisoners, such conditions seemed unbearable, but after what I'd endured in the Warsaw Ghetto, the Nuremberg camp was a walk in the park. With the bulk of the German ire focused on Soviet prisoners, I soon realized I could keep my head down, work hard at my assigned role in the munitions factory and reasonably expect to survive.

That's not to say I was disappointed when the Americans liberated the camp in April 1945. We heard whispers that they were coming, and the way the Germans fled as the Americans approached was a thing of beauty. But while my fellow prisoners were all delirious with joy, I was anxious for news of my homeland.

"What is happening in Poland?" I asked a translator, who was working with the Americans to guide us to Red Cross workers for food and medical assistance.

"The Red Army has liberated Poland," he told me, beaming.

"Liberated?" I repeated incredulously, but my heart sank. "So you're telling me we have overcome the Germans only to fall under Soviet rule."

"The government-in-exile is confident that they will be able to regain control of Poland through negotiations."

"The Soviets occupied half of Poland for the first few years of the war! They only lost that territory because of the German advance. They watched the Uprising fail when they could easily have intervened to help. Now that they have pushed the Germans out of Poland, do you really think they are simply going to leave again?"

I saw his smile fade.

"These American soldiers told me that there are countries all over the world who have offered to take Polish refugees," he said nervously. "You don't have to go back."

"Don't have to go back?" I repeated. "Poland is my *home*. Do you think I've survived everything this war has thrown at me only to give up on it? Besides, my girl is waiting for me there."

Unfortunately for Kacper, I had been right about his foot. The Red Cross doctor wanted to amputate it, but with thousands of urgent cases in the camp, he was going to have to wait for his turn.

The poor kid was utterly terrified and tried to convince the doctors to let him return to Poland to seek medical attention there. When we saw pictures of what was left of Warsaw in a newspaper, even Kacper realized this was going to be impossible.

"Will you stay?" he asked. "They say they won't let me leave until the stump heals."

I shook my head automatically.

"I need to get back to find my friends."

"Please, Roman," he whispered, his voice shaking with fear. "I don't want to be here on my own."

"You've been a pain in my ass since the first moment I met you, kid," I muttered, but even so, I could never leave him to face what lay ahead alone. I took a job washing linens in the camp laundry and moved into a dormitory with dozens of other Polish men. Most were planning to immigrate to whichever country would take them, unable to bear returning home. But home was all I *could* bear. Emilia was there, and I knew that she would be looking for me. I had to find some way to let her know I had survived.

At first, I thought this would be simple: I'd just send her a letter, address it to her old address in Warsaw. But at the camp administration office, a worker told me that the postal service in Warsaw wasn't operating.

"Have you seen the photos?" he said, grimacing. "Finding an address is all but impossible. The best you can do is to register with us and hope that your girlfriend registers with the Red Cross office in Warsaw, too."

I added Kacper's name along with mine to the list of Poles searching for their family members, and he promised to let me know if he heard anything. Within a few weeks, Kacper's parents had sent a message: they were safe and well, living with his uncle in refugee accommodation in a school hall in Warsaw and anxious for his return.

I spent the next four months in the Red Cross camp, waiting—for news of Emilia that would never come, for Kacper's surgery and, finally, waiting for his stump to heal.

By the time we were ready to leave at the end of September, I had only two things on my mind: reconnecting with the Resistance and building the future with Emilia that I had been living for.

36

Emilia

SARA THOUGHT THE BABY WAS DUE TO COME AT CHRISTMAS-time, so I would need to live at the convent for at least five months. The day she left me there, she reassured me that this was for the best.

"The routine of life in the convent will make the days pass quickly," she told me. Truda had made the journey with us to Marki and stayed for two nights to help me settle in.

"Are you sure you want to stay here?" she asked when it was finally time for her to go. She looked anxiously around the lobby of the convent, a fretful mother scanning the environs for danger. "I feel awful leaving you here all on your own."

"It's for the best," I told her numbly. "I want to stay here," I admitted, dropping my gaze. I didn't know how to explain that part of my determination to avoid that apartment was rooted in my desperation to avoid Roman. I missed him desperately, and I knew that he would be missing me. I trusted completely that he was doing whatever it took to get back to find me. If I remained at that apartment, I might open the door to Roman, and I'd have to see the hurt and anger in his eyes. I wasn't ready for that. Even the thought of Mr. Wójcik on the second floor seeing my swollen belly filled me with shame. Besides, how could I ever rebuild my life if anyone in the homes around us knew about the pregnancy? The only way I could get through the next phase of this ordeal was to suffer through it in hiding.

The convent operated on a regimented schedule that seldom varied. I would wake at seven, tidy my room and bathe, then take morning exercise with the Sisters, usually walking around the yards. After that we would share breakfast and then pray the matins.

The nuns would study the scriptures after that, but because my circumstances were unusual, I was encouraged to continue my general academic studies. Sister Agnieszka Gracja had worked as a teacher in her younger days, and the very first time I met her, she offered to help me catch up on my schooling.

"If you work hard, then by the time this is all over, you'll be a step closer to matriculation. And who knows? If Poland is rebuilt, the Soviets may allow us to operate universities again."

After that, mornings became about books and words, about math and science. I liked to play a game with myself, to pretend that I was at the convent purely so I could complete my schooling. As my clothes became tight, I liked to pretend that I had been overindulging in the bland convent food.

The Sisters were constantly looking for ways to contribute to the local community, and most had taken up knitting hats for children in the village. I joined in at first, unraveling damaged clothing the way I'd once done for Sara, but after Sister Renata learned I liked to draw and paint, she found a notepad and pencils and some old house paint and wooden boards. After that, while the circle of nuns knit in prayerful silence, I painted.

I found such comfort in capturing details of the convent. I painted the arches along the church hallways, marveling at the way the light and shadows marked their own story onto the two-hundred-year-old stone walls, a different story at each hour of the day. I sketched Sister Walentyna's hand as she held a knitting needle, trying to capture the sunspots and the freckles and the wrinkles. I painted a blue china bowl left empty on a table when the apples were gone, and then I sketched it again when the apples were replenished.

While I still wasn't ready to accept the reality of my situation, my art allowed me to ponder it from the side. I had always loved creating—drawing and painting were the voice of my soul. But in those months, three things saved me: the care of a group of nuns who loved me simply because I was a child of God; art, which allowed me to view the world through the lens of a child again; and Roman. In my darkest days, it was thoughts of Roman that kept me going.

I had no idea when or even if we would be reunited. Sometimes, I tried to force myself to consider the reality that he might not even have survived, but I never let myself dwell for long. He was too vibrant—too determined. I had to believe he would have found a way to survive after the Uprising, too.

There were now many complications and confusions to a relationship that had once felt pure, but the strength of my feelings was undeniable. He was always on my mind, and even there in the convent, I could daydream for hours about those wonderful weeks and months he and I had spent together. Something of my soul was bound to something of his, and until we built a life together, I would yearn for his return.

But even as I missed him, and even as I fretted for him, I sometimes found myself feeling anxious about our reunion. I tried to imagine telling him about that day in Lodz or him seeing my swollen belly.

Anxiety soon turned to dread when I realized that every single time I pictured those moments, I saw one inevitable outcome: Roman losing himself to anger, wanting to tear the world apart for me.

I began to realize that as deep as my love for him was, the attack had left me a long way from being able to face his unbridled rage.

Getting to the convent was not an easy journey from Warsaw. Sometimes, it took two or three hours each way. Truda, Mateusz and Sara usually walked to the edge of the city where the roads were clear, then tried to hitchhike with any cart or car that passed. Even so, they each visited as often as they could. The Sisters never looked at or acknowledged my growing belly, which helped me to ignore it, too. But once it began to swell in earnest in June, my parents struggled to look anywhere else.

The periods between their visits were the longest we had been apart since they had adopted me, and I missed them viscerally. I'd count down the minutes until they were due to arrive, but within minutes of their arrival, I resented the thick awkwardness of our interaction.

"Did you really just come here to look at it?" I snapped at Truda one day.

She startled guiltily, as if she'd been caught committing a mortal sin.

Sara, on the other hand, maintained her light touch even when it came to my pregnancy. She asked me narrow questions about my health—How are you feeling? Are you eating enough? Are you still tired? Do you need any larger clothes? Do you have any questions?—without ever once drawing attention to the fact that I was, in fact, pregnant.

I didn't use that word when I thought about my current status. I certainly didn't think about what the endgame was. I was tired and uncomfortable, and I was in a strange place, but I was safe, and I knew one day I would get to return to Warsaw.

By all accounts, the city was beginning to recover, repairing itself bit by bit, even though the Red Army was a constant presence on the streets in Warsaw, just as it had been in Lodz. My visitors told me that the uncertainty of the early days of the Soviet occupation was beginning to fade into a more predictable reality and that the immense number of Red Army soldiers on the streets was slowly dwindling, too—as if there was an unspoken acceptance from both sides that the Communists were now in charge. It seemed that the entire country was coming to grips with the reality that those soldiers were going to be a part of our lives for a long time. That thought left me sick to my stomach, even as I recognized that, sooner or later, I would have to learn to accept it, too.

Mateusz found work on a street crew, clearing the streets so machinery and vehicles could again travel freely. Truda redecorated the apartment as much as she could, given there was still no glass in the windowpanes.

"But don't worry," she assured me carefully, her gaze dropping to my belly, then shooting back to my face before settling on the wall behind me. "By the time you come home, it will be winter. One way or another, we will have fixed the window situation by then."

One night in September, I was lying in my sparse cell in the convent, looking up at the crucifix on the wall above me. The moon was full, and the room was too bright. I couldn't get comfortable, and I had been shifting and wriggling, trying to figure out how to make my alien body feel *mine* again. When I finally stilled, the wriggling continued, only now, *I* wasn't doing the wriggling. There was a distinct and startling shift in my belly.

Over two months had passed since Sara had gently told me I was pregnant, but for the very first time I was forced to confront the reality of what those words meant.

I was going to have a baby, but it could never be my baby. I could no more claim that child as my own than I could claim the destruction of Warsaw was for the best.

I tentatively reached down to skim my fingers over my belly for the first time. I was so careful to avoid touching that bump as it grew, but now, I let my fingers explore the new landscape. I felt the wriggling again and, this time, tried to picture what a baby inside me might look like.

Images swam in my imagination—the spitting, snarling hate of strangers in Red Army uniforms—and I broke out in a cold sweat. I rolled onto my side and curled my legs up, not protecting my belly but almost guarding myself against it. How could a child conceived in that way be anything but ugly and destructive?

The next day, I made myself a calendar. Sara had told me the baby would come at Christmastime, so I marked a box for every day until then.

One hundred and eleven days. I just had to survive one hundred and eleven more days until my body could be mine again, and I promised myself that, once it was all over, I would never so much as think of that baby ever again.

"Have you heard any news of Roman?" I asked my parents one day. They hadn't mentioned him since my move to the convent, and I couldn't help but wonder if they were trying to protect me from bad news. "If there's something wrong, you can tell me. I'd rather know."

"I promise, Emilia, we haven't heard a thing, but I don't think you need to worry," Mateusz said quietly. "Most of the insurgents were sent to camps in Germany. He's probably still trying to make his way back to Warsaw, and once he does... Well, you've seen the city. It may be some time before he surfaces."

"If he does find me...find you..." I drew in a deep breath, then closed my eyes "...you can tell him what has happened, but I don't want to see him yet. Please don't tell him where I am."

I opened my eyes just in time to see the glance they exchanged, but for a moment they were silent, until at the very same time Mateusz said, "That's your decision," and Truda said, "You should let him visit. He will try to help."

"He will want to tear this thing out of my body just as I do," I snapped at Truda, gesturing vaguely toward my belly. "You saw him that day at the convent. He was wild—out of control. I love Roman, but he doesn't know how *not* to fight, and he would approach all of this in the exact same way." I ran out of steam and slumped as I admitted, "I just cannot deal with *his* anger and mine at the same time."

Truda linked her hands and leaned forward across the table.

"Then, tell me, Emilia. What exactly do you want us to say to him when he returns?"

"Tell him the truth," I said, stiffening my spine and brushing my hair back from my face. "Tell him I love him, but that I need time to figure this out."

37

Roman

KACPER WAS SAFE WITH HIS FAMILY AT LONG LAST, AND having watched the emotional reunion he shared with his parents, I was more than ready for an emotional reunion of my own. I stood at the door to Piotr's apartment, glancing between that intact door and the gaping space where my old home used to be. There was a sheer drop down into the courtyard just a few feet from Piotr's door, a space now full of rubble, surrounding a surprisingly robust apple tree.

I raised my fist and knocked. There was movement inside the apartment, and then the door opened. Mateusz was there—dressed in a uniform I didn't recognize. He gasped, then he opened his arms and embraced me. He thumped me on the back and squeezed me tightly, then all but dragged me into the apartment.

"My God," he said. "It is so good to see you, son."

"And you, too," I said and grinned, but then I looked around the apartment, searching for Emilia.

"She is not here, but she's alive," Mateusz said, but there was something in his tone—something dark. A burst of adrenaline ran through me. I had been about to sit on the couch, but I froze halfway, my muscles locked.

"What happened?"

"I'll get the vodka, and then you and I need to talk."

I sat on the sofa, watching him search the kitchen cupboards, muttering about Truda reorganizing and the vodka being lost. My patience quickly wore thin.

"Tell me, Mateusz. Just tell me."

Mateusz turned. He leaned against the kitchen counter. He gave me a helpless look and then slumped as he murmured, "Roman, she's pregnant." Of all the things I had feared, Emilia finding someone else hadn't even factored into my anxieties. I was no stranger to rage, but the jealousy that shot through my body was entirely new. I was on my feet in a heartbeat, restless and ready to tear the world apart, but before I could say a word, Mateusz said firmly, "Sit *down*." His voice broke, and the anguish in his face cut through the fury. "Just sit down, and listen to me."

I sank slowly onto the sofa, realization dawning. I closed my eyes.

"No," I whispered. "Please, no."

"We were in Lodz. It was Red Army soldiers. They were…" He inhaled sharply, then shook his head. "It is bad, Roman. I am so sorry. It is like the light in her eyes has been extinguished. She is not in a good way."

"Where is she?"

"She is in hiding until the birth. She will have the baby, and Sara will find a family to adopt it."

"When can I see her?"

"Roman," he said pleadingly, "you *can't*. She doesn't want to see you, and I'll be honest with you—I didn't fully understand why until just now. She is not ready to deal with your anger until she has made sense of her own. A display of rage like yours just now? God, I hate to even think of how that would scare her. She is so fragile…so withdrawn. I think…for now, she has made the right decision."

I didn't even know how to explain the urgency I felt, to go comfort her, to help her heal. I could fix this—I knew I could—I just needed the chance to see her.

"But I—"

"*No,*" Mateusz said flatly. "Whatever you are thinking, no. We must respect her wishes. I won't tell you where she is."

Mateusz had scolded me for my anger, and so I pushed it down, but I was horrified to realize that something even worse was rising up instead. *Grief.* I was going to weep for her, and I couldn't do it in front of Mateusz.

I glanced at him hesitantly, and his eyes were full of understanding.

"Stay with us. You can take her room for as long as you need it."

"I'm tired," I said. My voice was thick with tears, barely even audible. Mateusz looked away, and I was grateful. "I just need to rest. It's been a long journey."

"Of course."

I walked up the stairs, choking on a sob as I reached the top. But when I came to the doorway, I saw the mural of the city across the length of the wall, and my eyes were drawn to the bottom-right corner, to a scene full of love and hope. The figures she'd drawn were clearly, undeniably us—sharing the future I had chosen to live for.

I closed the door behind me, sat on the floor near the mural and wept like a child.

"You have no idea what that girl has been through," Truda told me that night as she made up the bed under the mural in Emilia's room. Her movements were brisk, and she brushed at the sheet fiercely. "You're welcome to stay with us for as long as you wish, but I won't have you harping on about her. She has made her feelings clear, and she has enough to deal with without you bothering her. And *I* have enough to deal with without you bothering *me* about her. Do you understand?"

"Yes, Truda," I said. But I couldn't sleep that night, and once she and Mateusz had gone to bed, I walked the halls of the apartment with the lamp Mateusz had given me. In Uncle Piotr's old room, I found a scrap of paper and a pen.

Dear Emilia,

I'm sorry. I am just so sorry for everything that you have been through and for everything you are going through.

I am staying with your parents, but they have made it abundantly clear that you are not ready to see me and, of course, I will honor that. But I want you to know that I still dream of a future with you, and when you are ready to dream again, too, I will be here waiting.

They have given me your room for the time being. I could stare at the mural on your wall all day and night and never tire of it. The city is gone, but it lives on in your art. The power and beauty of it takes my breath away. I love the way you drew us. I love the way I can see the love in your eyes as you stare up at me on that wall.

Take all the time you need, Emilia. Do you remember the picture you painted for me with your words that day at the convent hospital? A family of our own, a home. I'll find a way to study—become a lawyer like my father. And you'll raise the children and keep the house, and you'll paint. God, how you'll paint!

Our future is worth waiting for, and it is also worth fighting for.

For now, it is my plan to find work to support myself while I reconnect with the Resistance. You know better than most that this war is not over for us, and it will not be over until we are free. I hope that you know I am committed to the fight. I hope that when you are ready, you will join me.

All my love,
Roman

On Saturday, when Mateusz and Truda began to prepare for the long journey to wherever Emilia was hiding, I asked them to take the letter.

"I don't know if this is a good idea," Mateusz said, staring at the note in my hand.

"You can read it," I said. "There is nothing in there that is secret. I just want her to know that I'm back and that I care about her. It even says that I understand why she won't see me."

Truda snatched the letter from me and gave me a sharp look.

"I'll read it on the way. If I think it is suitable, I'll give it to her."

When they returned later that afternoon, Truda found me in Emilia's bedroom.

"She took your letter," she said curtly. "She didn't want to reply."

38

Emilia

EVERY TIME THEY VISITED, TRUDA AND MATEUSZ BROUGHT
me a letter from Roman. I always read them, even if it sometimes took me a few days to find the courage to do so.

*Dear Emilia, I am staying in your room, and morning and night I stare
at your mural. Have I ever told you how breathtaking I find your talent? Every day I find new details to marvel at. Every day I try to find
the dance of the light and the shadow, and when I think I feel it, I
feel you with me...*

*Dear Emilia, I have exciting news—I've found a job. I'm working
on the same road crew as Mateusz. I can't wait until I can tell you
all about it. Warsaw is coming back to life, Emilia. We are sorting
through the rubble and rebuilding what we can. There is work to be
done, and the fight isn't over, but it feels good to be helping people
find homes again...*

Dear Emilia, Mateusz is applying for a grant to start a new textiles factory. I'm sure he will tell you all about it, but I'm helping him with the paperwork. Remember when you asked me if I wanted to be the kind of lawyer who does boring contracts? Maybe I should reconsider: it seems I'm pretty good at this. I miss you, and I can't wait to see you again. I hope you are growing stronger. Poland needs you, and I need you, too.

"We could stop bringing them," Truda offered uncertainly. She visited me alone in mid-October, on a weekday when Mateusz was working. "I don't think we could convince him to stop writing them, but there's no reason we should bring them if you don't want them."

I didn't know how to explain that I looked forward to those letters as much as I looked forward to her visits. I poured over the words again and again, trying to absorb his love for me right off the page.

"He can write," I said carefully. "I'm just not ready to see him or to reply."

I knew the sharpness of his pen and the pattern to his words. They always spoke of longing and affection and of feelings for me that had not changed, despite what I had been through. I often cried as I read them, wondering if he'd feel the same if I let him visit or if he'd be repulsed by my monstrous belly and the sadness and exhaustion I just couldn't shake.

But the letters always ended on a war cry. Every single time.

...while they are on our streets, we are not yet free. The fight has only just begun.

...so many seem resigned to a further occupation of Poland, but I cannot and I will not accept it.

...I am meeting people, making connections, just trying to figure out the best way to mobilize.

And every time I read that war cry, I was reminded of the violence in him—of the bloodlust and the desperation for revenge and freedom. It was completely understandable after everything he had seen and everything he had lost. Maybe I even loved that part of Roman, just as I loved the rest of him. His passion for justice and for a liberated Poland knew no bounds.

I just wasn't sure I could deal with his aggression in the way I always had. Every morning, I woke and hoped to find I felt differently. Every night, I prayed to God to make me stronger, so that we could be reunited.

I wanted to find peace, but I realized peace could only be found if I accepted my life would never be what it once was. That might mean accepting that my country would never be what it had been. Such an attitude, even if I could achieve it, would mean putting my life's path at odds with Roman's, because I knew he would *never* rest until Poland was governed once again by the Polish.

The rest of that mid-October visit with Truda unfolded as they always did. Her eyes dipped to my belly, and her questions would come rapid-fire, soothing and smothering me in equal measures.

"How are you feeling? Can I get you anything?"

"No, thank you."

"Are you eating? Sleeping well? Are the Sisters still taking good care of you?"

"Truda," I said, as gently as I could, "I promise you, I'm fine."

"You look so tired."

"I *am* so tired. It never stops moving," I muttered, rubbing my lower back. I felt like I was awake all the time now, the squirming and wriggling beneath my heart constant, as if the baby were determined to make sure I couldn't forget about it, even just for a moment of peace. As if it had consciously decided to torture me with its very existence.

Worse than that, I finally realized that even once I gave birth and the baby had gone to live with some other family, I would never forget it. Sometimes I would touch my belly with one hand, wanting to send thoughts of kindness, as if that would help it grow up to be a good person, as my other hand curled into a furious fist, resting on the sheet beside me. The balance of loving and hating the intruder in my belly was exhausting. It gradually dawned on me that even when the pregnancy was over I would be torn between relief and grief. It seemed that life wasn't finished with its cruel tricks.

When Sara came for her next visit, she was buzzing with excitement. She'd taken a job as a nurse at the newly reopened Warsaw Hospital. With a reliable income, she'd been able to rent a small apartment and had at last moved out of the orphanage.

"Sara, what happened to the records of the children we rescued from the ghetto?"

"I went and retrieved the jar, just after we moved you here. A woman named Miriam Liebman is now leading the project to restore the children to their families. She's a widow, the wife of a well-respected rabbi who died during the war. I check in on her every few weeks. So far she has managed to reunite only a handful of families." Sara bit her lip. "You and I both know that those deported on the trains will not be found."

"And... Eleonora Gorka?"

Sara smiled faintly.

"Roman asked after her, too, the moment he returned. Miriam has tried to make contact with Eleonora's foster family but has had no luck. We think they may have moved since we were last in touch with them." At my look of alarm, Sara hastened to reassure me. "This does not mean Eleonora is lost—it might just take a little while for Miriam and her team to track her down."

We sat in silence for a while, before Sara told me she had to go so she could be home before dark. As she got up to leave, she passed me a letter, and I knew it was from Roman. I tucked it into the pocket of my maternity smock without opening it. Unexpected tears filled my eyes, and I looked away from Sara, to the bookshelves behind her.

"I wish you could stay."

"Only a few months left to go," she said gently.

"Fifty-seven days," I said. She smiled.

"You know that babies don't come exactly when we want them to. He or she might be born anytime from mid-December all the way through to mid-January."

I groaned in frustration.

"Mid-*January*? God. This is never going to end."

"You seem out of sorts today."

"I feel it," I admitted, then sighed. "I don't even want to see Truda and Mateusz. I just don't know how to ask them to stop visiting me."

"But why?" Sara asked, eyebrows rising. "They are so worried about you."

"They look at my... Truda constantly looks at my..." I closed my eyes, struggling for words. Instead, I pointed out my stomach. "She constantly stares at it, and she bombards me with questions. Why can't I feel one way about *anything* anymore, Sara? I hate the baby, I worry about the baby. I miss Truda desperately, I hate it when she visits. It's all so hard." I opened my eyes, then gave Sara a half smile. "Yes, I know. I complain so much these days. It *is* tiresome."

Sara laughed softly.

"Pregnancy is a difficult thing under your circumstances. But I want to talk to you about Truda. For half of her life, she has been married to Mateusz. For half of her life, they have been hoping for a baby, and she has never fallen pregnant. And now, this awful thing has happened to you, and you have to *suffer* through a pregnancy. Surely you can see how complex that must be for her."

"She is jealous?"

Sara shook her head hastily.

"Not jealous. No one would want to be in your shoes. But... please don't be so hard on Truda. That's all I'm asking. The one experience she has dreamed of her whole life has been forced upon the very person she loves most in the world."

I hadn't thought about it like that. Not at all.

I was awake again all night, but now I was trying to ask myself hard questions—finally feeling courageous after months of feeling like a victim. Instead of avoiding thoughts of the baby, I forced myself to stare them down.

> *I am pregnant. I am going to give birth to a baby. That baby was conceived in violence. That baby will always be a reminder of the worst moments of my life. That baby has forced me to endure these months when my body is not my own.*
>
> *But it is not that baby's fault, and the baby is also part of me. Even when it is gone from my body, it will have a part of my heart. How do I learn to live not knowing if it is well? How do I know that I am handing it over to the right people? Who in Poland has the resources to care for a baby? Sara assured me she would find just the right family, but what if just the right family doesn't actually exist?*

I tossed these thoughts over in my mind, turning them this way and that, trying to understand the right way forward. One night, tortured by insomnia, I walked to the chapel. The convent halls were freezing at night, so I wrapped myself in robes, but my belly jutted out. I walked slowly, thinking about how, when the warm weather returned and winter was over, I would have parted from the baby and would never see it again.

I lit a candle in the chapel and then knelt at the altar to pray.

I don't know why You let this happen to me. I don't know how You could have brought life out of such an ugly situation. You have to give me wisdom because I don't know the way forward, and I don't know how to survive this.

I heard the door to the chapel open, and I looked up to see

Sister Agnieszka Gracja. She knelt beside me at the altar and lit another candle. When I rose, she rose.

"What were you praying about at this strange hour?" I finally asked her as we walked back to our cells. She smiled.

"I was asking God to ease your torment."

The next day was Saturday, and Truda again came alone. For the first hour of her visit, we made small talk about her week—the food she'd prepared, the chores she'd done, the curtains she was trying to sew with some fabric she found.

"Mateusz is trying to complete the grant application for his new business, but I know he is so sorry to miss you again," she told me. "He said he will come tomorrow if you want him to."

"Why are you two so good to me?" I asked her suddenly.

Truda looked at me, confusion in her eyes. She thought about this for a moment and then said softly, "You are the answer to more than a decade of prayer, Emilia. You are the ray of sunshine that came out of the darkest years of our lives."

"Will you adopt this baby?" I blurted, before I could change my mind. But as soon as the words left my mouth, I felt my tension ease. This was the answer to my prayer, and the answer to Sister Agnieszka Gracja's prayers, too. *This* was the way forward. Truda recoiled as if I'd struck her.

"What? Emilia, why?"

"I want the best for it." My voice began to waver. "And you and Mateusz are the best."

"But that will mean that you will need to see it," Truda said. She spoke carefully, but her voice was strained. "I couldn't do that to you. It is better that the baby goes to another home, so that you can forget about it."

"I thought that, too. I really did, but I will never forget about it. I hate the way that it was conceived, but I will always care about it." I stopped, and my gaze fell to the table as I whispered, "Plus, I want you to experience motherhood. You have waited so long."

"Silly girl." She sighed, shaking her head at me. "For half a lifetime I prayed for a child, and God heard those prayers and gave me a chatty, inquisitive eleven-year-old who has almost driven me crazy in the six years since. I have plenty of experience with motherhood. Don't do this for me." Her gaze softened, and she added gently, "Emilia, if you love this baby, you should raise it yourself."

"It was conceived in rape," I said stiffly. "How could I possibly love it enough?"

"The next time you leave this place, I want you to look closely at the children you see," Truda said. "See if you can identify which children were conceived in rape and which were conceived in love. There will be an entire generation of children in this country who were forced upon their mothers, and the lucky ones will grow up in love just the same." I hesitated, and Truda reached to take my hand. "Don't think of this as a child of war. Every child is simply born good, and as long as they grow up in a family who can raise them that way, the circumstances of their conception are irrelevant. You, Emilia Rabinek, are plenty capable of handling this challenge if you want to raise the baby yourself."

"But I want you and Mateusz to—"

She reached across the table and squeezed my hand.

"Do not do this for us, Emilia," she said flatly.

I exhaled shakily.

"I think I'm doing this for *me*," I said slowly, tears filling my eyes. "I can't raise it, Truda. I'm not ready, and I still have so much healing to do. But I'm going to see this child for the rest of my life, either with my eyes or in my dreams. I love it enough to know that I can't raise it and too much to give it away. Could *you* love this baby as if they were your own?"

My voice trailed off by the end of the question because I

already knew the answer. She had taken me into her life in a heartbeat, as if I had already lived in her heart forever, even at the most tumultuous time of her life. While our entire world changed, the fierceness of her love had never wavered. Not once.

Truda was not soft, and she was not always warm, but she loved in a way that was as constant as the rising and setting of the sun.

"You know I could," she said quietly.

"Please," I choked out. "Please, will you be this baby's mother?"

"If you are sure that this is what you want..."

"I am sure. Talk to Mateusz about it?"

"I already know what he'll say," she whispered, then she hesitated. "You can always change your mind. We can plan this, but if you decide to keep it—"

"Truda," I said, "I am as sure of this as I have ever been of anything in my life."

At the end of her visit, I walked her to the entrance to the convent, then I hesitated.

"What is it?" she asked.

"Just do me one favor." I drew in a deep breath, then said, "Please let me be the one to tell Roman."

39

Roman

"WHEN THE CITY OPENS UP PROPERLY, YOU SHOULD START looking for a job with a lawyer," Mateusz told me, as we cleared an alleyway. It was November, and some days we were working in the sleet or the snow. "Now that the war is over, it is time for us all to get back to the lives we were supposed to live."

"The war isn't over," I said impatiently. "We've just reached a new phase. The war won't be over until the Red Army is gone."

"They will install a Communist government, Roman," he told me carefully. "And you need to be careful, speaking like that. Mokotów Prison is already full of those who have tried to dissent. You should lie low."

"I will lie low when the streets are free again," I vowed. "Until then, the fight isn't over."

I was trying to reconnect with the Resistance but having little luck with the city in such disarray. I knew that Truda and Mateusz were less than sympathetic to my frustration, but at dinner one night, I couldn't help but vent.

"Most of the leaders of the AK died during the Uprising, and this was exactly the outcome the Soviets had hoped for. They stirred up the rebellion with promises of assistance, only to watch from a safe distance as the bloodbath took place. Did you know that the surviving AK leadership was instructed to register any fighter who returned to Warsaw? I was so lucky I stayed in Berlin with my friend and came back months later than the others, because otherwise I'd have been on that list, too. Almost every man registered has now been tortured or executed. The Soviets quashed the inevitable rebellion long before it could take shape. Are we really going to sit back and let them have Poland after that? It is madness!"

"We don't have a choice," Truda said matter-of-factly. "There is no path forward for a resistance. We are too scattered, and they already have too much power."

I shook my head. "I will never stop fighting. Not until Poland is free. I don't care what it costs me."

"It is times like this I think Emilia is wise to hold you at arm's length," Truda muttered, shooting me a glare. "If she lets you back into her life, it won't just be *you* who pays the price when you are arrested."

"She will want to fight with me when she is well again."

"You have not seen her," Mateusz said quietly. "She is not the same girl she was."

"She has always believed in what is right," I insisted. "Perhaps working to free our homeland will be the thing that helps her feel herself again."

"Or perhaps she is broken by years of fighting, as the rest of this country is," Truda said impatiently. "Some of us *want* to choose peace. Some of us are ready to accept this new reality. As imperfect as it may be, it is still preferable to active conflict."

I would not even entertain the thought. When their next visit to Emilia loomed, I poured my frustrations into a letter.

Dear Emilia,

If there is one thing I have learned, it is that you must guard your spirit. When a country is occupied, the invaders will always try to suppress that nation's soul. After all, it is our souls that inspire us to fight, even when our bodies would have us cower. Why do you think the Germans destroyed so much of our culture in Warsaw? Our museums, our libraries, our landmarks? They knew it would demoralize us.

I hope there is still fight in you, Emilia. After everything you have been through, I hope your spirit is still ready to rebel.

The truth is I am scared for Poland. I feel no fight at all in Warsaw now, and Warsaw has always been a city that knew how to rebel. Even when the odds were stacked against us, we were conspiring, trying to regain our freedom.

They can crush us, but they cannot break us—not as long as we are willing to rise. I want you to know that I will keep fighting until the Polish people are sovereign once again. I will do this not only for our country, not only for myself, but for you.

I hope you will join me in the fight when you're ready.

Love, Roman

I thought I had been vindicated when Mateusz returned from his visit to tell me that Emilia had read my letter and was ready, at last, to see me.

40

Emilia

IT HAD BEEN OVER A YEAR SINCE I HAD SEEN ROMAN.
Through his letters and from my conversations with Mateusz
and Truda, I knew the basics of what had happened to him since
the Uprising. Somehow, though, I repainted the image of him
that lived in my mind, removing the scars and the visible signs
of trauma. When he stepped into the lobby of the convent, I
was shocked by his appearance.

He was more muscular than I remembered, no doubt a side
effect of his work on the roads. But he carried one arm at an
odd angle, and I knew this was a result of the injury he had sustained in the ghetto. The right side of his face and neck were
scarred horribly from the burn he had suffered in the explosion.
His body was a road map of all he had endured, but worse than
that were the shadows in his eyes. He was haunted, just as he
had always been. I had forgotten that about him.

Roman had seen so much and survived so much that I
couldn't shake the thought that his memories would pursue him

for the rest of his life, ready to pop up at any moment and rock the foundations of his life. I held his latest letter in the pocket of my smock, and as he approached, I reached down and touched it with my fingertips, to remind myself why I had to be strong.

"It is so good to see you," he whispered. But he made no move to touch me, standing just out of reach and casting his eyes down my body, then back to my face. His gaze asked a million questions that I didn't have answers to. I took his hands in mine, squeezed them hard, then reached up to brush my lips against his. Behind us, Sister Walentyna cleared her throat. I hid a smile and stepped back, releasing his hands. A smile slowly transformed his face, easing the tension, brightening his eyes.

I hadn't planned the kiss. I feared that I was broken and that I'd never want to touch another man again, but I was still drawn to Roman.

I would always love him. Always.

"I don't know what I expected," he said quietly, as we walked to the library. "Sara... Truda and Mateusz. They just keep telling me that you aren't the same, but..."

"I'm not the same," I said abruptly. "I'll never be the same." He didn't reply.

In the library, we took the chairs by the windows, the ones I always sat on with my parents and Sara. Sister Renata wandered silently into the room and sat on the other side with her Bible. I hadn't ever had chaperones when my parents or Sara visited, but I didn't mind. I was nervous about what I had to do, and I was glad to have allies in the room, even if they were out of earshot.

"Thank you for your letters," I told Roman. "They've meant a lot to me over these last few months. I'm sorry I couldn't write back."

"That's okay. I was ready to wait as long as it took." He hesitated, then added quietly, "I *am* ready to wait."

I inhaled slowly, then rested my hands on my belly. I saw his eyes follow them, but not in the way that Truda's did. A flash of something almost menacing crossed his face.

"You are gearing up to fight the Soviet regime," I said.

"Of course I am. And I think I am finally getting somewhere. I met an AK fighter last week who has been involved in acts of sabotage. I'm joining his group for a meeting on Thursday."

"This occupation is different, Roman," I said softly. "Even when it seemed like the Germans had won, it never felt permanent, and their victory never felt inevitable. This is *different*."

He frowned at me, visibly frustrated.

"Poland should be governed by her people."

"In an ideal world, of course you are right. But the Soviets will simply install a pro-Communist government who will be loyal to Stalin. This is not war, Roman. This is just our life now."

"I can't accept that."

"I know, and I wouldn't expect you to," I said quietly. The confusion in Roman's gaze almost broke my heart. "You, my love, are more committed to justice than any other person I have ever met. You will fight until you win or it costs you your life." He nodded slowly, but his brows were still drawn down. "But…it's different for me. I love this country, and I will always try to build something beautiful here, but I want no part in any resistance now. The fight has left me. I have seen enough conflict and enough violence—I have felt violence *in* my body. All I want for the next phase of my life is to adjust and to find peace."

Roman shifted, a terse scowl on his face.

"Emilia, I *have* to—"

"I didn't ask you to come here to convince you not to fight," I said, interrupting him, then I sucked in a deep breath. "I wanted to tell you in person that we cannot be together."

His eyes widened, and for a minute I thought he was going to argue with me. But then he sighed deeply and said, "There have been many times in my life when I thought about giving up. I know the temptation of it. I know exactly how you are feeling. It seems easier to just accept your fate. But that is not *you*, and that is not how we regain our country."

"It is going to take me time to recover from the things I have been through this year, and then..." I squeezed my eyes, unable to look at him while I told him my plans for the baby "...and then I'm going to have to adjust to being a sister to this baby, because I have asked Truda and Mateusz to raise it."

Roman shifted forward to lean on the table between us. He spoke urgently as he whispered, "The best thing is to give this baby to a family far away from us. Otherwise, every time you see it, you're going to be reminded of what happened to you! Bringing this child into your family will mean bringing *those bastards* into your family!" I stiffened my spine, but I didn't argue. Instead, I simply watched as his frustration grew. He had no way of knowing that every harsh word he spoke was confirmation that I was making the right decision. "For us to be together, you would need me to accept your rapist's child, and then you want me to sit back and let the Soviets have their way with Poland?"

"Roman, I wish we could be together," I whispered sadly, shaking my head. "But I need peace now, and you will always seek upheaval. There is no middle ground between what you and I want for our lives. You have become a part of my family, and my parents love you as much as I do." I straightened and met his gaze, hardening my voice as I added, "But, Roman, I am telling you now, if you wish to *remain* in our family, you are going to have to find a way to accept this baby, too."

We fell into a tense silence. For long moments, the only sound was the noise Sister Renata made when she turned the pages of her book.

"I need to think about this," he eventually said, dropping his voice. He reached for my hand, but I pulled it away slowly, and

Roman sighed impatiently. "You need to let me think about all of it."

"Sometimes in life, there is compromise. Other times, there is none," I whispered, swallowing the lump in my throat. "You and I both know that this is one of those times."

I walked him to the door, Sister Walentyna once again hovering somewhere behind us, but there was no illicit contact for her to protest this time. Roman and I stood a foot apart, an ocean of hurt between us. His expression was desperate, but he made no move to touch me. He turned to walk away, but then he paused, and his voice was raw as he turned back to say, "I don't know how to fix this, but there has to be a way."

"You can't fix this," I said gently. I could see the tension in his body—his shoulders and arms were locked, as if he were ready to start a physical fight. I wasn't scared of him—I'd never been scared of him, after that first day—but even his posture confirmed my decision. "Stay safe, Roman. Please, stay safe."

Somehow, I knew he wouldn't.

Truda was excited and she couldn't hide it even if she tried. She knit beanies and little cardigans for the baby and walked all over the city collecting clothes and blankets for it. She told me that Mateusz had built a little crib and set it up in their bedroom.

"Unless...unless you think it should be in your room," she added, uncertainly.

"Why would I have *your* baby in my room?" I asked, injecting just enough attitude that I felt like a teenager again, instead of the worn husk of a woman I'd become. But the end was in sight, and I knew that once the baby was born, I would begin rebuilding myself from the ground up. In the meantime, all I had to do was get through each day, hoping that every twinge I felt was the beginning of the labor that would open the next chapter of my life.

We celebrated a subdued Christmas at the convent—a Franciscan order of nuns, and me, Mateusz, Truda and Sara. Roman was missing, although my parents told me he had been invited and politely declined. He had moved out of my bedroom and found lodging somewhere else. Mateusz still saw him at their job, but if my father knew the details of what *else* Roman was up to, he didn't share them with me.

I missed Roman, but I was accustomed to missing him. What was new was that I had to grieve the future I once thought we'd share. Sometimes I'd catch myself dreaming about a reunion, as if we hadn't already had one.

Even so, I was proud of myself for making that hard decision. I had grown strong enough to know what was best for me and to seek it out.

Sara and Truda moved into the convent during the last weeks of the year to await the birth. Sister Teodora had been a midwife but was in her eighties now and hadn't delivered a baby for more than a decade, so Sara was going to assist. The entire convent was on tenterhooks waiting for the delivery to start, but I was almost convinced the baby would never come. I reached the end of my countdown calendar on Christmas Day, and every day after that felt like a mockery. It hurt to sit, it hurt to stand, and sometimes when I walked I was convinced the baby was going to fall out. My irritability seemed to know no bounds. I was even cranky with the Sisters, who had been so hospitable to me for all of those months.

There was a special meal for New Year's Eve, but I couldn't bear to eat it, and I went to bed early but couldn't sleep. It was a bitterly cold night—the world was blanketed in a thick carpet of snow, but I felt hot, even as I walked the corridors, pacing through my frustration.

"Come on, baby," I muttered, rubbing my aching belly. "Get out of here. Your mama is dying to meet you." Since I had begun thinking of the baby as Truda's, my ambiguity toward it had disappeared. Her excitement was giving purpose to my pain, and in that purpose I found comfort.

As I turned at the end of the hallway outside of the convent cells, I was gripped by pain so intense I forgot to breathe. The tightening started in my back and worked its way all the way around my stomach, until I felt like I was being turned inside out. It didn't last long, but it was markedly more intense than any of the twinges I had felt over the pregnancy. When I could breathe again, I resumed my pacing, only to be knocked weak against a wall by another wave of pain, just a few minutes later.

This time, I cried out, and a door along the hallway opened. A whole mass of nuns filed out to check on me, with Sara and Truda close behind. Sister Agnieszka Gracja clasped her hands in joy.

"Emilia." She grinned, but then her gaze dropped to my feet, and she hurried toward me. "Let's get you off that rug just in case your water breaks."

The labor was so fast I barely had a chance to catch my breath between contractions. It was my labor—but it was also *our* labor, because Truda was with me for every moment. When I was in pain, I saw that pain in her eyes. When I rested between contractions, I saw her relax, too, even just briefly. And when I cried, she cried, as if she couldn't bear to see me suffering alone.

I always thought of her as a harsh woman, and she could be. But that night, we were as close as two women could be— mother and child, laboring together to bring life to the world. And as the sun rose over the snow-covered township below us, Truda's son at last made his way from my body into the world. Sister Teodora wrapped him in a blanket and moved to pass him to me, but I shook my head.

"No. His mother should hold him first."

When I saw new love dawn on Truda's face, and when I saw the gratitude in her eyes, I realized that although I would always suffer for what had happened to me, I would heal through knowing that something so glorious had come of it.

Truda had been patient and kind and generous and brave, and she had prayed and waited, and through war and grief and heartbreak and tragedy, God had finally granted her a miracle.

41

Roman

June 1946

MATEUSZ WON A SMALL GRANT FROM THE CITY TOWARD his new textiles business. It wasn't nearly enough to get up and running, but it was a start, and he applied for a loan to get the rest of the funds he needed. I would be his right-hand man until he was more established, but after that, we agreed that I would look for another job. I liked paperwork, but I didn't have a clue where to start with the actual textiles.

He and I were trying to find a suitable building, but commercial real estate was all but impossible to find. The rebuilding effort was focused on housing. While we searched, we worked out of an abandoned storefront. My desk was a singed door stacked on bricks, and when it rained, ash and muddy concrete dust dripped from gaps in the roof. A much more sensible solution would have been for us to set up in Uncle Piotr's old office in Mateusz's apartment, but he didn't suggest it, and I didn't ask.

Every moment of every day, Emilia was on my mind, but I hadn't seen her since that day at the convent, and I hadn't met baby Anatol, though Mateusz talked about him constantly. He didn't seem to notice that every single time the baby came up, I stiffened and tried to change the subject. He was so besotted with his son he couldn't help himself. I heard about Anatol's first smile. That he'd rolled over already, and that Sara said that was early for a baby to roll so he must be advanced. And then the baby was babbling, and Mateusz was sure he'd heard the sound *tatuś*, Polish for *Daddy*. I just couldn't understand how that family welcomed that baby, knowing what Emilia had been through. I was glad that I'd never met Anatol Rabinek. I couldn't imagine feeling any affection toward him whatsoever.

As chatty as Mateusz was in those months, I was reserved. I was nurturing something new, too—something I was immensely proud of. I'd joined with a small group of returned AK insurgents, and we'd begun to execute a series of acts of sabotage. We were trying to stir the spirit of our city toward a broader resistance, even if all we could do with our limited resources was to paint prodemocracy slogans onto whatever walls were standing or distribute crude propaganda in support of a rebellion.

I was still bewildered by how hard it was to rally support for the underground within the general population. I had participated in two uprisings, and each time, those around me rose in support of the rebellion without any prompting. Now, Warsaw seemed resigned to its fate.

"The people's referendum is coming," Mateusz remarked cheerfully, as we inspected a potential factory one day in May. "You see? We will get a say in our future."

"The *people's* referendum," I scoffed, kicking a burned brick with the tip of my boot. "It will be a farce, Mateusz." The referendum would ask a series of questions about the senate, the border and the nationalization of property, but it was a codified referendum that could almost have been one question: Do the people welcome the Communist regime? Pro-Communists

cheered the people to vote in support of all questions. Demo-
cratic groups campaigned for Poles to vote no.

My underground unit felt certain that before a single vote was
cast, the outcome of the referendum had been decided. Stalin
was the puppet master, working to embed the local Communist factions so deeply that we'd never unseat them, and while
the Kremlin controlled our leadership, Poland would not be
free. Emilia would not be free, whether or not she knew it. I
felt certain she would never heal until the Soviets were excised
from our land.

"We must work toward sovereignty," I said, although I knew
Mateusz had already conceded defeat. "The war will not end
until the Polish people govern our nation."

Mateusz smiled sadly and pointed out toward the street. Men
and women were demolishing ruins and removing the rubble,
and new buildings were shooting up. The sounds of hammers
and nails had replaced the sound of bullets and bombs.

"We are rebuilding," he said simply. "It *is* over."

"We are rebuilding a version of Poland with a Soviet veneer," I said, voice tight with fury. "It will never be over until
we chip off that veneer."

"Again we must agree to disagree, my friend," Mateusz said
sadly. He looked at the gaping hole in the roof of the factory
and sighed. "This place isn't going to work, either, is it?"

"No," I said, shaking my head. "The search continues."

42

Emilia

THERE WERE GOOD MOMENTS AND AWFUL MOMENTS IN the first few months of Anatol's life. One day, I came downstairs for a drink of water and found Truda sitting in the lounge just staring at the baby in her arms. Mateusz was on the sofa next to her, staring at her face. They both wore looks of sheer adoration, so pure and so intense that it brought tears to my eyes.

A few weeks later, Truda was holding Anatol in one arm, singing quietly as she stared down at him. I didn't see his smile—but I saw her reaction to it. Her entire face lit up, and she looked at me with tears in her eyes.

"Did you see that? He smiled at me! It was the most beautiful thing I've ever seen!"

"It was," I agreed, although I knew we were talking about different smiles.

In moments like that, I forgot I had had any part in Anatol's conception and birth. He was my baby brother and a gift from God to the parents I loved.

The worst moments were more difficult to navigate. I had to breastfeed Anatol—there was no alternative. Truda did not have milk, and it was difficult to get fresh food, let alone baby formula. The act of breastfeeding became physically easier with time, but it was emotionally challenging.

Sometimes, he'd latch to my breast, and I'd close my eyes and try to imagine I was somewhere else. I was terrified of bonding with him, but I was also anxious that I would see his biological father in his features. Every now and again, I became fixated on trying to remember what each of my attackers looked like. Was Anatol's father the younger one? Was it the one with the bulbous nose? Or was it the oldest one?

"Emilia, do you think you could watch Anatol for a few minutes while I run out to look for fresh vegetables for dinner?" Truda asked one day, and I looked to her in alarm.

"Can't you take him?"

She shot me a confused look and pointed to the freshly installed windowpane. "It's raining."

"I'll go, then."

"I'll only be five minutes. You'll be fine."

She fixed a scarf over her hair and left before I could raise another protest. I sat Anatol down on a blanket in the corner of the room and moved myself to the other side of it, dusting some shelves that didn't need dusting. After just a moment or two, he started to grizzle. I knew he didn't need milk—I'd only fed him an hour earlier. I ignored the sound for a while, but that felt cruel, and so I impatiently crossed the room to pick him up.

He settled immediately in my arms, looking up at me with such curious wonder that I caught myself looking right back at him.

"Don't be like them," I whispered to the baby. "Please be good inside."

He stuffed his tiny fist in his mouth, drool rolling down his chin. I sighed and jiggled him a little, turning my attention to the window.

Perhaps it was better that I felt wariness with Anatol. Perhaps that was better than the alternative, of bonding too strongly and struggling to let him go.

I knew that Roman and Mateusz were working on plans for a new business. Mateusz was anxious about what else Roman might be working on, especially with the referendum looming.

"He's obsessed," he told me, brow wrinkled with concern. "Every time it comes up, I feel like he's ready to explode. I'm worried he's going to get himself killed."

"So am I," I admitted. I hated the Soviet presence in Warsaw, too: every time I saw that uniform, some part of me wanted to revolt. But just as I taught myself to focus on rebuilding rather than the rubble, I learned to focus on the relative peacefulness of this new occupation, not the occupation itself.

Some days, I missed Roman so much I fiercely regretted pushing him away. But I knew I never could have dealt with Anatol's arrival if I was distracted by Roman working ever closer toward blowing up his life.

"And how are you doing, Emilia?" Mateusz asked me suddenly. It was Sunday morning, and we were walking to Mass, Truda two steps ahead of us, pushing Anatol in a stroller we'd found and restored.

"I'm okay."

"What will you do with your life?"

"When Anatol is older and Truda doesn't need me as much, I'm going to find a job. I don't know what exactly, but something creative. Uncle Piotr once told me that art is generous, and I like the idea of putting things out into the world to inspire people."

Mateusz smiled softly, then slid his arm around my shoulders and pulled me close for a hug.

"That sounds pretty good to me."

It was a warm summer morning, and the sky was a vibrant blue, the sun just beginning to bite. I was alive, and I *felt* alive. The future rolled out before me, a long and lonely road, but I wasn't afraid of it. I was almost ready to move on to the next chapter.

43

Roman

TWO DAYS BEFORE THE REFERENDUM, I WAS WORKING IN the abandoned storefront with Mateusz, trying to make the money he'd borrowed stretch as far as we could. There was a knock at the door, and without waiting for an invitation, a man opened it.

"Can I help you?" Mateusz asked, cordial as ever, but my heart began to pound. I looked around the storefront, trying to find a way out, but then the man stepped inside, and three more men entered behind him.

There were no uniforms, and they didn't identify themselves as members of the Polish Communist Secret Service—the *Urząd Bezpieczeństwa*, known as the UB. They didn't have to. It was evident in the hard set of their gazes as they looked between Mateusz and me. It was evident in their aggressive stances.

As for me, I had faced death more times than I could count, but I had never been afraid like I was in that moment. If they had approached me in the pitiful excuse for a room I was renting, I'd have raised my fists, ready to fight. If they'd pulled up alongside me as I walked home from the office, I'd have taunted them. If they'd raided my meetings with the AK insurgents, I'd have relished the confrontation.

But those men were in our makeshift office, and Mateusz was right there beside me. In a heartbeat, I understood that Emilia was right to push me from her life. If I'd had my way, we might have been engaged by now. It might have been *her* watching my arrest.

"I'll go willingly," I said, hoping to defuse the situation before Mateusz tried to defend me. "This has nothing to do with him."

One of the men grabbed me, twisting my bad arm behind me until I felt my shoulder pop out of its socket. One of the other men dug his hand into my hair as they dragged me toward the door. I didn't care one bit about my capture or that I was likely about to undergo an interrogation. All I cared about was that behind me, I heard fists beating against skin and Mateusz crying out in pain, pleading for his life.

"Please, leave him alone," I gasped. "He has nothing to do with this."

As if they hadn't heard me, the UB officers pushed me into the back seat of one of their two cars outside our shop. I looked out the window as the car began to move, only to see Mateusz raising his hands over his face, hopelessly trying to deflect the blows of the two men who remained behind.

44

Emilia

OUT ON THE STREETS, THE CITY WAS ADJUSTING TO THE
news that almost 70 percent of the country had voted yes to all
questions, just as the Communists had asked them to. But in
our apartment, Sara, Mateusz, Truda and I were sitting around
the dinner table, the results the last thing on our minds.

My parents and Sara were drinking vodka like it was water—
but while my visceral reaction to the scent of it had faded, I still
couldn't bear the taste. I nursed my third cup of tea instead.
Anatol was sleeping in a Moses basket under the table, oblivious to the tense conversation above him. We had electricity as
of the previous week, and the bulb that burned above us cast a
yellow glow around the room—a novelty after months of getting by with candles.

"We need to get him out," I whispered.

"There is only one way, Emilia. You know this. I've spoken
to the guards at the prison, and the bribe they want to free him
is more than we can afford." Mateusz spoke very carefully, as if

a harsh tone would shatter a carefully won peace accord. When he spoke, he whistled accidentally, still adjusting to the tooth he'd lost during the beating. The bruising on his face was fading, but it still broke my heart to look at him.

If we managed to free Roman, there was a good chance I would kill the man myself.

"We are *not* paying that bribe," Truda added, giving me a pointed look. I met her gaze, and she threw her hands up into the air. "So after everything we have been through, we finally have a chance to get back on our feet, and Emilia wants us to swap that chance for the life of a boy who is determined to be a martyr."

Mateusz sighed, rubbing his forehead wearily. He looked at me, pleading with me to understand. "Truda is right. Even if we rescue him today, he is just as likely to do something foolish and be imprisoned again tomorrow. That's not fair to anyone."

"If I were the one in that prison cell, would you rescue me?" I asked them quietly.

"You know we would," Mateusz said.

"His parents don't have the chance to help him. We are his family."

"You haven't seen him in months, Emilia," Sara reminded me gently. "For very good reason."

"I still care about him. And I know that you all still care about him. He is impulsive and stubborn, but he's special. I know that you all see that about him, too." I looked to Sara, who avoided my gaze. "You especially, Sara. Make them see sense!"

"The thought of him suffering turns me inside out," Sara said abruptly. "But I cannot ask your parents to sacrifice their future for him. Truda is right: for as long as we have known him, Roman has had more passion for this country than sense. Say your father spends the money he has borrowed rescuing Roman instead of setting up his factory. What do we do next week, when Roman is arrested again? Now you have no factory, no money and a loan to repay with no income to do so, and the outcome is the same."

I was so frustrated I could cry, but I could see the logic in what they were saying. But since we had learned that Roman was being interrogated at the infamous Mokotów Prison, desperation had overtaken me. The most likely outcome was that he would leave that place in a coffin.

I thought if I put distance between us, I could carry on if he were imprisoned, or worse. But there we were. The worst had finally happened, and I couldn't think of anything other than finding a way to help him.

"You really think we should just leave him there?" I asked incredulously. "He is *family*."

"I'm sorry, Emilia," Mateusz whispered numbly. "We really don't have a choice."

The next morning, I fed Anatol, then passed him over to Truda as I always did, but instead of commencing the day's chores, I told her I was going out.

"Where to?" she asked, her gaze narrowing.

"I'm going to see if I can find someone who can help Roman." I had no idea where to even start, but I could not do nothing.

"Emilia," she groaned, shaking her head. "This is a terrible idea! You were right all along. You *need* to let him go—"

But just then, the front door to our apartment flung open, and Mateusz rushed inside.

"What are you doing home?" Truda cried, but he continued past us toward their bedroom.

"It's Roman." He threw the words over his shoulder as he ran. I followed him and found him on his knees beside the bed. Truda was close behind us with Anatol in her arms.

"What are you doing?" she asked impatiently. Mateusz withdrew a suitcase from beneath his bed and threw it up onto the mattress. The color drained from Truda's face.

"Don't you even think about it!" she whispered furiously. When Mateusz continued unclasping the suitcase, Truda passed Anatol to me and stepped toward the bed. She caught his arm. "Mateusz, *no*."

"I went past the prison this morning to see if I could talk the guard into a more reasonable bribe," Mateusz said, shaking her off impatiently. He tipped the clothing out of the suitcase and onto the bed. "He told me that they have broken Roman's legs. The interrogation has gone nowhere, and they have only kept him alive because they assumed I was coming back with the money."

Truda and I simultaneously gasped. Mateusz reached into his pocket for his penknife to cut open the lining of the suitcase. Inside, there was a thickly stuffed envelope.

"You're going to pay it?" I whispered. Mateusz nodded silently. Truda swore ferociously as she took Anatol from my arms and stormed away, back to the living areas. "Why?" I asked Mateusz.

"You were right last night. Roman is family," he sighed. He stuffed the envelope into the waistband of his trousers, straightened and looked right into my eyes. "I could live with the guilt if I did nothing, but I couldn't live with the disappointment in your eyes."

I walked across the room to throw my arms around him. I pressed my cheek against his chest and closed my eyes.

"Mateusz... *Tato*..." I whispered. *Dad*. I had called him that before, but only when others were around who didn't know he wasn't my real father. As his arms contracted around my shoulders, I knew Mateusz and Truda had more than earned the titles of *Mother* and *Father*. "Thank you."

Mateusz kissed the top of my head, squeezed me close one more time, then gently released me.

"I'll try to get this young man of ours back. You stay here and make up the sofa for me."

"The sofa?" I said, surprised. "Won't he need a bed?"

"Oh, no," Mateusz said, wincing. "No, I expect he is going to need the hospital. The sofa is for me. After what I'm about to do, it's going to be a long time before Truda lets me back into the bed."

45

Roman

I WOKE TO BLINDING PAIN AND AN UNMISTAKABLE MEDICINAL grogginess. As the fog cleared, I looked around the room. Hospital beds, both occupied and vacant, lined the walls on both sides of a narrow ward. A nurse was checking the pulse of an elderly man in the bed opposite me.

I had no idea where I was. The last thing I remembered was the crunch of the sledgehammer as it hit my shin. Blessedly, I passed out after that.

Now, both of my legs were encased in plaster. My left leg was suspended above the bed, connected to a series of wires and pulleys. I startled when I realized that Emilia was sitting beside me, reading a newspaper. When she saw I was awake, she folded the newspaper and pursed her lips.

"How many times am I going to have to come sit vigil at your bedside, Roman Gorka?" she demanded.

"What are you doing here?" I asked, as I drank in the sight of her. Emilia had lost the gauntness that had plagued us all over the course of the war. Her cheeks had filled out, and a rosy glow had returned to her complexion. Her hair was out, all around her shoulders and stretched down to her waist, so much longer than the last time I'd seen her.

"I couldn't stay away," she said. She didn't seem nearly as pleased by this as I was.

"We lost the referendum," I surmised, glancing down at the headline of the paper under her arm. "We will regroup," I said, almost to myself. The interrogation had been so much more brutal than I'd anticipated. I hadn't given up any AK insurgents, but I couldn't help but wonder if I would have been as brave if I had known their real names. For situations just like this, we adopted the Gray Ranks convention of only using code names.

"Do you know how Mateusz got you out of that prison?" Emilia asked me flatly.

"Mateusz?" I said, frowning. I was still groggy enough that I hadn't wondered how I'd been rescued, but suddenly I panicked at the memory of UB officers beating him as they dragged me from our office. "Is he okay?"

"He's missing some teeth. His bruises have healed, but he's fine," she said impatiently. "Although God only knows how long that's going to be the case, because Truda is on the warpath, and it wouldn't surprise me if she killed him. He took the money he borrowed for the factory, and he used it to rescue you."

I was suddenly distracted from the pain in my legs by a burst of guilt so immense, it almost swamped me. I knew how much Mateusz was relying on that loan—his entire plan for supporting his family had been based around it. The shame was so intense that, for a minute, I couldn't speak. I wished he'd left me in the prison to die.

"I'll pay him back," I whispered.

"Do you remember the first drawing I ever gave you?" Emilia asked me suddenly.

"The fist," I said. "Of course."

"And the words beneath it?"

"Striving for justice is always worth the battle," I said, staring into her eyes. She shook her head.

"You forgot the most important part, Roman. The first part of that sentence said *There are many ways to fight.* We wanted the war to end, and it did for the rest of the world, but…for us? We here in Poland have only entered a new phase, and this phase will last years. Bullets and bombs have failed us. Maybe they have always failed us. You need a new strategy."

She had changed since the assault, but not in ways I would have expected. The idea of her suffering made me want to tear the world apart, but Emilia didn't seem angry. In fact, in the months since I had seen her at the convent, she had only grown stronger and more certain.

She was healing, I realized. Emilia Slaska continued to astound me.

"All of the violence and bloodshed and death and suffering, and what has been achieved? Nothing," she said in frustration. "No justice. No freedom. I understand the inclination to continue fighting, and believe me, I understand what it is like to want to hurt those who have hurt you. But it is a losing battle, Roman. You defeat one bad man, and another is there, ready to take his place. You need to fight the ideas that lead to bad men in the first place."

The war had been so destructive in Emilia's life, but it had never dampened the goodness of her spirit. From the first moment I met her, she had been finding ways to do good. And in the early months of our relationship, even in the lead-up to the Uprising, she had been vocal about her desire for revenge. But over time, she evolved beyond those instincts, and that was something I had failed to do.

"You will never know justice for what happened to you," I said unevenly. She blinked away tears as she nodded. "You are looking toward the future anyway. How?"

"When you killed Germans during the Uprisings, did that bring you healing?" she asked me gently.

"You know it didn't," I whispered.

Emilia reached forward and rested her hand over mine. I turned mine over, sliding our fingers together, and she squeezed gently.

"Maybe it's time to find another way."

Don't waste it, Chaim had said as he pushed me down into that manhole back in the ghetto. I'd let those words drive me through more years of conflict, but staring down at my fingers linked through Emilia's, it struck me that I might have misunderstood his dying wish. Had he really saved me so I could live to die another day for our cause? Or had he saved my life so I could *live* it?

"I don't know how else to live my life," I whispered to Emilia. She ran her thumb over the back of my hand and flashed me a breathtaking smile.

"You don't have to have all the answers today, Roman. We have all the time in the world to figure this out together."

46

Emilia

ROMAN WAS IN TRACTION FOR MONTHS, STUCK IN A HOS-
pital bed, reliant on others to care for him, with little to do but
think. When he was finally released, Sara took him in. Her
new apartment was a few blocks from City Hall, two Spartan
rooms on the third floor of a hastily repaired apartment block.
Roman was using a wheelchair while his legs further healed,
and the stairs that led to Sara's apartment were impossible for
him to navigate. She worked irregular shifts at the hospital, and
he was often at home alone all day, with only a radio and whatever books we could source to keep him company.

"Remember when we had libraries?" he said wistfully. "Entire buildings filled with books—all gone now. It seems crazy
that I never stopped to appreciate that before."

"The libraries will be rebuilt," I promised. "We will rebuild
them ourselves if we have to."

At home, money was tighter than ever—Mateusz was struggling to pay off the loan he'd taken and to support us at the

same time. He was resilient: he'd found work again on a construction crew and remained philosophical about our situation.

"I saved Roman's life, and I have a hunch that might be one of the best things I ever did," Mateusz said, shrugging. Truda was less forgiving.

"He better not let us down," she warned, shaking her head. "It's going to be a long time before I trust that boy again."

Anatol was gradually weaning, down to only a morning and a night feed as he learned to eat solid food, and my days were at last my own. I found a job as a receptionist for a newly reestablished newspaper. The pay was terrible, but I knew that every *zloty* helped my family, and for the first time in a long time, I felt useful and independent. Every evening, on my way home from work, I called in on Roman to bring him a copy of the newspaper.

At last there was no curfew, and the streets were safe again. I could stay for hours, as late as I wanted to, and we would parse the newspaper, discussing the news as the country reformed. I knew it still pained Roman to see the Communist regime in power, but his venom eased. He was refocusing on eking out a new life, instead of raging as he had done for so long.

"I've been thinking about what you said to me in the hospital that day, about finding another way," he said. "I think politics is the answer. It won't be easy, but if we take all of the principles we learned in the Uprisings—mobilizing, organizing, finding a common ground—and we put those skills into lobbying for change, maybe one day we could free this country peacefully."

"I like that," I said, nodding excitedly. "What does it look like? How do you start?"

"Well, first I get better," he said wryly, motioning toward his legs. "Then I wait for the universities to open, and probably study for a law degree."

"Following in your father's footsteps."

He smiled as he nodded.

"Just like I always wanted."

"You are a sight for sore eyes," he greeted me one day. He was in the kitchen, his wheelchair just behind him, leaning heavily on a cane with one hand as he stood at the stove, looking flustered and out of his depth.

"What on earth are you doing?"

"I'm trying to cook dinner for Sara." The kitchen was a scene of destruction—sausages burning in a frying pan, potatoes cut into inconsistent pieces on a chopping board, and he'd even managed to hack unmanageable slices from a loaf of bread. I surveyed all of this, then looked back to him, and he slumped hopelessly. "It's terrible, I know. Please help?"

Laughing, I joined him in the kitchen to repair the meal. He dropped back into the wheelchair to watch.

"I need to be better at this," he muttered. "I never learned."

I paused, suddenly realizing why he had no idea how to cook. Confined to the ghetto, his family had been forced to rely on rations. He probably couldn't even remember a time when his mother had cooked normal meals for him.

"Don't worry," I said lightly. "I'll teach you."

He struggled to adjust to his lack of independence, and he struggled to heal, but I could see him making great strides emotionally. It was evident in the way he spoke: the sharpness and the aggression had faded from his voice, leaving room for vulnerability. And this new version of Roman was a man I knew I could trust. Our relationship had been strictly platonic since I had welcomed him back into my life, but every day we edged closer to something more.

"We should have a Sunday lunch here," he said one day. "You and I can cook."

I laughed softly. "I'm not sure you're up to anything fancy yet, but I'll help."

"We should plan it for a day when Sara can be here."

"That sounds like a great idea."

"And…" He drew in a deep breath, then said, "Emilia, I need you to invite your family."

"Why?" I asked, then held my breath. This was the moment I had been waiting for, but this gesture had to come from his heart.

Roman's gaze was steady.

"Mateusz has come to visit me, and I've thanked him in person, but I haven't seen Truda, and I need to meet Anatol."

"Are you sure you're ready for this?"

He leaned forward and cupped my cheek in his palm, staring at me with such tenderness, my heart contracted in my chest.

"It's the next thing, love," he whispered. "There are a whole series of things I need to do, and this is the next thing."

The following Sunday, Roman and I made a simple meal of roast potatoes and vegetables. Sara baked an apple cake for dessert.

Mateusz entered the apartment first, shaking hands warmly with Roman, then embracing Sara and me. When Truda stepped in behind him, Anatol on her hip, she cast her eyes over the room, then her gaze settled on Roman. He crossed the room slowly and looked between her and Anatol, who at ten months old was already squirming and ready to be put onto the floor to scoot around this new and exciting space. But Truda just paused in the doorway, staring at Roman, her expression unfathomable. He let out a breath, then extended his hand. Truda shook it warily.

"Your family saved my life," Roman said steadily. "I will never forget that, and I will never let you down again."

Truda raised her chin, then cocked an eyebrow.

"Good," she said abruptly, then she sat the baby on the ground and walked around Roman to the kitchen. "Let me see these potatoes. Emilia always undercooks them. I want to make sure you've done them right."

After the stilted start, lunch was relaxed and easy. I looked around the table at the people I loved most in the world, alive and strong and healthy. Piotr was missing, but just as this thought struck me, Mateusz suddenly raised a glass of wine and said, "To Piotr."

And I felt my uncle there in spirit as we echoed the toast and tasted the wine. After a moment of silence, Roman caught my eye and smiled quietly.

"I never thought we'd be lucky enough to sit around a table together like this, to share in a meal of delicious food and wine, in a nice apartment in a city at peace."

"*Delicious* is a bit of a stretch, but I'll toast the rest of that," Mateusz laughed, nodding toward his undercooked potatoes. We all laughed, and to me, that moment of shared laughter sounded like music.

While Truda and Sara washed the dishes, Roman and I sat on the floor. Anatol was wary of strangers, but over lunch, he'd gradually warmed up to Roman. Now, he was sitting near us, trying to mouth Roman's cane.

"He's all you," Roman murmured quietly.

"He does look a lot like me," I admitted.

"I don't know what I expected, but it wasn't a tiny version of you," he said, then he looked at me. "Do you regret asking Truda and Mateusz to raise him?"

I shook my head hastily.

"I don't know how to explain it, but I don't love him as my son. He's my brother." My throat tightened. "If I could go back and change it, I'd have clung to Mateusz that day at the market, and none of this would have happened. But I can't, and so I choose to see Anatol as a miracle. God gave Truda the child she'd always wanted, and he gave me a brother to replace the one I lost. That's all. That's the only way I see it."

"Then, that's how I'll see it, too," Roman said softly, and he reached out a hand toward Anatol, who tentatively reached out and touched his fingers. "Hey there, little boy. Want to change the world with me?"

"I think you should let him learn how to walk and talk before you get him involved in politics."

"It doesn't hurt to start him young, Emilia." He grinned. "Poland is going to need this next generation to be smart."

"Then, that's how we should raise our children," I announced. Roman's eyebrows lifted in surprise, and a broad smile transformed his features.

"Our children," he repeated, as he reached to take my hand. "It's going to take me some time to pay Mateusz back. And I need to earn my degree, to set myself up. But I promise you, Emilia, I will work every day of my life to make you as happy as you can be."

I felt light—free and hopeful in a way that I hadn't in years, maybe since before the war.

"And I will do the same for you," I promised.

The road behind us was paved with tragedy and loss, but the future stretched before us—full of challenge, yes, but also endless possibilities and hope.

At long last, Roman and I were ready to fall into step together and see where life would lead us.

47

Roman

I FOUND A JOB AS A CLERK FOR A LAWYER WHO KNEW MY father, and I won a scholarship to commence my law degree at the newly reopened University of Warsaw. Around those responsibilities, I spent every spare minute with Emilia.

I was itching to propose but first needed to get my degree and start earning real money, and I needed to repay Mateusz. He was managing someone else's textiles factory and seemed to be getting by, but my conscience would never rest until I'd squared the debt. I warned Emilia that our wedding would be years away. "We have nothing but time," she'd said as she smiled at me, her green eyes alight with happiness.

One night, while I was sitting at the kitchen table studying, Sara sat opposite me knitting. Out of nowhere, she suddenly said, "Miriam Liebman called me today."

I looked up at her in surprise.

"Has she found Eleonora?"

Sara looked back at her knitting, her gaze pensive.

I frowned. "Sara, what is it?"

"Miriam finally managed to track her down. Eleonora's foster mother died this past winter. Her father was unable to care for her, and she's been placed in an orphanage. She also seems to have some health issues, likely a result of the malnutrition in her infancy."

I closed my textbook slowly, digesting this news.

"Will she find a new family?"

"It is unlikely," Sara murmured. "The orphanages have been full of children since the war, and the sick ones are hardly ever chosen. It's possible, I suppose, but she may be in the facility for some time."

"Can I go see her?"

"I wasn't sure I should tell you," Sara admitted, and her gaze dipped to my textbook, then back to my face. "Your life is busy enough as it is. I don't want you to feel compelled to complicate it further."

"She and I are all that remains of our entire family," I said simply. "If she needs me, I'll find a way to help her."

I borrowed a car from my boss, and before dawn the next morning, Emilia and I left the city to make the three-hour journey to Częstochowa.

"What do you plan to do for her?" Emilia asked.

"I have no idea," I admitted.

"Whatever you decide, I am with you all the way."

We found Eleonora sitting on the floor in the orphanage director's office, between a heavy oak desk and a set of leather chairs. It had been five years since I had seen my baby sister, and back then, she was so tiny I could have held her with one hand. Although no longer an infant, she was still so fragile, dressed in a knitted sweater and skirt that swam on her delicate frame. Her hair had been brushed and put into two ponytails on either side of her head, each tied with a red ribbon. When she turned and I saw her face, her features were so reminiscent of Dawidek's that my knees went weak.

"Eleonora, this is Mr. Gorka and Mrs. Gorka," Sister Irena said quietly.

"Oh, we aren't married," Emilia said.

"Yet," I added hastily, and I tore my gaze from my sister to Emilia. "We are engaged, and we plan to marry very soon."

The last time we'd spoken of an engagement, we'd been talking in terms of years, but the thought of this little girl, all alone in this crowded orphanage, was just about breaking my heart.

"Next weekend, in fact," Emilia said lightly, catching on so quickly that if I hadn't already been completely gone for her, I'd have fallen in love with her right then. Her gaze dropped down to Eleonora, and I saw an instant affection rise in her eyes. She took a step forward, then crouched beside my sister and withdrew a little caramel from her pocket. "Hi. I'm Emilia. It's very nice to meet you."

Eleonora looked at the candy, then up at Emilia, but she didn't respond. Unperturbed, Emilia dropped to sit on the carpet and unwrapped the candy, then motioned toward her mouth with it. Eleonora finally took the candy, but sniffed it suspiciously, then licked it and finally put it in her mouth. Her eyes widened, and finally she smiled.

"We have tried our best with this little one," Sister Irena said sadly. "But she came to us desperately underweight, and it doesn't matter how much we feed her, she is always skinny and catches every illness that goes around. She doesn't speak much, but the Sisters tell me she has been learning her letters and seems bright enough. I am hopeful that if she can find a stable home her health will recover."

I heard the nun's chatter, but my attention was fixed on Eleonora and Emilia. I hadn't dared to think about my family in years—it hurt too much to confront what I had lost. But as I watched Emilia form a bond with Eleonora, I thought about

395 of the warsaw orphan

my mother and Samuel and Dawidek and the warm, loving environment I had once taken for granted.

My life's work would be rebuilding Poland, but that work needed to start right at home—with rebuilding a family for Eleonora, Emilia and me. I sat on the floor beside Emilia, and I smiled at my baby sister. She looked at Emilia and me warily, as if she were ready to lash out at any moment.

It struck me that for all that I had lost and for all that I had been through, life still had immeasurable blessings in store for me. I thought of Chaim, as I often did in my happiest moments, and I sent a silent prayer that, wherever he was, he knew that I was grateful to him. *I won't waste it, Chaim. I won't waste a second of this life.*

"Hello, Eleonora," I said softly, as I stared into my sister's eyes. "You don't remember me, but I remember you, and I am never going to leave you again."

★ ★ ★ ★ ★

A NOTE FROM THE AUTHOR

In the winter of 2018, I was invited to speak at a book club near my hometown. As soon as I arrived, I joined a lively conversation about family histories—a key theme in the book I was there to discuss, *The Things We Cannot Say*. One of the book club members shared the story of an infant smuggled from a ghetto in Hungary in a suitcase. I found this particularly fascinating because when I first planned *The Things We Cannot Say*, I'd originally considered a different structure, with more of a focus on Emilia (who ultimately became a minor character in that book). I'd planned to see her leave her home village and go to work to help rescue children from the Warsaw Ghetto, just like real-life Polish resistance heroine Irena Sendler. In the process of writing an early draft of that book, I realized that I needed to keep the focus of that story on Tomasz and Alina, so I reworked the structure and discarded that subplot.

But at the book club in 2018, I started thinking about that idea again for the first time in years. As we shared lunch together, one of the women asked me if I'd ever considered writing a sequel to *The Things We Cannot Say*. I'd had that question before, so I gave my standard answer—no, because I felt I'd tied up the loose ends of Tomasz and Alina's story. "Well, what happened to Emilia?" she asked me. "Couldn't you just write her story next?" Sometimes the muse whispers, and sometimes it shouts. In hindsight, the reason I couldn't fit more of Emilia's story into *The Things We Cannot Say* was because she needed to be the star of her own book.

So, to Lou Hoffman, Wendy, Sue, Lisa, Sonya, Tina and Jane—thanks so much for inviting me to your book club. And an extra-special thanks to Marina Wood for the conversation that inspired me to write this book.

A recent survey conducted by the Jewish Material Claims Against Germany found that almost two-thirds of the American young adults surveyed did not know that six million Jews died during the Holocaust. More than 10 percent of those surveyed believed that Jews *caused* the Holocaust. I couldn't find comparable studies of young adults elsewhere, but I fear that for much of the world, the results would be similar. How can it be that our young people aren't aware of the unfathomable darkness the path of hatred and bigotry led our species to just seventy-five years ago? I do not believe it is the role of historical fiction to educate us about history. We novelists inevitably get things wrong, and sometimes we take liberties to massage our stories into place. I do, however, believe that great historical fiction should pique our curiosity and inspire us to educate ourselves. To that end, wherever it was possible in this book, I have tried to write a story that *could* have happened—and it is my hope that if you were not familiar with some of the events that take place in this book, you might spend time learning more about them. Those who were lost and those who survived deserve to be honored and remembered for their own sake, but also so that the horror they endured is never repeated.

Irena Sendler was a Polish nurse and social worker, and working with a team of other Polish women, she facilitated the rescue of more than 2,500 Jewish children from the Warsaw Ghetto during the occupation. I became fascinated by Irena after reading *Irena's Children* by Tilar J. Mazzeo and *Life in a Jar* by Jack Mayer. Emilia's resistance work, as well as the characters of

Matylda and Sara, was inspired by Irena and her team. Like Matylda, Irena was arrested by the Gestapo and interrogated—however, Irena was secretly rescued just before her planned execution. While Warsaw believed she was executed and posters were hung around the city to announce her death, Irena lived under a false identity in order to continue her work. Like Sara, Irena worked as a field nurse in a makeshift hospital during the Warsaw Uprising. And just like Sara when she stored the jar in Emilia's courtyard, Irena also kept a jar filled with slips of paper recording the details of the children her team had rescued. Like Sara, Irena buried her jar beneath an apple tree and later passed it to Jewish authorities in the hopes that families could be restored.

Another Polish hero I became fascinated by in the research for this book was Polish historian Emmanuel Ringelblum. While his story is not reflected in this novel, I couldn't have written it without his work. While trapped within the ghetto with his family, Ringelblum led a secret project to document the reality of daily life there. With a team of historians, scientists and others, he compiled an extraordinary collection of documents, including posters, decrees, commissioned papers, diaries, photographs, rations cards and personal accounts—in total, more than 25,000 pages. Shortly before the ghetto was destroyed, Ringelblum's Oyneg Shabes group buried the collection underground in three separate parts. One of these parts has never been found, but the other two were recovered in 1946 and 1950. The courage, persistence and dedication of the Oyneg Shabes group have given those of us in future generations some small measure of insight into what life was like within the ghetto walls.

Various exhibits at both the Warsaw Rising Museum and POLIN Museum of the History of Polish Jews inspired my interest in some of the issues and events covered in this book. An article by Joanna Ostrowska and Marcin Zaremba in *Polityka* magazine sparked my curiosity about the horrifying wave of sexual violence against Polish women during the Soviet occupation.

I loved writing this book, and I so hope you've enjoyed reading it. If you did, I'd be grateful if you could take the time to write a review online. You can do this at Goodreads.com, or if you purchased the book online, at the website where you made the purchase. Your review really does make a difference—it helps other readers to find my books. I love hearing from readers, too—if you'd like to get in touch with me, you can find all of my contact details on my website, www.kellyrimmer.com.

My Best,
Kelly

The following resources were invaluable in the research for this book:

Irena's Children: The Extraordinary Story of the Woman Who Saved 2,500 Children from the Warsaw Ghetto, by Tilar J. Mazzeo

Who Will Write Our History? Rediscovering a Hidden Archive from the Warsaw Ghetto, by Samuel D. Kassow

The Warsaw Ghetto Oyneg Shabes-Ringelblum Archive: Catalog and Guide, edited by Robert Moses Shapiro and Tadeusz Epsztein

Notes from the Warsaw Ghetto: The Journal of Emmanuel Ringelblum, by Emmanuel Ringelblum and edited by Jacob Sloan

The Yad Vashem online photo collections

Tunnel, Smuggle, Collect: A Holocaust Boy, by Jeffrey N. Gingold, an account of his father's and grandmother's experiences in Warsaw during the occupation, based on audio and video recordings of their memories

United States Holocaust Memorial Museum's online resources, particularly their incredible collection of first-person accounts

Jewish Virtual Library

Holocaust Research Project

The Warsaw Ghetto Uprising, by Marek Edelman

The Bravest Battle: The Twenty-Eight Days of The Warsaw Ghetto Uprising, by Dan Kurzman

Rising '44: The Battle for Warsaw, by Norman Davies

ACKNOWLEDGMENTS

To Iga Fatalska, thanks so much for your help with the Polish language aspects to this novel. Mindy, thanks for all of your help over the course of this year. To Aunty Lola—thanks for convincing me to walk all over Warsaw during those stinking-hot summer days of our trip in 2017. Maybe I complained at the time, especially on that one day when we did 40,000 steps, but I couldn't have written this book without the research I did on that trip and it turned out that seeing so much of Warsaw by foot was handy after all! To all of my writer pals—especially Sally Hepworth, Lisa Ireland, Kim Kelly, Pamela Cook and Vanessa Carnevale. At different times, each of you imparted some wisdom or encouragement that kept me going while I was working on this book, and I am so grateful to have your friendship and support.

Dan, Maxwell and Violette, yet again I am sorry for how impossible I am to live with when I'm writing, and I know this book was particularly tough. Thanks for loving me anyway. And to Mum and Dad, thanks for emergency babysitting, Tim Tams and cups of tea.

To my agent, Amy Tannenbaum, and the entire team at the Jane Rotrosen Agency. I am so honored and grateful to be working with you—and, Amy, thanks for always going the extra mile. And to Susan Swinwood and the team at Graydon

House, Harlequin and HarperCollins, you have made so many of my dreams come true and I am so thankful to know that my stories are in such capable and skilled hands.

To booksellers and librarians, you superstars who place my books in the hands of readers, thank you, thank you, thank you. And to the bloggers, bookstagrammers, reviewers and to anyone else who has recommended my books to someone else over the years—thank you so much for believing in my work and spreading the word.

And finally, to readers. I still sometimes pinch myself—it seems a dream that anyone wants to read my books. Thank you for journeying through these stories with me.

THE
WARSAW
ORPHAN

KELLY RIMMER

Reader's Guide

GRAYDON
HOUSE

1. Early in the story, Emilia can be wildly impulsive and determined, and is even willing to manipulate to get her own way. Did you find her to be a likable character anyway? If so, why?

2. When we first meet Roman, he is a young man trapped in an impossible situation, but to his own thinking he is "a prisoner by choice." What did he mean by this? Did you empathize with his decision to refuse to consider alternatives to remaining in the ghetto?

3. Roman initially refuses to engage with the Resistance, but eventually becomes fixated on fighting back. Why was this? Do you think he made the right decision at each point in time?

4. Why do you think Chaim saved Roman's life?

5. During the Warsaw Uprising, Uncle Piotr undergoes a period of transformation. After years of focusing on himself, he becomes determined to look after his family. What drives this? Why did it happen in that particular moment?

6. Emilia's thoughts on her unborn child also undergo a transformation. Did her ultimate decision seem realistic to

you, given her circumstances? Roman initially has a very different perspective. Were you sympathetic to his refusal to accept baby Anatol?

7. Piotr and Sara have a complex relationship that is tragically cut short. What do you think would have happened between them had Piotr survived?

8. Were you already familiar with the historical events that take place in this story? Is there any aspect to that history that you're planning to look into further?

9. Which characters in this book did you like best? Which did you like least? Why?

10. Which scene in *The Warsaw Orphan* affected you the most, and why? What emotions did that scene elicit?

11. Were you satisfied with the ending? What do you think happened next for Roman and Emilia?

12. Fiction set during World War II has been increasingly popular in the last few years. Why do you think readers are drawn to these kinds of stories in this present moment?

13. What will you remember most about *The Warsaw Orphan*?

14. Who would you recommend this book to?

15. Was this your first Kelly Rimmer book? If you've read any of her other titles, which did you prefer?